The Antic

The Antichrists
© 2013 Mark A. Roeder

All rights reserved. No part of this book may be used or reproduced by any means, graphic, electronic, or mechanical, including photocopying, recording, taping or by any information storage retrieval system without the written permission of the publisher except in the case of brief quotations embodied in critical articles and reviews.

This book is a work of fiction. Names, characters, places and incidents are products of the author's imagination or are used fictionally. Any resemblance to actual events or locales or persons, living or dead, is entirely coincidental. All trademarks are the property of their respective owners and no infringement is intended.

Cover Photo Credit: Papa1266 (model) and Sampete (background) on Dreamstime.com.

Cover Design: Ken Clark

ISBN-13: 978-1484147245

ISBN-10: 1484147243

All Rights Reserved

Printed in the United States of America

Acknowledgements

I'd like to thank Ken Clark and James Adkinson for all they've done, not only in getting this novel ready for publication, but many others as well. Ken created and runs my website, markroeder.com, as well as two Yahoo fan groups and a Facebook page. Jim puts an enormous amount of time and effort into correcting my many mistakes. I truly don't know what I'd do without the help of Ken and Jim.

Dedication

This novel is dedicated to all those who struggle to reconcile who they are with their religious beliefs.

"I like your Christ, I do not like your Christians. Your Christians are so unlike your Christ."—Mahatma Gandhi

Chapter One
Verona, Indiana
Late August 1983

I walked toward the bleachers under the penetrating gaze of eighty sets of eyes. I had half a mind to turn and run in the other direction, but I hadn't worked out and run all summer to get into shape just to turn tail and run before team tryouts even started.

I had no idea so many guys would try out for the football team! I guess I hadn't thought about it at all. I'd been so busy pushing myself to get ready for practices that I didn't think much about the actual tryouts. I tried not to look at the other guys and I took a seat on the bleachers at the side of the football field. I felt like a grade school kid who had wandered into the high school tryouts by mistake. I was 5'7" and weighed about 120. Some of the guys sitting there had to be at least 6'3" and 220.

I heard a couple of guys snicker behind me and I just knew they were laughing at me. Football? What was I thinking? I'd never played an organized sport in my life and I was starting out with high school football? I had lost my mind for sure.

It hadn't seemed like such a bad idea at the beginning of the summer. My older brothers had played ball when they were in high school. Both of them earned football scholarships and were now playing for Indiana University. The problem was that I was nothing like my older brothers. I was the runt of the family. It was as if all the good genes were used up on them and I got what was left. They were taller, stronger, better looking, and far more athletically inclined.

I should have talked to Thomas or Mitch about my lame-brained idea of playing football. They would have had the good sense to talk me out of it, but no, I'd kept it all to myself. During the summer, I'd gone on long runs, running further and further each day until I could run for miles. I'd worked out on my brother's old weight equipment. Dad had even remarked that I was looking fit. I'd almost told him I was going out for football. It was a good thing I didn't. He would probably have laughed before he could stop himself. The idea of me playing football truly was laughable.

"Hey, kid. I think you're in the wrong place."

I looked up. I recognized the guy speaking to me. He'd played varsity the year before and he was good. His name was... Myer. Shawn Myer.

"I'm not in the wrong place. I'm a freshman. I'm here for football tryouts."

"As what, the water boy?"

It wasn't Shawn who said that, but some guy behind me. Shawn scowled at him.

"Hey, I recognize you now. You're Mitch Gaylord's little brother."

"Little is right," said the guy behind me.

"Shut it, Caldemyer," Shawn said.

I could feel my face going red.

"Both your brothers were really good," Shawn said. "If Brendan hadn't been around, either of them could have made quarterback."

"A spot you're hoping for, right, Myer?" called out one of the guys.

"Maybe. I'll sure get no competition from you!"

"Burn! Good one, bro!" A slightly smaller version of Shawn gave him a high five. He was Shawn's younger brother, Tim. I recognized him from last year's games.

"I'm glad you came out. You have football genes," Shawn said.

"Jeans! Size, extra small!" called out the guy who had been talking trash before.

"One more comment from you, Cody, and I'm coming up there, ripping your head off, and pissing down your throat," Shawn growled.

Some of the guys laughed. Cody shut up.

The coaches came out with their clipboards, and one began to call out names. I was so nervous I trembled slightly. It seemed to take forever before he reached my name.

"Gaylord, Elijah."

The coach looked up hopefully.

"Here, coach!"

My voice cracked, making me sound like thirteen-year-old girl. A bunch of the guys laughed. The coach looked disappointed. He was no doubt expecting a natural born jock like Mitch or our older brother Thomas. Instead, there was only me, the runt of the litter.

After roll was called the coaches took turns speaking. They told us that over the next two or three days they were going to be selecting players for the varsity and junior varsity teams. "Not everyone will make the cut," were the words that stuck in my mind the most. Did I really think I had a chance? I was easily the smallest guy there. I'd put on muscle over the summer, but it didn't make me any taller and I was a lightweight compared to the others.

After a lot of talk, the coaches told us to run around the track until we were told to stop. I was glad to get off those bleachers. I felt like everyone was staring at me. If there was one thing I could do, it was run. I'd been doing it all summer. I remembered my first few runs. I was out of breath after running only a few blocks, but I kept at it. Each day I could run longer and further. By the beginning of August I could run for miles without getting winded.

I ran along with the other guys as we jogged around the track. I stayed to the outside because I was afraid of getting trampled. Most of the other guys could effortlessly look right over my head. I put all my worries out of my mind as I ran. That's one thing I loved about running. It allowed me to forget everything. I just ran, feeling the track under my sneakers and the wind on my face. Some of the guys near me began to breathe harder as we ran lap after lap. I smiled when some of the biggest, most muscular guys began to wheeze. I ran on with little effort. I could keep this up all day.

Some of the guys began to fall out, gasping for breath as they put their hands on their knees. I wondered if one of them was the Cody-kid who had been making fun of me earlier. I hoped so, but since I hadn't actually seen him I didn't know. The coaches kept us running until several of the guys dropped out. Even Shawn and Tim were breathing hard, but they hung in there. When one of the coaches waved us over to the bleachers I grinned at Shawn. My breathing was hardly fast at all.

The coaches explained various passing and receiving drills we'd be doing so they could check out our skills. We would also be running an obstacle course and doing some scrimmages. I didn't understand all of it. I'd watched my brothers play a lot of football games, but I'd never been to a practice. I didn't know a whole lot about passing or receiving, except what Mitch and Thomas had taught me. Realistically, my chances of making junior varsity were slim, but I was going to try.

We rotated through various stations while the coaches observed and made notes on the clipboards. Some, like the Myer brothers, were assured a spot on varsity. Others were hoping to make the jump from junior varsity to varsity. Then there were guys like me who hoped not to be cut on the very first day.

I didn't do so well with passing. I had fairly good form, but my distance was... well... pathetic. I saw one of the coaches make a mark on his clipboard. I hoped he wasn't crossing out my name. I did much better with receiving. The pass was a little high, but I leaped into the air and snagged it with my fingertips. I cradled it safely against my chest. Shawn saw me make the catch and nodded to me. I grinned like an idiot.

The obstacle course was tough. I didn't trip as I ran through the tires, but my tackle was... well, I didn't move the platform at all. I just kind of rebounded off of it and nearly landed on my butt. I missed the tire completely when I made my pass, but I did pretty good on the remainder of the course.

"Name?" one of the coaches called out when I finished.

"Gaylord."

The coach looked mildly surprised and I know what he was thinking. *This is a Gaylord? Where's the rest of him? Perhaps he's adopted.* I just hoped he didn't ask my name so he could cut me.

We scrimmaged next. I was placed opposite a guy twice my size, which wasn't a surprise since most of the guys were twice my size. He looked at me with concern, as if he feared he might kill me by accident if he plowed into me too hard. I have to admit I was plenty scared. I was wearing a helmet and shoulder pads, but I figured I was still in for some pain.

When the coach blew the whistle I leaned in low and rushed forward, but my opponent rammed into me and I went flying backward. My feet left the ground and I landed on my back. My opponent ran past me. I'd barely slowed him down.

I just lay there for a moment. Getting hit by a lineman hurt, but most of the pain was in my butt. I'd landed right on it. I pulled myself up and lined up against the buff jock again.

The coach blew the whistle. This time I darted to my opponent's right and slipped past him before he could nail me. I broke into the clear and ran a few paces. The quarterback was actually getting ready to pass to me, but he got sacked.

We ran scrimmage after scrimmage. The lineman across from me was wise to my plan and countered my attempts to get past him. I began faking in one direction before darting in the other. He caught onto that too, so I faked to the right, then left, then zipped past him on the right. He laid me out on my back several times, but I broke into the clear just as often. I kept hoping to receive the ball. We weren't running actual plays so the quarterback passed to whoever was open. Even when I made it past the line he never seemed to see me. Being small sucked. I was easily overlooked.

The coaches set us back down on the bleachers after more than two hours of various drills and scrimmages. The head coach announced that a list of those who were invited to continue with tryouts tomorrow would be posted outside the locker room within thirty minutes. I prayed I would be on that list. I wanted to play so bad I could taste it.

As I walked toward the locker room with the other guys, I was reminded once again that I was a runt. They all towered over me. One almost knocked me down by accident because he didn't see me.

"You should quit, kid. You're gonna get hurt if you play in a real game."

I looked to the side. It was the guy I'd been trying to get past during the scrimmages.

"I can take it."

"I was holding back today because I didn't want to hurt you, but if you're in a real game, the guy across from you won't pull any punches. He'll just nail you as hard as he can and keep on going."

"Then maybe he'll trip over me."

The boy laughed.

"I'm Lucas."

"I'm Elijah. Are you a senior?"

"Nope. I'm a sophomore."

My eyes grew a little wide. Lucas was about 6'2", 185, and all muscle. He was a sophomore? I was angry for a moment. Why did God stick me with such a little body? My anger soon passed to guilt. I had no right to complain. I was lucky God had given me what he had.

I was a little intimidated by the locker room. Guys were stripping down all around me—tossing their shirts, socks, and underwear in lockers and all over the benches. I felt even smaller than I had out on the field. I'd been in a locker room nearly every day for my middle school P.E. classes, but only with boys my age. Most of them were bigger than me, but these guys… they had big muscles and big… other stuff too. I hurried toward the showers. The sooner I got in and out the better.

There were too many guys in the showers at once and I even had to wait on a showerhead for a bit. I stood there in the steamy shower room feeling inferior. What was I doing here with all these big guys? Any of them could have snapped me like a twig. I was way out of my league. It would all be over soon enough. I'd be cut for sure. Sadness enveloped me. I didn't want to be cut. I wanted to play football!

I tried not to let my eyes fall on the naked guys around me, but they were everywhere. No matter where I looked I saw a bare chest or butt or an even more private spot. I began to have sinful thoughts so I tried to think of Jesus like they taught us in Sunday school.

I finally got a showerhead. I didn't have soap or shampoo, but at least I could wash off the sweat and dirt. Shawn Myer was on one side of me. His younger brother, Tim, was on the other. They were both very handsome and had beautifully muscled, lean bodies. I tried not to look, but I couldn't help myself. Horrible, sinful thoughts flooded my mind and I began to get an erection.

No. I was not going to let this happen. I went to church every Sunday with my parents and I went to Sunday school too. Lust was a sin and feeling lust when I looked at another boy… it was an abomination. I fought my unnatural lust as the hot water pounded down upon me. Shawn raised his arms to run his fingers through his hair and I got a look at his underarms. I turned my head from the sight and got a full frontal eyeful of Tim. Was he getting hard or was he always that big? I looked down. I was kind of hard and I wasn't big. I was smaller than my brothers down there too, not that I'd looked at them much, but when you shared a room and were often in the bathroom together you saw things.

Maybe football wasn't a good idea. I hadn't thought about the locker room or the showers. I didn't realize the feelings that would rise to the surface when all these big guys surrounded me. It was hard enough fighting temptation without naked jocks parading themselves in front of me.

I rinsed off quickly and got out of there. I grabbed a towel from the towel boy and dried off as fast as possible. Guys were talking and laughing and roughhousing all around me, but didn't pay any attention to me. I was glad of that. The last thing I wanted was attention when I had a semi. I pulled on my clothes and escaped from the locker room.

I lingered in the gym, waiting for the list to be posted. I wasn't sure why I bothered to stick around. A lot of the guys didn't. They were that sure they'd make the team. It was probably best if I was cut. I didn't know if I could handle being in the locker room and showers with all those built jocks. It was just too... No. I wouldn't even think about that!

One of the coaches posted the list. I nervously walked across the gym floor. A few guys were checking out the list, but it took me only moments to get a look at it. My eyes widened. There, written as clear as day, was "Gaylord, Elijah." I hadn't been cut! I had made it through the first day of tryouts!

"Congratulations."

I looked to my side. It was Tim Myer. I hoped he hadn't noticed me looking at him in the showers, but he gave no sign he had. He put his hand on my shoulder and squeezed. That's when I remembered he was... one of those. My brothers had told me so. I pulled away as quickly as I dared.

"Um...thanks."

I hurried away. How could I have forgotten? I'd been so worried about tryouts I hadn't thought for a moment about Shawn and Tim. They were both homosexuals! Maybe I didn't end up between them in the showers by accident. Maybe they wanted to get me between them, but no, I'd picked that spot because it was the only one available. I tried to relax. Still, I was going to watch my back. The Myer brothers might see me as an easy target. I didn't want to be molested.

I put such thoughts out of my mind. I had made it through the first day of tryouts! I almost could not believe it. I hadn't given tryouts that much thought before I walked out on the field, but once I was there I figured I was doomed. Somehow I had survived. The big question was could I make it through two more days without being cut?

I walked home, tired. Tryouts were tough and if I made the team practices would be tougher. I wondered if I could handle a grueling practice after sitting in class all day. If I was very lucky, I'd soon find out.

My father was just getting home from work as I walked up the front steps. Mom speared me with a glance and I knew I was in trouble.

"Where have you been? You should have been home from school hours ago."

Uh oh. I'd forgotten to tell my parents I'd be home late. I could pretty much come and go as I pleased *if* I let my parents in on my plans or checked in.

"What's this?" Dad asked as he walked in.

"I...uh. I'm sorry. I forgot to tell you. I went to football tryouts after school."

"You're trying out for the team?" asked my dad. He looked surprised, but pleased.

"Yes."

"I don't want you playing football. I've already been though six years of worrying about your brothers. Now, they're playing in college. Every day I fear I'll get a call that they've been hurt," Mom said.

"If the boy wants to play he should be given the chance. It will make a man out of him." Dad looked at me. "How did you do?"

"Not great... but I didn't get cut! There are still two more days, but I made it past the first."

"Well, we can't expect you to be like your brothers, but good job."

I knew exactly what he meant. Thomas and Mitch were big and strong. I was a runt. Still, I could tell he was at least a little proud of me. I grinned.

My father left the room. Mom still looked worried.

"Don't worry. I'll likely get cut. The other guys are a lot bigger than me."

"That's what worries me the most."

I realized my attempt at comforting my mother wasn't a success. I'd said exactly the wrong thing. I was glad she hadn't seen me getting knocked down during tryouts. At least I could count on my father to let me play if I survived. Mom might object, but Dad would let me play. He was up for anything that "would make me a man."

I went up to the room I'd once shared with my brothers. They had both departed for school only the day before. Thomas was a sophomore in college now and Mitch was a freshman. The room seemed empty without them.

The bedroom was fairly large and seemed especially big now that both my brothers were gone. I was not used to having so much space to myself. I wasn't accustomed to the privacy either.

I picked up a book and tried to read, but my mind wandered to football tryouts. I wondered if I'd survive tomorrow. I was amazed I hadn't been cut. Getting cut on the first day would've been humiliating, but not surprising. I paused. Had I really made it through the first day, or had the coaches let me remain in the running out of pity?

I really wasn't very good at tackling and my passes were weak. I doubted I'd ever pass a ball in a game, but tackling was a major part of football. If I couldn't help block, what possible use could I be to the team? Wanting to be on the team and being a useful part of the team were two entirely different things.

Mom called me down to supper about an hour later. I was starving! Tryouts made me hungry!

The kitchen table seemed so empty without my brothers. Last year had been a hard enough adjustment with Thomas gone, but now that both my brothers were away it was even more difficult.

"Are you sure you want to play football?" my mother asked as she passed a platter of pork chops to me. "If you're going out for the team just because your brother's played..."

"That's not why I'm trying out. I'm tired of not being athletic. I want to do something."

"Why not track or tennis?"

"I want to play on a real team. Thomas and Mitch are always talking about all the stuff they do with their teammates. Most of their friends in high school were other players. I want to be a part of that."

"I still think..."

"The boy has made his decision. I think we should support him," Dad said. "I just want you to know, son, that I won't be disappointed in you if you don't make the team."

I had a feeling he would be disappointed. I'd always been a disappointment to him. He'd never said so out loud, but I could see it in his eyes when he looked at me, especially if my brothers were around. Even if I'd been normal-sized instead of small I would still have looked pathetic compared to them.

"I've been working for this all summer long," I admitted for the first time. "That's why I've been working out and I've been running too."

"You have put on some muscle," Dad said proudly. I smiled.

"I know I'm not really big enough to play football, but it is something I want to try. I figure if I put everything I have into it I might make the team."

I wasn't nearly as confident as I tried to sound. Chances were that my football playing days would start on one day and end on the next.

"You just try your best, Son. If you don't make the football team perhaps you can try out for soccer or wrestling."

"Or track, tennis, or swimming," suggested Mom.

It was obvious my dad wanted me to play a rough, man's sport, while my mom wanted me to do something that avoided bodily contact, and therefore injury.

"I'm going to make the team," I said, pretending to be determined. I liked the way my father looked at me with approval when I spoke with confidence.

"That's my boy. We'll make a man out of you yet."

My mother shifted the talk away from football and onto what she might need to send my brothers for their dorm rooms. I knew she missed them. I missed them too. I listened to Mom while I ate my pork chops, mashed potatoes, and cooked apples. My mother was quite a good cook. She put a lot of time and effort into it. Both of my brothers were big eaters. I'd been eating more since I began to work out, but there was no way I could match either of my brothers!

I returned to my room after supper. Part of me wished I hadn't mentioned football tryouts. Now, I felt extra pressure to succeed. Dad would be disappointed that his youngest couldn't match the standards of his older sons. That's what I didn't like about being the youngest. Even if I succeeded in something, Thomas, Mitch, or both had already accomplished it. If I failed, it was yet more evidence that I was inferior. I really liked both my brothers, but sometimes I wished they weren't so good at *everything*. If they were football studs but failed academically, I would have had my niche. I would've been the smart one. But, no. Thomas and Mitch were great athletes, and they received nearly straight A's. I'd lived in their shadow my entire life.

I pulled out the books on football that I'd checked out of the library a few days before. I was trying to learn more about the game. I knew quite a bit from watching Thomas and Mitch play, but watching and playing were two very different things. I had attended nearly all of both my brother's high school games. I had even traveled down to Bloomington with my family to watch Thomas play for IU a couple of times. Still, there was plenty I didn't know.

I did my homework and studied on football until I grew sleepy. I stayed up a little longer thumbing through my brother's old football magazines, but soon I was too drowsy to keep my eyes open.

I set my alarm before I stripped down to my boxers and crawled into bed. As I lay there, my mind kept drifting to the Myer brothers. They were both very...fit. A lot of the other guys were well-built too. Some were on the heavy side, but most were lean and muscular like my brothers. I forced my thoughts in another direction. I didn't need to be thinking about the bodies of other guys, especially my brothers.

Shawn was gay. Everyone knew it. I don't know why I hadn't thought of that before tryouts. I guess I was too overwhelmed to think about anything. He had been really nice to me. He'd taken up for me when that Cody kid was trashing me. What was I going to do if Shawn was interested in me? How could I avoid him? Would he try to force himself on me? I'd heard homos did that. They lured boys into their cars or got them alone and then did things to them—bad things.

I laughed, not because of what homosexuals did to boys, but because the idea of Shawn being interested in me was ludicrous. I was nothing compared to him, but then maybe that was part of the attraction. Maybe he was into me because I was boyish. I shuddered to think about it. Great, just what I needed, something else to worry about.

Images of the naked guys in the locker room and the showers flowed through my mind. I couldn't stop the mental pictures. They just kept coming. Once again, I wondered if trying out for football was such a good idea.

I'd nearly forgotten to pray, so I clasped my hands and asked God to take my unnatural and sinful thoughts away. I also asked him to help me survive tryouts tomorrow. I stopped short of asking him to make sure I made the team. That was up to me. Instead, I asked him to do what was best for me. Whether I made the team or not, I knew it was God's will.

***

I was on the field for tryouts a few minutes early. Shawn said "hey" and I returned his greeting, but didn't encourage him. I was probably safe around him. He hadn't tried anything with my brothers so he probably wouldn't with me unless he did like the boyish type. I pushed that thought out of my mind. It wasn't right to think the worst of someone, even if they were destined to burn in Hell. Who knows? Maybe God even put the idea of playing football into my head so I could turn Shawn and Tim from their evil ways.

The second afternoon of tryouts involved some running and obstacle course work, but it was mostly a one-on-one skills test. The coaches paired those who had played last year with us hopefuls. Most, probably all, of those who had played before would be returning. I was paired with Tim Myer, which made me a little nervous, especially when he peeled off his shirt. Was he trying to seduce me? He sure looked good without a shirt. He was sweaty and his muscles gleamed in the sun. I had to stop myself from thinking about Tim's body and the possible danger he posed. God would protect me.

I did my best to impress Tim. He made notes on a clipboard that Coach Jordan had given him. I wondered what he was writing about me. I hoped it wasn't "throws like a girl" or "is too wimpy to play football." I tried to act tough. I even peeled off my shirt to show off my new muscles. Maybe my body would distract Tim when I messed up. I guessed there wasn't anything wrong with using his perversion to distract him, or was I somehow encouraging his sinful thoughts? I didn't have time to debate it and besides, it was hot! I was sweating up a storm.

We didn't stop until 6 p.m. I was starving! I felt like I could eat my weight in anything. The coaches announced that tryouts were over. Their new routine of using experienced players to help evaluate the newbies had streamlined the process so there would be no third day of tryouts. I was relieved, but disappointed too. If I'd made it to the third day and was then cut, at least I would've had three days to prove myself. I felt like I needed more time to impress the coaches with what I could do, and hopefully draw their minds away from what I hadn't done so well. It would have also meant one more day of working with the team. I might never get the chance again.

Unfortunately, the list would not be posted just a few minutes after tryouts this time. Since it was a Friday, I feared I'd have to wait until Monday to find out if I'd made the team, but Coach Jordan announced the list would be posted on the doors to the gymnasium the next day at noon.

Tim hadn't hinted one way or the other about what he thought of my abilities. I'd seen coaches nod when they watched me, but I'd also seen them frown. I was very much afraid my height would work against me. I could almost picture them saying "He has some skills, but he's just too small."

I hit the showers with the rest of the guys. There were fewer of us than the day before, but it was still crowded. I tried to face the wall most of the time to avoid temptation. I also didn't want to make eye contact with Shawn or Tim, just in case they were after me. I hurried through my shower, dried off, and got dressed in record time. I caught a few glimpses of naked guys, but not nearly so many as the day before. I was so worried about whether or not I'd make the cut that I didn't have to worry much about having unnatural thoughts. I felt as if God was with me, seeing me on my way.

I spent my Friday night trying unsuccessfully not to think about whether or not I'd made the team. After I turned in, I had a series of dreams about the final roster, or more precisely I several variations of the same dream. In each I checked out the roster on the gymnasium doors. Sometimes, my name was on the list, sometimes it wasn't. Sometimes, my name was on the varsity list and once I dreamed I'd been made quarterback! Another time, I was on the list, but I was listed as "water boy."

I rode my bike over to Verona High School right after lunch the next day. My ride to school was eerily similar to my dreams the night before. I didn't take it as a premonition. How could I? I think I'd dreamed every possibility!

I was thankful that no one was around as I walked up to the gymnasium doors. I had a feeling I might cry if I didn't make the team, and there was a very good chance indeed that I had been cut. I didn't even bother to read the varsity list, but ran my finger down the list of junior varsity players. My heart almost stopped when I read "Gaylord, Elijah." I was so shocked I just stood there reading my name over and over to make sure. I couldn't believe it! I had made the football team!

Chapter Two

I had a lot to be thankful for as I rode to church with my parents. I'd worked and prayed all summer and I had actually made the football team. I was apprehensive about our first practice on Monday, but I'd come too far to give up now. I'd run mile after mile and knocked out bench presses and curls like a crazy man all summer. I wasn't wasting all that sweat and toil. Even if I was destined to be little more than a bench warmer, I was still a football player and I'd have the jersey to prove it.

I stepped out of the car when we reached the Apostolic Faith Tabernacle. My dress shoes were uncomfortable, but it was the only day of the week I wore them. It was the only time I wore my suit and tie as well, unless there was a wedding or a funeral.

My parents took their usual pew and I slid in after them. I felt the absence of Thomas and Mitch yet again. I was used to them sitting between our parents and me. Our family always attended church together. I thought that might change when Thomas went off to college, but whenever he was home on a Sunday he came to church just like always.

The sermon was about Abraham and Isaac and how Abraham had such love for God that he willing to sacrifice his son to him. I knew the story well so hearing it again was a little like watching a rerun on television. Don't get me wrong. I was interested. I liked going to church. My family was extremely religious. Perhaps I wasn't as devoted as my parents, but that was only because they were extremely devoted. I believed in God and tried to live by the Bible. There were some Sunday mornings I would've liked to sleep in, but I didn't want to miss church. Even on the mornings I was almost too tired to get out of bed, I figured I owed God a lot and I could surely attend services. It wasn't even a sacrifice on my part. I liked church. I loved singing hymns and being surrounded by people who loved God as much as I did.

Near the end of the service, Pastor Walker announced he had a special surprise for us. Pastor Walker hadn't been with us long. He'd started less than a month before, replacing our old pastor who retired and moved to Florida. I didn't like him as well as our old pastor, but a lot of that was probably just that I wasn't used to him yet.

A mike was brought onto the stage and lowered so that it was only about three feet tall. I wondered at this until a small boy I recognized as a member of the congregation was led onto the stage by his mother. He was not more than five and was very cute in his little suit. His mother sat off to one side with an acoustic guitar. She nodded to her son and he began to sing.

"No homo ain't never going to make it to heaven. I know the Bible's right, and the perverts are wrong. Romans 1 and 27, no homo ain't never going to make it to heaven. All the fags will burn in Hell while us Christians laugh from above, no homo ain't never going to make it to heaven."

"That's my boy!" called out the kid's proud father from where he was standing near the front off to the right.

The song shocked me. It didn't seem very Christian. Only last week the sermon was about walking in the footsteps of Jesus and this little kid singing a song about homos burning in Hell didn't seem to fit with that. I seemed to be the only one in the congregation with doubts. Some parishioners were nodding their agreement and others were calling out "yea" and "sing it!"

When the boy finished his song the congregation clapped and cheered. The boy ran over to his father and they exchanged a high-five.

When the clapping calmed down the Pastor stepped up again.

"This Sunday we will be passing two collection plates. The first is so that we may continue the good work of the church, but the second is of equal importance. Our way of life is under attack. Good Christian values are besieged. Traditional marriage is in great danger. Please give generously so that we may fight to protect the sanctity of marriage and legally define it as between one man and one woman once and for all. I know you may think there is no danger, but a storm is brewing and we cannot wait until it is upon us to act. Mark my words, in years to come the homosexuals will attack the sanctity of marriage. They will mock it by demanding to be allowed to marry each other. By making our move now, we will preempt their unholy efforts."

Pastor Walker waited until the clapping calmed before he continued.

"Our Bible School classes will be holding a bake sale next Sunday to raise funds for the fight against gay marriage, so I urge all of you to bring your sweet tooth and your dollars for this most excellent cause. Next Sunday, we will also begin collecting items for our rummage sale. All proceeds from this sale will be donated to protect the sanctity of marriage. Together, we can make a difference and take back this good country from those who seek to pervert and profane it."

I had never heard of such a thing as gay marriage. I didn't think there was any threat. It seemed like there would have been something on the news about gays wanting to marry. Did the pastor think he could see into the future? I didn't see what the big deal was anyway. How could homos getting married threaten the sanctity of marriage?

The collection plates were passed as we sang a final hymn. I gazed at the stained glass windows, which pictured Christ and his disciples. I felt uncomfortable under their gaze so I focused on the candles burning by the altar instead. I loved listening to the voices of the congregation as we praised God with song.

The car was quiet on the short drive home. I thought about saying something about the little boy's song. It didn't seem right to me, but it was sung at church. Pastor Walker and the congregation obviously approved. I guess I just didn't understand. It had been the same when the sermons mentioned the crusaders killing the infidels in the name of God. I could never understand how anyone could be killed in God's name. "Thou shalt not kill" was even one of the Ten Commandments. I obviously had a lot to learn.

***

Monday afternoon, just after school, I joined my teammates in the gym. Both the varsity and junior varsity teams were present. Today was our first practice. It was the day we received our practice uniforms. I sat and waited while the varsity team received their uniforms and left for the locker room. I wondered if I'd ever be one of them. I doubted it. Even if I turned out to be talented my size would hold me back. It might have been wiser to go out for soccer where my size wouldn't have been as much of a liability, but my brothers had played football and I wanted to follow in their footsteps.

I watched as the Myer brothers received their uniforms. Shawn and Tim were both very handsome. They looked like such clean-cut boys, but they were homosexuals. I thought back to the song I'd heard in church. How could they choose a lifestyle that they knew would lead straight to Hell? Both of them had so much going for them. They had looks, talent, and nice builds. How could they destroy themselves by having sex with other guys, maybe even with each other?

My penis stirred in my shorts. The will is strong, but the body is weak. I would not give in as Shawn and Tim had done. I would not allow myself to become a pervert. Maybe I was lucky that I wasn't as built as the Myer brothers. Maybe that's what made them gay. Their good looks and muscular bodies might well have been their downfall. With such looks came opportunities and temptations.

I suddenly wondered about my own efforts to improve my body. Was I setting myself up for a fall? I was having more trouble with temptation than I had before I started working out. It was harder to keep my eyes from roving. It was harder to contain the lustful thoughts the devil put in my mind.

"Gaylord!"

I was startled by my name. I looked up. One of the assistant coaches was holding my uniform. I grinned, walked forward, and accepted it. The jersey felt silky in my hands. I almost couldn't believe I had a football uniform. I'd always admire my brother's uniforms, and now I had one of my own!

I walked across the giant V on the center of the gymnasium floor and into the locker room. I looked around the room, trying to select a locker from those that were not yet taken. The varsity team had come and gone, so a lot of the lockers were already reserved. I spotted Lucas Needmore ripping off his shirt and tossing it into his locker. He was the only guy on the team I sort of knew, so I took a locker next to his. I grabbed up the athletic tape, ripped off a section and slapped on the top of my locker. With a black marker I wrote "GAYLORD" in block letters.

I began to strip. Lucas was now completely naked. He was beautiful. I shoved the thought from my mind. I would not let myself think it. I would not follow that path. It was unnatural. Even that little boy in church knew as much. His song echoed in my mind; "No homo ain't ever going to make it to Heaven." I was going to make it to Heaven. I was determined to get there.

I needed to find a girl to date. Maybe now that I was on the football team I could do so. I would not make the mistake of the Myer brothers. I was going to work out and become just as muscular as them, but I was going to use my muscles to attract girls. Once I found a girl I could get rid of the sinful thoughts in my head. Even if I wasn't getting any action, the possibility of it would allow me to focus on females the way God intended.

I focused on stripping. I wanted to get into my uniform as quickly as possible, both because I couldn't wait to wear it and because I wanted to cover up my nakedness. It was not being naked that concerned me. It was being naked around guys who were physically superior to me. Even with the varsity players out of the locker room, I was still inferior to every guy there. I was so tired of being small.

I jumped as a locker door near me slammed with a loud clang. I looked to my side and then quickly back again. Cody Caldemyer was swearing under his breath. In the glimpse I'd had of him he looked mad enough to chew on nails. I was relieved when he left the locker room. I was having enough trouble trying to figure out how to wear my jock strap. I'd never worn one before.

"What's up his butt?" Kevin asked.

"He got cut from varsity," Lucas said. "Remember? He was on the varsity squad last year but he got sent down. He was in a lot of fights last year."

I swallowed hard. Cody didn't like me too much. Just what I needed—a guy who was known for brawling taking a dislike to me. Maybe I could make peace with him before he took a swing at me.

I managed to get my jock on without looking like I didn't know what I was doing. The pouch scrunched my stuff up uncomfortably. I wondered how guys who were big down there could stand it. I stole a look at Lucas. His jock was stretched out so much I could see part of his stuff. Lucas caught me looking.

"Uh...does that hurt?" I asked. I figured I'd better speak up before he suspected I was checking him out. I didn't want to lose the one sort-of friend I had on the team.

Lucas looked confused for a moment, but then he figured out what I was talking about.

"It was uncomfortable at first but then I got used to it. It's the price I have to pay for being hung like a horse."

My face turned red as the guys around me laughed.

"Keep dreaming, Needmore!" one of them called. "Your last name says it all, you *Need More* size!"

"I don't have to dream. I've got it where it counts!"

Lucas groped his package. I swallowed hard and struggled into my uniform, trying to ignore the stirring in my jock.

"Never wore a jock before?" Lucas asked quietly.

I shook my head. I was embarrassed by my lack of knowledge. I was a complete novice, surrounded by experts. Most of my teammates had probably already slept with girls.

"You'll get used to it. You'd hardly even notice once practice begins."

I nodded. I was overwhelmed. Bigger guys surrounded me, I didn't know how to wear a jock, and I could only guess what was coming up in my first football practice.

"Nervous?" Lucas asked.

"Yeah."

"You'll be fine. Practices are tough, but no one has died yet."

"I thought I was going to die my first practice," Kevin said.

"Ha! Ha! I remember," said Beck. "You spewed chunks all over the end zone."

"Never have pizza before the first practice," Kevin said, laughing.

"I shouldn't eat pizza?" I asked.

"You can eat it. Just don't eat too much of it," Kevin said.

"What you should do is drink milk, lots of milk," said Beck from the other side of the locker room.

"Don't listen to him," Lucas warned. "If you drink a lot of milk before practice you will be hurling."

"Sure, ruin the fun," Beck said.

"That's what I'm here for, to ruin your fun. Uh, I forgot your name. It's Becky, right?" Lucas asked.

"It's Beck, asshole."

"Oh yeah, slipped my mind."

Beck flipped Lucas off, but Lucas just laughed.

I felt out of place as I walked toward the football field with Lucas and the others. My uniform felt strange and my jock squeezed my stuff together. I felt like I didn't belong in my uniform. The way some of the guys were eyeing me I was certain they agreed.

We had a short team meeting. Most of it was about teamwork and sticking up for each other on and off the field. Coach Jordan also talked about cigarettes, chewing tobacco, and alcohol and how they were all bad for athletes. Some of the guys grinned slyly at each other about the alcohol. I bet they drank a lot. I'd never tried so much as one beer. I was not ashamed about that. Drinking was wrong.

Coach Jordan talked about getting ready for our first game and said we'd be spending at least a part of every other practice in the weight room. It might have been my imagination, but I felt like everyone looked at me when he talked about working out. I'd show them. Now that I was on the team I'd put on some real muscle. I thanked God I'd worked out all summer. Without those workouts I would've looked truly pathetic.

We started practice by running around the track. I was thankful I'd done a lot of running over the summer or I would've dropped dead right there on the track for sure. The coach kept us running a lot longer than he had during tryouts. A few of my teammates looked like they were in pain after a few laps, and some had to slow down almost to a walk well before coach called us off the track. Even I was huffing and puffing by the end.

Next, Coach had us do sit-ups. I felt like I'd been drafted into the army. I'd never done so many sit-ups before. My midsection began to ache and then finally to burn. Just when I thought I could do not a single sit-up more Coach called a halt and moved us onto our next exercise.

Cody looked at me and shook his head dismissively as we dropped to the ground to do pushups. It wasn't going to be easy getting along with him. He'd already decided I was too scrawny to play football. I just hoped he wasn't right.

Coach Jordan pushed us. He kept us doing pushups until my arms were shaking. I was so wobbly after a while I collapsed repeatedly. I didn't give up, but my form was horrible near the end. I was thankful when Coach told us to stand and run in place, bringing our knees up high. After running in place, we continued with a lot of exercises that were unfamiliar to me.

We spent most of the rest of the practice working on passes, which were not my strong point... not that I actually had a strong point. I was afraid Coach Jordan would walk over and tell me I wasn't right for the team after all. I noticed him watching me a few times when I made a clumsy pass. I could put a good spin on the ball, but I couldn't get it very far. Cody watched me, then shook his head with disapproval. My face darkened with anger. If I was bigger, I'd get up in his face and ask him what his problem was. That thought almost made me laugh. I wasn't a confrontational kind of guy. I probably wouldn't have gotten in Cody's face even if I was his size.

Coach worked us hard with drills. My muscles were screaming and I was gasping for breath near the end. We were constantly on the move. The only break I got was when I was waiting my turn to embarrass myself with my weak passes. I thought I might blow chunks like Kevin said he had the year before, but I managed not to do it. I was feeling kind of nauseous as we walked back toward the gym at the end of practice. My entire body hurt.

"Congratulations. You survived your first football practice," Lucas said as he walked near me.

I suddenly felt more nauseous than before. I actually thought I was gonna hurl. I held my hand over my mouth, but the feeling slowly subsided. I released a sigh of relief when I didn't lose my lunch.

"Does it get easier?" I asked.

"If you can't handle it, quit."

I looked behind me. It was Cody.

"I can handle it."

"I don't know what Coach was thinking putting a shrimp like you on the team. You'll be useless. You should quit before you embarrass yourself—more than you already have. You're pathetic."

"Shut it, Cody," Lucas warned.

"What is he, your pet? Or does Elijah do special favors for you?"

From the tone of Cody's voice I knew exactly what he meant. My face turned red. I wanted to turn around and clock him, but that wasn't a very Christian thing to do. He'd also kill me.

"I happen to like him and some people don't have to bribe others to be their friend."

"Ohhh!" said more than one guy around us. Cody was not happy. He shot me a dirty look and then shouldered past us.

"Why doesn't he like me?" I asked. "I've never done anything to him."

"Cody has a chip on his shoulder and a stick up his ass. I'm sure in grade school his teachers wrote 'Does not work and play well with others' on his report card," Lucas said.

I laughed.

"He may be right. I don't see how I'm going to be able to stop a 200-pound linebacker."

"If you can't stop him then slow him down. Grab onto his leg and refuse to let go," Lucas said.

"I may have to try that."

"I'm sure Coach Jordan picked you for a reason. He cut bigger guys while he kept you. He knows what he's doing."

"I hope so because I'm not sure I do."

"It is just your first day, Elijah."

"And I didn't hurl!"

"It that a crack?" Kevin called over to me.

"Hmm, you're a lot bigger than me so...no."

Kevin laughed.

"It was a crack," I whispered to Lucas.

"I heard that!" Kevin called back, but he didn't come to clobber me.

I liked most of my teammates. I didn't know most of them very well yet, but only Cody was hostile. The others ranged from indifferent to friendly. I liked Lucas the best. He looked out for me and he was just plain nice.

I was too exhausted to take much note of my naked teammates in the locker room or the showers. Or, perhaps my first football practice was beginning to make a man out of me. Soon, there would be girls in my life, or at least one girl.

I walked home alone. I could not remember ever having been so tired before. I wanted to lie down on the sidewalk and sleep. I was almost too tired to eat, but I was ravenously hungry. My mother had made vegetable soup. While I was sweating buckets on the football field hot soup would not have appealed to me at all, but the scent of it as I walked into the kitchen made my mouth water.

I sat down and ate a big bowl of soup. My parents had already eaten. We almost always ate as a family, but times were changing. My brothers were out of the house and football practice would put me home late most evenings. What's more, I'd never be sure when I was coming in. I missed Thomas and Mitch, and I kind of missed our family meals too. I guess I couldn't expect everything to remain the same indefinitely.

I was sleepy as I climbed the stairs to my room, but I didn't dare lie down until my homework was completed. If I did I'd slip into a coma and surely not awaken until the next morning.

I attacked my homework with what enthusiasm I could muster, although my true goal was getting finished so I could go to bed. Oddly enough I became more alert as I read and scribbled in my notebooks. By the time I had finished I wasn't sleepy. It was just as well. It wasn't even nine p.m. yet! Whoever heard of going to bed so early? Then, again I think I could have dropped right off if I'd tossed myself on the bed when I got home from practice.

I lay on my bed with my hands behind my head. My life was changing. I'd made the football team and had survived my first practice. If I could make it through one practice, I could surely make it through them all. I was close to becoming friends with Lucas and some of the other guys on the team seemed to like me, more or less. Cody had it in for me, but I had a feeling I could get along with everyone else. I was finally fitting in with the jocks. I almost couldn't believe it.

***

I was so sore the next morning I could barely move. It reminded me of the morning after my first work out. My muscles had screamed at me for abusing them then too. I painfully struggled to my feel and lurched toward the bathroom. My legs hurt, my shoulders hurt, my chest hurt, and even my butt hurt. I stripped off my boxers and climbed into the shower. The hot water massaged my sore muscles and I moaned with pleasure.

I shampooed my hair and soaped up. The pain in my muscles weakened to a dull ache. The pain was a pleasant reminder that I was on my way to being a jock. Football was just what I need to push myself. If I could just keep going I'd end up with a ripped body like Lucas, popularity, and a girlfriend. As a football player I could have it all.

It might have been my imagination, but I thought kids looked at me differently as I walked through the hallways the next morning. It probably was my imagination. We'd only had one practice and our first game was days away. No one outside of the team even knew I was on the team. Still, there was something going on. I felt better about myself than I had for a long time.

When lunchtime rolled around I gripped my tray as I looked toward the football table. My brothers had sat at that table in years past. Approaching it now was intimidating, but I forced myself forward. I was a member of the team. I had a right to sit there. I kept my feet moving and did not allow myself to veer off. I tried to project an outward confidence I did not feel. I faltered a few steps away, but I forced myself to keep going.

"What do you want?" Cody snarled when he spotted me.

"Here, there's a spot by me," said Kevin.

"You promise not blow chunks on me?"

"Ha. Ha. Very funny. Now sit your ass down."

I slid in beside Kevin. Lucas nodded at me over his burger.

"Want some milk? Kevin asked, wiggling his eyebrows.

"No thank you. I think that joke is over, Kevin."

Kevin laughed.

"Why are you so short?" Cody asked.

I shrugged.

"Maybe it's my high metabolism. I eat three times a day but my body eats six times a day."

"Do you even weigh a hundred pounds?"

"I weigh 120."

"Oh my God! I weighed that when I was twelve!" Cody said.

"Yeah, but it was because you had a fat ass," Lucas said.

"I have never been fat in my life. I'm all muscle."

Cody flexed his arms over his head and his muscles bulged. He noticed me looking so I looked away.

"Flex your arm," Cody said.

I pushed up my sleeve and flexed my right bicep. The muscle bulged.

"You must work out," Kevin said.

"Kevin is hot for Elijah," Cody said. "You're big ole homo, aren't you?"

Kevin sneered at Cody.

"You wouldn't talk like that if Shawn and Tim were sitting here," Lucas said.

"Maybe I would, but they always sit at the homo table with all the other faggots. I hear they all get together for weekend butt-fuck parties."

I felt my face pale slightly. I wasn't used to hanging out with guys who used words like that. If I used such words around my parent's they'd wash my mouth out with soap. I reminded myself that most people weren't as religious as my family. My parents had long ago explained that a lot of people didn't attend church. I almost couldn't believe it when they told me. Our former pastor had sometimes preached about the unfaithful. He said it was our job to save them. I looked around the table. I could just imagine the reaction I'd get if I tried to get any of my new teammates to go to church. Maybe my fear made me a bad Christian, but I just wanted to fit in. Maybe I could prove myself and then try to save my teammates one by one. Maybe that's even why God put me on the football team.

Lucas burped loudly and all the guys laughed, even me. It was so loud kids at neighboring tables looked in our direction. I hoped I didn't have to burp to fit in. I didn't know how.

"Mmm. Mmm. I want me some of that," Cody said as a leggy girl with a big chest walked past.

"What? You haven't already had some? The way you talk I thought you'd already banged every girl in school," Beck said.

"Nah, not every girl, just the hot ones. I leave the ugly ones for you guys."

"You're so full of shit," Lucas said, clearly amused.

"You're such an idiot for dating one girl, Lucas. How can you limit yourself like that? We're surrounded by all this fine pussy and you only get one, if you get her," Cody said.

My ears were burning. I could not believe the language spoken at this table.

"At least I won't end up with a sexually transmitted disease," Lucas said. "How is that gonorrhea coming?"

"Fuck you! I don't have gonorrhea or any other disease. All the disease is over at the faggot table. They've probably all got AIDS."

"My pastor says AIDS is God's punishment for homosexuality."

Cody stared at me. Why did I mention my pastor? Now he'd think I was a nerd. Cody laughed.

"He's probably right. It would be no loss if they all died."

"Tell that to the varsity team. Their coach just made Shawn quarterback."

"What the fuck?" Cody asked loudly. "What the hell is up with having a faggot quarterback? First Brendan and now that fudge packer. I bet he sodomizes his little brother every night."

"You're getting brave now that Brendan isn't around anymore," Lucas said.

"I wasn't afraid of that faggot."

"No?" Lucas grinned and Cody's face reddened slightly. I knew I was missing something.

"God! I hope we don't end up with a homo quarterback," Cody said.

"I doubt you'll be offered the position," Beck said.

"Shut the fuck up, asshole!" Cody said. Beck just laughed. It was contagious.

"What are you laughing at?" Cody asked, spearing me with his eyes. "I'd say you're the most likely out of any of us to be a fag."

I stopped laughing.

"Cody, stop picking on Elijah. He's a member of the team," Lucas said.

"A tiny member," Cody said, then laughed.

I had the feeling I had just been insulted, but I couldn't figure out how. Cody laughed louder when he saw the expression on my face.

"Not too bright either," Cody said.

"What?" I asked.

"Tiny member? Get it?" Cody asked.

I shook my head.

"It means you have a little dick. Cody is obsessed with dicks," Lucas said.

My face reddened with embarrassment and Cody's reddened with anger.

"What's wrong, Cody? You can dish it out but you can't take it?" Beck asked.

"I can take it. It's just more fun dishing it out." Cody grinned and laughed again. He was extremely attractive when he wasn't being a jerk. Unfortunately that wasn't too often.

Cody left me alone the rest of lunch. He almost seemed friendly at times—almost. Sitting there with the guys I felt like I really was part of the team. I was a member of the football team, but being a member and feeling like I belonged were two different things.

I noticed girls looking in our direction now and then—hot girls. I noticed boys giving our table a wide berth. I also noticed kids noticing that I was sitting with the football players. I'd just taken a huge step up in the hierarchy of VHS.

"Hey! Watch it!" Cody shouted.

Cody turned around and a very thin blond boy turned white with fear. Another kid had pushed him into Cody as the pair walked past. I vaguely remembered the boy who had bumped into Cody from my P.E. class.

"Sorry," the kid stammered.

"You should be, you little twerp."

"Lay off him, Cody," I said. I knew it was a mistake, but I didn't like to see anyone getting bullied. Cody turned on me.

"What did you say to me, you little shit?"

"I said lay off... or do you enjoy picking on guys half your size?"

Cody's face grew sullen.

"Asshole," he said.

The kid scurried off. Our table was momentarily quiet. I wondered if Cody would hunt me down and kick my butt between classes, but he gave no sign he had any such plans. He practically ignored me for the rest of lunch.

I'd expected the guys to spend most of their time talking about football, but they mostly talked about girls—which ones were easy and which were a waste of time. A few of the things said made my ears turn red, but I tried to pretend I thought nothing of it. If my parents knew what my teammates said at the lunch table they'd never allow me to sit with them, and would probably make me quit the team. It was a sin of omission, but I wasn't going to tell my parents about all the vulgar talk.

After lunch, I headed for my next class. I watched out of the corners of my eyes for Cody, just in case he came after me. Of course, there wasn't much I could do if he did, except try to outrun him. If Cody wanted to get me, he would. I couldn't hide from him in the locker room or showers or on the field.

I would've been smart to keep my mouth shut at lunch. Cody wouldn't have hit the kid who bumped into him, at least I don't think so, but I hated to see anyone bullied. Being on the small side I'd been targeted by bullies myself and I knew it wasn't fun. Even though Cody might get me I wasn't sorry I'd spoken up. God commanded the strong to protect the weak. I almost laughed at that, not that I was making fun of God because I'd never do that, but the thought of me being "the strong" was hilarious.

Kids really did look at me differently after lunch. They'd seen me sitting at the football table. I was at the junior varsity end, but I was still at the table. No one had noticed me much before, but now I was a football player and that gave me immediate status. I just hoped I could find my niche on the team. Lucas said Coach Jordan had picked me for a reason. I sure hoped he was right.

When I walked into the locker room to dress out for 7th period P.E. I spotted the kid Cody had yelled at during lunch. Now that I saw him again, I remembered him better. He was about three inches taller than me, but I bet he didn't weigh an ounce more. He was all legs and his torso was painfully slim. He was changing into his V.H.S. Phys. Ed. shirt so I could see his bare chest. He had no muscle. He was even thinner than I had been before I began to work out.

The boy noticed me looking at him and smiled shyly. He looked like he wanted to say something, but quickly looked away. I dressed out and joined the others in the gym. I paid attention during roll call and the boy answered to Morgan. At least now I knew his last name.

I'd never cared much for calisthenics, but compared to football practice it was easy! Jumping jacks were nothing. Thanks to my summer of working out I could do push-ups and sit-ups with ease. I almost laughed when some of my classmates whined about the push-ups. If this was football practice we'd just be getting started! I noticed Morgan having a lot of trouble. He couldn't even do them right. His skinny butt was way up in the air.

After calisthenics we ran out to the football field and then around the track. Again, the running we did in P.E. was nothing compared to what we did in football practice. No one in my P.E. class was on the team, but there were plenty of guys bigger and better built than me. Still, I noticed them puffing while I ran almost effortlessly.

Morgan was a good runner too. He wasn't out of breath at all as we ran. I fell in beside him and ran with him. He looked at me once and smiled shyly, but mostly he focused his attention ahead.

For the next couple of weeks we were learning about football in P.E. The timing was perfect for me. I'd studied on football during the summer and was still doing so, but there were some things I didn't get yet. I was sure I was the only guy on the team who didn't know all about the game.

Morgan looked intimidated as he lined up across from me for our scrimmage. He was taller than me, but I was better built. I smiled to put him at ease, something no player would ever do in a real game.

I rammed into Morgan when the ball was snapped, but I held back. Even so I sent him flying. I rushed past him, but the receiver fumbled the ball. On the next snap I took it even easier on Morgan. This was only P.E. and the kid was so light he was easy to push aside. Actually, he might have weighed as much as me, but with his long legs he had a much higher center of gravity. Morgan was not built for football.

I'd like to say that I was one of the best football players in my P.E. class, but the truth was that I wasn't. I didn't get a chance to handle the ball. I could get past Morgan, but the plays never lasted long enough for me to do much. I knew talent when I saw it and just about any boy in class could throw better than me. They were better at tackling too. If I weren't lined up against Morgan I would've been in trouble. I didn't let it get me down. I was starting at the bottom, but I was on the football team. I could only improve and I was determined to do so. I was not going to give up on the incredible opportunity I had before me.

Our P.E. teacher held Morgan back at the end of class so I lingered on the football field so I could talk to him. I didn't have long to wait. I stepped in beside him as he walked toward the gym.

"I'm Elijah," I said.

"Banshee."

"Banshee?"

"Yeah. My real name is Fred. How is that for boring?"

"Why are you called Banshee?

Banshee looked around, but the other guys were long gone, and our P.E. teacher was picking up markers on the football field. Banshee opened his mouth and let out a wailing scream that almost made me go in my pants.

"A Banshee is an Irish spirit that wails. I made that sound once when playing capture the flag with friends and they named me Banshee. The name stuck."

"That was freaky," I said.

Banshee grinned.

Thanks for taking up for me at lunch. I thought that guy was gonna kill me."

"Nah. I don't think he would've hit you."

"Well, thanks anyway."

"Don't mention it."

"So, you're a football player?"

"Yeah. Junior varsity."

"You kind of look like a football player."

"Me? I'm the smallest guy on the team."

"You look strong. You're sure better built than me, but then everyone is."

"I stared working out at the end of the last school year. My goal was to get on the football team."

"Congratulations. You succeeded."

"Thanks. I still don't know how I made the team. I'm so excited!"

Banshee and I talked all the way back to the gym and kept talking as we stripped and walked to the showers. I noticed Banshee looking at my arms and chest. I liked being looked at. It was the first time anyone had actually noticed the muscles I'd worked so hard to get.

We didn't talk much in the showers because the other guys were shouting and laughing and horsing around. I noticed something about the boys in my gym class. Most of them were nowhere near as built as my teammates. I actually had a better body than most of them, even though I was shorter. There was nothing I could do about my height, and thankfully I was still growing, but I was glad I'd put in all that time working out. I intended to continue.

I picked up a towel from the towel boy and walked back into the locker room while drying my hair. I spent a lot more time in the locker room these days. I was in there every day for P.E. and for football practice. All of the other kids had to use the lockers that all the P.E. classes shared, but since I was a football player I had my very own. I felt special.

I bid Banshee "goodbye" at the end of class and rushed off to my next. There was never quite enough time between classes, but that was mostly because I wasn't into carrying a lot of books. I stopped at my locker between almost every class.

I returned the locker room after school. I stripped down and changed into my practice uniform. I eyed Cody as he changed. He was all muscle. He could rip me apart with ease. A fight between us wouldn't be a fight at all. It would be a massacre. I bet if I hit him as hard as I could in the stomach and he wouldn't even feel it. All he had to do was tighten his six-pack and it would deflect my blow like a shield. Cody caught me looking at him and snarled. I quickly looked away. My heart beat faster. I just knew he was gonna kill me.

Cody slammed his locker and left the locker room, but not before glaring and pointing at me threateningly. None of the other guys saw him do it, which frightened me all the more. He was out to get me.

"You okay?" Lucas asked as he pulled on his jersey. If I had his muscles I wouldn't have been afraid of Cody.

"Yeah. I'm just hoping Coach doesn't kill any of us today."

"Look at the bright side. If you do drop dead, you'll always be remembered as the first football practice fatality at VHS."

"Thanks, that makes me feel so much better."

Lucas grinned.

I had some difficulty running at the beginning of practice. Coach Jordan made us run longer than the day before (and told us we'd be running more and more as the season progressed) but I was winded before we'd even run as many laps as the day before. I slowed my pace but still had difficulty breathing. Near the end I'd slowed to a jog and I was hurting.

The pushups got to me even more, especially when Coach made us do them with one hand. Lucas and Cody could do it, but the rest of us struggled. I couldn't keep my balance and kept falling over. It was extremely difficult to do even one pushup with only one arm! Yep, this was it. This was the day I was going to drop dead on the football field.

When we were all good and exhausted, coach led us back into the gym and to the weight room. Coach Jordan must've taken a sadistic pleasure out of tormenting us. I watched Lucas pump out bench presses as I waited my turn. He was using two hundred pounds and his chest and arms bulged like crazy. I wanted muscles like his so bad I couldn't stand it.

I was up next and Lucas was a hard act to follow. I was embarrassed to take off half the weights, but at least I could bench one hundred. When I started working out late in the spring, I could only lift about half that. I thanked God for my progress over the summer.

A hundred pounds was all I could handle and my arms trembled as I struggled to finish the last few reps.

Cody gave a dismissive snort as he walked past, but I didn't let him get to me. There wasn't much I could do about the fact Cody didn't like me. He had no reason not to like me. He just decided not to like me and that was that.

Some of my teammates looked surprised when they saw that I was benching a hundred pounds and were equally impressed at other amounts of weight I used for curls, military presses, and so forth. I wasn't as strong as my teammates, but they'd expected me to be a weakling.

I pushed myself a little too hard to impress the guys. Before the end of our weight session my arms were trembling. That wasn't my only problem. Most of my teammates were rather well built and some of them stripped off their shirts to work out. Seeing them naked in the locker room and showers was bad enough, but seeing the muscles of their arms and chest bulge and flex made me glad I was wearing a jock. Even so I feared some of the guys might notice the bulge in my pants. I tried to think of Jesus instead of my hunky teammates, but my attention kept getting drawn back to the hot guys around me.

I grew increasingly upset because I could not control the unnatural, perverted thoughts that rampaged through my mind. I almost felt like I was going to cry but there was no way I was going to cry in front of my teammates. Lucas noticed my pained expression so I quickly looked away and focused on a set of rows.

When Coach Jordan announced time was up Lucas lingered as the other guys headed for the showers. He held me back when I started to leave and soon it was just the two of us.

"Don't let Cody get to you. I saw the looks he was shooting you."

I couldn't tell Lucas the real reason I was upset so I pretended he was right. It wasn't exactly a lie, but it wasn't far from it. I didn't like lying.

"I just wish he would cut me some slack. I'm trying."

"Dude, you're doing great. I didn't know you could lift that much weight. You're a stud."

"In my dreams maybe."

Lucas laughed.

"Don't let Cody get you down. You are doing great and he's being a jerk. Once he gets over being sent down to junior varsity he'll probably chill out."

"Thanks."

Lucas left, but I remained behind for a while. I gazed around the room at all the weight equipment. Being on the football team felt unreal. I felt like I didn't belong in this place or with my teammates. How long would it take to me feel like I fit in?

Not fitting in was the least of my problems. Some of the guys on the team were so hot! Cody scared me, but he had the most incredible muscles and his... No. I couldn't let myself think about that.

I didn't know if I could remain on the team. I was willing to endure the physical punishment of practice, the humiliation of not being as big or strong as my teammates, and the taunts of Cody, but I couldn't stay on the team if it was going to set me on the path to Hell. I had never before had so much trouble fighting the perverted, sinful thoughts that sometimes forced their way into my mind. I was surrounded by temptation.

I headed for the locker room. Most of the guys were already getting dressed. I stripped and walked into the showers. Only a handful of guys were left and three more departed as I turned on the shower.

The hot water relaxed my tired muscles. I grinned. I actually had muscles! I might be small and I was nothing compared to my teammates, but I was no longer a scrawny little kid.

I saw Cody out of the corner of my eye. The was shampooing his hair and the suds ran down his smooth muscular chest, over his six pack, and right down to his... private parts. My own private parts stirred. I was about to look away, but Cody turned his back to me. He had wide, knotted shoulders, a back rippling with muscles, and the hottest butt! I had to turn from the sight because I was becoming visibly aroused. I could not let myself walk down that path. I had to fight it. I could not let my body betray me. It didn't know right from wrong. I did, and staring at naked guys in the showers was wrong.

I calmed myself down by looking only at the wall. I fought the temptation to turn and look. Somehow I managed it, but I wanted to look at Cody's naked body so badly!

I finished soaping up and rinsing off. I shut off the showerhead and turned. I almost walked right into Cody. He was so close I could feel his breath on my face. He shoved me up against the wall with his arm across my chest.

"I don't like you on the team, faggot. If you know what's good for you, you'll quit."

"I'm not a..."

Cody grabbed my throat with his free hand and squeezed. I couldn't breathe.

"I know what you are. I see you checking out the other guys. I see you checking me out. We don't need a sick, useless little pervert like you on the team."

I struggled to breathe, but I couldn't. I could feel my face turning blue. Cody finally released my throat, but kept me pinned against the wall. I gasped for breath.

"Do you have any idea what I could do to you right now, faggot," Cody snarled.

I tried to keep the tears from coming, but I was so scared.

"Yeah, that's it. Cry like a little baby. Even if you weren't a pillow-biter you wouldn't belong here. Football is a game for the strong, not puny little shits like you. You quit the team or I'll make your life a living hell."

Tears ran down my cheeks as I fought to keep from sobbing. I struggled, but I couldn't budge Cody's arm. He didn't look like he was putting out any effort at all to hold me in place. It made me feel weak and pathetic.

"Don't go crying to Lucas, either. You wouldn't want him to get hurt, would you?"

I shook my head. I trembled with fear. I tried to fight it, but I couldn't stop shaking. Cody grinned.

"Quit the team. There's no way you can make it anyway. Save yourself the trouble, the humiliation, and the pain."

Cody released me, but I was too scared to move. He turned to leave, but then turned back to me.

"Oh, one more thing. Don't sit at the team table anymore. You're not one of us. If you sit with us again I'll make you very, very sorry."

Cody walked out. I slid to the floor and began sobbing. I just sat there crying and shaking like a little baby. What was I thinking joining the football team? Cody was right. I didn't belong here. I wanted to belong, but wanting didn't make it so. Something else shook me up just as much. Cody seemed certain I was a homo. Had I given in to my perverted, unnatural thoughts to such an extent there was no turning back? Had I already lost my soul? I clasped my hands together.

"Dear God, Please make this go away. I don't want to be that. I just want to be normal. I'll do anything. Please take away my unnatural lust. Help me. Please. I'm desperate. Amen."

I felt a little better when I finished my prayer, but I was still very shaken and upset. I walked out of the shower room and picked up a towel. Luckily, the locker room was empty except for the towel boy. I could hear him cleaning up a couple of rows over. I quickly dried off, dressed, and departed.

I walked toward home slowly. Should I quit the team? I wanted to be on the team more than just about anything, but did I dare to stay? Cody would no doubt make my life a living Hell as he'd promised. He'd never liked me and now he hated me. If I was what he said I was, he had a right to hate me. Maybe he was my punishment for having sinful thoughts. My evil thoughts had attracted him to me. If I could eradicate those thoughts maybe Cody would leave me alone.

I walked to the park. I didn't want my parents to see me so upset. They would ask what was wrong and I'd have to lie. I didn't want to commit yet another sin. The list of my sins was already far, far too long.

When I reached the park I washed away the evidence of my tears in the water fountain. As the water flowed away from my eyes I looked up to see a boy gazing at me. He was about my age or perhaps just a bit older. What I noticed most were his kind eyes, but there was something about him... I wasn't sure what. It wasn't his appearance. His black, curly hair was a little long, but not unusually so. The boy's complexion was a little dark, but again nothing out of the ordinary. He wasn't especially tall or short. He was pleasant looking, but not strikingly handsome. He was dressed like any boy our age, but... there was something about him.

"God loves you just as you are, Elijah."

I gazed at the boy, too stunned to speak. Guys didn't talk like that.

"Do you go to my church?" I asked.

The boy shook his head.

"I have no need to attend your church to know the words I've spoken are true."

The boy spoke with such confidence that he made me feel a good deal better.

"What is your... name?" My voice trailed off. The boy was gone.

I looked all around, but I did not see him anywhere.

I walked toward home. I thought about what the boy said. God did love everyone. Did that really include me? I'd done some bad things in my life and the worst of all were the thoughts that had run through my head—unnatural thoughts. Could God actually love me when I was a pervert? I made up my mind right then and there to fight my unnatural thoughts with everything I had. I loved God too much to give up.

By the time I got home there was no evidence I had been upset or crying. I was still worried—about my ability to control my lust, about Cody's threats, and just about surviving football, but as

I didn't want to discuss any of it with my parents so I hid my fear. Was that a sin? Possibly, but what could I do?

Mom heated up my supper for me, except for the fried chicken, which I liked cold. There were mashed potatoes, green beans, and apple pie for dessert. I was ravenously hungry! Working out burned up tons of calories.

Luckily, my mother did not ask about football so I didn't have to skirt around my problems. She asked about my classes instead and I was able to truthfully tell her I was doing well. I had received an A on an algebra quiz and another on my first English assignment. I would have no trouble keeping myself eligible for football.

Supper was delicious, especially the apple pie. My mother even put a scoop of vanilla ice cream on top. Yum! I ate a lot more now, but I wasn't worried about getting fat. Football burned up tons of calories. If anything, I was probably losing weight. I had to be careful about that. I had almost no fat to lose.

I went upstairs to my room and worked on my homework. My muscles were extremely tired and sitting down felt wonderful. Reading was relaxing, even if it was for school. Writing took little effort. I had some trouble concentrating on algebra, but at least I didn't need my muscles for that. Still, I was sleepy by the time I finished my homework. I tired more easily now. Football practices wore me out!

Before turning in, I sat down on the edge of my bed and gave football some thought. Cody had promised to make my life a living hell if I didn't quit the team. I had no doubt he'd live up to that promise. My life would be easier without football. Practices were brutal and the workout today was tough. There were the temptations in the locker room and showers to consider too. That was the real danger. I might feel like a loser, quitter, and wimp for quitting the team, but if I didn't change my ways I was going to lose my soul.

My lower lip trembled as I thought about quitting the team. I loved being on the football team. Despite all the hard work, I loved it. I wanted to stay on the team, but how could I? What might Cody do to me if I didn't quit? I did not know if I could control myself in the locker room and showers either. I wanted to be a good Christian but I felt myself drawn to those guys... I frowned. I guess there was only one decision to make. I couldn't remain on the team. I was going to have to give up on my dream.

There was a knock at the door.

"Come in," I called out, hoping my voice didn't betray what I was feeling inside.

"Hey, sport. I bought you something."

"Yeah?" I asked. My father rarely bought me something for no reason.

"What do you think of this?"

Dad held out a brand new football, still in the box. I grinned, but then almost frowned again. Luckily, I caught myself in time.

"I'm darned proud of you for making the team and for hanging in there. I know practices are tough."

"Brutal," I said.

"Well, I'm very proud of you."

Dad hugged me.

"Thanks, Dad," I said.

Dad closed the door as he left. I stood there holding the football. There was no way I could quit now. Perhaps this was a sign from God. I'd just have to endure whatever Cody did to me and fight my sinful thoughts. I grinned. I was staying on the team.

Chapter Three

I hesitated as I came out of the lunch line. I looked toward the football table. I wasn't quitting the team. I didn't want to and I couldn't, not after Dad gave me that football and told me how proud he was of me. If I failed and was cut it was one thing, but I couldn't quit. Cody had warned me about what would happen if I didn't quit. Should I defy him further by sitting with the team after he told me not to dare doing so?

I gripped my tray tightly, trembling slightly with fear. Who did Cody think he was telling me where I could and could not sit? I had half a mind to march right over and sit down beside him.

He would kick my butt for sure if I did that, but then he likely would anyway when I showed up in the locker room to dress out. I took a step toward the football table, but then I spotted Banshee sitting all alone. He looked lonely and sad. It was God's wish that we love and be kind to each other. I changed directions and headed for Banshee. I could feel Cody's eyes on me as I walked away. He probably had a grin of triumph on his face. I was tired of him bullying me, but I needed to help Banshee more than I needed to defy Cody. Not getting beat up was a definite plus and made me doubt my motivation. Then again, I was a good person and could not let anyone suffer. Besides, I'd do my defying of Cody when I showed up for football practice.

"Mind if I sit here?" I asked.

Banshee looked up and immediately smiled at me.

"Please," he said, indicating the empty seat next to him.

"Looking forward to more football in gym?"

"Um... no. I'll be happier when we get to something a little less violent. Thanks for not killing me during our last class."

"Me?"

"You could've nailed me much harder, admit it."

"Yeah."

"Thought so. With your muscles you could've sent me flying."

I grinned. I wasn't used to anyone noticing my muscles.

"Why aren't you sitting at the football table?"

"Eh, they're too loud," I lied. *No. I've lied too much already.* "Actually, I was invited to leave."

"Your teammates kicked you out?"

"Just one of them. Cody, the guy who was giving you trouble yesterday."

"Oh, him. He didn't get mad because you stood up for me, did he?"

"Well, yeah, but he's been on me since I made the team. He told me I'd be very sorry if I sat with the team. He also threatened to make my life a living hell if I didn't quit the team, but I'm not quitting."

"So, why didn't you go ahead and sit with your teammates?"

"I was about to sit with them. I was scared of Cody, but I was about to do it anyway. Then I saw you sitting alone."

"I looked so pathetic you felt sorry for me?"

"Well… honestly, yes, but I also like you and I can always use a new friend. Sitting with you also gives me an excuse not to put my butt in danger by defying Cody. Maybe he won't be so angry I'm not quitting the team if I don't sit with them."

"A reasonable compromise. I don't think I'd have the courage to defy Cody. He's got muscles bulging out everywhere."

"Yeah, if he decides to beat me up I'm dead. I'm hoping that "making my life a living hell" will be limited to shoving me around and calling me names. That I can take."

"Yeah, that's not as bad."

Banshee sounded as if he talked from experience. I thought about asking him, but it was really none of my business.

"Well, I'm glad you came to sit with me. I get tired of eating alone."

"You could surely join other tables?"

"Maybe. I don't know. It's easier not to try."

"As of today, we're starting our own table."

"Yeah!"

I laughed. I liked this kid. He was cute too. He had beautiful blond hair and blue eyes. I stopped myself. No. I would not allow perverted thoughts into my head. Surely I could control my thoughts around Banshee. He was cute, yeah, but cute like a puppy or kitten. The boy had no muscles.

Banshee and I made fun of the fish sticks and what the cafeteria claimed was tartar sauce. We talked and laughed. I liked Banshee. I'd made the right choice when I came to his table.

I looked up and caught a glimpse of the boy from the park. He had so mysteriously appeared and then disappeared in the park I almost thought I'd imagined him, but no, he was walking with two girls, quietly talking. Whoever he was, he was quite real.

"Hey, you want to do something after school sometime?" Banshee asked.

"Um, yeah, but I have football practice every afternoon so a weekend would be better."

"Maybe this Saturday then?"

"Yeah, Saturday is good."

"Great!"

Banshee's enthusiasm made me feel like laughing, but I didn't because I feared he would think I was laughing at him. We talked through the rest of lunch and then headed for our next class.

Banshee and I stuck together in gym. I gave him some pointers while we were playing flag football, even though he was on the other team. We were once again pitted against each other and, while we made it look good, neither of us was using much force. We made a game out of looking as ferocious as possible without actually harming each other, like those stunt guys in movies. Some of the boys in class bought our act and we had to fight to keep from laughing.

I grew increasingly anxious as the end of the day grew nearer. I was sure Cody thought he'd scared me off when I didn't sit at the football table at lunch. Part of me was looking forward to showing him he couldn't bully me into quitting football, but most of me feared the consequences.

Last period ended and I made my way through the crowded hallways as kids rushed past to get out of school as quickly as possible. The halls with filled with loud voices and laughter, but I was quiet. I stopped by my locker to pick up the books I needed for that night and then headed toward my doom.

Anticipating Cody's reaction had kept me in a nervous state all afternoon, but now I was genuinely afraid. Cody did not want me on the team. He hadn't liked me from the beginning and now he was convinced I was a homo. The latter was mostly my own fault. I had checked out Cody and some of the other guys. I hadn't fought hard enough to control my unnatural desires and Cody was my punishment for sinning. Perhaps God had even put Cody in my life for the sole purpose of helping me to avoid temptation. I was going to fight my evil desires with everything I had. I'd asked for God's help. Surely, with his help I could force the perverted thoughts from my mind.

Walking into the gymnasium took effort, but stepping into the locker room was one of the hardest things I'd ever done in my entire life. I didn't see Cody at first. I spotted Beck pulling on his jersey, Lucas stripping off his shirt, and Kevin slipping on his jock. I didn't allow my gaze to linger on any of the male nudity that assaulted my eyes. I knew God helped those who helped themselves.

I felt someone staring at me and turned. Cody glared at me from across the locker room. He was completely naked, but I felt no lust, only fear. Cody mouthed, "You're dead" as he stood there flexing his muscles. He looked like a Greek hero as he stood there glaring at me. I don't think I'd ever been so scared in my entire life.

I swallowed hard as I headed for my locker. My hands trembled slightly as I worked the combination.

"How's it going, Elijah?" Lucas said, slapping me on the back hard enough I lurched forward. "We missed you at lunch today."

My eyes met Cody's. He was close enough to hear everything He dared me to say anything about his threats.

"Yeah. I saw this kid from my P.E. class sitting alone. He looked so sad so I sat with him instead. I figured you guys would survive without me."

"No! No! We can't make it without you! Please! Please come back!" Beck wailed as he clasped my knees.

"You are so weird," Lucas said.

"No. I'm such a badass I can do anything I want," Beck said.

"Yeah, you keep telling yourself that, buddy," Lucas said, patting Beck on the back.

"Kiss my ass," Beck said.

"That's your fetish, not mine, homo," Lucas said.

"Beck isn't a homo. He's just rated as "unfuckable" by all the girls," Kevin said.

"Fuck you, Kevin."

"Or maybe I'm wrong. You want me, don't you, Beck?"

"You wish, cock sucker."

I turned toward my locker and closed my eyes for a moment. I took a couple of breaths to calm myself. The insults my teammates hurled back and forth hurt. I reminded myself that the guys weren't talking to me. I wasn't a homo. Yes, I'd checked out my teammates and I had been attracted to them, but that was coming to an end. I wasn't going to allow myself to be like that. How could anyone choose to be like that? Everyone hated homos.

I stripped down and pulled on my uniform. When I turned around, Cody was looking at me with a sadistic grin on his face. His grin was far worse than his glare. I swallowed hard again. He was gonna kill me.

We headed for the field and began running around the track. I stayed with the pack, but kept my distance from Cody. I was winded too easily again so I slowed my pace. The last few laps were agony. My breath came hard and fast and my heart pounded, but that wasn't the worst of it. I felt so tired I didn't know if I could make it.

We ran a few drills next. My breathing slowed to normal, but I wanted to drop onto the grass and just lay there. I pushed myself. I wasn't giving up. I wasn't going to quit.

Coach Jordan and the old guys began teaching us newbies some plays. We practiced each of them on the field. I amazed myself when I managed to elude the lineman across from me break into the open not once, but twice. Lucas, our quarterback for this practice, noticed and selected me as his receiver. I was intimidated by the responsibility, but reminded myself that this was only practice.

Beck was lined up across from me. His size was intimidating, but at least he wasn't Cody. I was safe from Cody for the moment. He was the quarterback for the other team so chances were he'd get nowhere near me. Still, I kept an eye on him whenever I could.

As we moved into position, I knew I was going to have to play smart. Since we were learning a play there were no surprises. The other team knew exactly what we were going to try to do. I could only mix things up by the way I got around my opponent and what I did after I got my hands on the ball... *if* I managed to get in the clear, and *if* I managed to catch it.

I dodged to the right as Beck lunged for me. He shifted, but not fast enough. I might be small, but I was quick. I broke into the open, sprinted, and turned my head to find Lucas. Our eyes met and he dropped the ball right into my hands. I ran like my butt was on fire and made it to the eighteen-yard line before I was tackled from behind. When I returned to the huddle Lucas gave me a high five.

Lucas marked me as his intended receiver again. The other team probably wouldn't be expecting it because it was too obvious a move. At least that's how Lucas explained it. I moved into position but found myself facing not Beck, but Cody. Coach had switched quarterbacks. My eyes grew wide with fear.

"I'm gonna crush you like a bug," Cody whispered.

When the ball was snapped I darted to the left, but Cody followed my move. I tried to slide to the right, but Cody laid me out flat on my back and fell on me with every ounce of his bodyweight. The air was forced out of my lungs and my whole body hurt.

"Get used to it princess. This is only the beginning," Cody whispered before he climbed off me. He made a show of helping me to my feet.

I turned away for a moment because getting tackled hurt and I was afraid I might cry. I got myself under control and gathered in the huddle with the other guys.

"Elijah is a marked man, so you're it, Doug," Lucas said.

We lined up again. I tried to outthink Cody. I went to my left last time, so maybe I'd try to go to the right. Then again, wouldn't he be expecting that? Maybe I should go to the left again, but Cody knew that I knew he'd be expecting me to go to the right so maybe he was really expecting me to go to the left. Arrgh! Who knew that football required thinking?

I wasn't ready when the ball went into play. Cody dove in low and hit me hard, lifting me right up off the ground. He knocked me to the ground and nearly got to Lucas before Lucas could get rid of the ball.

I just lay there for a few seconds. Tears came to my eyes. I was in pain. Nothing was broken but I felt as if I'd stepped out in front of a truck. I wiped away the tears and slowly climbed to my feet. I tried to hide that I'd cried, but I think Lucas noticed as I joined the huddle. He didn't make me receiver again. He probably figured I'd just get clobbered again. He was most likely right.

I trembled slightly with fear as I lined up against Cody yet again. He stuck out his lower lip and made a trail down his cheek with his finger and then laughed at me. He grabbed my face guard for a moment and pulled me close to him.

"This is it, faggot. They're gonna carry you off this field on a stretcher."

I used every ounce of my willpower not to turn and run off the field. Cody meant business. He was going to hurt me and he was going to hurt me bad. I was not going to be a coward. I was not going to allow Cody to drive me away. I held my ground.

My heart pounded as Lucas called out numbers. I tried to outthink Cody, but it was hard to think knowing I was seconds away from broken bones. I was on the verge of panic. This was it. I was going to die right here on the football field.

"Hike!"

Cody came in low again. There was no time to go left or right. I did the only thing I could. I took a dangerous step forward and leaped into the air. Cody grabbed for me and very nearly got me, but he was too low. The bottom of my foot hit his back and I used Cody as a springboard. Suddenly, I was behind the defensive line, completely in the clear. Lucas spotted me and passed the ball. I caught it and ran like Cody was right behind me, which I feared might be the case.

I didn't look back to see if anyone was close. I just ran. I passed the thirty-yard line, then the twenty, then the ten. I crossed the goal line. I scored!

My team greeted me as I ran back toward them. They patted me on the back and cheered as if this was a game and not a practice. Cody glared at me. He was furious. Some of the guys laughed at him and asked why he played leapfrog with me instead of blocking me. That made Cody even angrier. I tried not to grin too much, but I couldn't believe I'd actually vaulted over Cody and managed to score!

Thankfully, Coach Jordan put us to work on some drills so I didn't have to face off against Cody again. I was going to do everything I could to avoid being positioned against Cody. He would kill me if he got the chance.

I stuck close to Lucas as we walked back toward the gym. I made sure to keep up with the group as everyone stripped and headed for the showers. I got in and out quickly. I didn't dare give Cody the opportunity to get me alone. Limiting my time in the showers also helped me to avoid temptation. I noticed the sleek, muscular bodies of my teammates, but I didn't let my thoughts turn to sex. My mind tried to go there, but every time it did I forced it in another direction. I thought of Jesus, chocolate cake, puppies, and anything else except what the perverted part of my mind tried to think.

I couldn't rush out of the locker room after dressing because Cody was almost finished dressing too and might've got me alone. I waited until some of the other guys were heading out and followed them. Cody sneered at me. He mouthed "You're pathetic", but I knew he was furious that he couldn't get his hands on me.

I was only postponing the inevitable. Cody would get me alone sooner or later. I figured later was better. Maybe he'd calm down and not be quite so mad. Maybe he'd have time to think about how he'd knocked me down and dropped on me during practice. Maybe he'd remember the grimace of pain on my face and not be so eager to hurt me even more. Maybe not, but I was going to avoid a beating as long as possible.

I began walking toward home. I wished I had a car, but I guess that wouldn't help. I wasn't old enough for my license yet. I didn't even have a learner's permit. Sometimes I thought I was doomed to be small and young forever.

I was a few blocks away from school when a black Trans Am slowed down as it passed. My heart leapt into my chest. Cody sneered at me from the driver's side!

The car stopped just up ahead. I panicked. I was hemmed in by a chain-link fence on my left the after school traffic to the right. Cody got out of his car and stomped toward me. I turned to run, but that's when I noticed another boy from school approaching from behind. I didn't know him, but I had a very bad feeling he was one of Cody's buddies. I was trapped. I was just about to try darting past Cody's accomplice when a blue car pulled up to the curve. A lady I didn't know was driving, but Banshee leaned over her from the passenger side.

"Need a lift?"

"Yes!" I said and ran for the car. I was in that backseat before Cody or his bud could even think of trying to stop me.

"Mom, this is Elijah. Elijah this is my mom," Banshee said as the car pulled away from the curb.

"It's very nice to meet you," I said as I met her eyes in the rearview mirror.

"It's very nice to meet you. Fred was just telling me about you."

Banshee twisted around and faced me.

"What'cha doin'? Is practice over?" Banshee asked.

"Yeah, we just finished."

"Elijah is on the football team," Banshee told his mom.

"Junior varsity," I explained. "I just started."

"Hey, if you want, you could come home with me for a while... if you want," Banshee said.

"I'll have to call my parents and I can't stay long. I have homework."

"But you can?"

"Sure."

Banshee grinned. He turned around and faced the front of the car. We were at his place in just a few minutes.

Banshee and I helped his mom carry in groceries, then I called my mom and told her where I was and when I'd be home. Banshee then led me upstairs and into his bedroom. It didn't look like any boy's room I'd been in, not that I'd been in a lot of them. There were posters of teen idols like Matt Dillon, Rob Lowe, C. Thomas Howell, and Corey Haim on the walls. Stuffed animals occupied much of the bed. I thought it odd, but didn't say anything. I walked over to the C. Thomas Howell poster.

"*The Outsiders* was a cool movie. I read the book," I said.

"Yeah, I love that movie. Ponyboy is my favorite character. C. Thomas Howell is soooo.... uh talented."

"Yeah, he's good. I could never be an actor."

"Have you tried?"

"No."

"Then how do you know?"

"Okay. I guess I should have said I'm not interested in being an actor."

"I wouldn't mind."

"Hey, thanks for stopping to offer me a ride. You don't realize it, but you saved my life."

"I did?"

"Did you see that big guy heading toward me? Cody? The blond who was giving you trouble the other day?"

"Yeah."

"He was going to kick my butt. I was going to run for it, but one of his buddies was closing in on me from the other direction. I was trapped until you showed up."

"Wow. I'm glad we stopped!"

"Me too."

"I guess he wasn't kidding when he said he was going to make your life a living hell."

"Oh, he wasn't kidding. Believe me he was quite serious."

"Why does he hate you so much?"

"I have no idea, but he's out to get me."

That was the truth as far as it went. I wasn't sure why he'd taken an instant dislike to me. I couldn't tell Banshee the main reason Cody hated me. If Banshee knew Cody thought I was a homo, our friendship would've been ruined before it began.

"Won't he be hard to avoid?"

"Very. He was knocking me around in practice today. It hurt."

"Looks like he'd pick on someone his own size."

"I'm an easier target. I can't hurt him much."

"Kick him in the balls."

I laughed.

"There was a bigger boy that just kept picking on me in grade school. I got tired of it so I kicked him in the balls. I got in trouble, but when the principal found out why I kicked him the boy who was picking on me got in bigger trouble."

"I'll keep that in mind. I hadn't thought of that. I'm not a fighter."

"Me either."

"I scored a touchdown today," I said to change the subject.

"Really?"

"Yeah. We were practicing plays. I got past Cody, Lucas passed me the ball and I took off running."

"Wow. I don't think I could ever play football. I'm way too skinny. Football players are so big."

"Except for me. I'm the smallest guy on the team by far. When I showed up for tryouts one of the guys told me I was in the wrong place. He wasn't being a jerk. He really thought I was some middle school kid who wandered into the wrong tryouts. I don't know if I'll ever get to play. I'm just not big enough."

"Well, you got past Cody and he's huge! You scored a touchdown! You're kind of built, too. You may not be too tall, but you've got muscle," Banshee said. He gazed at my biceps. "Flex your arm."

I did so and Banshee felt my bicep.

"Nice. Your arm is rock-hard. Look at this," he said and flexed his arm. Very little happened. "Not much there, is there?"

"Well, you could work out."

"Yeah, but I don't think I could ever put on much muscle so there isn't much point. I'm not the athletic type anyway."

"Working out is a lot of work."

"I bet."

I couldn't stay very long, but I enjoyed hanging out with Banshee and talking to him. He genuinely seemed to like me, which made me like him that much more. I'm glad I'd sat with him at lunch. I did it as much for myself as for him, but I'd gained a friend.

I headed home where Mom warmed up beef and noodles for me. Life at home had certainly changed. My parents and I rarely ate together. I guess that was because I had a life now. I just hoped my life didn't end in horrible tragedy, namely me being beat to death by a certain football player with a bad attitude.

***

I somehow managed to evade Cody for the rest of the week. He never once got me alone. He shouldered me in the hallways if I couldn't get away fast enough. He called me nasty names under this breath. He "accidentally" knocked me down once in the showers. He even managed to lay me out on my back again during practice. His abuse was getting to me, but at least he didn't beat the crap out of me.

Banshee and I hung out again on Saturday. Chicken Fillets was having its Grand Opening and giving away a free large drink with every order so we went there for a late lunch. Chicken Fillets was a national chain, but before today the closest one had been up in South Bend. I had a motive besides hunger for eating there. I wanted to get a weekend job. I'd already asked my dad and he said it was okay so long as I kept my grades up.

I had second thoughts about applying when I spotted a six-foot chicken handing out samples.

"That's kind of sick when you think about it," Banshee said after we'd passed.

"What is?"

"A chicken handing out samples of chicken. It borders on cannibalism."

"I never thought of that. I pity whoever is stuck in that costume—how humiliating."

We checked out the menu while we waited in line. There was quite a crowd. In addition to free drinks there was another chicken waddling around handing out small stuffed-toy chicks to kids and yet another was handing out cookies.

We placed our orders and then waited off to one side for our number to be called. I peeled an application from a pad on the wall while we waited.

"Are you thinking of getting a job here?" Banshee asked.

"Yeah. I could use some money."

"Who couldn't?"

"We could work here together."

"No, thank you. It is my life's ambition to never work in a fast food place."

Banshee looked me up and down.

"What?"

"I was just picturing how you'd look in a chicken costume."

"Not funny. Not funny at all."

Soon, our number was up and the boy behind the counter handed me a tray containing my Big Chicken Clucker sandwich, fries, and my large Pepsi. I picked out a table while Banshee waited on his Lil Peep sandwich, fries, and drink.

Banshee gazed at his sandwich cautiously as he sat down across from me.

"What's wrong?"

"Why couldn't they just call this a small chicken sandwich? Lil Peep—I feel like it's made from baby chicks."

"Well, it is."

Banshee jerked his head in my direction. I laughed.

"You're a jerk. I believed you for a moment!"

"I'm a football player. We're required to meet our jerk quota."

"Uh huh. Hey, if you work here I bet you'll get an employee discount."

"I don't think that's much of a plus. This tastes like the chicken sandwiches we get at school."

"I thought everyone loved Chicken Fillets! The commercials say everyone loves the food here so it *must* be true."

"Whoa! Do you know how much fat is in my sandwich?" I asked as I read the label.

"I don't see any fat from here."

I gave Banshee a "you're too stupid" look, but he only grinned.

"According to the wrapper, the Big Clucker contains 160% of the recommended daily allowance of fat. The Little Clucker has 135% and the Lil Peep has 100%."

"See! I ordered the right sandwich."

"Yeah, but your fries also contain 100% of the recommended daily allowance of fat."

"Oh no! I'll be fat in no time!" Banshee said.

"I thought chicken was supposed to be healthy."

"I guess deep frying it in lard adds a few calories. Besides, I don't think you have to worry about being overweight."

"No. I guess not," I said. "It's just scary reading about what's in your food. Don't even get me started on hot dogs."

"Hey, I have an idea for you, Elijah."

"What's that?"

"Don't read the labels!"

"And they say blonds are dumb."

"Hey!"

"Eat your baby chick sandwich and shut up."

"What if it really was made of baby chicks?"

"It's not."

"Yeah, but what if? That would be horrible."

"I'm sure the ASPCA would be all over Chicken Fillets if they made sandwiches out of baby chicks. You can relax. If you want to be extra safe, next time order the Little Chicken Clucker."

We ate and talked and then I filled out the application. The hardest part was references. How was I supposed to have references when I'd never worked before? I listed some teachers who particularly liked me. I hoped that was good enough.

I turned in my application and then Banshee and I departed.

"I hope you get the job. It will be worth it just to see you wear the uniform."

"Ugh! Don't mention that!"

The Chicken Fillets uniform was a black button-down shirt, which wasn't too bad, but the cap... the cap had chicken feathers printed on it, and worse, it had wings!

"I'm going to come in and take pictures of you if you get the job."

"And here I thought you were my friend. I want no picture of me wearing a headless chicken cap."

"Okay. If you're gonna whine I won't take your picture, but you owe me."

"Yeah. Yeah."

Banshee and I spent the entire day together. If I got the job it might be one of my last completely free Saturdays. Banshee liked to take long walks and talk about movies and books. That was fine by me, so we wandered aimlessly around Verona and chatted away like we'd known each other forever. Banshee wasn't into any sports, but he did like hearing about football practices. I liked talking about them, so we were a perfect match.

"A couple of the guys have hurled during practice," I said.

"Have you?"

"Not yet, but I came very, very close."

"Practices must be brutal."

"I think Coach Jordan believes in that old saying, 'That which does not kill you makes you stronger.' Either that or he's just trying to kill us."

"Maybe he is trying to bump you all off. Maybe he's jealous because his glory days are over and you're all young studs."

"Me? A stud?"

"Take a look in the mirror, Elijah."

I smiled. Banshee made me feel very good about myself.

"I'll come to the first game. Maybe I'll get to see you play."

"I doubt that. The chances of me getting game time in the very first game are practically nil. I'm surprised the back of my jersey doesn't have "Bench Warmer" written on it."

"You're such a pessimist!"

"No. I'm a realist. A pessimist wouldn't hope he'll get to play later in the season. He would just assume he'd never get to play."

"In any case, I'm coming to your first game and I hope to see you play."

"Thanks."

I took Banshee home with me and introduced him to my parents. I took him up to my room. I'd put up some football photos from magazines since I'd joined the team, but there wasn't much on my walls. Banshee noticed the framed picture of Jesus. He looked at it closely, then looked at me.

"What?" I asked.

"I was looking to see if it was autographed."

"Funny."

Banshee spotted the weight set that belonged to my brothers.

"Hey, show me some exercises."

"I thought you had no interest in working out."

"I just want to try it out. I don't plan on becoming a big stud like you."

"Hey, stop making fun of me."

"It was a compliment."

"Okay, I'll show you a few things, but if you get addicted to working out and get muscle bound don't blame me."

"Not a danger."

I showed Banshee how to do bench presses, military presses, and curls. I put on very light weights for him but he still struggled. He would've fallen over doing a military press if I hadn't been spotting him.

"You know what, Elijah?" Banshee asked when he stopped after three curls.

"What?"

"I suck at this. Lemme see you do some bench presses. Show me how an expert does it."

"I'm not an expert."

"You are, compared to me."

I loaded up the bar with 100 pounds. Banshee's eyes got big. I lay back on the bench, grasped the bar, and pumped out ten bench presses. Banshee watched my every move.

I sat up, breathing just a bit harder. Banshee reached out and ran his hand over my chest.

"You chest is so hard."

Banshee didn't draw his hand away immediately, but kept feeling my muscles for a few moments. The front of my jeans grew a little tighter and I began to breathe harder still.

Banshee gazed into my eyes. He leaned in, and before I realized what he was doing, kissed me on the lips.

My mouth dropped open in shock. I stood, took a quick step backward, and stared at him.

"Why did you do that?" I asked as fear and confusion consumed me.

"I've wanted to do that since I first saw you. You're beautiful, Elijah."

I wrinkled my nose.

"What are you saying?"

"I like you a lot. You like me too, don't you? I thought maybe we could be... boyfriends."

I looked at Banshee in disgust. How could I not have known?

"What's wrong?" he asked.

"Get away from me!"

"I don't understand."

"You're a homo?" I said with distaste.

"I'm gay but... aren't you?"

"No! How can you say that? That's disgusting! I'm not a pervert!"

"I'm not a pervert either. I'm just gay is all."

"I think you'd better go now."

"But..."

"Just go! Get out of here! I don't want you here!"

Banshee looked as if I'd struck him. Tears welled up in his eyes and rolled down his cheeks.

"I'm sorry," he croaked before he turned and ran from my room. I could hear his sobs as he rushed downstairs.

I sat on my bed, trying to ignore the throbbing sensation in my groin. No! I would not let Banshee turn me. I could not give in to the unnatural desires that the devil had placed in my mind to torment me.

I dropped onto my bed and cried into my pillow. I thought Banshee was my friend. How could he kiss me like that? How could a nice boy like him be *one of those*? Just when I thought I'd found a friend I discovered he wasn't what he seemed to be at all. He'd been lying to me, pretending to be normal when he was an abomination. It was disgusting. I would never speak to him again!

Chapter Four

The two angels arrived at Sodom in the evening, and Lot was sitting in the gateway of the city. When he saw them, he got up to meet them and bowed down with his face to the ground. "My lords," he said, "please turn aside to your servant's house. You can wash your feet and spend the night and then go on your way early in the morning."

"No," they answered, "we will spend the night in the square."

But he insisted so strongly that they did go with him and entered his house. He prepared a meal for them, baking bread without yeast, and they ate. Before they had gone to bed, all the men from every part of the city of Sodom — both young and old—surrounded the house. They called to Lot, "Where are the men who came to you tonight? Bring them out to us so that we can have sex with them."

Lot went outside to meet them and shut the door behind him and said, "No, my friends. Don't do this wicked thing. Look, I have two daughters who have never slept with a man. Let me bring them out to you, and you can do what you like with them. But don't do anything to these men, for they have come under the protection of my roof."

"Get out of our way," they replied. "This fellow came here as a foreigner, and now he wants to play the judge! We'll treat you worse than them." They kept bringing pressure on Lot and moved forward to break down the door.

But the men inside reached out and pulled Lot back into the house and shut the door. Then they struck the men who were at the door of the house, young and old, with blindness so that they could not find the door.

The two men said to Lot, "Do you have anyone else here— sons-in-law, sons or daughters, or anyone else in the city who belongs to you? Get them out of here, because we are going to destroy this place. The outcry to the LORD *against its people is so great that he has sent us to destroy it."*

So Lot went out and spoke to his sons-in-law, who were pledged to marry his daughters. He said, "Hurry and get out of this place, because the LORD *is about to destroy the city!" But his sons-in-law thought he was joking.*

With the coming of dawn, the angels urged Lot, saying, "Hurry! Take your wife and your two daughters who are here, or you will be swept away when the city is punished."

Pastor Walker looked up from the podium and gazed at us, making eye contact with as many of the congregation as possible before he spoke.

"I am sure you are all familiar with the story of Sodom and Gomorrah that I have just read. Sodom was a city of evil and brought destruction upon itself because it allowed perversion within its walls. I am speaking of homosexuals, the very men who came to Lot's home with the intention of performing unspeakable sexual perversions with his guests. These events took place over two millennia ago, but such perversions still plague us. They are here with us in our own wholesome town. The homosexuals have gained a foothold here, and the story of Sodom and Gomorrah could well be played out today in our very own Verona.

"Do not be fooled by the appearance of the homosexuals around us—these 'gays' as they call themselves. They hide among us, pretending to be normal. They appear as athletes in our schools and as 'plain ordinary citizens' that live next door, but they are anything but normal. They are unnatural perversions. They are an abomination and we must do everything we can to encourage them to leave our midst before God sends down his Angels to destroy Verona just as he did Sodom and Gomorrah all those centuries ago."

I thought of Shawn and Tim. They seemed normal. They had never been anything but kind to me. How could they be abominations? I thought of Banshee too. I'd been very angry and upset when he kissed me, but had he done such a bad thing? He was lonely and needed a friend. He shouldn't have kissed me, but was it really a perversion?

As I sat there, I grew doubtful. I'd often walked by the homo table at lunch. I gave it a wide berth, but those guys were always talking and laughing. I had the feeling that they'd welcome me or anyone else who wished to sit with them. I didn't get that feeling from most of the other tables. Perhaps that was their way of luring others in. Maybe they did pretend to be normal so they could lure in naïve boys like me. Was I being naïve? Was I falling for an act? Was Pastor Walker right? He *was* a pastor, after all.

"I cannot suggest or condone violence against these perversions of nature, but I can recommend constant vigilance. I assure you the danger is quite real. We must not allow ourselves to forget that these homosexuals are not like us. We are the righteous. They have chosen to forsake the path of God and all that is holy. Do not be lulled into acceptance by their seemingly normal behavior, for they are sinners who will lead you into sin. They will turn you if they can. They will recruit you. We will not be safe until the last of them are gone.

"But, what can we do?" Pastor Walker asked, looking out upon his congregation. "How do we remove these evil-ones, these abominations from our midst? They deserve death. There is no doubt of that. If we were back in the days of the Bible, we could deal with this menace even as the angels of God were sent down to Earth to do. We live in more complicated times now, my friends, and therefore cannot bring justice to those who might very well destroy us all.

"But, there is a solution. There is a way to exterminate homosexuality from the world without harming those who have descended into sin to practice their unnatural way of life. It is for God to punish these sinners, not us. We must love the sinners, even though we hate the sin.

"Homosexuals do not, and cannot reproduce. If they can be isolated and left to their own perversions they will die out naturally. No one need raise his hand against them in violence. Our government should round up all of these homosexuals and place them in camps surrounded with electrified fencing to keep them separate from those of us who are normal and follow God's path.

"Some of you may think this is cruelty, but it is not so. I am not talking about cruel concentration camps, but comfortable, pleasant living places where even these sinners may live out their lives. Once they are rounded up and separated from us, we may safely minister to them and seek to turn them from their evil ways. Some can doubtless be saved. Those who refuse to leave their evil ways behind can remain in the camps and live out their days in peace until the Lord's judgment comes for them.

"It is out duty to protect ourselves from these abominations, but as Christians it is also our duty to do all we can to save them from themselves. By placing them in camps we can save many. Those who have turned their back on God will eventually die. Either way, society will be rid of this menace once and for all, for once the homosexuals are contained their evil influence will be at an end."

I sat there stunned. Concentration camps for homosexuals? I'd read something about the concentration camps during WWII. It was the holocaust when thousands and thousands of Jews were murdered in the name of racial purity. There were camps for homosexuals then too. I felt uneasy sitting there in church as I never had before.

I noticed some of the parishioners looking at each other uncomfortably. Others had determined expressions as if they would give their last breath to make Pastor Walker's dream of a homosexual-free world come true. The pastor spoke of kindness and comfortable living arrangements, but concentration camps?

After church, I rode home with my parents, changed out of my suit, and then went for a long walk. It was the end of summer, still rather warm, but no longer quite hot. The leaves on the trees and all the vegetation had a tired look as if they were eager for the rest that came with autumn and the slumber of winter. I didn't heed their beauty as much as I usually did, for my heart was troubled.

I had gone to church all my life. I loved God. I tried to follow the teachings of Jesus, but lately... What I heard in church today was not love. How could Pastor Walker propose to round up a group of people and force them into concentration camps behind electrified fences? He made it sound as if they would be treated to a luxury resort, but "rounded up" meant "removal by force" and the electric fences meant imprisonment. I'd expected someone to stand up and challenge the idea, but no one did. Some looked uncomfortable, but that was the extent of the opposition.

Had there been preachers in Germany who proposed concentration camps for the Jews? I knew that before and during the Civil War there were pastors who stood up for slavery and condemned those who opposed it, calling them the enemies of God's plan. There were the crusades where thousands marched to kill others who did not share their beliefs. I was beginning to have doubts. Wasn't being a Christian supposed to be all about love?

Where was the love? Hate the sin, but love the sinner. The key word there was 'hate.'

I thought about what had happened with Banshee only the day before. I had turned my back on my only real friend. I'd tossed him out of my life just because he tried to show love for me. Where was my compassion? Where was my love? Where was the forgiveness I was supposed to show others? He, who Pastor Walker called an abomination, had shown love and I, a Christian, had yelled at him in anger, brought tears to his eyes, and ordered him away. I didn't feel like a Christian. I felt as if I'd done something horribly wrong.

I kept picturing Pastor Walker making his pitch for concentration camps for homosexuals. He stood behind the pulpit, a man of God preaching imprisonment and death for those who were different. As I walked I realized he was no man of God at all. How could he be if he preached hatred?

I was confused and alone. All my life I'd held onto my religion and let it guide me, but now... The very source of goodness in my life had gone bad. If I couldn't trust my pastor or my church who or what could I trust?

I'd always had faith, but now...

I thought of Banshee again and the look on his face when I told him to leave. All he'd done was kiss me and I went off on him and called him names. Even Jesus had kissed his disciples. Well, it wasn't the same. Banshee admitted he liked me. I thought about that for a moment. What was so bad about Banshee liking me? Liking was like loving and love was the basis of Christianity, at least I had always thought so. Now, I was not so sure.

***

I gazed at Banshee as he sat alone the next day at lunch. I wanted to go and sit with him, but how could I after I'd made him cry? I'd lost the only real friend I had. I felt as though I was losing everything. I didn't even look forward to going to church next Sunday. Nothing seemed right anymore.

I gripped my tray and looked around the cafeteria. I looked over at the football table. I made my decision. Cody already had it in for me so sitting with the team wouldn't make things any worse, or at least not much worse. Cody would make my life hell either way.

Cody glared at me as I sat down, but I pretended not to see him.

"You have returned!" Lucas said.

"It's just Elijah, not Patton," Beck said.

"Yeah. I'd like to see General Patton play football like Elijah."

"He scored one touchdown during practice, big deal," Cody said.

"He got past you," Lucas said, then laughed.

"Shut up."

"Oh, we struck a nerve," Lucas said. "I'm glad you have rejoined us, but weren't you sitting with that kid?"

"Yeah, but he... he's not what I thought he was."

"What is he then?" Cody asked. "Oh, I get it! You thought he was a boy, but he's a girl, and you don't like girls, do you Elijah?"

"Shut up, Cody."

"Oh! I struck a nerve. You are a homo, aren't you?"

"No! I'm not! I'm not friends with Banshee anymore because he tried to kiss me, okay? He's a faggot!"

My face blanched when I realized what I'd said.

Cody looked over at Banshee sitting alone.

"Yeah. He looks like a faggot. God, I hate fuckin' queers."

"Then don't fuck them," Kevin said, then laughed. Some of the other guys laughed too.

"Shut up, Kevin!"

Cody was pissed off. He glared at Banshee. I should have kept my mouth shut. I recognized the expression on Cody's face. He despised Banshee now just like he did me. Cody turned and looked into my eyes. He just stared at me.

"Maybe I was wrong about you. Maybe you're not a faggot after all."

I didn't know what to do, so I laughed, but it wasn't funny. I'd just betrayed someone who had considered me a friend. I'd placed him in danger to save face with my buddies. I should've changed my name to Judas right then and there. I felt less and less like a Christian with every step I took. Why was everything going so horribly wrong?

***

I sat with the team for the rest of the week while Banshee sat alone. He looked sadder and lonelier than ever. A couple times during lunch periods his eyes met mine and I could read the pain in them. I'd made his life worse. He had been lonely before, but I'd offered him friendship and then jerked it away. I was a horrible, horrible person.

I avoided Banshee in gym class. I felt so guilty I couldn't even look him in the eyes. Then Thursday, Banshee showed up for P.E. with a black eye. I would've been afraid to ask how he got it even if I'd been talking to him. I feared I knew.

Cody didn't harass me as much. He wasn't friendly, but he didn't push me around either. I guess all it took to get him off my back was to call another kid a... homosexual. That's not the word I almost used, but I wasn't using the F-word for homosexual again. I couldn't believe I'd said it out loud even once. I couldn't believe I'd said it about someone who had been my friend.

***

My breath came harder than usual as I ran around the track. I needed to pay more attention to my pace. It wasn't like me to get winded, but I'd been getting winded a lot lately. I'd done a lot better during the summer than I was doing now. I had been more tired than usual lately, too. The practices and workouts were wearing me down. I needed to learn how to pace my entire life.

I was relieved on Friday when I watched Casper from the homo table walk over and sit down by Banshee. They talked for a few minutes, and then Banshee picked up his tray and followed Casper back to his friends. Cody noticed and his eyes narrowed.

He looked at me and shook his head in disgust. I feared for Banshee.

I worried about Banshee the rest of the day. I feared what Cody might do to him. I thought about trying to talk Cody out of any violence he might be planning, but I was scared he'd turn on me again. I was a coward.

Just after school, I spotted Shawn walking with his boyfriend, Tristan. They were openly a couple. I didn't understand how they could do that. I didn't understand how they could cope with everyone knowing what they were.

I was afraid to approach. I almost walked away without doing so, but then I reminded myself that Banshee had saved me once. Was I going to stand by and do nothing while he got hurt?

I took a deep breath and walked up to Shawn and Tristan.

"I've got to talk to you," I said.

Shawn looked at me. His face grew concerned.

"Are you okay?" he asked.

"I am, but... I'm afraid for Banshee."

I didn't tell him all the details. I was too ashamed to admit what I'd done. I didn't want him to know another boy had kissed me either. It might tempt him. I told him only what was important; that Cody knew Banshee was a homo and that Cody had it in for him.

"I'm afraid he'll hurt him bad. I don't want Banshee to get hurt."

"You're a good friend," Shawn said.

My lower lip trembled, but I bit it to maintain control. Friend? I was the worst friend ever. Shawn looked at me with a question in his eyes.

"You two hung out for a while didn't you?"

"We did, but... we can't be friends anymore. You'll look out for him, won't you? Please?"

"Of course I will," said Shawn.

"Thank you."

I walked away as quickly as I dared. I could feel Shawn and Tristan looking at me. I didn't know what Shawn would do to protect Banshee. Maybe he'd guard him. Maybe he'd confront Cody and threaten him. If he confronted Cody, then Cody might discover I'd gone to Shawn. If he did, I was back to being as good as dead. I didn't ask Shawn not to keep my name out of it. If I got hurt it was only what I deserved.

***

I reported to Chicken Fillets for orientation on Saturday afternoon at 2 p.m. I was about to begin my first real job. I almost messed up when I met Andy, the manager. He couldn't have been more than twenty. When he was introduced as the manager I almost laughed and said "For real?" but caught myself in time. He didn't look as if he had a sense of humor.

I was stuffed into a tiny room to attend Chicken Fillets University. No. I'm not kidding. That's what the manager called it just before he pushed play on a VCR and left me to myself. I sat and watched the tape. I was welcomed to the Chicken Fillets family. Chicken Fillets "a restaurant based on good, old, family values." The tape spoke of the competitive pay, extra perks such as half priced meals while I was working, and the possibilities for advancement. I, too, could someday be at the head of the pecking order and manage a Chicken Fillets. The tape had barely started and I was already rolling my eyes at the chicken references.

The tape lingered a good fifteen minutes on the evils of unions and how I should avoid the propaganda of those who wanted a hefty percentage of my wages as dues and would give me nothing in return. "Here at Chicken Fillets the wages are above industry standard and we give you more in benefits and advancement opportunities than restaurants that have been infiltrated by unions." Those whose lives had been ruined by unions treated me to testimonials. I wanted to shout at the screen "Yeah! I get it! Unions bad! Chicken Fillets good!"

The manager returned not long after the tape ended, but stayed only long enough to insert another. This one was all about safety in the workplace. That tape was followed by one on serving customers with a smile. I was bored out of my mind but at least I was getting paid a whopping $3.35 an hour to watch videotapes.

I finally escaped Chicken Fillets University when the manager turned me over to Skip, a kid I vaguely recognized from school. Skip was just a little older than me, probably sixteen. He gave me a tour of the kitchen and work area. I'd been hired to work the counter, but Skip said I might be called on to help in the back if the need arose. He warned me to stay clear of the deep fryers which were hot enough to cause third degree burns. Next, Skip instructed me on cleanup procedures and how to wash my hands (like I didn't already know that).

After my tour Skip took me back to Andy, who presented me with my official Chicken Fillets cap, two black Chicken Fillets shirts, and a large canary yellow apron that read, "Peep in Training." I was allowed to use the Chicken Fillets University room to change, but it was hardly necessary. All I was doing was changing shirts. I was used to getting naked in front of the entire football team. I suppose stripping in the back of Chicken Fillets wasn't the same.

There was a small mirror on the wall. The shirt looked okay, but the cap...let's just say I should've been paid extra just to wear it. The apron was the worst. It couldn't have been a brighter yellow unless it was neon, and "Peep in Training" was written in such huge letters I felt like a walking billboard. I knew I was going to die of embarrassment if anyone I knew came into the restaurant.

As I'd been instructed, I returned to Skip for training as soon as I'd changed. Skip took one look at my bright yellow apron and nearly laughed out loud.

"I have good news for you," Skip said. "You only have to wear that apron on your first day."

"Whew," I said.

"Okay. When you start your shift, the first thing you do is report to Andy to get your drawer. It will be loaded with $40, mostly in change."

"That's all?"

"Yeah. Most people pay in small bills so it's rare to run out of change. If you do, just call for Andy."

We stopped at the manager's office. It was a small room about the size of Chicken Fillets University and contained only a small desk, a chair, a filing cabinet, and a large safe. Andy had our cash drawer waiting on us.

Skip took me to the counter where other Chicken Fillet employees were busily taking orders. Skip explained the log in procedure and how I'd be given my own personal code. None of it seemed too difficult until I got a look at the cash register. I panicked. There were at least fifty buttons, and not one of them made any sense to me. Skip noticed the look on my face.

"It's not as difficult as it looks. Within a couple of days you'll have it down. Before long you won't even have to look at the register as you type in orders. The buttons actually do make sense. "BCC" is the button you push for a Big Chicken Clucker sandwich. "SFF" stands for small French fry. "LP" means Little Peep sandwich."

Skip put the register into training mode, which meant we could press buttons without orders actually going back to the kitchen. Skip explained how the register was laid out and how it was color-coded. I began to relax.

Skip placed a few "orders" while I tried to figure out which buttons to push. I was slow and got lost, but Skip was patient. Still, I got frustrated.

"Relax. Everyone has a tough time their first day. You should have been here before the grand opening when everyone was new. Training was chaos."

I liked Skip. While Andy looked like he might yell at me if I made the least mistake, Skip didn't take Chicken Fillets so seriously. I had a feeling he thought the cap was ridiculous too.

"Okay. I'm going to open up and take some orders. Just watch what I do. After a while, I'll put you on the register, but don't worry, I'll be right here."

I stood just to the side as Skip took the register out of training mode and opened up our section of the counter for orders. I was amazed at how fast he could type orders into the register as customers rattled them off.

Every order had a number, and the number flashed when it was ready. When the first order number began to flash Skip took me to the back counter.

"If it's a to-go order, take a bag and grab up all the items. There is a list right on the screen here so you can make sure you're filling the order properly. We move fast, especially when it's busy, but take the time to get the order right. Some customers get very angry if you mess up an order, especially if it's a to-go order and they don't discover the error until they get home. Mistakes on eat-in orders aren't as bad, but we still try to avoid them."

I noticed that Skip always asked if the customer would like fries with their order. There was something in the training tape about that too.

"Uh, I'm always supposed to ask if a customer wants fries, right? What if they only order fries? Do I still have to ask?"

Skip laughed.

"No. You only ask if they'd like fries if they didn't order fries."

"Oh!"

I shadowed Skip for an hour, then he put me on the register. I was so nervous I trembled as I took the order of a grandmother and her three grandchildren. One of the kids changed what they wanted after I'd already entered the order.

"What do I do?" I asked, panicking.

"Relax. The order doesn't go to the kitchen until you press the "Send Order" button. To remove an item, just push that item's button and then press "Remove." Customers change their minds all the time."

My hands shook as I removed the items and put on the new items. I read the order back and I didn't have it right. I was visibly upset.

"It's okay, dear," said the grandmother placing the order. "I think you're doing fine for your first day."

"You're my first customer," I said.

Skip helped me get the order right. I looked over and noticed Andy watching.

"Am I going to get fired?" I asked when the grandmother and her grandkids departed.

"No. Everyone messes up at first. Just don't get in such a hurry. The speed will come with experience."

I got the next two orders right and I didn't have to ask for help. I screwed up the order after that, somehow leaving off two large fries. The customer was kind of ticked off because it was a to-go order, and they didn't notice the missing fries until they got to their car, but Skip smoothed things over by showing them they hadn't been charged for fries and by giving them two orders of fries for free.

"We can do that? Give stuff away?" I asked when the customer was gone.

"You can't just give away free food to friends, but you can to keep a customer happy. Instead of that lady leaving angry because you messed up her order and she had to come back inside, now she'll be pleased because we gave her free fries. That means she'll be back. She's probably happy now that you messed up her order."

Things went easier when I calmed down and didn't try to match Skip's speed. I even started to learn the register. The layout actually did make sense once I began to learn the abbreviations.

I noticed Andy watching me a few times. Luckily, it was when I wasn't messing up. I was making fewer and fewer mistakes. One guy was really nasty. He barked his order and was just plain rude, but I just kept smiling and told him to have a nice day. Andy caught my eye when my rude customer left. He smiled and nodded.

"Sometimes, I want to grab a customer and smash his face into the counter," Skip whispered. I laughed.

Skip's shift ended at the same time as mine. He showed me how to close down the register and then take the cash drawer back to Andy, where we counted the money. Andy had removed cash from our drawer a couple of times during the afternoon, but there was still a whole lot of money in there.

I was amazed when Skip showed me how to count the paper bills. He didn't actually count them. He just took the stack of ones out of the drawer and put them on a scale. The scale showed dollar amounts instead of pounds and ounces.

"That's accurate?" I asked.

"It gets it right every time," Skip said.

Our drawer came up twenty-three cents short. I was scared for a moment, but Andy didn't seem upset. I guessed little errors were okay. I wondered how I'd messed up. I thought I counted all the change out correctly.

"You did a good job, Elijah. Next Saturday you can fly solo, but help will be close at hand," Andy said.

"Thank you, sir."

Skip took off. I turned in my bright yellow "Peep in Training" apron and changed back into my own shirt. I walked out of Chicken Fillets carrying my two black shirts and winged cap. I smiled as I walked home. I'd put in five hours and I was down for eight hours the following Saturday. For the first time ever I was making my own money.

o   ***

I went to church with my parents as always on Sunday. I felt a little better as we sang hymns. During the prayer I prayed for God to protect Banshee from Cody and to forgive me for being a horrible friend. I wanted to tell Banshee I was sorry, but I couldn't even make myself look him in the eyes.

"God created Adam and Eve. He created man and then a woman to be his companion. This is how nature was meant to be—one man and one woman. There are those among us who would pervert God's law by flouting tradition. Two men or two women together was not God's plan. Two men cannot procreate, neither can two women. Such unions are obviously unnatural so why are they tolerated? I will tell you why, because homosexuals have infiltrated every level of our society," Pastor Walker stated. "Homosexuals are in our schools teaching children. They are running day care centers and leading Scout Troops. They have so successfully integrated themselves into our society that some have begun to accept their perverted lifestyle as normal. We, the good Christians of not only this church, but all churches, must combat this threat to the very fabric of our society. Last week, I talked about camps to isolate the homosexuals. How do we bring this about? By voting! The elections are coming up. It is the duty of every good Christian to resister to vote and to vote his conscience. At the end of the service today, please pick up a church bulletin. In it

you will find the voting records of our local, state, and federal representatives, as well as information on new candidates. I am not here to tell you who you should vote for. I am but a simple man of God after all. What I ask is that you take a long, hard look at the candidates and vote for what you know is right.

We must take other steps as well, and some of those steps are close to home. We must weed out homosexuality before it has a chance to gain roots. Homosexuality is a choice. It is a chosen lifestyle. Many claim is it not, but do not let yourselves be fooled. Those who practice this deviant lifestyle do so because they have chosen to follow the path of depravity. Look to your own children. Watch them with a critical eye and be ever vigilant for signs that they might be setting foot on the wrong path. Effeminate toddlers must be taught be tough. They must be taught to learn to withstand pain. I know such measures are difficult for soft-hearted parents, but if you spare the rod you spoil the child. In this case the stakes are much higher. You are fighting for the immortal soul of your sons. A black eye or a cracked wrist is a small price to pay for salvation. Some rough treatment now from the hands of loving parents will prevent your sons from being bashed later by those who do not possess Christian attitudes.

"Girls too are at risk. Butch girls must be made to soften up. They must not try to be boys. They should not play sports and they should, at least in church and at formal events, wear dresses.

"God designed us to be male or female before we were even created. When anyone expresses gender dissatisfaction in words or deeds they are sinning against God. Boys who are feminine and girls who are masculine are as guilty of sin as those who commit adultery. Do not tolerate such in your home. You must be strong so that your children will be as God intended them to be. If it takes force, then so be it.

> "Men ought to act like men, and women ought to act like women. Living out gender distinctions glorifies God. The homosexuals fly in the face of this. Those God-hating abominations need to be wiped from the face of the Earth. Be vigilant. They will come for your children. They will seek to turn them. Sometimes the attack will be direct. Sometimes it will be more insidious. Some teach what they call 'toleration.' Do not be fooled. It is nothing but a recruitment tactic. Beware even thoughts. Thinking sinful thoughts is the same as sinning. Thinking about committing a sin is a sin committed. Make no mistake, we are in a battle for the hearts, minds, and souls of our children."

Now he was telling parents to beat their sons if they weren't masculine enough? That's the message I received from his comments about a "black eye" or "cracked wrist." Force girls to be feminine? The pastor seemed to think he was God. I had once looked forward to coming to church, now I could not wait to get out. I felt as if everything I believed was being stood on its head.

As the service continued I thought about what the pastor said about thought and sin. When I'd lusted after guys in the showers at school it was the same as having sex with them? How could that be true? It seemed to me there was a very big difference between thinking about sex and having sex. If what the pastor said was true then thinking about killing someone was the same as killing someone. That made so sense at all. If I thought about killing someone his or her life continued. If I killed them they were dead. There was a big difference between dead and not dead.

The pastor ranted on about the homosexuals and how they had to be stopped and controlled now because they were already demanding rights. It seemed to me that rights didn't have to be demanded. I'd looked up the word "right" in the dictionary very recently for some schoolwork and one of the definitions was "morally good." Homosexuals had to be stopped before they could demand what was morally good?

I was quiet on the ride home. I felt as if my world had been turned upside down. I felt like someone had kicked my gyroscope and now I was unbalanced and couldn't tell up from down. Mom even asked if I was feeling okay.

I took off my suit and hung it in the closet, then went out for a walk as I had the previous Sunday. I used to come home from church feeling uplifted. I felt as if God was a part of my life and I'd just touched base with him. Now...

God was supposed to love everyone, but our pastor preached hate. It wasn't just him either. I'd seen the parishioners nodding and agreeing with "yea" and "amen." Pastor Walker whipped up the congregation into a homo-hating frenzy. Were homosexuals really that bad? Compared to rape and murder having sex with another guy seemed kind of tame and yet Pastor Walker ranted about homosexually as if it was worse than both. The Bible did say it was wrong, but was it *that* wrong?

I thought about Shawn, Tim, and Banshee. I was supposed to hate them? I didn't know if I could do that. Hate was wrong.

A tear ran down my cheek. I couldn't make sense of any of it. I felt lost and alone. I'd always trusted that God was with me. I'd always believed God loved everyone, but it seemed it wasn't so. Didn't God create everyone? If he created everyone, he created the homosexuals. How could he create them and then not love them? The pastor said homosexuality was a choice, but I wasn't so sure about that. When I looked at guys like Lucas and Cody in the showers my whole body reacted. I didn't want to desire them, but I did. I closed my eyes for a moment; half fearful lightning would strike me for acknowledging my lust. I didn't want to desire other guys. I'd even prayed to God to take my unnatural lust away from me, but it wasn't gone. I tried to fight it, but it wouldn't go away. I tried to ignore it, but it wouldn't be ignored. How could God do this to me? I'd always gone to church. I'd always tried to be a good Christian. How could he make me feel these feelings and then hate me for it?

"Faggot!"

My breath caught in my throat for a moment. I thought someone was yelling at me, but no. I was walking in downtown Verona and the voice came out of an alley. In a few seconds Banshee came tearing out of the alley. He hid himself behind a display of clearance garden plants in front of the hardware store. My eyes met his. Tears ran down his cheeks and he trembled.

Cody burst out of the alley. His chest heaved. He panted. He looked up the street in one direction and then the other with narrowed eyes. Then, he noticed me.

"Did you see that little faggot? Did you see where he went? I'm gonna kick his ass."

If what Pastor Walker said was right, then as a good Christian I had to turn Banshee in. I had to let Cody beat him up and should probably join in myself. If I didn't tell the truth... If I didn't tell Cody where Banshee was hiding... If I didn't help him beat Banshee I'd go to Hell for it.

I looked at Banshee for a moment. He'd drawn his knees up to his chin and was rocking back and forth, silently sobbing. He looked at me with tear filled eyes and pleaded with me to protect him. I made my decision. I'd go to Hell.

"Yeah. He tore down the street that way, then cut back to the left," I said, pointing south.

"Thanks, man!"

Cody took off. I looked at Banshee again. I started to speak, but no words came. Our eyes met and we just gazed at each other. I turned away from him and walked away.

My eyes filled with tears. I knew what I'd just done, but how could I have done any differently? My religion taught me to love others, but then demanded that I allow a boy to be abused. The two demands were incompatible and I was caught in the middle. In my heart I felt I'd done what was right, but Pastor Walker would not agree. I didn't want to go to Hell, but what else could I do? My very faith demanded it. I felt betrayed by that faith. I'd been set up for a fall and I had fallen. It was a trap from which there was no escape.

I walked to the high school and out to the football field. I sat down on the bleachers. A slight wind blew over the empty field, carrying with it the scent of recently mown grass. The football stands felt lonely and too quiet. I'd sat in the stands when they were filled with screaming, yelling fans and the band blaring out fight songs. Now, there was only the sound of the wind, like a lonely wail pleading for companionship.

"I don't want to go to church anymore."

I don't know why I said it out loud. Maybe it was because I needed to hear something besides the wind. Maybe I just needed to say it out loud to make the thought real.

I thought about Banshee, his eyes full of tears, hiding behind the display in front of the hardware store. I thought about Lucas and how magnificent he looked when he stood in the showers naked, rivulets of water streaming down his hard muscled body. I thought about Shawn and how he'd stood up for me, a kid he didn't even know. I thought of my pastor, standing up in front of the congregation, his face contorted with hatred as he preached against the homosexuals. My mind was spinning. It was so filled with images I wanted to scream.

I remembered Banshee's kiss. I remembered how wonderful it had been in that split second before the shock cleared from my mind and I pushed him away. I remembered how badly I'd wanted him to kiss me and how badly I'd wanted to kiss him back. The memories came flooding it as if they'd finally burst through a dam they had long struggled to overwhelm.

I looked up. The mysterious boy who I'd seen in the park some days before was standing in front of me. He gazed at me with compassion in his kind eyes.

"This is a difficult time for you," he said.

I nodded. I had no idea how this boy knew what I was experiencing, but at the moment it didn't matter.

"God has turned his back on me," I said. I would not have said it to any other. The guys on my team would've thought I was weird and... I didn't have other friends.

"No. God never turns his back on anyone, Elijah."

I peered at the boy. He spoke with such confidence. There was such peace about him. How did he know my name? Had he been asking about me?

"Who are you?" I asked.

"I'm Jesus," he said.

I just stared at him for a few moments. I'd only met one other boy named that. He was Hispanic and he'd pronounced it "Hey-Seuss." I reached out my hand and Jesus took it. He did not shake it, but took it in both his hands and held it for a few moments. No other boy would have done so. Any other boy would have been afraid of being called a fag.

"I'm Elijah."

I didn't know what to say, so I said nothing more.

"Do not despair. You will find your path soon. God loves you whether you turn left or right and whether or not you go to church, but I advise that you not give up on your church, not yet."

"How do you know these things?" I asked. It was as he could read my mind.

Jesus did not answer. He just smiled at me and yet I felt as if he had answered. I felt comforted. I closed my eyes for a moment as a feeling of peace flowed through me. When I opened them again Jesus was gone.

I stood quickly. I looked in every direction and even under the stands, but I could find him nowhere. He'd disappeared, just like before. If I had not spotted him at school speaking with others I might have thought I'd imagined him.

I sat back down. I felt very strange and yet I felt peaceful. I felt as if everything was going to be okay. I didn't actually see how everything could be okay, but I felt that way regardless.

Chapter Five

The next day at school I spotted Banshee between classes. I didn't see any evidence of a black eye, so I figured he'd escaped from Cody. I wondered why Cody hated homosexuals so much. I didn't think he was particularly religious. I knew for a fact he did not attend my church. Perhaps he was just a bully, and yet that didn't seem quite right either. I couldn't figure him out, but then I couldn't figure myself out either.

I sat with the guys at lunch. Cody greeted me with a "Hey, man" and even slapped me on the back. As usual the guys talked about girls and football, mostly about girls. The language they used made my ears burn, but I guess I'd led a sheltered life.

I didn't join in the football talk much because I did not yet know what I was talking about. I didn't join in the girl talk at all because I knew far less about girls than I did about football.

"I bet he's a virgin," Beck said.

"Huh? What?" I asked, when I noticed everyone was looking at me. I'd been playing with my green beans and wondering if the beef and noodles would taste as bad as it looked.

"Are you a virgin, Elijah?"

"I, uh, uh..."

"He's a virgin," Cody said, then laughed.

I could feel my face go red. I started to protest I wasn't a virgin, but that would've been a lie. I had never done anything sexual except for... well, you probably know.

"Virgin! Virgin!" the guys chanted. I wanted to crawl under the table. I was sure my face was completely red.

"I say we make it our goal to help Elijah get some before the end of the football season," Cody said. "Don't worry. Your teammates will help you get a girl. I know a lot of sluts."

"That's because sluts are the only girls Cody can get!" Kevin said.

"Shut up, faggot. I can get any girl. I have the bod!"

Cody stood and flexed his biceps. His arms rippled with muscle. I was glad I was sitting down because I instantly had a huge bulge in my pants. I couldn't help it—it just happened. It was like breathing or sneezing. I didn't consciously bring it on. My body just reacted. It was as if my eyes were directly to connected to my... private parts.

I focused my attention on my beef and noodles, hoping the topic of my virginity passed quickly. It did. Apparently my virginity was only good for a quick laugh or maybe I wasn't the only virgin at the table and the others feared they might be scrutinized next.

I looked over at Banshee sitting at the homo table. He was smiling and laughing. I was glad Casper had invited him to join the rest of them, but should I be glad? Wouldn't being with homosexuals only lead to further temptation for Banshee? Once again, my religion was at odds with itself. Pastor Walker would say that Casper lured Banshee into a perverted lifestyle and yet what I saw on the day Casper walked over to the table where Banshee sat alone was quite a different thing. Casper offered Banshee friendship and the companionship of his friends. It was a very Christian thing to do. How could an act be good or evil depending on how one viewed it?

Banshee caught me at the entrance to the locker room right after I'd dressed out for our gym class. He motioned me to the side.

"Listen, I know you don't like me, but thanks for not giving me away yesterday. Cody would have beaten the crap out of me. Thank you."

Banshee was gone before I had a chance to speak. It was just as well. I didn't know what to say to him. I wanted to tell him that I didn't dislike him, but I didn't know how to explain myself. I didn't even understand myself right now. I had all these thoughts, feelings, and doubts. Not long ago, I thought I had things all figured out, but now... now I knew nothing.

I watched Banshee during P.E. class. We were still playing football. He was clearly out of his element and yet he tried. I'd always heard that gays were effeminate, but Banshee wasn't. He was no jock and yet he got right back up after being knocked down and tried again. That took courage. Banshee wasn't short, but he was so thin that most guys easily outweighed him. He went up against the bigger guys with no sign of hesitation. I knew he had to be frightened or at least apprehensive, but he plowed ahead.

Wasn't the very definition of courage to go ahead and do what needed to be done even when you are afraid?

Some of our classmates gave Banshee a hard time. They weren't out to beat him up like Cody, but I heard one boy keep chanting "faggot" under this breath whenever he was around Banshee. Another had pretended to bump into Banshee in the locker room, "accidentally" shoving Banshee into a locker. Some of the guys laughed. I didn't think it was funny. I knew they were doing it because Banshee had started sitting at the homo table. He hadn't been sitting there long, but long enough that everyone had a chance to see him. The guys knew, or at least suspected he was gay, and that's all it took to make him a target.

The boys in our P.E. class didn't get violent with Banshee, but some of them weren't very nice. Most didn't give him any trouble, but I wondered how he dealt with those who called him names and pushed him around. It was further evidence of his courage. A boy like Banshee had to have courage just to come to school.

Football practice was brutal. I really think Coach Jordan was trying to kill us. I got so fatigued running drills I just wanted to lie down on the field and sleep. Our first game was coming up, but I knew I wouldn't get to play. I could run fast and I could catch the ball well, but my blocking abilities were almost nil and Cody said I threw like a girl. Cody wasn't being nasty when he said that. He was just being honest. I was quite sure a lot of girls could throw better than me. Footballs are hard to throw. I could often get a decent spin on the ball, but even my best passes only went a few feet. I would never be the quarterback, that was for sure. At least I hadn't been cut from the team. That was my constant fear.

My days became a routine. School, football practice, then homework. I sat with the team every day at lunch. Cody stopped giving me crap during practices. We weren't buddies, but he was no longer my tormentor. Practices didn't vary much. We ran around the track, then ran the same drills, then practiced plays. Every other day we hit the weight room. I wasn't pleased with my progress. I hadn't increased my weight on a single exercise. In fact, I had to back off. I felt like I was getting weaker instead of stronger. I had increasing difficulty with running, pushups, sit-ups and other exercises too. It all should've come easier, but it didn't. It was just another way in which my life no longer made sense. The only thing I could truly count on was gravity, and I wasn't so sure that wouldn't fail me too.

***

I arrived at Chicken Fillets a little before 10 a.m. on Saturday morning for my first full day of work. There would be no union-bashing videotapes, no bright yellow aprons, just taking and filling orders.

I collected my cash drawer from Andy and walked to the front. I was glad to see my register was next to Skip's. If I got in a jam he'd be right there to help me. I managed to sign in with my code and get my register up and running with no problems. Moments later I took my first order of the day. It was an order for large fries, nothing else, just fries. Skip and I exchanged a look, grinned, and I managed to keep from asking, "Would you like fries with that?"

Customers filed in steadily for the first half-hour and I had no trouble keeping up. I had to ask Skip how to cancel an item again, but other than that I managed quite well. Business picked up after 11:30 and by noon Chicken Fillets was a madhouse. The lines grew longer and the customers more impatient. I tried to hurry and got flustered.

"Chill out, no one will die if they have to wait thirty seconds more for their Big Chicken Clucker," Skip leaned over and whispered to me.

I took a deep breath to calm myself then grinned.

"Can I take your order?" I asked my next customer.

"That's "May I take your order?"" the lady at the counter corrected.

"English teacher?" I asked.

She smiled and laughed.

"May I take your order?" I asked.

When I had filled the English teacher's order and the next customer stepped up I said, "May I take your order?" before the teacher was out of earshot. She turned and grinned at me. I winked back.

I made some mistakes, but most I corrected easily. Skip had to help me out a couple more times, but I didn't do too badly for my first day. I didn't have any rude customers, but one lady came in with four small children and they were all screaming so much I had trouble hearing her order.

My half-hour "lunch" break came at 2:30. I'd had a late breakfast and no lunch, so I was starving. There weren't many customers in the restaurant just then so I was able to step right up to the counter. I ordered a Big Chicken Clucker, large fries, and a large Coke. At half-price my meal was cheap.

I found a table in the corner and ate my sandwich and fries while gazing outside. The front of the restaurant was nicely landscaped with boxwood, hostas, and pink and purple petunias. I put Chicken Fillets out of my mind as I looked at the little garden. I grinned. I usually didn't eat out a lot because of the cost, but my meal was only $1.50. Now that I was working I had more cash, or would once I got a paycheck. I could afford to splurge a little.

I could afford other things now too. I wasn't going to go crazy and spend all my money. There wouldn't be all that much money considering I only worked for a few hours on Saturdays, but if I wanted a tape or a poster I could buy it. I planned to save half of what I made. I figured if I started doing that now it would be easier to keep doing it later. Once I got into college I'd probably need every cent I earned to pay for expenses, even if my parents paid most of the costs. I had only a few years to work while I had no expenses.

I dipped a French fry into catsup. The fries were really good here. I don't think they quite matched Burger Dude's, but since Verona didn't have a Burger Dude it didn't matter. Verona didn't have much in the way of fast food, but there were some good restaurants. I loved Ofarim's and Café Moffatt.

It felt good to sit down and get off my feet. Standing in one place most of the time was rough on the feet. I did get to walk a few steps to gather each order, but my job involved too much standing in one spot. It was sure going to feel good when I could go home and lie on my bed for a while.

All too soon it was time to get back to work, but every minute I worked was five more cents in my pocket. A nickel wasn't that much, but it added up. I just wished I didn't have to wait so long to get paid. I wouldn't get my first paycheck until the next

Saturday. My first paycheck would be a big one. I'd get paid for today and my orientation. That would be $43.55, minus taxes. Dad said I could expect to lose about 20% to taxes, but that would leave me more than $30 and I might even get a tax refund come next April. That would be nice!

I made fewer mistakes after my lunch than before. We kept busy. Skip said that was a good thing because the busier we were the faster time passed. I think he was right. When the supper rush hit between 4:30 and 6:30 p.m. it seemed like only twenty minutes went by during those two hours. I got off at 6:30 so I was finished!

Just a few minutes before my quitting time I closed down my register and took the drawer back to Andy. I had exactly the right amount of cash in my drawer! I'd counted out so many ones, halves, quarters, dimes, nickels, and pennies I was surprised I hadn't made any mistakes. Then again, perhaps I had made mistakes, but my mistakes just happened to even out.

When I walked out of Chicken Fillets I felt sad. I actually missed the customers and the other workers. I found myself thinking about who would be working there until it closed at 10 p.m. I almost wished I could work there instead of going to school, but I didn't think making Chicken Fillets my life would be a wise idea. It was kind of fun one day a week, but full-time? I didn't think I'd like that much. For one thing, I knew I'd get sick of hearing all those chicken phrases all the time.

When I arrived I greeted Mom, walked upstairs, took off my shoes and socks and dropped onto my bed. I wasn't sleepy, but getting off my feet felt so good I let out a loud "ahhh!"

I was pleased with myself. I had successfully completed my first real day on the job. I didn't mess anything up too badly and no one yelled at me. If the rest of my days at Chicken Fillets went as smoothly I'd be happy.

***

A red Mustang pulled up in front of the house and honked the horn. I stood up from where I'd been waiting on the front steps. I approached the car, opened the door, and climbed in.

"Nice car," I said.

"Thanks. It was my sixteenth birthday present. It's three years old, but new enough for me," said Lucas.

"Any Mustang is cool," I said.

Lucas pulled away from the curb.

"Thanks for giving me a ride."

"No problem. I remember what it was like to be a pathetic fifteen-year-old without wheels."

"That was what, last year?"

"Yep, ancient history."

"So who will be at this party?"

"Some of the football team, both varsity and us. More importantly for you, girls."

"Why more importantly for me?"

"You are a virgin, right?"

"Yeah," I admitted. I turned slightly red.

"Don't be embarrassed. Everyone is a virgin for a while."

"I've been one for a long while. How long were you a virgin?"

"Fourteen years."

"You had sex when you were *fourteen*?"

"Don't sound so shocked. It's not that unusual."

"Um... what did you do, exactly?"

"Exactly?"

I could feel my face grow warmer.

"Well, not exactly! I don't mean details. Did you go all the way or...?"

"By my definition losing ones virginity requires going all the way."

"So you did?"

"Yes, with an older woman."

"How much older?"

"She was nineteen."

"Isn't that a felony?"

"Maybe, but what do I care? It was so hot!"

"Who was she?"

"My babysitter."

"Are you kidding me?"

"Nope."

"Seriously?"

"What did I just say?"

"Oh my gosh! I can't believe that! I mean, I believe you, but..."

"Yeah. Fucking awesome, huh?"

"Well, most people would call her a child molester."

"I wasn't a child. I was a horny, horny boy who knew exactly what was going on. It took me weeks to seduce her."

"So you made the moves?"

"Yep."

"At fourteen?"

"You're really stuck on that number. Aren't you?"

"It just seems kind of... sick."

"Sick? It was the best experience of my entire life! We did it every time she sat with me. Unfortunately, it was only a few months before Mom and Dad decided I didn't need a babysitter. I didn't need one, of course, but my parents were always paranoid I'd fall down the steps or someone would break in while they were gone."

"So instead..."

"I had sex repeatedly with a hot, hot nineteen-year-old girl. She taught me so much."

"Wow. I can't believe that happened."

"Lots of stuff goes on behind closed doors you probably wouldn't believe. I could tell you stories, but if you turn any redder you're gonna start to glow."

"I guess you think I'm naïve and pathetic, huh?"

"Naïve, maybe. Pathetic, no. I'm sure you aren't the only virgin on the team, not that the others would admit it. Everyone makes up stories. Probably half of the hookups you hear about in the locker room are pure fiction."

"It's still embarrassing for everyone to know I'm a virgin."

"It's not a big deal, man. So what if you haven't screwed a girl yet? Everyone gets to things in their own time. I'll tell you my deep, dark secret if you promise to keep it to yourself."

"Of course I will."

Lucas looked at me as if deciding whether or not he could trust me. He was silent for several moments before he finally spoke.

"I've never played miniature golf."

"That's it? *That's* your deep, dark secret?"

Lucas laughed.

"You were expecting something perverted that you could whack off to later. Admit it."

"I was not! I..."

"Don't even try to tell me you don't jerk off. There are only two kinds of guys; those who admit to jerking off and those who lie about it."

I grinned.

"If that's your deep, dark secret you must be truly boring," I said.

"Yeah? Well what's yours, Mr. Mysterious?"

"You already know mine, not that it's a secret any longer. I'm a virgin. You owe me a deep, dark secret."

Lucas was quiet for a while. He was quiet so long I thought he wasn't going to say anything.

"I'll tell you, but you really have to keep quiet about it. You can't tell anyone and I mean no one, okay?"

"This isn't going to be something stupid, is it? Like you've never played Monopoly?"

"Everyone has played Monopoly."

"You know what I mean!"

"No. This is a true secret."

"Okay. I promise. I won't tell anyone."

"You know Shawn Myer, who plays on the varsity team?"

"Yeah. I don't know him, but I know who he is. I've talked to him."

I began to sense where this was going and the front of my jeans grew a little tighter.

"About a year ago, at a party, we messed around."

"Really?"

"Yeah. I was kind of drunk and this girl had been teasing me all night. She would make out and she felt me up, but she wouldn't do anything more. I was all worked up. You know? She left me high and dry and just plain left the party. I went out back to get some air. Shawn was out there talking to some guy, but soon we were alone. I knew he was gay and I was in need. He was single then so... I told him I heard guys gave better head than girls."

"Wow."

"Yeah. We kind edged around the topic a while and then he asked if I wanted to find out if guys are better. I told him I did. We went out and sat in a glider in the dark. Shawn pulled it out of my pants. I pulled his out too. We began stroking each other and then he leaned over and took mine in his mouth."

"Was he good?" I asked before I could stop myself.

"He was so much better than any girl I'd had it wasn't even funny. I only lasted for about three minutes and he swallowed it."

"Wow."

"I figured I owed him. I didn't want to blow him, so I jerked him off. I'd never touched another guy like that. How's that for a deep, dark secret?"

"That definitely qualifies. I'm surprised you told me."

"I trust you."

"I appreciate that."

"I also wanted you to know that we all have secrets, so being a virgin really isn't a big deal."

"Thanks."

"Have you ever messed with a guy?" Lucas asked.

"No."

"Would you?"

I fought to control my breath. My zipper was under such a strain I feared it would rip.

"I might," I said.

"Yeah?"

"Yeah."

The air between us was thick with sexual tension. It might have been my imagination, but I thought Lucas was breathing a little harder too. I half expected to feel his hand on my leg, but it didn't happen.

I felt silly. How could I think even for a moment that Lucas was going to come onto me? He had a girlfriend and he's lost his virginity at fourteen. I'd seen him making out with his girl and I believed his story. The idea of him coming onto me was ridiculous.

I wondered what I would've done if Lucas had put his hand on my leg. I wondered how far I would've let it go. In those fleeting moments images of pressing my lips to his had entered my mind. Would I have done for Lucas what Shawn had?

I felt like a pervert and yet as if I had no choice in the matter. I couldn't control how I felt. I couldn't control my breathing and I sure couldn't control what was happening in my pants. My body had gotten excited at the prospect of something happening. I didn't choose for it to be that way. I didn't try to make it happen. I wasn't indulging in a fantasy to excite myself. It just happened.

"Is your girlfriend going to be at this party?" I asked.

"No."

"She lets you come alone?"

"Hey! She doesn't own me. I'm not one of those guys who are whipped. Besides, I'm not sure that..." Lucas grew quiet.

"What?"

"Well, I told you my deep, dark secret so I guess it won't hurt to tell you this. I'm not sure how much longer we'll be going together. I kind of think she's cheating on me."

"On *you*?" I asked incredulously.

Lucas looked at me and grinned. I realized I'd given something away, but I guess a bit of hero worship was no big deal.

"Yeah. I've seen her with this older guy in town. I don't know his name, but he's twenty-something and he's built. They seem way too close, if you know what I mean. I think they're messing around."

"Maybe you should say something."

"No. If I'm wrong it will piss her off. If I'm right she can just deny it. It's not like I've been completely faithful either. There was a girl this summer... I shouldn't have, but I couldn't help myself."

Lucas turned and looked at me a moment.

"I'd better shut up. You're going to know all my secrets soon."

"I'll never talk," I said.

"Yeah. I know."

I grinned.

The party was at Kevin's place. It was chaperoned by his parents, which was why I was allowed to come. Even so, the music was kind of loud as we got out of the car and approached the front door. The door was open. Kevin opened the screen door for us and welcomed us inside.

I recognized several guys from the team and a few varsity players too. There were lots of girls as well. The party had been going on a while from the looks of it. I also doubted very much that Kevin's parents were anywhere around, but I didn't ask. If they weren't there I didn't want to know.

I was handed some punch in a plastic cup. I took a small sip and nearly started coughing. I looked at Lucas.

"Vodka," he said.

Most of the kids at the party were drinking like they thought the vodka-laced punch was the greatest thing ever, but in truth it was downright nasty. I wanted to fit in and not look like a complete loser so I took a small sip now and then while making it look as if I was drinking much more. If I came home drunk I might never be allowed to go out again. At least the vodka had no scent to it. I guess whoever made the punch used it because it couldn't be detected on the breath.

Lucas wandered off. I mingled among the guys. I blushed when I noticed two different girls gazing at me like I was worth looking at. I wasn't used to that. I felt the vodka taking effect. I began to feel a little giddy. I knew I seriously had to watch it. If I wasn't careful I'd mellow to the point where I thought nothing of drinking more and more. I went into the kitchen. A couple was just leaving and I was alone for a few moments. I quickly dumped my punch down the drain. I found some grape juice in the refrigerator that looked just like the punch and filled my cup.

I returned to the living room. Cody was talking to a large group of guys and girls. When I walked near he nabbed me, put his arm over my shoulder, and held me close.

"This guy! This guy!" Cody said, pointing to me and laughing. "He's really small. I don't mean his dick, girls. I mean he's short, but he's fast. You should see him in practice. Mini-Gaylord here... he ran right over the top of me. It was like leap frog. This boy is a frog!"

Cody was wasted. I could smell something on his breath, so he'd been drinking more than the punch.

"Hey! Hey!" Cody said, catching Lucas' arm as he walked by. "First game... we should take Mini-Gaylord here and throw him over the offensive line. Yeah! Throw him!"

Cody busted up laughing, releasing me when he doubled over. He fell on the floor and rolled over onto this back, still laughing. Lucas rolled his eyes and walked on. The rest of the group laughed with Cody. At least he was a funny drunk.

No one else was as far gone as Cody, but most were more tipsy than me. I felt a little warm and a little too happy, so I knew I was just a little drunk, but I'd stopped drinking before it was too late.

Beck and a girl were making out on one end of the couch. I didn't know the girl's name, but that didn't mean anything. I knew the names of only those few girls who were in my classes. Some of the girls at the party were cheerleaders. Others were the more popular girls at school. Still others... well, they were girls with reputations, if you know what I mean. I didn't pay that much attention to rumors, but I still heard them.

I sat there feeling unusually happy. I listened to the music and watched my teammates and the girls. There wasn't a single guy there who wasn't a football player. Cody kept talking a little too loudly, but just about everything he said was funny. At the moment, he had his arms over the shoulders of two girls and was telling a story about his failed attempt at learning how to rollerblade.

A girl blocked my view and I looked up into her eyes. She had uncommonly pretty blue eyes. She took my hand and pulled me to my feet, then wrapped her arms around me and began swaying to the music. I was so shocked I just let her hold me and dance. Lucas caught my eye and nodded, so I put my arms around her and danced with her.

I didn't know how to dance, so I just did what she did. She was blond and pretty and just a little taller than me. She had a big chest and she smelled nice.

I kind of liked dancing. I'd never danced with a girl before. I'd never danced before, period. Maybe this was the beginning of something. Maybe I'd stop having thoughts about guys if I had girls to dance with.

My eyes widened as I felt her hands on my butt. She groped my butt! I didn't know what to do so I just kept dancing.

"I'm Elijah," I said.

"I'm Allison."

Allison nuzzled my neck, then brought her lips to mine and kissed me. I didn't like it, but I tried to make myself like it. I kissed her back.

Allison ran her hands down my chest, feeling my muscles. I kind of liked that, but... not really. My eyes locked with Lucas' over her shoulder. He nodded toward the hallway. I nervously led Allison away from the living room and down the hall. I didn't want to do this, but Lucas was watching and this was my chance to make myself normal.

I felt guilty. Nice boys weren't supposed to mess around with girls. Messing around with other boys was way worse, but messing around with girls wasn't allowed either. Perhaps it would be better to sin a little with a girl than a lot with a guy. I didn't know.

Allison opened a door and pulled me into an empty bedroom. It had to be Kevin's. There were football posters on the walls as well as centerfolds from swimsuit issues of *Sports Illustrated*. Allison locked the door and began pawing me. We kissed and I tried to get into it, but it wasn't happening. Nothing was happening down in my pants either. When Banshee had kissed me the reaction down below was immediate and definite, but nothing was happening now.

I panicked. In the back of my mind I'd always told myself that once I was with a girl everything would be okay, but it wasn't okay. I didn't want to be doing this, and what would happen if she felt me down there?

I had my answer almost immediately. Allison groped me. My mind raced to find an explanation. I couldn't think of anything, except...

"You're so hot!" I said and sloppily kissed Allison. "You know that? You. Are. So. Hot," I said, poking her in the chest with my finger to emphasize each word.

I stumbled and Allison had to steady me. I smiled at her with a lopsided grin. I did my best to mimic Cody when he was drunk.

"I wanna do it... so bad!" I said, shaking my head and then laughing. I wasn't acting like me at all, but that was the point. I had to sell my drunken act and sell it fast.

Allison giggled, then laughed. She really had been drinking a lot.

"I didn't think you'd be so bold. They told me you were a virgin."

"Yeah! Except for that girl last summer! Summer... yeah. We just... Mmm."

I thrust my hips forward, feeling so very vulgar, but Allison laughed.

"Come on, let's do it!" I said.

I started to unfasten my belt. Allison groped me again, but I was completely soft.

"I don't think it's gonna work with that," she said.

I looked down and frowned.

"Maybe I drank too much?"

"Maybe you drank way too much."

"Oh. Oh. I'm sorry, baby. I wanna make you feel so good."

"You're so sweet."

"I'm not sweet. I'm an aminal. An naminal. An animal."

Allison laughed again. I guess I was wrong when I told Banshee I couldn't act. I was giving a great performance.

"Hey! Hey! You won't tell will you? That I couldn't? If the guys hear..."

"Shh!" she said. "No one will ever know."

"Thanks!" I said very loudly. "Hey! Hey! Let's give em a show!"

I leaped up on the bed and began jumping up and down.

"Mmm! Mmm! Yeah baby! Oh!" I said.

Allison giggled.

"Harder! Oh yes! Oh yes, Elijah! Harder! You're an animal!"

We giggled. I jumped up and down and we both moaned loudly. The bed squeaked with my every leap. I jumped up and down as fast as I could, then slowed down and jumped higher and higher while we both moaned, groaned, and called out to each other. We reached a crescendo and then abruptly stopped.

We were both out of breath as we made for the door. Allison stopped me before we went out.

"That was the most fun I've ever had in a bedroom with a guy," she said, then giggled. "Here."

She unzipped my pants, then tucked my shirt in so that the tail came out the fly. I looked down and laughed. It was a nice touch. Allison opened the door and rejoined the party. I walked in a few moments later.

"It's always the fuckin' quiet ones!" Cody said when he spotted me.

"Quiet, hell! We could hear that out here," Lucas said.

I staggered and gave Cody a thumbs up and a lopsided grin. Lucas patted me on the back.

"Congratulations. You are no longer a virgin," he said.

"Yeah!" I said much too loudly then staggered again. Lucas helped me to the couch where it all began.

I sat there grinning, giving a low-key drunken performance while I caught my breath. I felt like a liar for making everyone think I'd just done it with Allison, but I couldn't let the guys know I couldn't get it up for a girl. I'm just glad Allison bought my drunken excuse. I didn't want her to know what I was and I also didn't want her to think she was unattractive. Getting drunk was a bad thing, but pretending to be drunk had just gotten me out of what could've been a huge mess.

I felt guilty. I'd done a lot of things tonight I shouldn't have done. I was going to have to do some heavy duty praying when I got home. I hoped God would understand. It wasn't easy being fifteen.

I'd remembered to bring along my "punch" when I returned from the bedroom with Allison, so kept sipping and pretending I was drunk. I turned into a quiet drunk, as that didn't take as much acting. Cody had quieted down too, but he was still laughing and talking a lot.

There were a lot of couples making out and some disappeared from time to time. I didn't have to guess what they were doing. My parents would've had a fit if they knew what kind of party this was, but I wasn't going to tell them. I felt wicked being there, but I had not drunk much, and I hadn't done what everyone thought I'd done with Allison. I guess I was pretty deep into the sin of being untruthful, but what else could I do?

I very nearly nodded off. It must've been the vodka because the music was loud and so was much of the talking. I came back to my senses when I felt someone shake my shoulder. It was Cody.

"Hey, Mini-Gaylord."

"Hey," I said. Cody was far-gone. I almost laughed at the drunken expression on his face.

"It's stuffy in here," he said and pulled off his shirt.

I tried not to look, but how could I not? Cody had an incredible body. I noticed plenty of others checking him out and not all of them were girls. I figured I was safe if other guys were looking. Guys did like to size themselves up against other guys after all.

"Allison said she never had such a good time in bed before," Cody said.

"Yeah, that's what she told me." I grinned, and then giggled.

"You dog you!"

I laughed.

"Damn, it's hot in here. Let's go outside for a while."

I shrugged and followed Cody through the crowded living room, the kitchen, and out the back door. I could barely see Cody's bare back in front of me as he navigated the large back yard. He finally found what he was seeking and sank down on a glider. I sat beside him.

"Yeah, this is better," Cody said.

I could make out Cody better as my eyes adjusted to the light. There was just a bit of moonlight and it tinted his bare chest ever so slightly blue. The shadows made his muscles even more defined. I breathed a little harder gazing at Cody's bare torso. I wanted to reach over and touch him so bad I couldn't stand it, but I didn't dare.

"I am sooo wasted," Cody said.

The way Cody slurred his words made me believe it. He wasn't putting on an act like me. He was drunk.

"All those girls in there make me so fuckin' horny."

I blushed at Cody's use of the F-word, but of course he couldn't tell in the dark. Cody and the other players lived in a different world than mine.

I swallowed hard when Cody began to rub himself. He was looking up at the moon and idling groping. Did all jocks so freely touch themselves when they were around other jocks?

"Man, I gotta stroke."

I couldn't believe it. Cody pulled down his pants and began slowly jerking off as he sat right beside me. I got so hard my pants were bulging.

"Don't be shy, man. I've seen it before." Cody laughed.

I couldn't believe I did it, but I pushed down my pants and began jerking too.

"Man, everyone could hear you doing Allison. Made me wanna grab a girl and do her right there with everyone watching."

I had to go real slow because I had never been so turned on in my entire life. Cody Caldemyer, one of the hottest guys in school, was sitting next to me practically naked stroking himself. I didn't even pretend not to watch. I was mesmerized.

Cody kept looking over and watching me too. I'd heard guys did this kind of thing together, guys who weren't homos, but I hadn't believed it until now. I felt very self-conscious when Cody looked at me, but mostly he just gazed up at the moon.

"Man, my head hurts."

Cody stretched his arms over his head, looked and me again, then reached out and put his hand around my penis. I was so shocked and surprised I almost yelped in fright, but it felt so good I immediately lost myself in the feeling. I summoned all the courage I had and began stroking Cody too. I was so turned on there was no stopping.

After only a few moments, Cody leaned over and pulled my penis into his mouth. He slid his lips up and down and then I lost control. I moaned loudly and my eyes rolled back in my head with pleasure.

Cody pulled off, gave himself a few strokes, and then he moaned loudly too. I watched his body convulse during his orgasm. I'd never seen another guy get off before.

Cody stood when he was finished and pulled up his pants. I pulled mine up quickly too.

"Come on, let's go back in."

That was all he said. I absolutely could not believe Cody Caldemyer had given me head!

My mind was reeling so much I didn't have to fake drunkenness. I stumbled as I walked back into the living room and almost fell into Lucas. He turned to me and laughed.

"I'd better get you home. I think you've had enough."

"Yeah! Enough vodka and enough Allison!" Cody said loudly, then laughed.

I followed Lucas out, still in a state of disbelief. I expected to wake up at any moment. We climbed in the Mustang and closed the doors.

"Should you be driving?" I asked.

"I only had a little, unlike you."

"I didn't really have that much. I just get drunk easy I guess."

"At least you recover fast. You seem to be sobering up quickly."

"I guess I'm blessed. Ha! Ha!"

Lucas shook his head.

"We're not late, are we? If I don't get home by the time I promised my parents my butt will be in a sling."

"You're okay. We should even have a few minutes to spare."

We were quiet on the way home. I had too many thoughts racing through my mind to talk and Lucas seemed equally thoughtful. Before I knew it he'd pulled up in front of my place.

"Thanks for taking me. I had a good time."

"You're welcome and everyone at the party knows you had a good time." Lucas laughed again.

"Yeah, I guess so. Nite, man!"

"Nite!"

I slammed the door. Lucas pulled away as I walked up the sidewalk. When I entered the front door I thanked God I'd controlled my drinking. There was no evidence at all I'd done anything I wasn't supposed to do.

I went up to my room, undressed, and dropped onto my bed. I was sleepy, but I mainly wanted to lie there and think. I still couldn't believe Cody had given me head. I was shocked when he groped himself and then began masturbating, but I never dreamed he'd touch me and then blow me! Cody had hated me when he thought I was a homo, but now he'd turned around and did something that homos do. He was drunk, but still...

Mostly, I thought about how good it had been, even before Cody went down on me. Sitting there in the moonlight, stroking each other was the most intensely pleasurable thing I'd ever done in my life. It wasn't just that it felt good either. It was thrilling and fun and I felt like I was truly being myself for the first time ever.

I frowned. What did that say about me? Sex outside of marriage was a sin and what I'd done with Cody... According to Pastor Walker guys went to Hell for that. Pastor Walker... I didn't get him. He said such hateful things. He was a pastor and yet he didn't seem like one. Should I really pay attention to his words? I felt like I was committing a sin for doubting him, but he'd said such un-Christian things lately. He felt... false.

I grew afraid, not of Hell, but of Cody. What would happen when he sobered up and remembered what we'd done? Would he blame me? Would he call me a homo and say I'd tried to turn him? Would he beat me up? I might be in some very real danger for all I knew. I remembered how Cody had treated me when he thought I was gay. I remembered how he'd chased Banshee and would have beat him up if I hadn't concealed him. Cody didn't like homos. I had no idea how he'd react when he remembered what we'd done.

I was responsible for my own actions. I had no one to blame but myself if Cody beat me senseless. I'd committed a whole string of sins. I'd lied. I'd drank. I'd committed homosexual acts. I felt as if I'd fallen and wasn't a good Christian anymore, but I was so confused I wasn't sure I even knew how to be a good Christian.

I clasped my hands and prayed for forgiveness and even more for guidance. I prayed about church, and Banshee, and Cody, and the party. I prayed until I fell asleep.

Chapter Six

I didn't want to go to church. I felt guilty for not wanting to go, but my church had turned on me. What I'd always thought was the house of God... wasn't. Every Sunday the pastor had been preaching hate against homosexuals and most of the congregation seemed to agree. Time and again the pastor talked about perverts choosing homosexuality, but when I was near Lucas or Cody or another attractive boy there was no choice to be made. My body reacted in no uncertain terms. I did nothing to make it happen. I'd fought it with everything I had and yet it was still there.

I thought about what had happened the night before with Cody. Maybe none of it would've happened if I hadn't been drinking, but the truth was I hadn't drunk very much. Cody was drunk, but I wasn't. I knew what I was doing. If I could blame what I'd done, and what I'd allowed Cody to do, on drunkenness it would've been easier, but I couldn't do that. I had to take responsibility.

I'd felt guilty the night before, but what I remembered now with clarity was how natural it felt to be with Cody. When he touched me it felt as if it was meant to be. I felt instinct kick in. It was like my body was designed to react exactly as it had.

I'd committed some sins last night. I'd lied and I'd drunk, but the more I thought about it, the more I was certain that what I'd done with Cody was no sin. It was just nature.

Pastor Walker looked so sanctimonious standing behind his podium as we entered the church. My eyes narrowed. He'd made me feel guilty about something I shouldn't have felt guilty about at all. He'd harmed me with his words and he had been trying to harm others like me. He was inciting the congregation to commit violence against gays. He would deny it was violence, but concentration camps for gays? That was violence to be sure.

I wasn't too pleased with God at the moment, either. I thought he loved everyone, but he'd stuck me with desires for members of my own sex and he was going to send me to Hell for it—for something that wasn't even a sin? How was that fair? I began to suspect that God wasn't good and kind and loving. Maybe he was sadistic. A sadistic God made more sense than a kind and loving God. The world was filled with pain, suffering, sickness, and despair. Cruel acts were committed daily. The strong trampled the weak and few seemed to care. If God loved everyone there would be no such things as sickness, sadness, grief, or pain. Such things could only be the creation of a cruel God.

What about me? I felt like God had set me up. I was coming to understand that being gay wasn't a choice at all. I didn't try to get turned on by guys like Lucas and Cody. It just happened. I'd even tried hard not to get turned on by them, but there was no stopping it. God made me gay and he made being a gay a sin, so I had definitely been set up. It wasn't fair. I had no choice in the matter. I didn't even understand why being gay was a sin. It didn't make any sense.

I took my seat in the pew by my parents, sitting where we always sat. The congregation began to sing a hymn. I'd always loved signing the hymns but now it left me feeling empty. It was as if all the meaning had been drained away. I'd lost my faith in God and with that went everything.

Pastor Walker began his sermon. As I suspected, it was another diatribe against homosexuals.

"Do not lie with a man as one lies with a woman; that is detestable." These are not my words, but the words of the Bible, Leviticus 18:22.

"If a man lies with a man as one lies with a woman, both of them have done what is detestable. They must be put to death; their blood will be on their own heads." Again, these are not my words, but the words of the Bible, Leviticus 20:13.

A few weeks ago, I suggested that camps be created to separate homosexuals from normal members of society, but as you can see from Leviticus I have erred in my kindness for what the Bible says is quite clear, "They must be put to death." Homosexuals should be put to death here as they were in Israel. If this was done, there would be none of this "coming out of the closet." Homosexuals would either remain hidden from the view of good Christians or they would be executed.

You may be asking yourself if I'm telling you to go out and kill homosexuals. No, I am not, but the government should. They won't, but they should. I know such violence is detestable, but it is God's idea, not mine, and I'm not ashamed of it.

""Love your neighbor as yourself." Matthew 22:37-39.""

It was not Pastor Walker who spoke these words. I did not know who spoke them and neither did anyone else. The voice was that of a young male, clear and confident.

"We love because God first loved us. If anyone says, "I love God," yet hates his brother, he is a liar. For anyone who does not love his brother, whom he has seen, cannot love God, whom he has not seen. Whoever loves God must also love his brother." 1 John 4:19-20."

A gasp ran through the congregation as a very young man stepped forward. My breath caught in my throat. It was Jesus! It was the boy who had come to me in the park and on the bleachers by the football field.

Pastor Walker glared at Jesus.

"Sit down and be quiet, or leave," the pastor said.

"What is wrong, Pastor? Cannot you refute my words? You stand behind your podium and preach hatred and murder and claim it is not your words, but God's. The message of God is one of love and only love."

"The Bible clearly states that homosexuals are to be put to death."

"The Bible nowhere mentions homosexuals. The word did not exist until recent times. If you knew your Bible you would also know that the texts you cited referred to ritual sex performed to worship a foreign god. Toevah, translated as abomination refers to cultic behavior, idolatry, and foreign ritual. It refers only to behavior concerned with worshipping a foreign god. It refers to cultic prostitution and nothing more.

"The Bible commands many things. Do you stone rebellious children to death? Do you sell your neighbors into slavery? No, you do not do these things and yet you condemn gays."

""Justice—justice shall you pursue." Deuteronomy 16:20," Pastor Walker said.

"Yes. "Justice—justice shall you pursue." Discrimination against gays is injustice and therefore in violation of Biblical law. Imprisonment and murder are both injustice and therefore also in violation of Biblical law and yet you stand there and preach both. You resemble more the Pharisees than that the one you call Lord."

The congregation, including me, was speechless. No one had ever dared to argue with Pastor Walker, much less a sixteen-year-old boy. I gazed at Jesus. He was so calm, serene, and confident while the pastor quaked with anger.

"The devil can cite Scripture for his purpose, be gone devil!" Pastor Walker shouted.

"Scripture is filled with love, but you have preached hatred. Christian religion commands you to love your neighbor, and it imposes an extra obligation on the strong to protect the weak and work for their welfare. Gays are God's lambs. You were charged with protecting them instead you have persecuted them."

"Remove him!" screamed the pastor. "Remove him and his blasphemy!"

A handful of men in the congregation stepped from their pews and toward Jesus, but did not approach too closely. They were afraid.

"This is your warning, Pastor. Repent from your sinful ways. Repent from the sins you have committed standing behind that pulpit. I shall return in one week. I hope to find a better man."

Jesus turned and walked slowly and calmly to the exit. When he had departed all eyes turned on Pastor Walker.

"Someone call the police," the pastor said. "The boy is obviously demented. He is likely a danger to himself and to others. I think we shall stop our service here today. I'm sure this intrusion has upset us all."

With that, Pastor Walker rushed into his backroom and the congregation exploded. Everyone was talking at once. I smiled. I had not wanted to come to church today, but I would not have missed it for the world. I did not know who this Jesus-kid was, but he was sure living up to his name.

I sat in the back of the car as Dad drove us home from church. I noticed my parents weren't talking. They usually chatted on the way home, but today—nothing. A question burned on my lips, but I was afraid to ask it. My parents were very religious; much more so than I'd ever been, especially now that I was having serious doubts.

"What did you think about that boy who interrupted the service?" I blurted out finally. The question was likely a mistake, but I had to know.

Neither of my parents answered for several long moments.

"I think he made some valid points," Dad said.

"I think he was right," said Mom.

Dad looked at Mom for a moment, somewhat surprised.

"Pastor Walker has been a bit... extreme in recent weeks," Mom said. "This crusade of his against homosexuals. It's just... too much."

"I think it's wrong," I said. "Concentration camps? Executions?"

"Camps, not concentration camps," Dad said.

"No matter what name the pastor put on it, the camps he was talking about were concentration camps, just like in Nazi Germany and today he was talking about killing people. It's wrong."

Mom and Dad looked at each other again. They didn't know what to say. I guess it was hard for them to agree with me. The pastor was the leader of the church.

"I think Pastor Walker needs to stop being so extreme and get back to teaching about the Scriptures," Mom said.

I sat in the back seat amazed. I was afraid my parents might go along with whatever Pastor Walker said just because he was the pastor. Their disapproval might not seem like much, but for my parents it was a major rebellion.

We said nothing more the rest of the short drive home. Once there, I went up to my room, changed out of my suit and tie and into a pair of running shorts and a VHS Football tee shirt. I felt like running. I had some things to think about. I did a lot of my thinking while I walked, but sometimes I needed to run. This was one of those days.

I smiled as I tightened the laces of my sneakers and ran down to the stairs. I was beginning to feel like a jock. I'd been playing at it all summer long with my runs and workouts, but now

I was actually on the football team and I was getting buff. I wasn't tall and I wasn't built, but I was toned and defined.

I jogged down the front sidewalk, then turned south and began to run. I set a steady pace, not too fast because I wanted to cover some distance today. As I ran block after block my mind cleared of random thoughts and I was able to focus.

I felt as if my whole world was changing. For as long as I could remember, religion had guided me and shown me the way. Lately, my doubts had been growing. Pastor Walker was rather extreme, but most of the congregation seemed to agree with him when he talked about putting homosexuals in concentration camps. They even agreed when he preached that the government should kill homosexuals. I'd read about the Nazi concentration camps. I knew what had happened there. How could those who called themselves Christians condone such a thing? Did Christianity condone it too? I didn't even understand how God could allow something as horrible as a concentration camp to exist. It made me wonder if God existed at all. I didn't like having such doubts. I didn't like feeling as if my religion had betrayed me. I felt like I'd been lied to for years and Christianity wasn't at all what it represented itself to be. It was filled with hypocrisy. It spoke of kindness, love, and helping others when it was actually filled with violence and hatred.

I had gone to church today with great reluctance. I wasn't even sure I ever wanted to go again. It was such a radical thought I couldn't even openly ponder it, but in the back of my mind I had thought of giving up on church. Now, everything had changed again. Jesus, the boy from school, had appeared. I was amazed he had challenged the pastor, but the words he spoke seemed far more Christian than anything that had come from the pulpit of late. Jesus gave me something to hold onto. I heard in his words what I'd once heard from my church, and I realized I didn't truly want to give up on church or on God. Jesus said he would return. All thoughts of not attending church vanished from my mind. I wanted to hear what Jesus had to say. I wanted to see what happened.

While I was thinking these thoughts I'd ran past the town limits of Verona and into the countryside. Instead of homes and businesses, there were cornfields and forests on the sides of the blacktop road. I loved the smell of the air out here. It was the scent of green, growing things. It was the scent of trees.

My breathing became increasingly labored as I ran. I tried to push on, but I couldn't. I was forced to slow down. I had a slight headache too. I hoped I wasn't getting sick. Our first game was Friday night. I wouldn't get to play, but I wanted to be there to sit on the bench. It might sound pathetic, but sitting on that bench was a big deal to me. My brothers had sat there before me. I'd always been up in the stands. I knew I couldn't match what my bigger, stronger brothers had done, but at least I could sit on that bench as a player for VHS.

I was so out of breath by the time I reached the Selby Farm I had to stop running and walk. I should've been able to run further. Near the end of the summer I'd worked my way up to running a good three miles past the Selby Farm and then back home again. I knew practices were wearing me out, but I'd had all of Saturday and most of Sunday to rest. True, I'd been on my feet for hours yesterday at Chicken Fillets, but standing in one place isn't physically taxing like running.

I gazed over at the two-story farmhouse and the big barn. I could see a boy riding shirtless on a tractor. It had to be Ethan Selby. I didn't know him. He'd graduated from VHS before my high school years, but I'd seen him in town. Even with his shirt on I could tell he was built. I'd seen his name on the big wrestling banner in the gym and on a plaque in a showcase near the front of the school. He was the best wrestler ever at VHS.

I had wondered before how a boy like Ethan could be a homosexual. There was no doubt he was one. He didn't try to hide it. Everyone knew. Just like Shawn and Tim and a few others at school, Ethan was open about what he was and most of the kids at school didn't seem to care. Of course, most of them weren't Christians. Only the bullies hated homosexuals—bullies and Christians. How odd that Christians and bullies had that in common, but if my pastor represented Christianity, then I guess it wasn't so surprising. Lately, Pastor Walker had been a bully too.

I didn't wonder anymore how a boy like Ethan could be gay. I knew. He just was. It was as simple as that. I understood because I was like him. I was what I was. At least that's what I was coming to understand. Part of me still fought it. Years of going to church had so drummed into my head that homosexuality was sinful that it was hard to give up on the idea. I guess I didn't know for sure one way or another, but my ideas were changing.

My mind drifted to Cody once more. He confused me. He had hated me because he thought I was gay. He'd chased down Banshee and was going to beat him up when he found out Banshee was a homosexual. Then, last night, he'd performed a homosexual act. It didn't make any sense. I wasn't looking forward to school tomorrow. I was very much afraid of what Cody might do.

I turned and walked back toward home. I was having trouble catching my breath. I felt really tired too, more so than I should have. I guess I needed to cut down on my running distance now that I was an active member of the football team. We ran plenty during practices so I didn't need to do any outside running. Today had been more about thinking than running, but my thoughts were as labored as my breathing. Nothing made much sense anymore.

***

I walked into school tired. I'd gone to bed early, but I felt like I'd turned in late. Mom had even asked me if I was sick, but I didn't feel warm, didn't have a sore throat and I felt fine—just tired.

I tensed when I spotted Cody at his locker, but when he turned and noticed me he smiled at me and nodded. I nodded back and hurried on. I was still scared of what he might do. He didn't seem belligerent, but I wasn't taking any chances.

I didn't sense any hostility from Cody at lunch either. We didn't directly interact as we ate our Salisbury steak, mashed potatoes, green beans, and apple crisp, but when our eyes met there was no hostility in them. The talk at the table was mostly football and girls. It was the same every day. Near the end of lunch an arm-wrestling completion began. I stayed clear of that. I had no need of humiliation.

I was a bit jumpy all day, but Cody didn't ambush me. He hadn't so much as frowned at me, but I still feared he'd blame Saturday night's sexual encounter on me. I didn't want to go back to the days when I lived in fear of Cody beating me to a pulp.

I put Cody out of my mind as I dressed out for 7th period P.E. Banshee's eyes met mine. I read the sadness there. It was always there when he looked at me. I'd put it there. I was confused about

God and church, but I still had my beliefs. I'd hurt Banshee. I'd overreacted. I'd greeted love with hatred and hadn't been a good Christian. It was time to do something about that. I'd been too ashamed to tell Banshee I was sorry. I'd been a coward and I'd let him suffer because I was afraid. I had to make things right.

I hurried after Banshee as he left the locker room. I caught up to him as he entered the gym and pulled him to the side. He looked about anxiously.

"Listen, um... we need to talk. I have some things to say to you."

Banshee swallowed and looked slightly fearful but said nothing.

"I can't talk here. How about after school? I have football practice, but maybe we could meet somewhere... the park... at... maybe seven?"

"I'll meet you at Ofarim's," Banshee said.

"Okay, Ofarim's at seven."

I hurried on into the gym and lined up for calisthenics. I felt better, but also afraid. I wasn't looking forward to my talk with Banshee, but it was something I had to do. He wasn't eager to meet me, but I couldn't blame him. I'm hurt him and he was likely angry. I owed him an explanation and a chance to yell me if he wanted.

Banshee eyed me now and then during gym. We were moving from football into track. I was good at sprints, but I couldn't quite cut it during distance events. I watched as Banshee sailed past me during the 1600 meter. That run left quite a few of the guys huffing and puffing since it was nearly a mile, but I should've been able to perform much better. I grew frustrated during the last lap and slowed to little more than a jog. I'd run for miles during the summer but now I couldn't even run the 1600 without gasping for breath like I was completely out of shape. I felt unusually tired as I crossed the finish line. I was glad our next event was the shot put. I knew I couldn't throw it far, but at least I didn't have to run.

***

I was nervous as I entered the locker room before football practice. I pulled off my shirt and jeans as my teammates stripped. Lucas was right next to me and I was struck yet again by the beauty of his torso. He had a smooth, muscular chest that tapered down into six-pack abs. He even had the beginnings of an eight-pack. The symmetry of his body was perfect. From his broad-shoulders and rippling biceps all the way down to his bubble butt and muscular legs. Lucas was what every guy wanted to be. I'd almost sell my soul to look like that. I immediately regretted my last thought. No. I wouldn't sell my soul, not for anything. My soul was in enough danger already.

"Hey!" Cody yelled as he came up behind me and grabbed my shoulder.

I flinched and turned to face Cody. This was it. He was going to deck me in front of everyone.

"Sorry to scare you, man," Cody said, then laughed. "I promise not to bite." Cody gnashed his teeth.

"You better hope he doesn't bite. I don't think he's had his rabies shot yet," Beck said.

I stood there completely naked for a few moments, my heart pounding in my chest, but Cody gave no sign he was angry. I peered at him, searching his eyes for some clue.

"What?" Cody asked.

"Nothing."

"Are you gonna dress out or do you plan on running laps naked?" Cody asked as he pulled off his own shirt.

The sight of Cody's bare chest aroused me, as did the bulge in his jeans. I almost couldn't believe I'd had my hands on what was hidden in those pants.

"Um...I guess I'll wear clothes this time," I said.

I quickly grabbed my jock and slipped it on. I had to conceal my increasing arousal.

"On behalf of us all, thank you," Kevin said.

"Yeah right, Kevin. I bet you like looking at Elijah naked, you homo," Cody said, then laughed.

"You wish."

The guys laughed. I wondered how Cody could so easily joke around about homos after he'd given me head at the party on Saturday night. I still almost couldn't believe it happened. In fact, I was beginning to wonder if I'd dreamed it. I had been a little drunk that night—for the very first time in in my life. Maybe I nodded off while Cody and I were out talking alone in the backyard and dreamed the whole thing. That was a more rational explanation than what I thought had happened.

I looked at Cody again. He gave no indication that anything had happened between us. I'd feared his wrath all day. I'd feared him blaming me for what had happened, but he wasn't angry. It was as if nothing had happened at all. There was no acknowledgment of what we'd done, not even a significant gaze. Cody didn't shrug off our sexual encounter with an "I was so drunk at that party." Cody acted as if he really didn't remember. I didn't think he was capable of that level of acting, so I began to wonder if the whole thing hadn't taken place in my head. But, it had really happened, hadn't it? I just didn't know anymore.

Running laps was a killer. Coach Jordan noticed I was having trouble and pulled me to off the track before I was finished. My breathing was unusually labored, and I was hurting so much I had tears in my eyes.

"Do you smoke, Gaylord?" Coach asked.

"No, Coach. I've never smoked."

"Listen, you're new. You have to learn to pace yourself."

"I know about pacing. I ran all summer."

"That's not what I'm talking about. I mean pacing your entire life. Guys your age think they're immortal. They think they can keep going with little or no sleep and that nothing can touch them. Guys my age know better, but when you're young it's easy to think you're invulnerable. You look really worn down, Gaylord. I think you're pushing yourself too hard. You need to ease up and get more sleep. Rest is extremely important."

"Maybe I haven't been getting enough sleep. It's hard between practices and school work and everything else."

"Yes, I know. It is difficult, but you need to take better care of yourself. Eat healthy. Don't try to exist on junk food. Drink plenty of water and remember to get plenty of sleep."

"Okay, Coach. Thanks."

"Go ahead and head for the weight room. The guys are about finished here."

I walked back toward the gym. Coach was probably right. I wasn't getting enough sleep. I did eat a little too much junk food. I knew I should drink more water too. I needed to make some adjustments in my life if I was going to survive football. I knew it was going to be hard, but I had no idea it would be so exhausting!

I was in the weight room alone for about five minutes. I set my weight for the bench press and started in. I stopped after one rep to check the weight stack. It felt too heavy, but the weight was correct. I lay back on the bench and started again. I got through five reps and then had to stop. My arms trembled and I was breathing harder than I should've been. What was wrong with me? I felt like I kept getting weaker instead of stronger. I reluctantly lowered my weight. I completed my reps, but it wasn't easy. I wanted to catch up to Lucas and Cody, but instead I was going in the opposite direction!

My teammates filtered in and soon the weight room was filled with the clanging of weight plates and the grunts of teenagers pushing their bodies to the limit. I took it easier. I just couldn't cut it today so I didn't try. I cut my weight on every exercise, but my workout was still a struggle.

Most of the guys worked out shirtless and they were sexy, but Lucas and Cody looked like heroes who stepped out of an ancient Greek myth. Those two were beyond handsome, beyond built. I wondered what it would feel like to be that good looking and have that incredible of a body. I'd never know. I guessed I was okay looking, but I wasn't handsome like those two. As for my body... at my current rate I was never even going to get close to being built.

I struggled through my workout, but I was proud of one thing. I never once thought about giving up. This had been the hardest day I'd experienced so far, but I definitely wasn't thinking about quitting the team. That would never happen. I might get cut from the team or kicked off, but I wasn't going to walk off.

I began to feel nauseous as I was doing seated rows. My head kind of hurt and I didn't feel good at all. Right in the middle of my set I got off the machine and hurried to the restroom. I only just made it to a toilet before I hurled.

I stayed in the restroom for a while. I felt like I might throw up again. I wet a paper towel and put in on my forehead. That made me feel a little better, but my head still hurt.

I began to feel less nauseous, so I returned to the weight room. I didn't go back to working out. I wasn't up to it. I told Coach I wasn't feeling very good. He sent me to the locker room.

The locker room was eerily quiet. I don't think I'd ever been in there alone before. It was usually crowded with guys talking, laughing, and slamming metal doors. I stripped out of my uniform and walked to the showers. The shower room was just as eerie. The only sound was the water cascading from my lone showerhead. As I worked shampoo into my hair scenes from psycho flashed in my mind, which was funny in a way because I'd never watched it. I'd just heard about the stabbing scene in the shower.

I turned around quickly when I thought I heard something, but no one was there. I didn't need a psycho stalking me. I could create one with my own mind.

I usually like a hot shower, but today I wanted a cool shower. It eased the slight pain in my head and made me feel less nauseous. I took my time in the showers. Being in there alone was a luxury. I soaped up my entire body and watched the suds as they ran down the drain.

I began to feel better, not exactly good, but good enough. The nausea all but disappeared and my headache did too. The absence of pain is pleasure so even my mood improved. I wasn't going to let myself get down. I was just having an off day.

I heard a noise behind me again. I turned and this time there was someone there. It was Cody. My heart began to beat faster as he approached. He didn't look happy. This was it. He blamed me for what happened between us on Saturday night and he was going to kick my ass for it. I backed away as he approached, but I knew there was no escape. We were alone and with his powerful muscles he could do anything to me he wanted.

Cody came nearer, then stepped up to a showerhead a couple down from mine and turned on the hot water.

"I pushed my weight up to 220 on the bench press today, but that bastard Lucas did the same."

I heaved a sigh of relief.

"I had to lower my weight," I admitted. "I also had to hurl. Coach says I'm not eating right or getting enough sleep."

"You don't look good. You're kind of pale. Working out sucks when you're sick, but I work though the pain so I can have an arm like this."

Cody flexed his left bicep. His entire arm rippled with muscle. The sight aroused me so I had to turn away from him. I also changed the water temperature from cool to cold.

Other guys began to come in. I left, picked up a towel from the towel boy, and headed for the locker room. I was just sure Cody was going to get me in the shower room but again nothing had happened. We were completely alone and he did nothing. He also said nothing about Saturday night. I again wondered if I hadn't dreamed the whole thing. Cody Caldemyer giving me head? That sure seemed more like a dream that anything that would actually happen.

I dressed and headed out of the locker room. I stopped by the nearest payphone and called Mom. I told her about my plans to meet Banshee at Ofarim's and said I was going to study in the library until it was time to meet him at 7 p.m. Mom was fine with it. I knew she would be. My parents never had to hassle me about getting my schoolwork done so they weren't worried.

The library was only a few blocks from Ofarim's so I worked on my assignments while I waited for 7 p.m. to draw near. It was after 5:30 when I got out of practice, so I didn't have a lot of time to kill. I wanted to use the time to do homework. I'd be up until midnight if I was with Banshee too long. Our meeting was likely to be a short one. I doubted he wanted to have anything to do with me.

I put my books in my backpack a little before 7 p.m. and walked to Ofarim's. I was feeling a lot better. I was tired, but my headache and nausea were gone. Sitting quietly in the library had helped.

I spotted Banshee entering Ofarim's when I was a block away. When I entered I found him seated in a booth talking to Shawn. I'd forgotten they both sat at the homo table. I don't know how I'd forgotten. It wasn't that long ago that I'd asked Shawn to look out for Banshee because Cody was after him.

"Hey, man," Shawn said as I entered and took a seat across from Banshee. "How is practice going for you?"

"It's going to kill me," I said.

"I know the feeling, but at least you don't have to work after practice."

"I only work on Saturdays."

"Jerk."

I smiled.

"What would you like to drink?"

"Gimme a Coke," I said. I was starving so I planned to order whether Banshee did or not. "You going to get anything?" I asked.

"I think I'll just get a milkshake."

"I'm buying," I said.

Banshee looked surprised.

"Um, thanks."

I took a moment to look around Ofarim's. Truthfully, I was stalling, but I did like the atmosphere of the burger and ice cream joint. The jukebox with its neon lights gave the place an almost 1950s feel, but Ofarim's was more modern. The booths were comfortable and there was a nice view of the park across the street.

There were a few other customers, but Banshee had picked a booth in the corner. No one else was near. We were free to talk so I figured I'd better get started.

"Listen, I asked you here to apologize," I said.

"Elijah, I know I shouldn't have kissed you, but I thought I was picking up signals. I thought you wanted me to kiss you."

"Actually, I came to apologize to *you*," I said.

"You did?"

"Yes."

Banshee looked relieved. Shawn arrived just then with my Coke and an ice water for Banshee. I ordered a double-cheeseburger and large fries. Banshee ordered a chocolate shake.

"So, you're not still mad that I kissed you? I'll be honest; I didn't want to meet you in park because I was afraid you were setting me up. I thought you and some of your football buddies might jump me."

"I've been a bigger jerk than I thought," I said, frowning. "I would never do that to you or to anyone. You didn't do anything wrong and... I probably was sending signals. I didn't mean to do so, but I can see where you might have thought I wanted to kiss you."

"I was stupid for thinking you were gay. It's just that you were so nice to me and sometimes when you looked at me you looked... interested."

"Um... well... actually... you weren't stupid. I think that I am... gay."

Banshee stared at me.

"Then why did you yell at me?"

"I was confused and... well, I'm still sorting things out. I don't want to be a homo, but I think I am one. You have to understand that my family is extremely religious and I've always been taught in church that homosexuality is a sin. Our pastor said gays were out to turn straight boys so..."

"When I kissed you, you thought I was trying to turn you?"

"That's part of it. It's not just my family that's religious. I am too. I thought being gay was a sin and that all homosexuals were destined for Hell. I had these feelings... these desires, but I hoped it was just a phase. It's especially difficult in the locker room and showers after football practice. Lucas and Cody..."

I realized I was going on about my dilemma when I was there to apologize to Banshee. I looked up. Banshee grinned at me.

"I'd give twenty bucks for a look at either of them naked."

His comment made me burst out laughing.

"I was fighting what I thought of as evil. You kissed me and it was like the Devil was tempting me through you. That and... well in that moment you kissed me... I liked it. I was mad at myself for liking it and mad at you for showing me I liked it. I should never have yelled at you like that. I should never have told you to leave. I should have told you then what I'm telling you now, but I couldn't because I wasn't as far along in thinking things out."

"I just thought I'd made a huge mistake and kissed a straight boy."

"You kissed a messed up boy who wasn't sure what he was. I'm not entirely sure now, but I'm pretty sure. Maybe I am sure and I can't admit it to myself."

"It sounds as if you're admitting it to me."

"It's hard for me. I guess it's hard for anyone, but for my entire life my church has told me that homosexuality is a sin. I've always gone to church. I've tried so hard to be a good Christian that being faced with being something that is sinful is just too much."

"I'm sorry it's been so hard on you."

I wanted to tell Banshee about the horrible things our pastor had been saying. I wanted to talk about how that made me feel, but this wasn't about me.

"I'm really sorry for what I did. I had my reasons, but it was still wrong. I hurt you. You were kind to me and I hurt you."

"You did hurt me. I was so happy when you started hanging out with me. I thought we were becoming friends and maybe more than friends then I felt like you hated me."

"I didn't hate you. I was wrong and stupid. We were becoming friends, until I messed it up. Can you forgive me?"

"I forgive you."

"Why is it that all you gay boys act more Christian than Christians?"

"I can't speak for us all, but the boys I've been sitting with try to be kind to others. I think that being on the receiving end of abuse makes gay boys more compassionate toward others."

I paused. I hadn't thought about that. Could it be that God made me gay so that I would be more compassionate?

"I haven't forgotten that you didn't tell Cody where I was hiding that day he was after me," Banshee said.

"You saved me once, so I figured I owed you. I don't want to see anyone hurt, either."

Shawn brought my burger and fries and Banshee's chocolate shake. We spent a good deal of our time eating instead of talking. We both had a lot to think about.

"If you're interested... if I haven't messed up everything so bad you don't like me anymore... maybe we could try hanging out again?"

"What about your football buddies? Cody doesn't like gays. I take it he doesn't know about you."

My mind flashed back to Saturday night for a moment.

"I haven't told anyone what I've just told you. I can't sit at the homo table with you, but we could do things outside of school. If my teammates see us... I'll just cross that bridge when I come to it."

"Are you sure?"

"Yeah. I like you and... I kind of need someone to talk to."

Tears welled up in my eyes for a moment, but I wiped them away quickly. Banshee smiled at me sadly.

"It will be okay," he said. "I know it's rough, but it will be okay. I'm doing pretty well and I'm not even a football stud like you."

That made me laugh. I liked Banshee a lot.

"Football stud. Yeah, right. I was just crying."

"You weren't crying. Your eyes got watery. It doesn't count unless tears roll down your cheek."

I smiled.

"I'm sorry I put this off," I said. "I figured you were going to be angry with me, but I wanted to explain and give you a chance to yell at me if you wanted."

"I wish you'd talked to me sooner, but then again, maybe not. I don't think you were ready until now. If you hadn't put it off, our reunion might not have worked out so well."

"Perhaps. What's it like sitting at the homo table?" I asked.

"It's a blast! Those guys are so much fun. They're good looking too, which doesn't hurt. Shawn is so built and Tim isn't far behind him. The only problem is they are all attached. You knew Casper is Brendan's boyfriend, right? The quarterback and team captain from last year?"

"Everyone knows that."

"Casper is so lucky. Have you seen, Brendan? Oh! My! God!"

I had to stop myself from asking Banshee not to say "God" like that. He didn't know it was wrong. Since he didn't know, maybe it wasn't. Either way I wasn't going to mess up what we were starting... again.

"He's very fit."

"He's beyond fit. Casper showed me a picture of Brendan shirtless. I think I drooled on it."

I laughed even as I turned a bit red.

"Sorry. This is too much, isn't it? You're confused and I'm talking to you like you've been hooking up with guys or dating."

"Well, I'm not exactly comfortable and I'm not exactly sure about myself... I think I am, but... how do you know you're into guys and not girls?"

"How do you feel when you see Cody or Lucas naked? Does your heart beat faster? Do you start getting hard?"

I blushed.

"Both," I said quietly.

"How about when you're around girls? Do any of them make your pants dance?"

I shook my head.

"You may be confused, but your body isn't. It *knows*."

"My pastor says homosexuality is a choice."

"That's complete bullshit."

"I think you're right. I've fought hard against feeling things for other guys, but it hasn't worked."

"Of course it hasn't worked. Trying to change who you are attracted to is like trying to will yourself taller or trying to transform yourself into an eagle. You can try all you want, but you can't change what you are."

"I'm beginning to doubt a lot of what my pastor says. I've even begun to doubt God, and I feel horrible about that."

"Why do you doubt God?"

"He made me like this and He hates me for it. It's cruel."

"That does sound cruel, but are you so sure He hates you for it?"

"The Bible says so. Well, maybe it does. I'm not so sure about that now either." I thought back to what Jesus, the Jesus who goes to VHS, said. It made sense.

"I don't want to put down your religion, but I don't believe in the Bible."

I was shocked. Banshee read the expression on my face.

"I'm not saying I know for sure, but I just don't believe it's God's word. Men wrote it, not God. It contradicts itself repeatedly. It says slavery is a good thing. It just doesn't seem very Godly to me. I think it's merely a tool used to justify hatred and prejudice."

I began to get angry, but then I calmed myself down. Banshee was entitled to his opinion and I wasn't sure of anything anymore.

"I don't know," I said.

"I don't know either. I think too many people claim to know too much. I think if there is a God he's probably so unlike what we can imagine he's not even a he. He's beyond that. I don't think anyone knows anything about God. I know I don't. I have some ideas, but that's all they are, ideas. I just try to be nice to other people. That's my religion right there."

"That's the basis for Christianity," I said.

"I think the world would be a better place if everyone just stuck to the idea of being kind to others and forgot all the rest."

"I don't know about that."

"I don't claim to know anything. That's just what I think."

I didn't want to get into a discussion about what had been going on recently in my church, so I said nothing more on the subject.

"What's it like sitting at the football table?" Banshee asked.

"It's fun, but some of the things they say... whoa."

"Like what?"

"Stuff about girls. If my parents knew the things they said and the language they used I'd never be allowed to sit there. They'd probably even make me quit the team."

"That bad, huh?"

"Sometimes I turn red," I admitted.

Banshee laughed.

I ate my burger and fries while Banshee drank his chocolate shake. I enjoyed talking to him even more than I remembered. I'd asked him to meet me so I could apologize. I didn't expect it to be a pleasant experience, but I was having a good time.

"Has Cody given you any more trouble? I asked.

"He pushes me around when he gets the chance and he calls me names. I'm careful about where I go alone. The guys watch out for me too. I didn't know they were doing it at first, but then I began noticing at least one of them always seemed to be around, Shawn or Tim especially."

"I uh, told Shawn that Cody was after you and asked him to look out for you," I said.

"You did?"

"Yeah, right after that day you had to hide from him downtown."

Banshee smiled.

"Thank you, Elijah. I wasn't sure why you didn't tell him where I was hiding that day. I was afraid you'd jerk me out onto the sidewalk and help him beat me up."

I frowned. I hated that I'd made Banshee feel that way about me.

"It's okay," Banshee said. "Don't be down on yourself. I'm glad we've talked. Now I understand why you reacted the way you did. I shouldn't have kissed you, but I wasn't thinking about the consequences. You're so handsome and so nice and I just couldn't stop myself."

Banshee's face turned slightly red.

"Sorry, I'm doing it again. I'm acting without thinking. You probably don't want another guy telling you he thinks you're attractive."

"It's okay. I... I don't want to be gay, but it's becoming pretty obvious that I am. Praying hasn't worked. Trying to change myself hasn't worked. No matter what I do my feelings remain the same. I'm religious like I said. I don't want to get into why, but I haven't been all that happy with God lately."

"Relationship difficulties?" Banshee asked. He laughed, then his expression changed to that of a little boy who knew he'd just said something he shouldn't have. I smiled.

"It's okay. You're not far wrong. Despite the difficulties, I still think God would help me if he could. I'm wondering if he's not helping me to change because he doesn't want me to change. That, more than anything else, makes we feel that I am gay, but that it's okay. Maybe I was meant to be gay."

"I think you were meant to be gay, just like me. I tried to fight it too at first, but not only did I fail, I realized I was lying to people and hurting them."

"Is that why you sat alone and kept to yourself?"

"Yeah. I didn't want to lie and I didn't want to hurt anyone, so I closed myself off. I realize now that was a mistake too."

"How did you hurt other people, if you don't mind my asking?"

"I tried to make myself straight by dating a girl. I was thirteen. I liked spending time with her, but I didn't have any feelings for her beyond friendship. She had feelings, strong feelings, for me. I kept trying to force myself to fall in love with her. I kept trying to force myself to want her, but I couldn't. When we kissed all I felt was revulsion. I tried to hide it, but she caught on. We broke up. I broke her heart. I never felt so bad about anything in my life. That's when I decided to quit fighting what I was and just admit to myself I liked boys. I wasn't ready to tell others the truth, so I closed myself off. Then you came along."

"And I hurt you."

"Yeah, but then Casper came and talked me into sitting with his friends. Now, you and I are here talking and I hope we can do it again."

"I'd like that a lot."

I smiled. I'd come to apologize, but I was leaving with a friend.

Chapter Seven

There was no football practice after school on Friday because it was a game night. I almost couldn't believe our first game was at hand. We were only the JV team and I'd likely only be a benchwarmer, but I was both excited and anxious. The game wasn't until seven, so I went home for supper. Dad came in about five so we all ate together. We hadn't done that for quite a while. It used to be an every night thing before my brothers took off for college, except when they had a game or a practice that ran too long. My whole world was changing. I liked this little piece of familiarity. I liked the meatloaf, mashed potatoes, baked beans, hot yeast rolls, and especially the peach cobbler even better!

"Are you excited about tonight?" Dad asked.

"Yeah."

"I'm glad to see you playing football, son. The Gaylord's have a long history in football. Your great grandfather played for Knute Rockne, you know."

"He knows dear," Mom said. We'd all heard that fact from the family history more times than we could count.

"It's not all ancient history either. I played football in college. I'm so proud of your brothers for playing college ball."

"Even with them going to IU instead of Notre Dame?" I teased.

"They're men now. They are free to make their own decisions, even if their father is a Notre Dame man."

"We're coming to your game tonight," Mom announced.

"You are? I mean, that's great, but..."

"What?" Dad asked.

"Well, I'm one of the new guys on the team and I'm also the smallest. I probably won't get to play."

"You are still on the football team, son. We want to be there in case you get to play. If you don't, we still want to be there. We're proud of you. We know you worked very hard to make the team and we're proud of you for that alone."

"We would have been proud of you even if you hadn't made the team. I've never seen you put so much effort into something before. Now, here you are on the football team and working a part-time job. My baby is growing up," Mom said, getting a little weepy.

"This is just my freshman year of high school," I pointed out to make Mom feel better.

Dad began reminiscing about my brother's high school football days. Both of them had been great players, although not quite quarterback material. I don't know how I would've managed if they'd both been the quarterback in their time. It was hard enough standing in their shadow as it was.

After supper, I tried to rest but it was hard to lie there when butterflies were flitting around in my stomach. I didn't know why I was nervous. Sitting on the bench wasn't that difficult. There was no way Coach Jordan would play me the first game. I'd learned a lot during practices, but I was still at the bottom of the ladder. I was just one step above the water boy.

There was pre-game bonfire at six. It was tradition. At 5:30 I got up. I walked over to the mirror and stripped off my shirt. I flexed my muscles. I actually had muscles now. I was nothing compared to either of my brothers, but I was getting into shape.

If only I could be six inches taller.

I sighed and pulled my shirt back on. There was no use in whining about my height. I might grow a little more yet. I could only wait and see. I would either grow or I wouldn't. There was nothing I could do about it.

I ran downstairs, told Mom I was heading out, and then did just that. I walked toward the high school, excited and nervous. It almost didn't seem real. I wondered what it was like to be really good at something. Both Thomas and Mitch had been excellent football players. I remembered Brendan, the quarterback last year. He was incredible. He had a passing arm that was unbelievable. He passed like a pro. He was just as good at racing down the field. He had a way of dodging the defense that was unreal and could he run fast!

Brendan. He was a homo and he'd never made a secret of it. Everyone knew he was gay and that Casper was his boyfriend. Not many guys had been down on Brendan. Most idolized him, at least secretly. Mitch joked that he suspected being a homo gave Brendan superpowers. If it did, where were mine?

I paused for a moment before walking on. I was a homo, wasn't I? My slight experience with that girl at the party told me I had zero interest in girls. My intense reaction to Cody during the same party made my interest in guys certain. It wasn't just hero worship. Sure, when I looked at boys like Lucas and Cody I wished I could look more like them and be more like them, but what I felt went much further than that. I had been edging closer to admitting the truth to myself and then I found myself telling Banshee was I was pretty sure I was gay. I guess there really was no question about it anymore. I was a homo and I just had to deal with it.

I put it out of my mind. I didn't want to think about being gay just now. This was my first ever football game as a player. Tonight, play or not, I'd get to wear my game jersey and sit with the team.

I could see the bonfire out near the football field as I approached. There were loads of kids and plenty of older people milling around. It was kind of weird seeing teachers outside of the classroom. Sometimes, I didn't think of them as real people, which is stupid I know, but when I spotted one of my teachers buying groceries or eating in Ofarim's or Café Moffatt it just seemed odd.

I joined the members of the team who were gathering around the fire. As soon as I stepped into the circle of my teammates I became part of the center of attention. Guys kept coming up to encourage us to beat the crap out of the other team. Girls flirted with some of the guys and boys gazed at us, wishing, if only for a moment, that they were us.

Most of the attention went to others, of course. I was definitely not an A-list celebrity of the JV team. The JV team wasn't even A-list. The varsity team held that position. Still, I was a football player at a pre-game bonfire. For the first time in my life I was at the center of things.

I saw one of Cody's buddies slip him a drink from his Coke, which I was quite sure was as much whiskey or some other alcohol as it was Coca-Cola. Disguising alcohol in soft drink cans was a very old trick. No one offered me any, which was a relief. I probably would have coughed and sputtered and looked totally uncool. I remembered the punch at the party. It was nasty.

Wood smoke scented the air and there was just enough of a chill to make the warmth of the bonfire welcome. I talked with the other players and a few other kids until it was time for us to go in and suit up. As we left the bonfire for the locker room the crowd began chanting "Football! Football!" and my teammates began whooping and hollering. I was amused until I realized I was yelling right along with my teammates.

So this is what it feels like to be on a team, I thought to myself.

My heart began to beat faster as we stripped in the locker room and put on our uniforms. The air was filled with testosterone and I feared my jock would not be able to conceal my excitement. Lucas helped me put on my pads. He already had his on, but hadn't slipped on his jersey yet. The sight of him wearing those pads with his bare chest showing... if I didn't believe God existed before then I would have upon seeing Lucas. He was beautiful.

When we were both suited up, Lucas closed in on me. I could smell his cologne. I wondered if that was the scent his girlfriend smelled right before he kissed her.

"Don't get upset if you don't get to play tonight. It may be the third or forth game before you get on the field. You're a freshman and you're new."

"I don't expect to play. Like you said, I'm a freshman and new. I'm also the smallest guy on the team."

"That would be Lucas!" Cody said. "Oh wait, you weren't talking about your dick, were you?"

"Hey, Cody. Why don't you play for the other team so I can kick your ass," Lucas said.

"Kiss my ass? You can kiss my ass if you want, Lucas. Here!"

Cody began to unfasten his laces.

"Keep your big butt in your pants, Caldemyer," Lucas said.

"My butt's not big! What I've got big is right up front." Cody groped himself and I felt a stirring in my jock.

"As I was saying before the idiot interrupted," Lucas said. "Don't get upset about not playing. It means nothing. Yeah, you are kind of small for football, but you're also a great receiver."

Cody began to open his mouth, but Lucas glared at him.

"Shut it, Caldemyer."

Cody laughed.

Coach Jordan stepped into the locker room and called us out on the field. I felt taller than I ever had before. Lucas Needmore called me a great receiver and he meant it.

I loved wearing my football uniform. The pads made me look a lot bigger. They made it harder to pass through doorways too. I banged my right shoulder into the wall as we left the locker room. The pads sure worked. I didn't feel it at all.

We walked up to the football field. The stands were crowded with fans and the band was playing. We warmed up to get our muscles limber. Our opponents did the same at the other end of the field. Coach Jordan pulled us into a huddle, gave us a pep talk, and then gave us the lowdown on the opposing team. The Razorbacks were tough, probably the toughest opponents we'd face all season. Their varsity team had almost won state the year before and their JV team was better than most varsity teams. Coach was expecting a tough battle. After hearing all that I was certain I would not be getting on the field.

The first string took the field. Among them were Lucas, Cody, and Beck. Coach hadn't picked a permanent quarterback yet, but Lucas and Cody were the frontrunners. I didn't think I'd want to be quarterback even if I had the talent. It was too much pressure. The coach might set up the plays but the quarterback had to make it happen and had to be ready to change the play in an instant as conditions changed. If the team won the quarterback was a hero, but if it lost he could easily get blamed for the mistakes of others.

I took a seat on the bench. I'd never had such a great seat before. If nothing else, sitting on the bench gave me a great view of the action. I couldn't help but feel a little special as I sat there. Only a select few could sit on that bench and I was one of them.

I looked behind me. The crowd was talking and laughing and yelling while waiting for the game to start. Guys were snuggling with their girlfriends. I spotted Tim and Dane sitting close together. Tim was on the Varsity team. I guess he was a big enough football nut to come and watch the JV team play. As I watched, Tim and Dane gazed at each other and grinned. I smiled before I remembered what the Bible said about homosexuals.

Then, I remembered my growing doubts about the teachings of the church. Tim and Dane leaned in and kissed. They obviously loved each other. How could any love be wrong?

I turned and looked out onto the field. I didn't want a silent battle raging in my head just now. I watched Lucas, Cody and the others huddle up and then take their places. Part of me wanted to be out there with them. Part of me was glad I was sitting safe on the bench.

The game went wrong from the start. Cody was sacked on the very first play. Our receiver was taken down on the next play the moment he caught the ball. I'd watched quite a bit of football in the years my brothers played. I wasn't an expert but I could tell we were getting our butts kicked not because we weren't a good team or weren't playing well, but because our opponents were just that good. The Razorback linemen were bigger than ours. Our biggest lineman was not quite as large as their smallest. Most of the linemen on the other team looked too big to be in high school. I could just imagine what one of those guys would have done to me if I were across from him.

At the end of the half the score was 0-21. Our guys were playing well, but just couldn't penetrate the Razorback defense. On the two occasions someone did get through they didn't make it far. The situation was just as bad when we were on defense. Our guys could not hold theirs back. It had to be scary on the line. I thought it was bad when I'd faced off against Cody during my first practice, but most of the Razorback linemen were a lot bigger than Cody.

The second half was just as bad. Our guys managed to hold the Razorbacks back a little better, but there was no stopping those guys for long. Lucas was getting his turn as quarterback, but there wasn't much he could do. The receivers couldn't get past the Razorbacks so most of the time Lucas had nowhere to throw the ball. He just tore out and went for any opening he could find. He even made it past the defensive line a couple of times, but never came close to making a touchdown.

I think Lucas was the only player we had who was as good as the Razorback players. I could not believe those guys. I'd seen them play last year and they'd destroyed our team then too.

The minutes ticked away until there were only four left. Beck had to be carted off the field on a stretcher. Lucas jogged over to

Coach Jordan. The two spoke briefly and then Lucas walked back onto the field.

"Gaylord! You're in!"

For a moment, I was in a daze. I knew the coach had called out my name, but it didn't quite register. I hadn't dreamed of getting to play in the first game. Well, I'd dreamed but I didn't think it would happen. I grabbed my helmet and ran out to join my teammates who were forming a huddle.

Lucas began setting up his play then time slowed down as Lucas looked at me and continued speaking.

"I'm going to pass to Elijah. Elijah, as soon as the ball is snapped I want you to fall back and get right behind Cody and Kevin. Cody and Kevin, I want you to plow between the guys blocking you. Don't tackle them, deflect them to the side. Elijah, you zip through the opening. You're gonna have to be fast because when you drop back that's going to leave one of their lineman free. I hope he'll come after me, but if he sees what we're doing he may be after you."

I swallowed hard and tried not to let my fear show.

"Just push them aside, huh? Have you seen the guy I've been trying to block? If he was green he'd look just like the Incredible Hulk," said Cody.

"I thought you said you loved a challenge. I know this is risky guys, but what have we got to lose?" Lucas asked.

"Consciousness?" Kevin said, then laughed.

"Let's make it happen guys. They are kicking out asses all over the field."

Lucas hung back just a moment after he broke he huddle.

"I know you can do this, Elijah. You're small enough to get by them. Take any opening you can find. Use your speed. You can't match their strength, but you can outmaneuver them. Get into the clear and I'll drop the ball right into your hands."

I nodded. I was incapable of speech. I hoped the wild fear that coursed through me didn't show in my eyes. I was so scared I was afraid I'd wet my pants.

I took my position. The lineman across from me actually laughed. He wasn't trying to be mean or cruel. He just couldn't help himself. The idea of me blocking him was so ridiculous that he couldn't do anything but laugh. He was huge! I couldn't see anything but him. I was so terrified I trembled, but it wasn't so much the fear of the giant across from me as it was fear I'd screw up the play. I wanted to show the guys I could do this. I wanted them to see I deserved to be on the team. I guess, mostly, I wanted to prove to myself I deserved to be here. I knew my parents were somewhere up on the stands watching too. Their eyes were on me, even if I couldn't see them.

I listened for 34 as Lucas began to call out numbers. I knew it was coming soon. Then, there it was, followed almost instantly by "hike."

I zipped behind Cody and Kevin. They surged forward, but didn't get far. They ran into a wall of muscle. They wedged themselves between the Razorbacks. There was only a space of about six inches between them. I knew that was as good as it was going to get. I ran forward and jammed through the space sideways. I got stuck, somehow pushed through, and then stumbled. An enormous lineman reached for me. I dove for the ground and rolled. He overshot me. I jumped up and sprinted, zigzagging to dodge the Razorback defense. I broke into the open, turned and looked to find Lucas even as I ran. He was dodging Razorbacks but he spotted me. He passed the ball and just as he promised he dropped it right into my hands. I tucked it into my chest and ran as if my life depended on it. It quite likely did.

I'd love to tell you how I dodged this way and that, got past the entire Razorback defense, and scored the only touchdown of the game. Oh how I'd love to tell you about that! But, it didn't happen. What did happen was almost as good. The crowd roared. There hadn't been much to cheer during the game, and anyone from our team breaking through and making it more than two yards was cause for celebration. I made it to the forty-yard line. I almost got nailed right there, but I dodged at the last second and slipped by the enormous lineman that tried to tackle me. I made it to the thirty-yard line. I could hear the crowd begin chanting "Gaylord! Gaylord!" I swear it happened. I'm not making it up. I got to the twenty-five and then the twenty. I began to hope I'd actually make it, but twenty yards is a mile when you're being pursued by guys two and three times your size.

There were only two defenders between the goal line and me but they were both closing fast. There was one to either side of the field. No matter how I dodged they kept on me and closed in.

I sprinted, but I knew I couldn't pass them before they reached me. Just before they closed on me from either side I lowered my shoulder and aimed for the gap between. I closed my eyes as we collided. My body was buffeted back and forth as I slipped between them. I stumbled, regained my balance, and took one step forward before they took me down from behind. I'd made it to the ten-yard line.

I just lay there on my stomach for a few moments, in less pain than I'd imagined. There was the goal line, so very close. I felt like crying. I pulled myself to my feet. The crowd was still cheering, even though I hadn't made it.

"Damn you're fast, kid," said the guy who had taken me down.

I laughed and hobbled back toward my teammates. Lucas and Cody slapped me on the back and so did plenty of the others. It hurt, but I didn't mind. I was probably grinning like an idiot, but my face guard hid my expression from most. You might think the crowd and my teammates were overly excited since I didn't score a touchdown, but my almost-touchdown had been the highlight of the game for Verona. As for me, getting that close to making a touchdown was like single-handedly winning the Super Bowl. I might never get that close to scoring again.

Time was running out fast so Lucas huddled us up.

"Let's fake them out," he said. "That play was the closest we've come to scoring, so let's make them think were going to try it again. Elijah, Cody, and Kevin, do exactly what you did last time. They'll likely be waiting for it so you probably won't get far, but maybe we'll get lucky. Elijah, if you do make it through, run into the end zone and I'll pass to you. Now, here's the real play. Doug, when I hike the ball, you drop back and try to run around the left side. With any luck the Razorbacks will be focusing on Elijah on the right. If you can get into the clear, I'll get you the ball. Got it?"

Everyone voiced their understanding and the huddle broke up. The clock down to just seconds now. There was no way to win the game. This was our last chance to score.

Lucas hiked the ball. He was right. The Razorbacks were ready for us to run the same play. When I dropped in behind Cody and Kevin the lineman who had been facing me was on my tail. I darted back to the right to keep from being flattened and found myself momentarily in the clear. The Razorback's were all over me then. It seemed like half the team turned in my direction. I was hit hard and went down. I couldn't breathe and I saw stars. My breathing returned to normal when the linebacker who had knocked me down climbed off. The clock ran out. I looked up at the scoreboard, but the score had not changed. We lost 0-28.

I hobbled over to join the rest of my teammates. I was in pain. I wondered if I'd ever be able to walk right again. Kevin filled me in on what had happened as we headed for the locker room. When I darted to the right to escape getting nailed so much attention was focused on me that Doug was able to make it into the clear. Lucas passed to him, but Doug was knocked down just as he caught the ball, and he dropped it. The play hadn't worked, but it had come close.

Coach Jordan gave us a pep talk in the locker room. You might think he'd yell at us since we lost so spectacularly, but he said he was extremely pleased with our performance against the toughest team we were likely to face the entire season. He even told me I did a good job.

My uniform was dirty and smelly as I pulled it off. I headed for the showers with the other guys. The hot water eased the pain in my muscles. I hurt all over but particularly my butt. I'd landed on it hard twice.

I shampooed my hair and soaped up. The guys were talking and laughing. Kevin did an impression of me darting from side to side in the play that lead to my almost-touchdown.

"Mini-Gaylord has the moves and the speed," Cody said.

My nickname was set. I was to be Mini-Gaylord ever after. It wasn't the best as nicknames go, but it wasn't so bad either. It was much better than the things Cody had called me during the first couple of practices.

I walked out of the showers and back into the locker room surrounded by my wet, naked teammates. As I was pulling on my underwear Lucas and Cody came back from the showers and stood to either side of me. I stole looks of their magnificent bodies. Their muscles made me want to feel them all over. I glanced at Cody's stuff. I almost couldn't believe I'd touched him, there. I wanted to do it again.

Lucas gave me a ride home. He said it was the least he could do after my almost-touchdown. I rode in the back because his girlfriend was in the front. When we climbed in the car she leaned over and gave him a lingering kiss. I was kind of turned on, but I felt like a pervert for watching.

When I got home Mom and Dad were waiting on me. They'd stopped at the grocery and bought me a chocolate cake.

"This is to celebrate the stellar beginning of your football career," Dad said.

"Stellar?"

"I know you didn't score, but I don't think either of your brothers could have done what you did on that field. I never realized you were so fast."

"It's from running from Thomas and Mitch all the time!" I said, then grinned.

Mom and Dad laughed.

"Being small helps me run fast. The guys have nicknamed me "Mini-Gaylord."

"They must like you if they gave you a nickname. We're very proud of you. I know it took courage to face those huge players."

"I can't believe boys that big are in high school," Mom said.

"Remember the Razorback varsity team from last year? They were even bigger," I said.

"Thank goodness you aren't on the Varsity team. I was so afraid you'd get hurt. When that huge guy knocked you down..."

"It's okay, Mom. That's what the padding is for. I hardly felt it."

I wondered if white lies were a sin. The truth was getting tackled was a painful experience!

The cake was well worth the price of my sore body. The cake was moist and the icing was so creamy. Yum! I ate two big slices with lots of vanilla ice cream.

I went upstairs to my room. It was only a little after ten, but I was sleepy and tired. I brushed my teeth, then climbed into bed. I lay there on my back with my arms behind my head for a few minutes reliving my almost-touchdown. I still don't see how I managed to squeeze between Cody and Kevin and make it into the clear. There were legs and arms and big bodies everywhere. Four different Razorbacks almost got me, but I managed to just barely evade them. I'd felt like an acrobat as I twisted and turned and dodged and darted. If only I could have made it a few more yards and made a touchdown during my very first game! That would've been something to tell Thomas and Mitch! They would never have believed it. I giggled. I bet they'd never believe I'd almost scored a touchdown against the Razorbacks either.

I grew increasingly drowsy. I tried stay awake because I wanted to think about the game some more. I wanted to etch every part of it in my memory. I wasn't successful. My eyes closed and soon I was fast asleep.

Chapter Eight

On Saturday, I was back behind the counter of Chicken Fillets again. I started at 9 a.m. so I had to get up earlier than I would have liked. It was the first time I'd worked breakfast. Up until 11 a.m. Chicken Fillets had a breakfast menu which included items like the "Cluckin' Chicken Breakfast Burrito" and the "Peep's Scratches Egg Sandwich." I really wondered who made the names up. They seriously needed a life.

My day was going well until Cody, Kevin, Beck, and Doug came in as a group. Jocks are always more dangerous when they travel in a pack. I knew my teammates wouldn't give me too much trouble, but I wasn't looking forward to them seeing me in my winged cap. Cody actually laughed when he spotted me.

"Nice hat, Mini-Gaylord. You should wear that to school."

I wanted to say something smart, but I couldn't because the manager was standing too close and might hear.

"Maybe I can get you one," I said instead.

"Mmm, that's okay, really!" Cody said. "Hey, don't you have to cluck like a chicken when we place an order."

"No. I do not."

"That is a shame."

"What can I get you?" I asked.

"Okay, I guess we've tormented you enough. Lemme think..."

The guys placed their orders. They snickered some as they stepped away from the counter, but that was the extent of their torment. I was relieved. I was glad they didn't see my on my orientation day when I had to wear the canary yellow "Peep in Training" apron. They would've really given me a hard time about that.

I mostly liked my job at Chicken Fillets. The manager took everything too seriously, but then I guess that's what managers did. I liked talking with the customers and making them happy. The stuff I didn't like, such as the ridiculous cap I was forced to wear and the even more ridiculous chicken terminology, wasn't so bad.

Chicken Fillets went way overboard with the chicken theme. As a new employee I was considered a "Peep." I was a member of the "coop", but I was at the bottom of the "pecking order." If I continued on I would soon become a "bantam" then a "cockerel." If I really dedicated myself I get promoted to "rooster." The truly embarrassing part was that our rank in the pecking order was printed right on our nametag. Of course, most customers didn't notice or care, but I still felt stupid wearing a nametag that said "Elijah Peep." It made Peep sound like my last name.

The manager sent me out to wash tables. When I was near my teammates I began to hear a noise. I couldn't make out what it was until I drew closer. When I realized the source I rolled my eyes. Cody and the others took turns saying "peep!" then laughing. I walked over to their table and crossed my arms.

"Watch it guys, the Peep is pissed. We may be in for a severe pecking," Beck said.

"You know, if I was you, I'd be very careful about what I said to a guy who handles my food," I warned.

Cody looked at his Big Chicken Clucker suspiciously.

"Maybe he slipped in the back and added some "special sauce" to your sandwich, Cody," Kevin said.

"Ewww!" the guys said.

I didn't get it, but I pretended I did.

"Be afraid. Be very afraid," I said, then walked off. The guys laughed.

A lot of kids from school and even teachers came in to Chicken Fillets. In a way, it was humiliating to be working behind the counter of a fast food restaurant, but then I was fifteen and this was my first job. I began to feel a little self-conscious, but then I thought about the situation from the other side. I had never looked down on anyone for working in a fast food restaurant. I'd never thought anyone was pathetic because they had to ask, "Would you like fries with that?" Pretty much everyone had a job and when you got right down to it no job was that much more important than any other. Okay, a surgeon saving a patient was more important than a guy like me who served chicken sandwiches, but I bet I was pretty important to someone who came in really hungry. A lot of people could do my job, but what if no one did it? How would anyone get their food then?

Chicken Fillets was busy all day so the time zipped by. Before I knew it my shift was up. As much as I enjoyed working, I liked not working even more. My weekend truly started when I took off my winged cap and walked out the door.

***

There were more people in church on Sunday than usual. It didn't take a genius to guess why. Jesus said he would return and everyone was waiting to see what happened. Pastor Walker looked slightly nervous as he took the podium, but there was no sign of Jesus. I was going to be disappointed if he didn't show.

"I have been criticized by outsiders after my last few sermons, but I stand by what I said. The Bible is clear in its denunciation of homosexuals..." Pastor Walker began.

"Jonathan loved David so much he gave up his kingdom for him," said a voice I recognized.

Everyone looked to the center aisle. There stood Jesus. I had not see him arrive, and from the looks on the faces of the other parishioners neither had anyone else. I learned later that the pastor had people watching the doors to stop Jesus, but either he'd slipped by them or someone let him in.

"David and Jonathan loved each other and expressed that love physically. You would call them homosexuals. David possessed God's favor. Surely I do not need to remind you of the story of David and Goliath. This denunciation you speak of... where do you find it?"

"Sodom and Gomorrah," Pastor Walker said simply.

"You speak in ignorance," Jesus said. Some of the parishioners gasped.

Pastor Walker motioned to some men sitting near the front. They stood and moved toward Jesus. I tensed, but Jesus stood his ground. He did no more than gaze at them and they silently backed off. Pastor Walker was incensed.

"Who are you to question me? You are a child! You have no right to be here."

"All have the right to enter the house of the Lord. I say again you speak in ignorance. Cruelty and inhospitality are the sins of

Sodom. Sodom's wickedness was brutality, injustice, and deceit, but never homosexuality. Sodom was known for oppression of the poor, crushing the needy, and ethical wickedness, but never for sexual immorality. The Bible has NEVER linked the story of Sodom with homosexuality."

"You obviously know nothing! Genesis 19 says, "...all the men from every part of the city of Sodom—both young and old—surrounded the house. They called to Lot, "Where are the men who came to you tonight? Bring them out to us so that we can have sex with them.""

"If you would study the story which you quote so frequently, you would know that it does not say "all the men" but rather "mankind" which refers not only to adult males, but to men, women, and children. The people of Sodom were so wicked that all of them, male and female, young and old alike, surrounded the home of Lot and demanded to abuse his guests, a most heinous crime, especially in Lot's time."

I could tell by the pastor's expression that he did indeed know this, but had intentionally used the convenient mistranslation. What Jesus had revealed changed everything. I had felt betrayed by God because he made me gay then hated me for it, but I'd known only half the truth. God did make me gay, but he did not hate me. I had been betrayed, but not by God. People like Pastor Walker had twisted the words of the Bible to fit their own prejudices. They were the betrayers. They were the evildoers.

I felt a huge weight lift from my shoulders.

"The Bible clearly forbids homosexuality!" Pastor Walker shouted as if saying it loud made it true. Jesus spoke calmly in response.

"Do you know so little of the book you quote each Sunday?" Jesus asked. "Current sexual categories such as homosexuality and heterosexuality are of recent creation. The term "sodomy" didn't exist until the 11th century. Claiming "the Bible forbids homosexuality" is as ignorant as claiming "the Bible forbids the use of the telephone."

"The denouncements of homosexuality of which you speak exist only through intentional mistranslation and distortion, but there is evidence of God's love for those you label as an abomination.

"The story of the faithful centurion (Matthew 8:5-13 and Luke 7:1-10) speaks of a centurion, who begs Jesus to heal his servant, who anyone living in that time would have known was the centurion's pais (boy companion). The centurion asked Jesus to heal his lover. It was common practice for a centurion to have younger male servants who acted as concubines. Jesus did as he was asked because God's love is unconditional."

"Now you promote child molestation!" shouted the pastor.

Jesus ignored the insult and the ignorance.

"We, who God has created, have an obligation to live out, as fully as possible, the nature with which God has created us, whatever that nature be. Birds were meant to be birds and fish were meant to be fish. Homosexuals were meant to be homosexuals. To attempt to be other than what one was created to be is not only unhealthy, but an insult to God. Homosexuals love in the only way they can love and thus that love is their only path to God. Blocking that path is an enormous evil."

"I say again that the Bible denounces homosexuality!" Pastor Walker said.

"Yes, you say it again and again, but the falsehood will be no more true if repeated a million times than it was the first time you uttered it. One of the purposes of gays is to test the kindness and love of Christians. You have failed the test utterly. You have misused your position and lied to your flock. You have preached violence against those you should have aided," Jesus said.

Jesus quietly turned and walked from the church. I noticed that just before he parted he shook the dust from his feet. I heard a gasp from the lips of more than one who also took note.

There was much talking and whispering as Pastor Walker tried to quiet the congregation. He began another tirade against homosexuals, calling again for concentration camps and asking for donations to further the cause. I saw more than a few parishioners exchange glances. There was a time when no one would have questioned the pastor, but now that Jesus had done so many began to wonder about his message of hate. Some even stood up and walked out. The pastor faltered and once again services ended early.

As I often did on Sundays, I took a walk after changing out of my suit. I started out running, but I was winded even before I reached the edge of town. I would've thought my stamina would have been increased by football practices, but instead they drained my strength. I felt tired a lot now.

Walking was easier than running. My thoughts were more walking than running thoughts anyway. That is, I had things to ponder slowly rather than racing thoughts that made me feel as if I needed to hurry to keep up.

I thought about the hateful things Pastor Walker preached and how Jesus had spoken only of acceptance and love. The pastor was supposed to be the leader of the church, but his sermons of late weren't very Christian. All he did was attack homosexuals as if he had a personal vendetta and wanted us all to join. I was thinking very seriously about leaving our church. I didn't know if my parents would allow it, but I honestly did not want to be a part of it anymore.

As these thoughts went through my mind, I looked up and saw Jesus standing up ahead on the sidewalk as if he was waiting on me. He was dressed like any other boy of our age, but he was unlike any other. I felt at peace even as I neared him. My inner turmoil was stilled. I walked up to him and gazed into his eyes.

"Are you... are you Jesus?" I asked.

"Of course I am. That is my name."

"Yes, but are you *THE* Jesus."

I know it sounds utterly ridiculous, but the boy who stood before me just seemed so Jesus-like.

"What does it matter? I am who I am. You believe in what I say, do you not?"

I nodded.

"I think God loves everyone," I said. "I don't think he cares about race or sex or whether one is heterosexual or homosexual. But, there is so much I don't understand. Why are there such hateful things in the Bible?"

Jesus began walking and I walked by his side.

"The Bible was written by many different men over many centuries. Many of these men wrote not for love of God but for their own purposes. Most of the Bible is now lost, and what remains has been translated and often mistranslated time and again. The text has become corrupted."

"So it's not actually God's word, is it? That's what my friend said."

"He was correct. There is only one word that is God's word—love. All other words are unnecessary distractions at best and perversions at worst."

"I'm thinking about leaving my church," I said. I looked at Jesus fearfully.

"The sermons of your pastor have created doubts in your mind. You now question your faith."

"Yes. I even questioned God for a time, but then I heard what you said. Still, I question my faith," I said.

Tears welled up in my eyes. Jesus turned to me and caressed my cheek for a moment.

"That is because you have a kind and innocent heart."

"So it's okay to question my faith?"

"You should always question it."

"But, isn't faith not questioning, but blindly following?"

"Those are dangerous thoughts. Blinding following has led to many wars, horrible injustices, and terrible hardships. Faith is about believing and about hoping. It's about love and understanding."

"I understand... a little."

"I do not expect you to understand more than a little. We are speaking of the spiritual realm. Words do not exist to discuss it adequately. At best we may only grasp with words at the edges of the true meaning. Your heart is another matter. With your heart you may know without knowing."

"I don't like the things Pastor Walker has been saying. I think he's wrong. I think what he's been preaching is un-Christian. That's why I've been thinking about leaving. Do you think I should?"

"That is entirely your decision, not mine, but consider this; by leaving your church you may be throwing out the baby with the bathwater."

"Meaning all the reasons I used to love attending church are still there and if I depart I will lose them?"

"You cannot experience what you love about your church if you are not there to experience it. Perhaps it is for you to stand up for what you believe instead of running away."

I peered at Jesus. He wasn't giving me easy answers. He turned and smiled at me. He was so beautiful, although he had not seemed beautiful before.

"You are going through a difficult time in your life, but remember that you are never alone. The path in front of you will be difficult, but you will never be alone."

I turned to look across the street. I saw Banshee sitting on a stone wall, looking in my direction. I turned back to Jesus... but he was gone. I looked around for a moment, but I knew I would not find him.

I turned my attention back to Banshee. He waved. I crossed the street and sat down beside him.

"Did you see the boy I was talking to across the street?" I asked.

"Sure. You were talking to Jesus. That's probably a big thing for you, being a church-goer and all." Banshee laughed.

I ignored his comment because I had a more important question to ask.

"Did you see him leave?"

"No. You looked at me and I was paying attention to you. When I looked again he was gone."

"He always does that! I never see him come and I never see him go."

"Now that you mention it, that has been my experience as well."

"You know him?"

"I don't know him, but I have talked to him, a few times in fact."

"About what?"

"Personal stuff, problems. When I'm feeling at my worst, he shows up and we talk."

"Don't you think that's odd?"

"He's a nice guy."

"Yeah, but he shows up when you need him the most?"

"You have done the same."

"I have?"

"That day you came and sat with me in the cafeteria? I was really down. I was so lonely I was on the edge of tears. Why all the questions about Jesus?"

I didn't answer. I just sat there.

"Well?"

"I think he is... Jesus."

"Uh, yeah. That is his name."

"No. I think he is Jesus. The Jesus from the Bible."

Banshee gazed at me and said nothing.

"You think I'm nuts, don't you?" I asked.

"He is always there when I need him the most. There is something about him so... maybe."

"You really don't think I'm crazy? I kind of think I'm crazy."

"Oh, I think you're nuts, but it has nothing to do with Jesus."

"Ha. Ha."

Banshee grinned.

I hopped up and began walking. Banshee joined me. I told him all about what Pastor Walker had been preaching in church and how Jesus had shown up twice now to dispute his words.

"It's like in the Bible when Jesus challenged the Pharisees," I said.

"The what?"

"They were members of an ancient Jewish religion. The name has come to stand for self-righteous and hypocrite. Jesus dared to challenge those highly placed in the Jewish religion. He pointed out their errors and their hypocrisy."

"He called them on their crap, huh?"

"Yeah, and he's doing the same thing in my church now."

"Maybe you should get his autograph."

"Seriously. What if it's really him?"

"Then I'd say you're part of something pretty special, but…"

"But what?"

"It's fine to talk to me about this stuff, but I don't think you should talk to others about it. I don't think you're crazy, but others might. What would you think if someone told you that *THE* Jesus went to their school and showed up at their church?"

"I see your point. It is pretty crazy, isn't it?"

"Yeah, but… he does *feel* like Jesus, if you know what I mean."

"Does that mean you're becoming a believer?"

"It means I'll keep an open mind."

"Good enough."

"Hey, if you're done talking about Jesus…"

"I guess I'm done talking about him for now, although I'm far from finished thinking about him."

"I think you need a rest from the heavy theological thoughts. I was at the game on Friday night. You kicked ass!"

I laughed.

"Don't you mean I got my butt kicked?"

"No. I mean exactly what I said. I absolutely could not believe it when you got past all those huge dudes, caught the ball, and dodged and darted your way down the field. You almost scored a touchdown!"

It was my turn to grin.

"I couldn't believe it either."

"That was amazing. I was cheering for you so loud I almost went hoarse. Everyone was cheering."

"I heard the crowd chanting my name. That was intense."

"Yeah. Listen, I've been thinking. Everyone is going to know who you are now. You're a jock and you're bound to become more popular. It's cool if you just want to be friends outside of school. I'll understand if you don't want to be seen with me. Since I began sitting at the homo table I'm sure it's obvious to all that I'm gay."

I stopped, turned to Banshee, and looked directly into his eyes.

"I'm not hiding our friendship. I won't do that to you. You mean too much to me for that."

"Cody won't like it."

"I'll just have to deal with Cody."

"A lot of people will think you're a homo."

"Well, I am."

"You don't want people to know, do you?"

"No. I'm not ready for that just yet. I'm still getting used to the idea myself."

"So, I think we should..."

"No. If I hide my friendship with you it would be as though I'm ashamed to be your friend. I'm not. I've done too much lying. I don't want to go on lying."

"You'll have to lie to hide that you're gay."

"I know, but... maybe I won't lie. If someone asks I'll tell them the truth."

"Or, you could tell them it's none of their business, which is also the truth."

"True."

We began walking side by side again. Banshee gazed at me.

"Thanks."

"Thank you for giving me a second chance."

***

I didn't even make it into school on Monday morning before I noticed people looking at me. Once inside I noted it more and more. Someone would spot me, and then nudge their friends. Guys I didn't know passed me in the halls and said, "Good job, Gaylord!" A couple even said we might have scored if Coach had put me in for the whole game. I've gotta admit my chest swelled with pride. No one had ever paid attention to be before Friday night. Kids I shared classes with barely knew my name. Now I felt like a celebrity.

"Don't get too used to it."

"Huh?" I asked, turning.

"Don't get too used to the fame. Soon you'll fade into the crowd and be just another football player," Beck said.

"I can live with that. Being just another football player is a lot more fame that I'm used to."

Beck laughed and moved on.

I was patted on the back all morning long. Guys yelled, "Yeah! Gaylord!" and girls noticed I existed for the first time. It figured girls would finally take an interest in me right after I figured out I wasn't interested in them.

At lunch, I took my tray of cheese ravioli, garlic cheddar biscuit, broccoli, and applesauce and walked toward the football table.

"Here is the hero of last Friday's game!" Cody said.

"I'm about the kind of hero you'd expect for a game we lost without scoring," I said.

"I guess he hasn't gotten a big head, guys. Cancel the swirlee we had planned for after practice," said Lucas.

"Funny."

"Who says we were kidding?" Lucas said. I eyed him, but couldn't figure out if he was serious or not.

"Sure, pick on the little guy," I said.

Cody began to open his mouth.

"Don't say it," warned Lucas.

"I wasn't going to say anything about your little dick."

"You know, your putdown would be more effective if everyone here hadn't repeatedly seen me naked."

"Slut."

"You know what I mean, jerk."

Cody laughed. Lucas and Cody were getting along a lot better now. They were rivals for quarterback and there was tension between them, but mostly they just insulted each other. I think they had a good time doing it.

"I'll admit something, Elijah," said Cody. "When you made the team, I thought the coaches were out of their minds. I figured you'd be totally useless."

"So now you think I'm just mostly useless?"

"Yeah, that's about right."

"If you weren't twice my size I'd pound you," I said.

"I do like your spunk," Cody said.

"Sounds like a sexual comment to me," Kevin pointed out.

I could feel my face grow warm and hoped I wasn't blushing. Kevin's comment hit way too close to home. Cody wasn't fazed a bit. I seriously began to wonder if I hadn't dreamed what happened between Cody and me.

"You pervert. Keep your fantasies to yourself," Cody said.

The guys laughed, but I was uncomfortable. The comments weren't directed at me and yet they were. I was gay. I had come to accept that. I was likely the only homo on the team. Lucas had admitted to messing around with another guy once and Cody had given me head... if that actually happened and I wasn't quite sure anymore. That didn't make either of them gay. Maybe Cody was gay and maybe he wasn't. I was totally confused about that. I was confused about so many things. That was me, Mr. Confusion. My point is that the guys joked around about homos a lot and I was uncomfortable sitting there listening to it. I was verbally attacked weekly in church and I was hit with verbal abuse when I was with my team. Why did so many people think there was something wrong with me?

"My fantasies center around being ravished by the cheerleaders. They corner me after a game, jump on me, rip my clothes off, and..."

"You've put a lot of thought into this, haven't you, Kevin?" asked Lucas.

"While he's whacking it," Beck said.

"At least I don't whack to fantasies about my mom," Kevin countered.

"I've seen Beck's mom. She's a babe," said Lucas.

"Dude!" Beck said.

"Well, she's hot! I'd do her in a heartbeat."

"Me too, man!" Cody said.

"We could double-team her," Lucas said.

"Would you shut up about my mom?" Beck asked.

"Just take it as a compliment. Your mom is hot," Lucas said.

"You guys are sick."

"Come on. I bet there are moms you'd stick in it if you got the chance," Cody said.

"Well...."

"I thought so."

I seriously could not believe some of the things said at the football table. I shouldn't have been surprised at anything they said, but they continued to shock me.

My teammates spent the rest of lunch talking about whose mom was hot. I was very glad none of them had met my mom. I did not want to hear them talk about her. None of the guys liked it much when the talk was about their mom, but they loved spelling out what they'd do with the other moms. I had to fight to keep from blushing and I wasn't entirely successful. My teammates were barbarians.

I spotted Jesus in the hallway while I was heading for 7th period P.E. He was quietly talking to a boy who was crying. I was probably crazy for thinking he was the real Jesus, but he sure acted like I'd expect Jesus to act if he came back as a high school boy. I guess the idea was ludicrous. If Jesus did return why would be come back as a high school kid and why would he pick Verona, Indiana? A far more reasonable explanation is that my classmate was a kind boy who cared for others. Maybe he even tried to live up to his name. I sure wasn't going to tell anyone else my theory. Banshee hadn't thought I was loony, but I bet just about anyone else would.

I put thoughts of Jesus out of my mind and headed for the gym. The locker room before and after P.E. was a completely different place than it was before and after football practices. It was just as loud, but there wasn't nearly as much vulgar talk about girls or insults about homos. The guys in P.E. just wanted to get in and out so they wouldn't be late. For my teammates, the locker room was like a clubhouse where we all hung out to have fun.

There was another big difference—the guys in my P.E. class weren't nearly as hot. Most of them weren't hot at all.

Banshee smiled at me as he pulled off his shirt and tossed it in his locker. I was already completely naked, but he didn't take the opportunity to check me out. He was interested in me and not just my body. I hoped we could become close friends.

I thought of something as I was pulling on my VHS P.E. uniform. The guys in P.E. didn't hassle Banshee. He'd been sitting at the homo table long enough for everyone know he was gay, but the guys didn't bully or torment him in the locker room. I wondered if I'd be so lucky if my teammates found out about me.

Banshee and I walked out into the gym together and stood next to each other. Calisthenics were not my favorite thing. Jumping jacks seemed kind of pointless, and the rest of it wasn't too thrilling either. Pushups and setups were okay, but I much preferred working out with weights.

I stood up too fast after my sit-ups and felt lightheaded for a moment. My vision even blacked out for a second. It didn't last long enough to be scary, but it was a weird sensation. Banshee noticed and even extended his hand toward me to steady me, but drew it back when he saw I was okay.

We were still doing our unit on track. We jogged out to the football field and ran a few laps. I had enjoyed getting outside and running through town and the countryside during the summer, but now running was different. More often than not I couldn't catch my breath. I was relieved when we were called over to the high jump.

I quickly learned I would never be a track star. I already knew I couldn't throw the shot-put very far, but I was more inept on the high jump. I couldn't keep from knocking the bar off no matter how low it was placed. Banshee was much more talented at the high jump. His height probably had something to do with that. I was so tired of being short, but it wasn't right to be ungrateful. I needed to be thankful for what I had. That wasn't always easy, especially when I was a good four inches shorter than most of the other freshmen.

***

Running at the beginning of football practice was much harder than running in gym. Coach kept pushing us, making us running further and further each day. I was becoming increasingly frustrated. During the first practices I could keep on going while the bigger guys were huffing and puffing. It made me feel as if I had an advantage in at least one small way. Now, running made me feel like a weakling. I couldn't keep up, especially after we'd run a few laps.

Today was my worst running experience yet. I was out of breath before we were halfway finished and I was so tired I had to fight to keep my feet moving forward. My chest hurt and my head hurt. I was in enough pain that tears began to run down my cheeks. I pushed myself to keep going. The truly frustrating thing was what I'd run considerably further during the summer without half the effort. My eyes were so filled with tears I had to keep wiping them away to see where I was going. I hoped none of the guys noticing me crying. I felt like a big crybaby but I couldn't help it.

When Coach called us over to the bleachers I was truly grateful. I dropped down onto a bleacher and fought to catch my breath. Lucas looked concerned when he spotted me. There was no hiding the evidence I'd been crying. Luckily, I didn't have to explain because Coach Jordan started in reviewing the game last Friday night.

My breath calmed. I prayed Coach would keep talking for a good, long time. I tried to listen. I smiled when he mentioned my almost-touchdown, then my head began to hurt worse than ever. I felt nauseous and dizzy and began to pitch forward. I felt someone catch me in his arms and then everything went black.

I woke up to a bright light shining into one of my eyes and then the other. I was lying down, but I had no idea where I was or how I'd got there. I began to sit up, but a hand on my chest gently pushed me back down.

"Just lie still. You're in Memorial Hospital in South Bend."

"Wha-what?"

"How many fingers do I have up?" asked a guy in a white coat.

"Three."

"Can you tell me your name?"

"Elijah Gaylord. Why are you asking me this? I didn't hit my head did I?"

"What's the last thing you remember?"

I was annoyed he didn't answer my question, but I was too disoriented to argue.

"I was sitting on the bleachers. We'd just been running around the track. I felt nauseous and dizzy. My vision blacked out and I felt myself falling. Did I hit my head?"

"No. One of your teammates caught you."

Lucas. I bet it was Lucas.

There were three people in white coats around my bed in the curtained off room. There were wires stuck to my chest and a machine with a screen kept beeping. The light was too bright and I was scared. The doctors or whatever they were talked among themselves using terms I mostly didn't understand.

"Am I okay?" I asked.

"You are now. Have you blacked out before?"

"No. Yes. I stood up too fast in gym today and everything went black for a moment, but I didn't pass out. I've had something like that happen a few times recently."

"How is your general health?"

"I've been getting tired really easily. I feel sort of weak most of the time. When I run, I can't run as far and it's hard to catch my breath."

"Any nausea like you experienced before you blacked out?"

"Yeah, when I was running and a couple of times before I guess."

"How do you feel now?"

"Really tired."

There were more questions. I shivered. I wasn't wearing a shirt and it was too chilly in the room. I wasn't quite as scared now. I didn't know what had happened exactly, but I felt okay. No one seemed to think I was going to die.

The questions stopped. I closed my eyes. I was so very tired. I could hear talking and the beeping of machines. I felt drowsy and wondered if they'd sedated me. I dropped off right there in the emergency room, although it wasn't until I woke up in a hospital room that I learned the ER is where I'd been when I woke up the first time.

I was disoriented again when I woke up some time later, but this time someone was holding my hand. Slowly, I recognized my mom.

"Hi, honey," she said.

"Hi."

Mom smoothed back the hair on my head. Dad stepped into view.

"How are you feeling, Elijah?" he asked.

"Really tired. What's wrong with me?"

"Maybe just exhaustion, but the doctors want to run some tests," Mom said.

"Tomorrow we're taking a trip to the IU Medical Center in Indianapolis," Dad said, trying to make it sound like a field trip.

"Why?"

"The doctor thinks it would be a good idea for you to have a CT Scan. It's an X-Ray that looks at your entire body."

"Am I that sick?" I asked.

My parents exchanged a look that did not put me at ease.

"We don't know what's wrong, Elijah. That's why you're going to be checked out. It may be something simple or it may be nothing. We'll just have to wait and see."

Nothing? I didn't black out from nothing. Mom and Dad were trying to act like they weren't concerned, but they weren't very good at acting. I was scared again, not too much, but I felt uneasy, like something bad was about to happen. I mostly felt tired. A nurse came in and gave me a couple of pills to help me sleep, but I hardly needed them. I felt like I could doze off again at any moment. I grew increasingly drowsy and soon I was asleep.

I felt better the next morning, except that I was awakened too early. Mom and Dad were both still there. I was allowed to dress so maybe I wasn't too bad off. I wasn't going to miss my hospital gown. I hadn't really paid much attention to it until I got up to dress, but what I'd heard about hospital gowns were true.

They didn't close up properly in the back. If I had walked down the hallway in mine everyone would've seen my butt.

In only a few minutes I was wheeled downstairs and out to a van. Mom and Dad said they would meet me at the IU Medical Center in Indianapolis. I didn't know why I had to ride down in a hospital van and not with them, but I was anxious enough about my CT scan I didn't think on it much.

The ride was boring. I was still tired. I was hungry too, but I couldn't have anything to eat until after my scan. I tried to nap on the way, but was only partly successful. Most of the time I watched the scenery pass outside. There wasn't a lot to see besides flat fields and some homes and businesses, at least until we got to Kokomo. Then, I saw a Burger King, a McDonald's, a Kentucky Fried Chicken, and lots of other restaurants. Seeing all those restaurants made me hungrier than ever.

I tried to take my mind off my hunger by wondering what the guys thought when I toppled over during practice. I wondered if they were freaked out and if kids were now talking about me at school. I must have been out cold until I woke up in the ER. The team must've wondered what was going on when they couldn't wake me up. I wondered about that now, too. I didn't think exhaustion could knock me out like that.

At the medical center there were lots of hallways. I was glad an orderly was pushing me in a wheelchair because I would've got lost for sure. My parents waited in a waiting room while I was taken to a room that looked a lot like an ER. I had to change into another hospital gown and then they hooked me up to more beeping machines. I was in that room a good long while before I was put back in the wheelchair and taken on yet another ride. My parents went along with me as far as they could, then sat in yet another waiting room while I was wheeled in for my CT Scan.

This room wasn't like the others. There were lots of screens and wires and this big tube in the middle of the room that looked like a super-thick donut. I was helped onto a cold platform that led into the hole of the donut. I'd eaten a lot of donuts in my time, and now it looked like the donut was going to eat me.

"Have you ever had a CT Scan before?" a lady, who was dressed like a doctor and maybe was one, asked.

"No."

"It won't hurt, but some find it a bit claustrophobic. It helps if you close your eyes. The scanner will scan your body. It's like an X-ray, except your entire body will be scanned. It will allow us to see what's going on inside without touching you. It will take several minutes. It's important that you hold still."

I didn't think holding still was going to be a problem since I was strapped in. That frightened me a little, but I'd had an X-ray once and there actually was nothing to it. I couldn't even tell anything had happened.

"Just relax and the machine will do the rest. Some patients even fall asleep during their scan. Are you ready?"

"Yeah."

The platform began to move slowly into the donut. I could hear a weird whirring sound, but I didn't know if it was the scanner or some other piece of equipment in the room. I felt just a little like I was in Dr. Frankenstein's laboratory. I tensed up a little as I slid into the donut. There wasn't much room in there. I wasn't claustrophobic, but I could get panicky if I couldn't move my arms. I couldn't at the moment, but I reminded myself it was because of the straps and not from being trapped in an enclosed space.

I began to relax. It was kind of cool in the donut. It was certainly a new experience for me. I relaxed and my fear left me. It definitely didn't hurt.

I didn't know how long I was in there, but it felt like hours. There was nothing to do but lie there so it was boring after a while. Eventually, the donut spit me out; I was unstrapped and put back in to a wheelchair. I was taken back to the room where I'd changed and allowed back into my street clothes. Mom and Dad joined me as an orderly pushed me down the hallways and I was surprised when I was wheeled right outside.

"That's it?" I asked as the orderly departed and my parents began to walk me to the car.

"Are you disappointed you don't get to spend the night?" Dad asked with a smile.

"Not at all. Hospitals are too cold."

"We'll have to wait a few days for the results. Now, all we need to do is go home," Dad said.

"Wrong," I said.

"Wrong?"

"We have to stop somewhere and eat. I'm starving!"

Chapter Nine

I went back to school on Wednesday. Other that looking pale and still feeling tired there wasn't anything obviously wrong with me. The doctors told me to take it easy during football practices, but said otherwise there was no reason I couldn't go on as usual.

I felt slightly like a freak show as I walked into school. A lot of kids were staring at me. No doubt word had spread that I'd been carted off from football practice in an ambulance.

"Are you okay?"

I turned at the sound of Banshee's voice.

"I guess you heard, huh?"

"I heard a lot of things: you had a heart attack, you collapsed while running laps, you passed out and blood came out of your mouth... There were some other rumors, too, and none of them were good."

"The truth is less dramatic. I blacked out during football practice and didn't come around until I was in the ER in South Bend. I didn't have a heart attack and blood didn't come out of my mouth. I just slumped over and one of the guys caught me."

"That's still scary. Are you okay? Did they find out why you blacked out?"

"I'm really tired, but I'm okay. They ran a CT scan but the results haven't come back. My parents are worried. They're pretending they aren't and I'm pretending I buy their act."

"If you need to talk, you know I'm here," said Banshee.

"Thanks. I think football practice wore me down. I'm under doctor's orders to take it easy. That will probably fix me up."

"I sure hope so. I'd better get to class. Let's hang out soon, okay?"

"Sounds good."

I headed for my locker, wondering how much catching up I had to do. I'd only missed a day, but I liked to keep on top of things. I wasn't a procrastinator. I liked to get work out of the way.

"Why were you talking to the fag?"

I knew that voice. It was Cody. I was digging in the bottom of my locker for a notebook. I slowly stood up.

"He asked if I was okay."

"He probably wants to butt fuck you, man."

"Banshee is a nice guy."

"I wouldn't be seen talking to him if I was you. People will wonder."

"Let them wonder."

"So, I guess you didn't die."

"And they say blonds are dumb. You figured that all out by yourself, didn't you, Cody?"

"Don't make me pound you, jerk. Next time you keel over I'm just gonna let you fall and bust your head."

"So that was you I felt catching me when I blacked out?"

"You remember that, huh?"

"It's the last thing I do remember. I was out cold until I woke up in the ER."

"I'm not surprised. Coach tried smelling salts on you and you didn't move. We thought you were dead but then we noticed you breathing. You missed your chance at fame. If you'd dropped dead everyone would've been talking about you for years."

"I think I'd rather live without the fame."

"So, they figure out why you keeled over?"

"No."

"Figures. Doctors know nothing. Well, I'm glad you're not dead."

"You're going soft, Cody."

"Yeah, well, I'm not admitting to anyone else I'm glad you're not dead." Cody laughed.

I breathed a sigh of relief when Cody departed. I was afraid he was going to jump on my butt some more for talking to Banshee. His reaction had been mild. Maybe I could ease Cody into the idea of Banshee and me being friends. I doubted it, but maybe.

Passing out during football practice had a lot of fringe benefits. The girls, especially, paid a lot of attention to me. Girls I didn't know came up to me and hugged me and told me they were glad I was okay. Beck and Kevin witnessed me getting a hug from a girl they drooled over. They looked jealous, so I hugged her back. I guess I'm just a little bit evil. I wondered if the girls would've paid any attention to me at all if I wasn't a football player.

I was relieved to discover assignments had been light the day before, at least in my morning classes. I could easily catch up.

"There's the faker," Beck said as I approached the table with my tray of spaghetti, garlic toast, zucchini squash, and applesauce.

"Yeah, you should have seen the little actor all over Darcie Swanson. I think he faked the whole thing just to get some action," Kevin said.

"Come on, guys. You know Mini-Gaylord isn't bright enough to think of something like that," Cody said.

"Thanks so much."

"How are you?" Lucas asked.

"I'm okay, but I have to take it easy. Doctor's orders."

"It isn't enough he gets to ride in an ambulance and have girls fawn on him, now he gets to be a slacker too," Doug said.

"If it's any consolation, I don't even remember the ambulance ride."

"We are glad you're okay. We thought you were dead for a few seconds there," Lucas said.

"Maybe I was and I came back from the dead."

"I knew it! He's a zombie! Protect your brains guys!" Beck shouted.

"You'll be safe at least," Lucas said.

Beck looked confused, but then he got it.

"Hey!"

"I'm glad I'm not a zombie. There's a zombie famine at this table for sure."

"Watch it, Mini-Gaylord. Bad things happen in the locker room to those who insult us," Kevin said.

"That means Kevin will molest you," Doug said.

"Don't make me pound you."

"See what I mean?" Doug asked.

"That's not what I meant!"

Doug laughed.

"To think I could have died and missed all this," I said.

"You know you'd miss us," Lucas said.

"Yeah, sure," I said in my best insincere tone.

"Let's give him a few days to recover and then think about that swirlee idea again," Cody said.

I tried to give Cody the evil eye, but my grin ruined it.

My afternoon was uneventful. I presented my doctor's note to my P.E. teacher and thankfully that got me out of running and calisthenics. We were still on our track unit, so there was nothing I could do. My doctor's note was good for a week, so I was going to remember to bring homework to P.E. unless we moved onto something I could participate in.

I felt a little guilty sitting there doing nothing while everyone else ran around the track. Banshee stuck his tongue out at me every time he passed and made us both laugh. I was so glad everything was okay between us.

I dressed out for football practice. Coach Jordan told me to take it easy and only participate as far as I felt I could. When the team ran at the beginning of practice I jogged around the track. I set an easy pace and when I began breathing harder I slowed down. I even walked part of the time.

I participated in the passing and receiving drills, but stayed away from the tackling dummies. I avoided the dummies more out of a desire to escape humiliation than anything. The "dummies" were big pads around a steel pole on a sled weighed down with heavy weights. Guys like Lucas and Cody could shove them backwards two or three feet when they slammed into them, but I only bounced off. It made me feel as if I was repeatedly running into a brick wall. I was relieved I didn't have to deal with that for a few days.

I settled back into school and practices and it was nice to be able to take it easy for a while. I hoped a few days off from strenuous physical exertion would allow me to get back to normal, but I was still tired. I got dizzy a few times too, but I didn't tell my parents, even though I was supposed to tell them about any dizziness or headaches. I had one headache, but I didn't want to worry my parents with it.

I was surprised on Friday afternoon when my mom showed up at my P.E. class. Neither of my parents had ever come to school before. I was scared that something had happened to Dad at first, but Mom had come to pick me up for a doctor's appointment. My lab results had come in.

I was a little frightened as I went into the locker room to change back into my jeans and tee-shirt. Mom had said nothing about a doctor's appointment before I left for school. I thought the hospital would call our house with the results, and that would be that. The bad feeling I'd had in the hospital returned.

Mom looked scared as she drove me to my appointment, but she didn't let on. I pretended to be unconcerned because I didn't want to upset her. I was worried, but at the same time I trusted God to take care of me. He wouldn't let anything too bad happen to me. Then again, horrible things happened every day. Where was God then? I don't mean that I had no faith in God. My faith had been slipping, but then Jesus appeared. I was still confused, but I was coming to understand the problem wasn't God. The problem was Pastor Walker.

We didn't have to wait for our appointment with Dr. Peters. That was unusual. So was the fact that I was asked to wait in the waiting room while Mom went in alone. My sense of doom increased. I must have set there twenty minutes before a nurse called me back. I was shown to an examining room. The nurse took my blood pressure (I always hated that!), wrote it down on a chart, and left me alone in the room.

Dr. Peters entered alone a few moments later. I wondered where Mom was, but she followed only a few seconds later. Her eyes were red. I knew she'd been crying. Mom sat down beside me and took my hand. Dr. Peters sat down across from us.

"So?" I asked. I couldn't bear the waiting. The news was obviously bad or Mom wouldn't have been crying. I wanted to hear it and get it over with.

Dr. Peters looked at me gravely and sadly.

"The CT scan revealed a mass in your brain," Dr. Peters said. "You have cancer."

Mom sobbed despite her best efforts not to do so. I looked blankly ahead. I felt like I was watching an after school special. What was happening felt unreal.

"That's why I get dizzy and have headaches. That's why I blacked out."

"Yes."

I didn't know a great deal about cancer, but I knew it was extremely bad. Sometimes it killed people. I'd heard about chemotherapy and how sick it made people and how their hair fell out. I didn't want to experience any of that.

"So... what happens now?" I asked.

"You go home. You go to school. You live your life."

"That's it? Don't I have to go through that chemotherapy stuff?"

"In your case it would do no good. The tumor is already much too far along. We can treat you for it, but that would only make the time you have left unpleasant."

The time I had left... I was going to die. Everyone died, but... I was going to die soon.

"Can I see it?" I asked.

Dr. Peters looked at Mom. She nodded. My doctor pulled a small stack of thick sheets out of my file and handed them to me. I looked through them. It was weird looking inside my own head. I could see my brain and I could see a big lump that wasn't supposed to be there. It was so large I wondered why I couldn't feel it. I looked at Mom.

"Could I talk to Dr. Peters alone?" I asked.

Mom looked surprised, but nodded. She got up, dabbling her eyes with a Kleenex, and left the room. I wanted her to leave because I didn't want to make this any harder on her than it had to be. I'm sure she already knew the details and there was no reason she had to listen to it again.

"How long before I die?" I asked Dr. Peters when Mom was gone.

"In as little as a month or as long as four months."

A month? I might not even make it to Halloween, let alone Christmas? This wasn't an afterschool special. Kids in TV shows always got six months. At best I had four.

"Will it hurt? I don't mean dying. I mean, will I have more headaches? What's going to happen?"

"Your headaches and the dizziness will get worse. I'm going to prescribe some medication for you. One prescription will be for pain, another to reduce your nausea, and another will help control the dizziness. We will try to control the symptoms so you can go on and live normally as long as you can."

"What will happen at the end?"

"Are you sure you want to know this?"

I nodded.

"As the tumor increases in size it will put more pressure on your brain. The headaches will get much worse. At that point we'll probably begin treating you with morphine."

Morphine. That was powerful stuff and highly addictive. I guess the addictive part didn't matter since I wasn't going to live very long.

"You'll begin to have trouble controlling your body. During the last three or four days you'll likely be unable to walk on your own. During the last couple of days you'll be unable to walk at all."

"I'm really worried about Mom and Dad," I said. That's when tears welled up in my eyes.

Dr. Peters squeezed my knee.

"It will be hard on them, but they will survive. You can make it easier on them by taking care of yourself. I want you to take your medication whenever you need it. The longer we can control the symptoms, the better. I'm going to give you some information for counseling as well as numbers you can call for help."

Dr. Peters picked up a folder he'd carried in with him. He took out his pen and began writing inside.

"This is my office number and my home phone number. I want you to call me if you begin experiencing any additional symptoms or any pain the medications can't control. I also want you to call me if you need any help or just need to talk."

"Thank you," I said. I took the folder at looked at the numbers. I laughed. "I can read your handwriting! That's the first time I've ever been able to read your handwriting."

Dr. Peters actually began laughing. We walked out into the hallway together, still laughing. Mom was sitting there in a chair. I don't think she knew what to make of it, but I actually saw her smile for a moment. The smile was soon gone, but I was going to make her smile all I could before I died.

Mom was crying as she drove to the drug store. She kept trying not to cry, but couldn't stop the tears. She more or less got herself under control by the time she parked the car. She smiled at me and patted me on the knee and we went inside together to get my prescriptions filled.

"If you'd like anything, get it," Mom said while she filled my prescriptions. From the tone of her voice I'm sure I could have filled a cart full of stuff. I picked out a giant-sized Hersey chocolate bar with almonds. My grandfather had once told me all chocolate bars were that size when he was a kid. I don't know if he was serious or not. I also got a Yoo-hoo. I figured I might as well choc-out.

It was too quiet on the way home, but what was there to say? When we arrived I put both the Hershey bar and the Yoo-hoo in the refrigerator. I liked them both cold and I wanted to save them for after supper. I went upstairs to my room. I heard Mom crying before I shut my door.

I just sat on the edge of my bed for a while. I was in a daze. Everything still felt unreal. Maybe that's why I wasn't too upset. I should've been upset. I was going to die and it wasn't going to be pretty near the end.

I was really worried about Mom and Dad. I was the one who was sick, but they had to deal with me dying. I felt guilty, although it's not like I had a choice. The worst thing I was I didn't know how to make it okay. I didn't want Mom and Dad to suffer. I'd take my medication like Dr. Peters asked. With its help I could hide my pain, at least for a while. After that...

I went downstairs. Mom quickly dabbed her eyes with another Kleenex.

"I'm going to go out for a while and walk," I said. "I'll come back before supper."

"Are you sure you..." Mom began, but then stopped herself. "Okay, dear. Be careful."

Mom almost started bawling again. I walked over to her and hugged her.

"It's going to okay," I said. I thought about adding something about going to Heaven and all of us being together again someday, but I figured that wasn't such a good idea.

I gave my mom a kiss on the cheek and went outside.

I walked aimlessly for just a bit, but then I realized it was about time for school to let out. I headed in that direction. I wasn't going to football practice. I wasn't ready for that just yet. I headed for VHS because I wanted to talk to Banshee.

I didn't know what Banshee had last period, but I did know where his locker was located. I arrived just as school was letting out and headed straight for his locker. He appeared about five minutes later, looking very surprised.

"Is that offer to hang out still good?" I asked.

"Sure it is."

I smiled, but from the expression on Banshee's face I knew he could tell something was wrong.

I thought about walking out to the soccer fields, but I didn't want to take a chance of seeing any of my teammates as they made their way to the football field. I didn't feel up to talking to any of them and I didn't want to explain why I wasn't going to practice today.

"Let's walk to the park," I said.

We didn't speak as we walked out of the school. We didn't speak as we walked down the sidewalk either. I wanted to talk to Banshee, but I didn't know how to begin.

"Did you get some bad news?" Banshee asked.

"Yeah."

"How bad?"

"Real, real bad," I said.

I began to lose control then. Suddenly everything became real. My lower lip began to tremble and I had to bite it to keep from crying. Tears filled my eyes and one rolled down my cheek.

"I'm so sorry," Banshee said.

"I have cancer," I said. "A brain tumor."

"Oh." Banshee said nothing more for several moments, but then spoke again. "So I guess you have to do chemo and all that?"

I shook my head, and then looked at him.

"It's too late."

Now Banshee's lower lip trembled and his eyes filled with tears. He began to cry and quickly wiped his tears away.

"If I'm lucky, I have four months. If I'm not, maybe just one."

Banshee looked stunned.

"There's nothing they can do?"

I shook my head.

"If it had been caught early, it might have been possible to remove it, but it they try now it would most likely kill me."

"I'm so sorry. I wish there was something I could say to make it better."

"Thanks. I'm still kind of in shock. You never think it's going to happen to you, you know?"

Banshee nodded.

"I don't think I'll mind dying so much, but there's so much I wanted to do. I thought I had plenty of time, but now I don't."

I looked at Banshee walking beside me. Tears were still running down his cheeks.

"I'm sorry. I shouldn't be laying all this on you. I just needed to talk to someone. I can't talk to my parents. Mom is so upset already. My doctor gave me a number I can call, and his number too, but I need to talk to someone my age, you know?"

"Don't be sorry. We're friends, aren't we?"

"I haven't been a very good friend."

"Don't bring that up. That's the past and you had your reasons. I understand. If our situations were reversed, I'd likely have done the same. You have been a good friend. I'm glad you picked me when you needed someone to talk to. It means a lot to me. I just... I just don't want to lose you."

Banshee began sobbing. I reached over, put my hand on his shoulder, and pulled him close in a one-arm hug.

We walked to the park and set on a wooden bench under an enormous oak tree.

"This is a nightmare," Banshee said. "I hope I wake up soon."

"That would be nice. A lot of my life has seemed like a dream lately, making the football team especially, almost scoring a touchdown, fooling around with Cody at that..."

I looked quickly at Banshee. I hadn't meant to say that last part.

"Cody? Cody Caldemyer? The guy who was going to bash you and then was going to bash me? You fooled around with him?"

"Uh, yeah, but you can't tell anyone. I didn't mean for it to slip out."

"That hypocrite. What happened?"

"Promise you won't tell *and* not to tell Cody that you know?"

"Yeah, I promise."

"Lucas took me to a team party at Kevin's house. There was a lot of drinking and making out. I didn't drink very much. I mostly just pretended. Cody drank a lot. We went out in the back yard, sat in a glider, and watched the moon. One thing led to another and then we started... um... jerking off. Then, we were jerking each other off, and then Cody leaned over and gave me head."

"Cody Caldemyer, homophobe extraordinaire, sucked you off?"

"Yeah."

"He's such an asshole. He was going to beat both of us up for being gay and he's a cock-sucker."

I grimaced at Banshee's choice of words.

"Cody is... complicated. He is a horrible jerk sometimes, but he's a good guy mostly."

"Do you guys hook up a lot?"

"No. We just did that once. It's weird. It's as if it never happened. I'm not even sure he remembers it."

"Don't fall for that."

"For what?"

"The "I was drunk" routine. Guys use it to dismiss all sorts of things. Cody obviously isn't as straight as he pretends. I bet he planned the whole thing."

"It didn't seem planned."

"I bet it was. Either that or he saw his chance and took it. Now, he's using the fact he was drunk to rationalize it and pretend he doesn't remember."

"I don't know, but we're teammates. We might not quite be friends, but we're friendly."

"Yeah, real friendly," Banshee said, then giggled. "I can't believe you did it with Cody. He's hot! He's a jerk, but he's hot. Is he big?"

I blushed, but nodded.

"How big?"

"It's not like I measured! Can we stop talking about this?"

"You're so cute when you're embarrassed. You can get it on with one of your football buddies but you can't talk about it? Just tell me."

"I don't know. Eight inches maybe."

"Nice."

I shot Banshee an annoyed looked.

"Okay. Okay. We can talk about something else."

We both went quiet. For a few moments we'd both forgotten I was dying, but there it was again—stark reality staring us in the face.

"I'm worried about my parents. This is going to be hard for them and I don't think I can make it okay. My family is religious. I don't think of death as an end so much as a change. Still, I'm not going to be here and it's going to be a long time before we're together again. I'm not entirely sure about life after death either. I believe in it, but I don't know for sure if it's what I've been taught to believe. What if there's nothing? What if we just cease to exist when we die?"

"That wouldn't be so bad, would it? Think about it. If you cease to exist, it's not as though you'll be sad or lonely or missing anyone. There will be no fear or pain. You won't exist at all. I don't know what I believe. I don't like the idea of anyone else ceasing to exist, but for myself I don't think I'd mind that much. Not having to worry about anything actually sounds pretty good. I'm not saying I want to die, but it's comforting to think that when I die I won't be lonely, or sad, or afraid, or any of the rest. There won't be any bullies. There won't be anyone who wants to hurt me. Of course, the whole idea of Heaven is pretty sweet. I think I'd like that better."

I actually laughed for a moment.

"At least now I know why I've been so tired. It was so frustrating because it didn't make sense. Everything started going backward. I couldn't run as far and I couldn't lift as much weight. I guess I'll never be as buff as Lucas or Cody now. That was my goal. I wanted to look like them."

"You look great just as you are."

"I'm okay I guess."

"You're better than okay. You are hot. Believe me. I know. I'm a homo!"

I laughed again. I had found out an hour ago I was dying, but Banshee could still make me laugh.

"You know what? Let's stop talking about this. I'm tired of talking about it. Let's just do something."

"I'll do *anything* you want, sexy," Banshee said in a pretend seductive tone. He was being goofy, but I knew he also meant it.

"Let's get some ice cream. I love ice cream. I just want to sit, eat ice cream, and pretend today didn't happen."

"Okay, let's do it. I'm good at pretending. Apparently, so is Cody."

"Banshee..." I growled.

He laughed.

"Come on," Banshee said. He pulled me up off the bench and together we walked across the street to Ofarim's.

Banshee and I spent a good hour in Ofarim's. We each ordered a hot fudge sundae and then sat there talking long after we'd devoured our ice cream. Banshee entertained me with some of the goings-on at the homo table. He made sitting with the gay boys sound like so much fun I wished I could join them. I told him some of the things said at the football table, except I didn't use the same language. I didn't think I could say those words out loud!

Banshee walked me home when we left Ofarim's. We talked and laughed, and for stretches of time I forgot that I didn't have much time left. I just enjoyed being with Banshee, hearing the sound of his voice, and his laugh. It was the best part of the worst afternoon of my entire life, but it would've been the best part of many afternoons that were a good deal better. Banshee had become a good friend.

When we reached my house, Banshee gave me a hug. We just stood there holding each other for several moments. When we released each other at last I turned and walked up the front steps. I gave Banshee a wave just before I stepped inside.

Dad was home. He was sitting the living room. His eyes were red. I knew he'd been crying. I couldn't recall ever seeing my dad cry before. When I walked in he stood and hugged me close.

"I love you so much. You know that, don't you?"

"Of course I know it," I said into his chest. "I love you too."

"Come on, your mom almost has supper ready. She's frying chicken and she made mashed potatoes and baked beans."

"Mmm, those are some of my favorites."

Mom's eyes were red when Dad and I walked into the kitchen, but she smiled at me.

"It's almost ready. I hoped you'd be getting home soon."

Before long we were all sitting around the kitchen table eating. I wished Thomas and Mitch were there too. I paused for a moment. I wondered how my brothers would take the news. I stopped eating for a few moments.

"Let's not tell Thomas and Mitch until they come home from school to visit, okay? I think they'll be better off not knowing until then," I said.

Mom and Dad looked at each other. They were likely both thinking they wished *they* didn't know.

"I think that's a good idea, Elijah. They'll be home for a visit very soon. We'll tell them then," said Dad.

"How are you feeling?" Mom asked.

"I'm fine. I don't need any of my pills yet."

"You let me know when you do."

"I'd like to keep them in my room if you don't mind. I promised Dr. Peters I'd take them when I needed them. He gave me his home phone number. Can you believe that?"

"I guess you can keep them and I'm not surprised that Dr. Peter's gave you his number. He's always told us to call him at home if we really need him."

I was relieved Mom was going to let me keep my prescriptions. I didn't want to have to ask her for them. When I started taking them, I wanted to hide that I needed them as long as possible. I didn't want Mom and Dad to worry.

"Do you need a few days off from school? You can stay home if you want. You really don't have to…" Mom trailed off for a moment. She almost said something about going to school not mattering anymore but she caught herself. I pretended not to notice. "… But, I'm sure you'll want to be with your friends. Still, a day or two wouldn't hurt."

"No. I want to go. I like school mostly, especially football practice."

Mom and Dad looked at each other.

"About football… your mother and I think it might be a good idea if you gave that up. Practices are very taxing and we don't want you getting worn down."

My face fell. I felt like crying. Give up football?

"I worked so hard to make the team. Thomas and Mitch played football, so did you and grandfather, and great-grandfather. The guys on the team are my friends. I like being a part of the team. Please don't make me quit."

"You're not going to be able to play, sweetheart," Mom said, on the verge of tears.

"I might be able to play, for a little while. I never expected to get to play much. I didn't even know if I'd get to play at all. I promise I'll take it easy. I'll only do what I feel I can do. I won't push myself. I don't have much time left to play football. Please. Let me do this. I don't want to stop living my life because I'm going to die soon."

Mom lost control. I felt horrible for making her cry. I guess I shouldn't have said that last part about dying soon, but I couldn't give up football.

"He is right," Dad said. "The worst thing he could do is give up the things he loves."

"But, what if he gets hurt?" Mom said, her eyes full of pain.

"Mom, nothing that happens to me on the field is going to make me any worse."

"Don't push yourself," Mom said. "Take it easy. If you feel yourself getting too tired sit down and rest, no matter what anyone says."

"I will."

Mom didn't look happy about the idea, but she couldn't say no.

"It will be okay, Mom," I said.

"He'll be fine," Dad said.

Dad and I were lying and Mom knew it. I wasn't going to be okay, but I didn't want to stop living my life, especially now that I had so little life left to live. With that in mind, I enjoyed my fried chicken, mashed potatoes, and baked beans. Mom had made chocolate cake for dessert, with lots of icing just like I liked it. I had an extra-big slice, then went upstairs to rest.

I lay back on my bed and looked at the ceiling. Why was it that nothing in my life seemed quite real anymore? It wasn't the cancer. Things felt unreal before that. I was a football player, I was gay, and Jesus went to my high school. Things didn't get much more unreal than that.

I thought about Jesus. I was looking forward to Sunday. I had no idea if Jesus would be back again, but I hoped he showed up if Pastor Walker started gay bashing again, as he probably would. My views on homosexuals had changed and not just because I'd realized I was one. I thought of Banshee and his compassion and kindness. I thought of Casper on that day he went over and offered a lonely Banshee friendship. I thought of me too. I hadn't been able to bear seeing Banshee alone and suffering. I'd messed up things after that and thankfully fixed them since, but I'm reached out to Banshee because I was compassionate and a good person. That might sound immodest, but it is also true. I was gay and I was a good person. The two were not mutually exclusive as Pastor Walker and others would have me believe.

I wondered how long I had left. Would I have four months or only one? A month wasn't very long, just over four weeks. I guess I could count on a month and anything beyond that would be a bonus. I didn't have long, so I wanted to make sure I worked in everything I really wanted to do. I thought of my Hershey bar and Yoo-Hoo in the refrigerator, but I was much too full of chocolate cake. I'd save those for later. I wasn't *that* short on time, not yet.

I wanted to continue with football. I wanted to sit with the guys. I wanted to keep hanging out with Banshee too. There wasn't much I wanted to do that I wasn't already doing. I guess I had a better life than I'd thought. I couldn't think of anything I wanted to add to it. I was going to eat more chocolate, but other than that I mostly just wanted to keep going as long as I could.

I wondered how much it would hurt near the end. I guess my prescriptions would help with that. When the pain grew too severe, Dr. Peters said I'd be put on morphine. I almost wished that, near the end, they could give me far too much and get it over with, but I don't think God would like me picking the time of my death. That was his job.

I lay there and thought about Heaven and Hell. According to Pastor Walker I was going to Hell. I would've been really scared if I believed it. The words Jesus had spoken in church had changed everything. He made me realize I was wrong about a lot of things. I was wrong because I'd been taught wrong. The truth made far more sense. I was relieved that God didn't make me gay and damn me for it. He made me gay, just as he makes all things, but I wasn't going to be damned. No one would be damned for being what they were meant to be. I was glad that things were right between God and me again. I guess I could've been angry he gave me cancer; only I didn't think God gave it to me. It's something that happened because it had to happen. I didn't understand why, but that didn't matter. If I had to have cancer, that's the way it was. I wasn't going to spend my last days angry with God. He'd been with me all these years and I wasn't going to part ways with him now.

My teammates would probably think I was a total nerd for being so religious, if they knew that is. I didn't hide that I went to church, but it was something we didn't talk about. Church was not a likely topic at the football table. My ears still burned sometimes when I listened to my teammates talk about girls, but in a way weren't they showing appreciation and thankfulness for God's creations? Still, I wished they weren't so vulgar.

I yawned. I was sleepy. I undressed before I got too tired and set my alarm for the morning. I didn't have to go to school tomorrow. I didn't have to go ever again if I didn't want to, but what was I going to do? Sit at home and think about dying? I wanted to be with my friends. I wanted to be with my team. Being there would help me forget what was going to happen. Everyone died sooner or later after all. Some of us just died a lot sooner than we'd expected.

I turned off the light and lay there thinking as I slowly grew drowsier and drowsier. I wondered if that was what death was like. Maybe when I died I'd just get more and more sleepy and then, instead of falling asleep, I'd just pass away.

Chapter Ten

I looked pale. That's what I noticed when I looked in the mirror the next morning. It didn't scare me. I knew what was wrong with me. Knowing was better than not knowing even though the truth was bad. I guess how I looked didn't matter all that much. I'd never been as good looking as guys like Lucas and Cody. Even without their amazing bodies they were sexy and hot. Their features alone made them well worth looking at. I wasn't nearly as good-looking as either of them and never would be. So what did it matter if I looked sickly?

I hadn't thought to ask Banshee to keep my illness a secret. I didn't really want the whole school talking about me, but I wouldn't be able to hide it for long. I was going to have to tell Coach Jordan. My teammates would have to know too. Otherwise, they'd wonder why I wasn't doing much in practice. I was going to do what I could do, but even before I found out what was wrong with me I'd been forced scale back. I just couldn't cut it anymore.

I was surprised when Dad said he was driving me to school. I soon found out why. He was going to talk to the principal and Coach Jordan and tell them what was wrong with me. They needed to know. I hadn't thought about it, but my cancer was going to affect a lot of people beyond my family. It had already affected Banshee. I hated to make him cry.

I walked into school with Dad. We paused before we went our separate ways. I could tell Dad wanted to hug me, but feared he'd embarrass me. I turned to him and gave him a hug.

"I love you," I said.

"I love you too, Son."

I smiled, then turned and walked down the hallway. Banshee waited for me by my locker. He looked sad, but smiled when he saw me. I didn't know it then, but Banshee was going to be waiting by my locker every morning.

"How are you?"

"Tired, but I'm going to have to get used to that. I feel good mostly."

"If there's anything you need..."

"I'm not confined to a wheelchair yet."

I knew I'd said the wrong thing. Banshee looked like I'd slapped him.

"I'm sorry. I just mean you don't have to worry about me so much. I feel pretty good and if I start to get a headache I have some of my hydrocodone tablets with me."

"Hydrocodone?"

"Think of it as aspirin on steroids. I have an even stronger painkiller at home, but the doctor said it would make me loopy."

"How will anyone know?"

"Jerk... but that's more like it. Please don't treat me like I'm fragile."

"I'm just worried about you."

"I'll tell you what. If you won't treat me like an invalid, I'll be honest with you about how I'm feeling. When things get bad, I'll tell you."

"Deal," Banshee said. "Can I walk you to class?"

"Yes."

We walked along together through the hallways. Cody spotted us. He glared at Banshee and looked none too pleased with me.

"Don't worry about him," I said. "Don't let him catch you alone either. I'll talk to him."

I felt better with Banshee at my side. Even though there was nothing he could do, just knowing he was there was comforting. It was good to have friends.

It might've just been my imagination, but I felt like everyone was looking at me. None of them knew what was wrong with me yet, but I *had* been carted off from football practice a few days before. So much had happened since my blackout I'd almost forgotten it. Everyone else soon would too.

I smiled when Mr. Hahn, my social studies teacher, began talking about our research paper that was due at the end of the school year. I didn't have to do it. I wasn't going to be around at the end of the year. My smiled quickly faded. I looked around at the other students, the posters on the walls, and the chalkboards. All this would still be here when the school year ended, but I wouldn't be. I'd be long gone. I wondered if anyone would even remember me. Banshee would. I smiled. Knowing someone would remember me made me feel better. Banshee was a truly good friend.

Cody gave me the cold shoulder at lunch. The guys gave me a hard time for missing practice. I told them I'd gone home sick with diarrhea. I figured that would keep them from asking questions, and it did. I'd have to tell the team about my cancer soon, but I didn't want to tell them just yet.

Banshee and I talked and laughed as we dressed out for P.E. I could tell by the look in his eyes he was worried about me, but he didn't ask how I was feeling or treat me like I was made of glass.

Mr. Wells pulled me to the side when I came out of the locker room and told me the principal had informed him of my condition. He told me to participate as much or as little as I felt like. His words of advice were, "Just have fun."

I could've skipped out on calisthenics entirely, but I went ahead and did the jumping jacks, pushups, and sit-ups. When it came to running I took it easy. I ran slowly enough to keep my breath from coming too fast. I certainly didn't feel up to any running events, so I volunteered to assist Mr. Wells. He gave me a measuring tape and a clipboard and put me in charge of the long jump. When everyone had finished that, Mr. Wells had me take over the high jump. It was a lot more fun setting the height of the pole and recording scores than it was trying to make it over that bar.

I wasn't worn out after P.E., which made the afternoon far more pleasant. The pleasantness ended when I walked into the locker room. Cody had just dressed out. He slammed his locker and looked down at me as I sat on the bench taking off my shoes.

"Why are you hanging out with that faggot?" he growled.

"Because he's my friend," I said. I was through with hiding my friendship with Banshee. I guess I never had actually hid it, but I didn't advertise it either.

"You're friends with a faggot? I warned you about that. I told you it would make guys wonder about you."

"Back off, Cody. Who Elijah chooses to have as a friend is none of your business," Lucas said.

Lucas had his shirt off. He looked intimidating with all those muscles.

"Yeah? What are you going to do about it?" snarled Cody.

Lucas stepped up nose to nose with Cody.

"You want to go?" Lucas asked. His muscles were tensed and ready. Cody glared into his eyes.

"No! Just stop it!" I said.

They both looked at me.

"I don't want you two fighting over this! I appreciate you standing up for me Lucas, but guys please don't fight. Cody, just leave me alone, okay? What's it to you if I have a gay friend? It doesn't hurt you. Banshee's a nice guy."

Lucas and Cody stepped away from each other, but still eyed each other.

"I should kick that little faggot's ass," Cody said.

"Leave him alone, please."

"Why should I?"

"Because I'm asking you to."

Cody didn't look convinced.

"Consider it my dying wish," I said. I shouldn't have said it, but I was upset and I was worried about Banshee. I didn't want Cody to hurt him in some macho effort to make himself look tough.

"Yeah, right," Cody said with a small laugh. "There's a problem with that. You aren't dying."

"Yes, I am," I said quietly.

Cody began to laugh at my joke, but then he noticed the expression on my face. I looked down at the floor, fighting back tears.

"No, that's stupid. You're not dying. You're just fifteen. What could you be dying of..."

Cody's voice trailed off. I looked up at him. Tears rimmed my eyes. The color drained from Cody's face.

"Elijah?" Lucas asked.

The locker room had gone silent. The whole team was looking at me.

"I wasn't going to tell you yet, but you'll find out soon enough anyway. I have a brain tumor. That's what made me black out during practice. I don't have a lot of time left. Cody, please leave Banshee alone. He's my friend and he's the only one I can talk to about what's happening to me."

Tears welled up in my eyes. They suddenly welled up in Cody's too.

"I'm sorry," Cody said. "I didn't know. I... I'm sorry. I won't bother him."

I felt like saying he shouldn't have bothered him anyway, but I didn't want to get into that.

"I'm really sorry Elijah," Lucas said, putting his hand on my shoulder. "Are you okay? Is there anything we can do?"

"Yeah. There's something all of you can do," I said looking around at my teammates. "Don't start treating me different, okay? I'm not going to be able to do as much during practice, but everything else will be just the same. I don't want to be the freak with cancer. I just want to be one of you. So make smart-alecky remarks like you always do Beck, and Cody... go on being a jerk. Being on this team means so much to me. I just want to be with you guys while I can."

All of my teammates looked like they might cry. I bet that was a first. These guys did not cry, at least not in public. There was a long uncomfortable silence.

"Well, are you going to dress out or not?" Kevin asked at last.

Cody looked down at me. He hesitated, but then spoke.

"Yeah, hurry up dick-head. If Coach makes us run extra laps because you're late I'll kick your skinny little ass."

I grinned and pulled off my shirt. The guys once again started changing into their practice uniforms and began to head to the field. Both Lucas and Cody held back. Before long we were alone in the locker room.

"I'm sorry I gave you a hard time. I'm an asshole sometimes," Cody said.

"Yeah, you are. You've also been cool to me... mostly."

"You can do treatments, right?" Lucas asked. "Chemo? They can operate on you or something can't they?"

I slowly shook my head.

"It's too late. My doctor said that if I'm lucky I'll have four months. If I'm not lucky, maybe just one."

Lucas sank down on the bench beside me.

"Shit. Is he sure?"

I nodded.

"I feel like such an asshole," Cody said, sitting down on the other side of me and banging the back of his head against the locker.

Lucas looked at Cody, but refrained from saying anything. I guess he figured Cody was suffering enough.

"I wish I could have kept it a secret, but it will get harder and harder to hide," I said.

"I'm glad you told us," Lucas said.

"I'm glad I know what's wrong with me. At least I now know why I've been getting weaker and why I get winded so easily. I was so frustrated about that. It didn't make any sense. I kept telling myself practices were wearing me down, but they aren't that brutal."

"Don't let Coach hear you say that," Lucas said and grinned.

"Hey, I can say it. I only have to do what I feel like. It's the rest of you who will suffer. Hmm, maybe I'll tell him practices are way too easy."

Lucas and Cody looked at each other.

"Swirlee," they said at the same time.

They jumped up, grabbed me, and pulled me toward the restroom.

"Guys! Guys! Come on, guys! I was just kidding!"

I struggled, but it was totally useless. They dragged me into the restroom and opened a stall door. They took me by the shoulders and began to pick me up, but then set me back down. My heart was racing. I actually thought they were going to do it!

"Still gonna tell the coach practices are too easy?" Cody asked.

"Um.... No." I laughed.

"Come on. Coach will chew our asses out if we're late," Lucas said.

"Come on, squirt," Cody said as he put his arm around my shoulders and pulled me toward the door.

"Who you callin' squirt?"

"Well it's not Lucas, so you figure it out."

"At least I *can* figure it out. I'm not blond," I said.

"You know, it's a short trip back to the toilet," threatened Cody.

"I'm not scared of you."

Cody glared at me.

"Okay! Okay! I'm scared!"

Cody laughed. The three of us walked to the football field together.

I joined the team as we ran around the track, but I didn't even try to keep up. I ran along as fast as I could without losing my breath. I already missed being able to keep up with the pack, but I was just glad I could run. I really did love to run. I was going to miss it.

I began to get upset, but I stopped myself. I wasn't going to spend whatever time I had left feeling sorry for myself or thinking about what I was soon to lose. I was going to do what I'd always done—enjoy what I had—right here and right now—as much as I could. I didn't know how many times I'd get to run on this track before I was unable to run. What had been a daily event was now something precious. I was going to enjoy running with the team while I could. My time was short and this time would never come again.

I had to stop long before Coach pulled the team from the track. Coach Jordan waved me over.

"I've been informed about your condition. I'm truly sorry, Elijah, and I admire you greatly for staying on the team."

"I know I won't be able to do all that much, but I want to do what I can. You don't know what being on this team means to me. Thank you so much for giving me a chance. I even got to play and that's something I'll remember for the rest of my life. I guess that doesn't mean as much as it once did, but you made my dream come true."

"Thank you, but Lucas is the one who actually made that dream come true. He asked me to put you in the game and he obviously knew what he was doing."

I smiled.

"I'm still thankful for just getting to be here and be a part of things. I never thought I'd make it, but I did."

"Yes, you did. I saw something special in you during practices. I saw a fire that I don't see in many players. I can see I was right."

"Thanks, Coach."

Coach blew his whistle and the guys jogged over, huffing and puffing. I sat down between Lucas and Cody.

"Slacker," Cody whispered and elbowed me. I giggled.

Coach Jordan and the experienced members of the team taught us some new plays. I even had my chance at receiver a couple of times. I didn't hold back, but raced down the field just as I would've in a real game. I snagged the ball both times. I was just sorry it was only a drill and I couldn't run right on to the goal line and score.

I mostly took it easy. I was tired at the end of practice, but then I was always tired. I wasn't as worn out as I had been. In the showers, I allowed myself the luxury of looking around, not that I was obvious. I'd admitted to myself I was gay so I figured I might as well enjoy the scenery. There was some fine scenery in the showers, especially with Lucas and Cody in there. Cody caught me looking, but didn't say anything about it. I was a little more careful after that.

Some of the guys acted a little odd around me, not because they noticed me checking them out, but because they knew I had cancer. It was probably a little unnerving being around someone who was going to die soon. I figured they'd get used to the idea and things would more or less be back to normal.

I grinned as I walked toward home. I'd had a good day. I started to get a headache mid-way through the afternoon, but I took one of my aspirin-on-steroids and then I was fine. I was going to get through this.

I paused. I wasn't though, not really. There was no getting through this. At the end waited death. I'd never feared death, but it had always been an elusive, future something. Now it was coming up fast. I still wasn't afraid, just sorry I didn't have more time.

I thanked God I was feeling good. I'd spent time with Banshee and my football buddies today. I'd stopped what looked to be a knockdown, drag-out brawl between Lucas and Cody. I'd had a great practice. Best of all, Cody had promised never to bother Banshee again. I couldn't wait to tell Banshee! Yeah, this was a good day. I wonder if I would have realized that if I didn't have so few days left.

I was in such a good mood when I got home that it made Mom smile. She didn't fuss over me too much as she heated up pork chops, mashed potatoes, and cooked apples.

"Are those cookies I smell?" I asked.

"Yes and you can have some after you eat your supper."

"I'll be happy to eat my weight in cookies. I'm starved!"

"You didn't push yourself too hard during practice, did you?"

"No. I took it easy in P.E. and during football practice. I didn't run at all in P.E., and I only ran until I started getting out of breath during practice. I've never felt better after a practice."

"That's wonderful," said Mom.

My supper was soon ready and I sat down to eat. I told Mom some about my day as I ate, but mostly I just ate. I finished off a couple of pork chops and lots of mashed potatoes and cooked apples. Then I hit the cookies hard, especially since they were chocolate chip with pecans. My favorite!

I ate too many cookies, but I figured what the heck? It's not like they were going to kill me. Eating all the chocolate I wanted was one of my top priorities and I decided to add cookies to that list. That made me think of the Hershey bar and Yoo-Hoo that were still in the refrigerator. I left the chocolate bar for the moment, but grabbed the Yoo-Hoo and a couple more cookies and headed up to my room.

I momentarily thought of blowing off my homework, but what was I going to do, ignore my schoolwork and sit in class confused and bored? I was probably better off keeping things as normal as possible. Homework wasn't so hard anyway. It was just one of those things I didn't like because I had to do it. Now that I didn't have to do it, I kind of liked it.

My next day at school was more normal than the previous one had been. I gave Banshee the good news he didn't have to hide from Cody anymore. He almost couldn't believe I'd convinced Cody to leave him alone, but then I told him the whole story of what went down in the locker room.

***

Before I knew it, the weekend had arrived. I decided to keep my job. One might think working at Chicken Fillets was a poor way to spend one's final days on Earth, but it was only for few hours on Saturday and making my own money made me feel good about myself. I was also now free to spend it all on me, me, me!

Okay, I'm actually not that greedy, but I figured if I really wanted something and could afford it, I'd buy it. I'd draw up an unofficial will and leave all my cool stuff to Banshee, Lucas, and the guys on my team. I doubted my parents would want my junk around after I was gone. It would just be a reminder that I wasn't there anymore.

I'd told Banshee when I was scheduled for a lunch break, so he came in to join me. I took his order, then clocked out and ordered my own. I joined Banshee in a quiet booth.

"How is work?"

"Lovely, but there will be no talking about work on my lunch break."

"Okay. Um… any hot guys come in?"

"Do you think of anything other than guys?" I asked.

"Sometimes older men. You know, your dad is kind of hot."

"Do not go there!"

Banshee laughed.

"Yeah. He is old enough to be my dad."

"He is *my* dad, so shut up!"

"Oh! I passed Cody on the way here."

"What did he do?"

"He smiled at me and nodded."

"That's much better than hunting you down with intent to kill."

"Yes, I do prefer the friendly greeting over possible murder. Thank you again."

"What are friends for?"

"Um... hooking me up with your football buddies?"

I cocked my head and gave Banshee a look I hoped came off as "Yeah, right!"

"Come on, there has to be a couple of gay guys on your team."

"Maybe, but I don't know who they are."

"You could ask around."

"Yeah, that's a great idea," I said sarcastically.

"Hey, it is!"

"If you think it's such a brilliant idea, you come in and ask them."

"I'm not on the team. Damn, it would be worth it if they were changing when I came in. Dude, you are so lucky. You get naked with the hottest guys in school every day!"

"Actually, I think most of the hottest guys are on the varsity team, except for Lucas and Cody."

"Yeah, I wanna see Shawn and Tim naked, preferably together."

"Eww. They're brothers."

"Come on. Doesn't that turn you on?"

"Uh, remember, I go to church."

"So? You're religious. You're not dead."

Banshee realized what he'd said and suddenly looked frightened.

"Would you relax? I'm okay, unless this Big Chicken Clucker gets me."

"What a way to go," Banshee said. He paused again and swallowed hard.

"You don't have to tip-toe around death," I said. "I'm going to die. Everyone is going to die sooner or later. Nothing can change that. Stop being so self-conscious."

"I just don't want to remind you."

"Thanks, but I know I'm going to die soon. It's kind of hard to forget that kind of thing."

"How can you just talk about it like that?"

"Ignoring it won't change anything. I don't want to die, but I'm not afraid to die either. I'm also curious to see what's going to happen. As Peter Pan said; "To die will be an excellent adventure.""

Banshee looked like he was on the verge of crying. It was funny in a way. *I* was the one who was dying and *he* was the one on the verge of tears. Then again, maybe it made sense. I'd soon be moving on to eternal life or oblivion. Either way my troubles would be over. Banshee would still be here in Verona, without me.

"Let's talk about something else. I don't really want to spend my lunch break on heavy topics."

Banshee didn't say anything for a bit. Then, a mischievous glint came into his eyes.

"So, who has the hottest butt, Lucas or Cody?"

"Back to guys?"

"I can't think of anything else. Besides, guys are one of my favorite topics. Answer the question."

"Who says I've looked?"

"Don't pull that 'I'm too good of a Christian to check out boys in the locker room' crap. You've looked. How could you not?"

"I'd say it's a tie."

"Who has the best body?"

"Tie."

"Who the most hung?"

"Would you stop?"

"Who?"

"Lucas, at least when he's um... not erect."

"What? You haven't hooked up with Lucas?" Banshee asked, shocked.

"What makes you think I would have hooked up with Lucas? Do you think I'm some kind of slut? Even if I had the chance..." I looked at Banshee. He was laughing. "I hate you."

"You are far too easy to fluster."

"Yeah, well. Quit taking advantage of that."

"Okay, I'll try to control myself. When is your next game?"

"Next Friday."

"Cool. I will be there to watch my favorite player."

"Lucas? He made quarterback you know."

"Not Lucas, you!"

"Eh. Well, the chances of me getting to play are poor. My appearance in the first game was a fluke."

"A fluke that nearly led to a touchdown."

"Yeah, but a fluke nonetheless. I'm not exactly a valuable player when I'm in top form, and I'm nowhere near top form."

Banshee looked concerned again. I knew I'd said the wrong thing.

"I'm okay. I'm not much weaker than I was, but I can't exactly go up against a linebacker who weighs 220 now can I?"

"It's not something I'd want to do."

"I had my time on the field. Now, I just enjoy being with the guys, plus I get one of the best views of the games. I'm close to the action."

"Maybe I should have volunteered for water boy. I would've had a good vantage point from there too."

"Ha! I know what vantage point you want. You want to hang out in the locker room and check out naked jocks."

"Oh yeah!"

I laughed.

"You really should have put in for towel boy. He's the one who gets an eyeful."

"Yeah?"

"Yeah. We pass by him twice every day—naked: Once, on the way to the showers, and then again to pick up a towel. He has a good view coming *and* going, and when he hands out towels he has a close-up view of *everything*."

"Does he check you out?"

"Yeah," I said and laughed.

"You should hook up with him."

"I'm not real comfortable with the whole hooking up thing."

Banshee gave me a look that reminded me I'd hooked up with Cody.

"That just... happened, and he started it!"

"You sound like a grade school boy trying to talk his way out of getting in trouble for fighting."

"Well, I didn't know it was going to happen and when it started happening I couldn't stop myself."

Banshee coughed "slut" into his fist.

"I'm just kidding, but you can't tell me you don't think about hooking up with you-know-who again," Banshee said.

"Okay, I think about it, but I don't know if it's right."

"It felt right the first time didn't it?"

"Well, yeah."

"So?"

"Well... you know I'm religious."

"We covered that. What is it with you church-goers? Is everything a sin?"

"Not everything."

"Only stuff that's fun, then?"

I was getting slightly annoyed.

"Okay. I'm sorry. I'm not making fun of your religion. Well, I guess I am making fun of it, but I respect your beliefs, even though I don't agree with some of them. I'm just saying we're talking about something that is perfectly natural. We were created to do it."

"You make it sound like we were made solely to have sex."

"No, but it's a part of what we are. If it wasn't, there wouldn't be any of us. I just think that a lot of churches make a big stink about something that isn't wrong to begin with."

I was silent for several moments because I was coming to the same conclusion and I wasn't sure I wanted to admit it.

"Ha! Ha! You agree with me! I can read it on your face."

I jerked my head up. My surprised expression was clear to read.

"Yeah, I'm right. You think it's all bullshit too."

"I do feel that my church has gotten way off track. We should be focusing on being kind to others and helping those who need help the most, but lately all the pastor does is attack gays. He's obsessed."

"So..."

"That doesn't mean it's okay for me to hook up with every guy in sight."

"When did I suggest you do that?"

"I guess you didn't."

"I'm just saying that you shouldn't feel guilty about doing a little exploring. Who is it going to hurt?"

"There are consequences to every action."

"Yeah, and most likely the consequences of hooking up with some guy who is interested in you would be positive."

"You're like a little devil sitting on my shoulder, tempting me."

"I'm just here to make sure you have fun. Oh! Speaking of fun, I have been authorized to invite you to a wiener-roast, hayride, and scary story telling session tomorrow night."

"Wiener roast? Sounds painful."

"You have a dirty mind for a guy who goes to church every Sunday."

"Where? Who will be there?"

"It's at the Selby farm, and most of the gay boys of Verona will be there, including a rather hunky football player who is coming home from IU to visit his boyfriend."

"I don't know…"

"It will be fun."

"I don't know if my parents will let me go. Everyone knows about those boys on the Selby farm…"

"You make it sound like an orgy. It's a wiener-roast. It's not like one of your football parties where everyone hooks up and drinks until they puke."

"My parents don't know about me and I don't want them to know. They will wonder why I want to go and I know they won't let me go."

"So don't tell them where you are going. Tell them you will be hanging out with some of the football players and that there will be no drinking."

"You want me to lie?"

"How is that a lie? Brendan, Shawn, and Tim will all be there. They're football players, and there will be no alcohol, believe me. Ethan's uncle would not allow it.

"Come on. You can meet the guys. I think it will make you feel better about yourself. If you spend time with them you'll see that they're just ordinary guys who happen to be attracted to guys instead of girls. I'm willing to bet they're a whole lot nicer than most of your football buddies."

"I guess it wouldn't hurt."

"It's a date then."

My time was soon up, but I went back to work in a great mood. Banshee waved as he departed. I couldn't wait until I could see him again. I was a little nervous about the wiener-roast, but I looked forward to it as well. I was glad I had Banshee to push me into doing things I would otherwise have been reluctant to try. At last, I was going to meet the gay boys of Verona.

Chapter Eleven

I gazed at the stained-glass window behind the pulpit as I sat with my parents in our usual pew. There was Jesus, with arms outspread as if drawing all those near to be embraced with love and kindness. That's the feeling church had given me when I was a boy. I felt as if I was being embraced with love and kindness. Then, Pastor Walker arrived and began preaching hate. His words made me hate what I was. His words made me hate myself. Then, I began to question his words, my faith, and the goodwill of God. I'd come perilously close to turning my back on my religion and on God, but then Jesus had rebuked the pastor and reminded me of what church was all about. I looked at the stained-glass Jesus standing silent. I thought about the Jesus I knew. I truly wondered if Jesus had come to walk among us again as he had done so very long ago. I guess it didn't really matter, because the boy who had walked into our church these past Sundays had restored my faith. I would not make the mistake of throwing out the baby with the bathwater.

I braced myself as Pastor Walker stepped up to the pulpit after the congregation sang a hymn. He would no doubt unleash yet another diatribe against homosexuals. I found it hard not to hate him for the harm he had done to me. He had not attacked me personally, but every word he said against homosexuals was a blow to my self-worth. Who knows what I would have done if Jesus had not come to speak out for me and all others like me? I wondered if he would return yet again today.

"It has come to my attention that a valued member of our congregation needs our prayers," Pastor Walker began. He glanced at me and I grew fearful. Had he found out about me? Was he going to denounce me and ask the congregation to pray for my soul? "Young Elijah Gaylord has been stricken with a serious illness. He has brain cancer."

Murmuring went through the pews. Many looked in my direction even as they tried not to let on they were looking. I was uncomfortable, but I was not under attack as I had suspected.

"The doctors have little hope for his condition. His only hope is prayer. It is time for all of us to gather together in his time of need and pray that the tumor that threatens his life will disappear."

I was stunned as Pastor Walker actually said a prayer for me. I had come to think of him as... not quite evil... but not a good person in the least. I was reminded that no one was all bad or good. Pastor Walker had said such hateful things, but I believed he genuinely hoped that I would recover.

Mom squeezed my hand. There were tears in her eyes. I knew she hoped the prayers would work, but I didn't believe they would. It's not that I didn't have faith, but I knew people died of cancer every day. Why should I be any different? I figured it was my time to go and cancer was the way it was going to happen.

"It is a true shame that good, Christian, young men like Elijah are struck with cancer while those who are far less deserving prosper. You might ask how God can allow one of our own to be stricken with disease while Godless homosexuals spread sin among us and live lives of depravity. You might even begin to question God's motives, but do not do so. God places stumbling blocks in our path so that we might overcome them and be stronger.

"Homosexuals are a test for all good Christians. They are a perversion, but they are more insidious than that. They infiltrate society and tempt our youth with their world of easy sex and drugs. They are the stumbling block of our time. We must rise above them and extend our hand to help the weak who might otherwise succumb to the temptations they offer. We must also be ever ready to reach out to the fallen and help them save themselves before it is too late. Homosexuals are the scourges of humanity. We must fight against them with every weapon at our disposal. We must save those who can be saved and wipe the rest from the face of the Earth."

I knew Pastor Walker would get around to gay bashing. I didn't like that he used my cancer as a springboard for his latest attack.

"As you are all no doubt aware, I have been criticized of late for my sermons against the evils of homosexuality. I am not alone in recognizing this more heinous threat. There is evidence of resisting this evil everywhere. You need only turn to your Sunday paper to see it for yourself. Just this morning an article has appeared proving this in no uncertain terms. In the past, Chicken Fillets, a family-owned national chain, has donated over 2 million dollars to groups who fight the insidious homosexual agenda. Many have denounced these donations to good Christian groups, but today Cathy Daniels, the president of Chicken Fillets, and a woman I might add, has stated that Chicken Fillets is highly supportive of the family and believes in the Biblical definition of family. God created Adam and Eve, not Adam and Steve. Cathy Daniels makes no apologies for the Christian beliefs of her company. She states that she is "guilty as charged" for donations to Christian groups and that her company is determined to stay the course and continue on this path no matter how powerful the opposition. Here we have a major company, with franchisees in cities all across the U.S. including our own Verona, that is standing up for good wholesome Christian values in the face of unwarranted criticism. I am happy to announce that our own church has just received a sizable donation from Chicken Fillets to continue our good work against the homosexuals. Mrs. Daniels herself called me only a few days ago and told me she had heard about my sermons and the wonderful song a child sang for us to lead the way. God be praised."

I felt sick to my stomach. I worked for a company that did that? No more. I would not wear that ridiculous winged cap another day. I would play no part in such a horrible campaign of hate.

"Mrs. Daniels expects to be attacked by the homosexuals for her stance, and we must be ready to stand behind her. Mark my words, the homosexuals will attack, and when they do we shall be ready to join the battle on the side of the righteous.

"The homosexual threat is very real. Even large companies realize this fact. Companies such as Chicken Fillets are often accused of greed and caring only about profit, but as you can see it is not so. Some stand for good Christian values. We must all fight against the homosexuals. I know this sounds harsh, but it is not so. It is for us to hate the sin, but love the sinner."

"The key word in your statement is hate."

The entire congregation turned at the sound of the now familiar, young, male voice. Jesus stood in the aisle calmly gazing at Pastor Walker.

"There is no love in your words. You speak of millions spent to bring harm to others. Where is the Christian charity in that? Children go hungry, the sick without care, and many wander the streets homeless, and you stand there and applaud pouring out gold not to help those who need it, but to hurl hatred at those who have done you no harm."

Pastor Walker trembled with rage.

"I will tolerate your presence no longer!" screamed the pastor. "I..."

Pastor Walker fell silent. The congregation gasped. The pastor's lips moved, indeed it was evident he was shouting, but no words came out.

"You were correct in one thing," Jesus said. "One of the purposes of gays is to act as a stumbling block for the church. Gays are indeed the rock on which the church will break if it does not halt its prejudice and discrimination. Any interpretation of scripture that harms or oppresses people cannot be the right interpretation. Where there is suffering, conscience calls upon us to alleviate it. Suffering surrounds us and yet how many good Christians raise their hand to make things better for their fellow man?"

Jesus stared straight at Pastor Walker who held his hands at his throat in fear.

"I say to you now Pastor Walker, repent before it is too late."

The windows darkened and thunder rumbled outside. Many looked about in fear.

"Remove him!" screamed Pastor Walker, regaining his voice at last. He immediately fell silent. When I turned to look at Jesus again he was gone.

"We must guard against further intrusions," Pastor Walker said, clearly shaken. "I wish to meet with the deacons immediately after the services so that we may look to our own security. This... this lunatic cannot be allowed admittance to the church again."

Most of the parishioners looked at each other in doubt. I wasn't one of them. I looked at the darkness outside the windows. This latest confrontation erased any doubts that lingered in my mind. Jesus went to my high school.

***

A black Cutlass Supreme pulled up in front of the house. The passenger door opened and Banshee stepped out. I hurried down the front walk to the car. Tim and Dane were in the backseat and Tristan was scooted up against Shawn, who was driving. I didn't know any of them well, but I knew who they were.

"You can have the front. I'll sit in the back," Banshee said and hopped into the backseat before I could answer.

I dropped in beside Tristan.

"In case you don't know everyone, this is my boyfriend Tristan and the blond in the back attached to my brother's face is Dane," Shawn said as he put the car into gear and pulled out.

"Hi," Tristan said and shook my hand. Dane waved without taking his lips away from Tim's.

I looked back at Banshee. My apprehension was clear to read in my eyes.

"It's okay," he mouthed.

"Hi," I said to Tristan. "Thanks for giving me a ride."

I had never been so near so many gay boys at once. I don't know that I could have handled it even a few short weeks before, but I reminded myself that I was a gay boy too, and there was nothing to fear.

Tim and Dane made out in the back. Shawn and Tristan carried on a conversation about Jazz music of all things. Banshee scooted up so he could talk to me more easily.

"You'll love the farm. It's peaceful and beautiful. I've been out there before in the evening. There are all these crickets and frogs singing. You can hear them in the distance. Sometimes owls hoot and there are also whip-poor-wills and Bob Whites. I love the wood smoke. It smells so good."

"Banshee is a regular nature boy," Shawn said.

"Hey, I'd never been to the country before you guys took me to the farm," Banshee said.

"It's only a couple of miles out of town," Shawn said.

"Yeah, but it's still a different world. How about you Elijah? Have you been in the country before?"

"I used to go running out past the Selby farm. I guess that counts."

"Eh. You can't see anything running," Banshee said. "You jocks don't know how to live."

"Watch it," Shawn said.

"If it makes you angry you can spank me," Banshee said.

"Watch it," Tristan said.

Banshee laughed. I could see where this group had a lot of fun.

It took little time to reach the Selby farm. There were a few cars parked out in front of the farmhouse. I could see a bonfire out toward a large barn. Banshee took my hand when we got out and pulled me toward the fire. I could hear the frogs croaking in the distance and insects as well. The insects didn't sound like crickets to me. They sounded more like weird aliens that would sneak up and suck my brains out. I was just a little afraid, but I tried not to let it show.

Standing by the fire was a tall, muscular young man with light brown hair that I immediately recognized. I'd watched him play football at VHS in previous years. He was Brendan Brewer who now played for IU. He was a legend in VHS football. He noticed me gawking at him, walked to me, and extended his hand.

"You're Mitch's little brother, aren't you?"

"Uh, yeah," I said.

"You should come down and catch a game. I wouldn't be surprised if both your brothers got some game time soon. I heard about that play you made. Your brothers were so excited they told the entire team."

"They did?"

"Yeah. They said you'd never played football before and they didn't even know you were interested."

"Well, I, uh, tried out for the team just to see if I could make it. I never dreamed I'd actually be on the team or get to play."

"Well, I'm impressed. You've got guts and talent."

"Thanks!"

Brendan turned his attention back to Casper, his boyfriend. Casper was my size. He was much smaller than Brendan, but from the way Brendan looked at him I knew size had nothing to do with how he felt about him.

I was in a daze. I sat down on a bale of straw near the fire.

"Are you okay?" Banshee asked.

"I can't believe Brendan Brewer said I impressed him and I can't believe my brothers have been telling the entire IU football team about my almost-touchdown."

"Believe it."

Banshee smiled at me. He took me by the hand and pulled me to my feet. He introduced me to Ethan, Nathan, and Nathan's little brother, Dave. I remembered watching Ethan wrestle when I was in middle school. I'd thought he was about the hottest guy ever in his wrestling singlet. If anything, he was even hotter now. Next, I met Scotty Jackson, who I recognized from school and his performance in *Willy Wonka and the Chocolate Factory* the previous fall.

Shawn introduced us to members of the gang that even Banshee hadn't met yet—Brandon, Jon, Marc, and Dorian. Brendan wasn't the only one visiting from college. I didn't know it, but I'd been invited to a reunion of sorts. Half of those present were in their first or second year of college and most seemed to go to IU down in Bloomington.

I didn't know most of the guys, which made sense because I was a freshman this year and many of them had graduated the year before. I did recognize Dorian. I'd seen him in both *The Picture of Dorian Gray* and *Willy Wonka*.

Dorian struck me as very feminine. I'm not being judgmental. It's just an observation. He was really too pretty to be a boy and he sounded a little like a girl. He was with Marc, a handsome skater-boy type. They made an odd couple, but then perhaps not so odd as Brendan and Casper or Ethan and Nathan. Maybe there was something to the idea of opposites attract. I mentioned as much to Banshee.

"Now, Brandon and Jon *look* like they should be a couple," I said. "I can see why they date."

Tristan overheard me and laughed. He leaned in and whispered.

"They aren't a couple. They aren't even gay."

"Really?" I asked. "I could have sworn they were."

Tristan laughed even louder, but wouldn't tell anyone what he was laughing about. I was relieved. Both Brandon and Jon were built, and either could have kicked my butt with ease.

Evening was fast approaching when we arrived and now the stars were appearing one by one above us. There were no streetlights here and the stars were soon clearly visible even though it was not yet dark. In only a few minutes more the last orange glow of the sun disappeared in the west and darkness reigned. The night noises grew ever louder and I drew closer to the fire.

"Are you okay?" asked Banshee.

"I don't like that sound from the woods. It's creepy. It sounds like aliens."

"Those are cicadas," Banshee said. "They're flying insects about the size of your thumb. I promise they aren't aliens."

Ethan handed out long pointed sticks. We impaled hot dogs on them and held them near the fire. I'd never roasted wieners before, so I watched the others to see how it was done. When the breeze changed direction I sometimes got wood smoke in my eyes, but I loved the scent of it. I loved the popping and cracking of the burning logs and the red hot glow of the embers. The warmth felt good since there was a chill was in the air.

The faces of the young men around me were lit solely by the flames. Everyone looked wild and mysterious. I was pleased that I had the chance to experience this... and to think I almost hadn't come!

It wasn't so much roasting wieners that was enjoyable as it was the whole campfire atmosphere. I had never before sat around a campfire. I'd had never known the joy of warmth from a fire on a chilly night. At home when it got cold we just turned up the thermostat, and it was not at all the same. I loved the light of the flames and the way they danced and moved. It was as if the flames were themselves alive.

"I feel almost as if I'm in the past," I said. "I bet the Indians sat around campfires like this. Do you think there were Native Americans on this farm?"

"I know for a fact they were here. There was a village down the hill and a little to the west, where our furthest cornfields now lay," Ethan said. "My great, great grandfather knew Native

Americans personally. Some of my ancestors are Native Americans."

"That's really cool," I said.

"There are a lot of Native American legends, some of which took place right here on this farm," Jon said.

"No. I don't want to hear scarecrow stories!" Dorian said.

"Don't even think about it!" Marc said.

I remembered then the big scare last year around Halloween when people saw scarecrows walking around. Some boys had been murdered and Dorian had gone missing. There had been a massive search to find him. I'd nearly forgotten, although I don't see how.

"Would *I* do that to you?" Jon asked.

"Yes!" called out nearly everyone.

Jon put his hand on his chest to express his innocence. He sure didn't look innocent, although he was very handsome with his black hair, dark eyes, and finely arched eyebrows.

"I was thinking of another legend. One I've never told you about. The legend of the changeling."

Dorian was sitting with Marc on the next bale of straw. He drew in close to him and Marc put his arm around him. Dorian's fear was contagious. I moved just a little closer to Banshee while trying to keep it from looking as if I was doing so.

"The changeling lived in these woods," Jon began. "Before Ethan's ancestors arrived this entire area was a forest. Two hundred years ago only the Native Americans lived on what was one day to be the Selby Farm, but they were not the first inhabitants of this place. The changeling watched the first Native Americans arrive in these woods centuries ago. The changeling was older than the trees, older that most of the hills. The changeling had been here so long I don't know if it even remembered its history. It was a creature left over from some forgotten age. Perhaps it had existed from the very beginning. No one knows, but it watched the Native Americans arrive and later still observed the first settlers to come upon this land.

"The changeling was not violent at first. It was curious about the strange people who had entered its lands. It watched them build homes out of small saplings and the bark from trees. It often disguised itself as a tree, a rock, or even grass, for it could become anything it wished with ease. It listened to the villagers as they talked around their campfires. In this way it learned their language and their customs. The changeling did not like that the Native Americans killed the bison and the deer, but it saw them giving thanks to the animals they killed. It learned their belief that those animals would come upon the Earth to live and be hunted again. For these reasons the changeling did not interfere and allowed the Native Americans to live in peace.

"Soon, the changeling walked among the people, for it could make itself one of them if it chose. It could make itself young or old, male or female. It could take any form and do it so well it could fool a person's brother, mother, or child. Sometimes it appeared as a member of a distant clan and lived among the villagers for weeks on end. The changeling adopted the people as its own, for it had been lonely.

"Then, a horrible tragedy befell a young mother of the tribe. Her two-year-old took sick and died from one of the many diseases to be found in those times. The changeling discovered the death before any of the tribe and secretly buried the body and took the place of the dead child to spare its mother the terrible grief it had seen too many times before.

"This act of kindness was rewarded, for as the changeling pretended to grow to adolescence and beyond, it had a family for the first time, or at least the first time it could remember.

"The changeling did not age, but those around it did. It was saddened when its newfound family members died over the years. It too pretended to age and then one day disappeared. It was assumed by the tribe that the old man had gone away to die alone.

"The changeling had not actually gone. It came back and watched over the village. When tragedy struck again, as it did all too often in that long ago time, the changeling again took the form of one who had died. It assumed the place of twelve-year-old boy who had been killed when he fell from the uppermost branches of a tree. The boy's parents never learned of his death because the changeling became him. The changeling repeated this scene countless times. The years and then centuries wore on, and the changeling was always here.

"Then, different men, pale men, some with hair the color of corn silk, came, and soon there was violence like never before.

The pale men took what they wanted, including the land which all villagers knew could not be owned by anyone. The changeling protected the village by assuming the form of strange and monstrous beasts to scare away the invaders, but there were too many of them.

"The invaders attacked the village slaughtering many, including the adopted family of the changeling. The changeling also pretended to die, and when the villagers went west in search of less hostile neighbors it remained behind with but one thought on its mind—revenge.

"A strange plague struck the settlers of the area or at least the settlers thought it a plague, but they were wrong. It was no sickness that took life after life, but the changeling who slipped in cabins undetected and silently killed those it found there.

"No matter how many lives the changeling took, it was not enough to erase its grief or assuage its anger, so its attacks became more gruesome. No longer did the settlers believe sickness carried their loved ones away for the evidence was clear. Some victims were stabbed, some hacked, and some crushed. Memory turned to the monstrous creatures that had been sighted before the Native peoples were slaughtered or driven out. Many feared that one or more of these creatures had remained or returned, and soon all doors were barred at night.

"There was no stopping the changeling. It could enter a cabin in the form of a brother or sister, the family dog, or even something so small as a fly. No matter how firmly the door was barricaded, the changeling could enter if it desired and it forever craved revenge.

"The changeling went on undiscovered for some time until it made an error. It was perhaps inevitable that it slip up eventually in all its long years and at last it did so. The changeling entered the cabin in the guise of a family friend and once inside slaughtered all it found there with the ax that rested by hearth, or so it thought. There was one survivor. A boy who was awakened by the commotion had the good sense to lie quiet, out of sight and out of mind. His bright eyes witnessed the horrible murder of his family, and witnessed something else too; the changeling altering its form from that of the family friend to its natural state, invisibility. The boy thought his imagination had run wild, but then he saw the door open and shut, seemingly on its own. He knew that whatever had appeared as the family friend was something far different, something that could assume other shapes and then make itself invisible.

"At first no one believed the boy, but as the attacks continued and no other explanation sufficed, the settlers came to first believe in and then fear the changeling. That's what they called it for they finally realized what it could do. They developed elaborate schemes to make certain of the identity of those entering their homes. Even family members would be asked questions that they and no other could answer. The settlers became paranoid and lived their lives in fear.

"It was at this time that the killings lessened in number and finally slowed so that only one or two deaths a year occurred. Many thought it was due to the precautions taken, but others believed that the changeling was satisfied for the moment because those who had driven out the Native Americans had made themselves prisoners. Still others believed that all those who had killed the villagers had been killed themselves, and the changeling's revenge was at an end. None of the reasons quite sufficed, for down through the years there have been many strange and unexplained deaths. There have been murders, unexplainable and some even seemingly impossible, and yet they occurred. Decades upon decades have passed, but many believe the changeling is still here.

"The most recent unexplained murder took place right where we're sitting. It was some decades ago, in the 1930s I believe. A group of teens was sitting around a campfire roasting hot dogs, just as we are now. They were sitting on bales of straw when one of them felt something strange. Bizarre and impossible as it seemed, the boy felt a hand coming out of the bale of straw itself. Before he had time to shout a warning, before he even had a chance to scream, it reached out and GRABBED HIM!!"

I let out a blood-curdling scream and jumped to my feet. Right as Jon said "GRABBED HIM!", a hand grabbed my butt. Banshee screamed and jumped to his feet too and I knew he'd also been grabbed. Most of those around the circle looked like they'd nearly wet their pants, mostly likely because our scream had taken them by surprise. Jon and Brandon were the only ones who didn't scream. They were far too busy laughing their butts off. While Jon kept our attention, Brandon had slipped away, approached us from behind in the darkness, and grabbed us when it would most terrify us.

"I hate you guys!" I said, but Brandon and Jon only laughed louder.

My heart pounded in my chest and my breath came hard and fast as if I'd been running. Slowly, my heart and breath returned to normal.

"Sorry, Elijah and Banshee. Jon and Brandon are always looking for new victims. We should have warned you," said Shawn.

"Think of it as an initiation," Ethan said.

"That would've been really funny if you'd done it to someone else!" I grinned.

"You never know when the changeling will strike," Jon said. "Sometimes, on early autumn nights, it even takes the form of a vicious killer chicken."

Some of the guys laughed again, but I didn't get.

"You're just a regular comedian, aren't you Jon?" Dorian asked.

Jon flapped his arms like a chicken.

"Please, don't do anything to remind me of a chicken," I said.

"Oh yeah, you work at Chicken Fillets don't you?" Nathan said.

"I worked there. Technically I still do. I haven't quit yet, but after what I heard today I'm out of there."

The guys looked confused so I explained the massive donations to anti-gay groups.

"I refuse to be a part of that," I said. "I was already getting sick of all the chicken phrases."

"I'll never eat there again. Chicken Fillets can keep its greasy-ass chicken," Brandon said. "I think it's time to spread the word. Boycott Chicken Fillets!"

"Some might argue that Chicken Fillets has the right to do whatever it wants with its money," Tristan said.

"Oh, they have every right to donate to whatever slimy group they wish, even the Neo-Nazis and the KKK, and I have every right never to eat there again and to try to convince others not to eat there either," Brandon said.

"If you're finished with your political activism, I have marshmallows!" Ethan said.

Jon popped one into his mouth.

"Tastes like chicken," he said.

"You're an idiot Jon. You really are. Tastes like chicken my ass," Brandon said.

"Hmm, who knows your ass tastes like chicken? Oh wait, you date those skanky girls no one else will touch," Jon said.

"I date hot girls and I don't have to pay by the hour!"

"Girls? When they're over sixty they aren't girls anymore."

"Oh, that reminds me. Your mom says, "hi"," Brandon said.

"We used to listen to this sort of thing every day at lunch," Tristan told Banshee. "Be thankful you missed it."

"Ha! We were the best thing about VHS! Weren't we Jon?"

"We sure were. God knows the place had nothing else going for it," Jon said, putting his arm around Brandon's shoulder.

"This is the point where they start making out," Shawn said.

"You wish!" Brandon said.

I impaled a few marshmallows on my stick and held it over the fire. Brandon and Jon had managed to get my mind off Jon's scary story. When Brandon grabbed me from behind, or perhaps I should say grabbed my behind, I thought the changeling had got me.

I noticed Tim and Dane weren't talking much. They were roasting wieners and marshmallows like everyone else, but they spent every spare moment making out. Casper noticed me watching them and I felt like a voyeur.

"Do they do that all the time?" I asked.

"*All* the time," Casper said.

Tim overheard us. He pulled his lips from Dane's for a moment and grinned at us.

"We do take time out to breathe occasionally," he said and then went back to making out with his boyfriend.

The sight excited me. Tim was seriously hot and Dane was sexy as he could be with his curly blond hair and ice-blue eyes. I was glad I was sitting down or my excitement would have been obvious. I was afraid of what Brandon and Jon would've said had they noticed. I had the feeling they'd gleefully tease and torment me.

I thought back to what had happened with Cody. I wanted to do that again. I felt a little guilty for that, but then why should I? What was wrong with it? Seriously? I was beginning to suspect that many of the sins listed in the Bible weren't sins at all. I didn't remember anything about what Cody and I had done being mentioned anywhere in the Bible. Even if it was, what would that mean? The Bible also said that eating pork was forbidden, but our church sold pork chop dinners to raise money only last summer. The Bible said planting two crops in one field was forbidden. Did that mean everyone who had a garden was going to Hell? I was fast learning that I needed to think for myself when deciding what was right and wrong.

Banshee and I didn't talk a lot. We were too busy listening to the older guys talk about college. It sounded like a dream world of parties and football games and freedom. I almost laughed at myself. All the drinking that went on at the parties would probably scandalize me. Still, I couldn't wait until...

I suddenly felt as if I might cry. For a while I'd forgotten I was sick. I'd forgotten I wouldn't live to finish my freshman year of high school. I'd never go to college. I'd never get to experience any of that world or a great many other things.

I took a deep breath. I drew in the scent of the wood smoke. I tasted my perfectly toasted marshmallow. I listened to the voices of the boys chatting around me and gazed upon their handsome faces. I looked up to the stars shining overhead. There were a lot of things I would never get to experience, but I wasn't going to allow myself to throw away what I had here and now. I couldn't stop what was going to happen, but I could hold onto the present and get everything I could out of it. Tomorrow was uncertain, but I had tonight. I had this bonfire and all these new friends. I wasn't going to waste the time I had with regrets. I was going to enjoy each precious moment.

Banshee looked at me and smiled. I reached over and took his hand. I wouldn't have been so bold anywhere else, but here I knew it was okay. I looked around at the boys who surrounded me. All of them, except for Brandon, Jon, and Dave were the spawn of Satan according to Pastor Walker. What I saw was a group of guys who cared about each other, even loved each other. There was far more Christianity here than there was in my church.

As the night grew chiller, Banshee and I drew closer together. He'd become a good friend in a very short time. I was fast coming to think of all these guys as my friends, even though I barely knew most of them. They were so open, accepting, and kind. I noticed also that none of them mentioned my cancer. I was quite sure they knew, but they didn't bring it up. I appreciated that. I didn't want to be thought of as the boy with cancer. I just wanted to be Elijah while I could.

Shawn and Tristan sat close together, sometimes leaning over and touching their heads together. Brendan had his arm around Casper. Ethan and Nathan sat so close they were touching. Marc and Dorian grinned at each other. Tim and Dane were joined at the lips. All of the gay boys of Verona had such wonderful relationships.

A new wave of sadness hit me, one I could not easily push to the side. I didn't want anyone to notice, so I put my stick to the side and walked slowly over toward a wooden fence. I stood there and looked up at the stars while I cried silent tears.

I felt a hand on my shoulder. I looked to my side, although I already knew it was Banshee. He drew in close and wrapped one arm around my waist. I wiped my tears away, but they were still coming.

"What's wrong?"

"I'm just having a little pity party for myself. I was looking around at all the happy couples and realized I'd never have a boyfriend."

"Maybe you will."

"Who would want to date a guy who'll be dead in four months—or less? No one will want to set themselves up for that sort of pain. Even being my friend is costly." I turned my head and looked up at Banshee. "Thanks for being my friend. I know it's going to cost you a lot. It's already costing you."

"The cost may be great, but you're still a bargain. I know what I'm letting myself in for and I also know that being with you is worth it. I wouldn't give up on the boyfriend either. I'd apply for the position myself only... I think we make better friends."

Banshee squeezed me even closer. I turned toward him. He hugged me close, leaned down, and kissed me on the lips. We stood there just holding each other for a while, then Banshee took my hand and led me back to the fire. No one mentioned my red eyes. The only acknowledgement was Tristan smiling at me sadly. I felt so safe in this place. Part of me wish I could stay here forever.

I saw Brendan walking toward the farmhouse to grab another bag of marshmallows. I told Banshee I'd be right back and followed him. I waited until he went inside then came back out before I approached.

"Could we talk?" I asked.

"Sure."

Instead of heading back toward the campfire, Brendan led me to a fence that overlooked a garden. The moon was shining bright and cast a blue hue over the flowers and vegetables.

"My brothers don't know about me yet, about my cancer I mean."

"And you want me to keep it a secret?"

"Yeah. I don't want word getting back to them. They'll have to know sometime, but Mom and Dad and I talked about it and we don't want to tell them until we have to. It's going to be hard on them. I don't want to ruin things for them, you know?"

Brendan nodded.

"Just don't wait until it's too late. I'm sure there are things you want to tell them and things they'll want to say to you too."

"Yeah. I know. They'll be home from school for a visit soon enough or we'll go down and visit them. I just want to give them a little longer without knowing."

"You are unusually thoughtful of others. Thomas and Mitch are lucky to have such a great little brother."

"I'm lucky to have such wonderful big brothers. They've always been good to me, even though I'm the runt of the litter."

"If you heard them talk about you I bet you wouldn't feel like the runt of the litter. I talked earlier about them telling all the guys about what you did in the game, but they talk about you often. They talk about how smart you are and how you don't let anything stand in your way when there's something you want to accomplish. They are extremely impressed with you making the team."

"Yeah, Mitch told me that on the phone."

"They're very proud of you and I don't blame them. I'd be proud to have a little brother like you too. I never had a brother. These guys are the closest I'll get," Brendan said, nodding toward the young men sitting around the campfire.

I smiled, but then my smile faded.

"I'm not looking forward to telling them, although I figure my dad will do the actual telling."

"They're strong. It won't be easy, but they can take it. They are a lot like you, after all."

"Thanks."

"How are you doing?"

"I'm okay. Knowing I'm going to die isn't so bad really. We're all going to die. I'm just going to do it sooner than I expected and *I know* it's coming soon. Most people don't know how much time they have left. I do."

"If you need to talk or just need someone, any of these guys will be here for you," Brendan said, indicating his friends again. "Of course, I think you have a very good buddy in Banshee. It's obvious he cares a lot about you. Are you two a couple?"

I shook my head. I wondered what tipped Brendan off. He knew I was gay, or was at least pretty sure. I guess it didn't matter. I was gay and I wasn't ashamed of it. I was as God meant me to be.

"We're just good friends. I don't have a boyfriend."

"A good friend can be worth just as much as a boyfriend. In Casper I have both. I'm very lucky."

"I guess I'm very lucky too. I don't know what I'd do without Banshee."

"I'll let the guys know not to tell your brothers about your condition. Several of us go to IU, you know."

"Yeah. They'll have to be told soon. I hope my parents and I are doing the right thing."

"I think you are. If I had a brother, I think I'd rather not know until I had to know."

"That's kind of what I thought."

Brendan gazed at me.

"I wish there was something I could say or do to make things better for you."

"Thanks, but I don't actually believe death is an end. I think I'll still exist. I'll still be me. I just won't be here. That's the tough part, knowing I won't be with my brothers and Banshee. I also believe I will be with them again, but it will be a long wait."

"Yeah. I'm not religious, but I don't believe anyone or anything stops existing. I think we go on. Our bodies are just... transportation. Our bodies will die, but our spirit or soul or whatever won't cease to exist."

"Think I should freak out Brandon and Jon by telling them I'll be watching them in the showers after I die? It would serve them right for scaring the crap out of me."

"That's a good plan, except I don't think they care who stares. Now, if you threatened to hover around and scare off girls... that would frighten them."

I laughed.

"Thanks, Brendan."

"You're welcome. I meant what I said. I'm here for you if you need me, and the same is true of any of these guys. We help each other out. You're one of us. We'll be there for you when you need us."

Brendan's last words were so touching they almost made me cry, but I managed to control myself.

"Come on, let's get back to the wiener roast. I think I need another marshmallow," I said.

Brendan put his hand on my shoulder and led me back to the campfire. I resumed snuggling with Banshee because it was even chillier than before.

I sat there with the guys, listening to them talk and laugh and insult each other. Part of me wished I could join the homo table and be with those who still went to VHS. If I sat at the homo table I'd be instantly marked as gay, but that's not what held me back. I couldn't sit with these guys unless I gave up sitting at the football table and I'd worked far too hard for the right to sit there to give it up. It was just too bad I couldn't sit in two places at once.

I had to be back home by 11 p.m. I didn't want to leave, but I was getting really tired anyway. Jon was beginning a tale about the werewolves of Verona, so it was probably a good time to get out of there anyway. His stories scared me!

Nathan drove us home in an old Ford pickup from the 1950s. It was so cool riding in that old truck. He dropped me off first and I made it inside just a little before 11. Mom was waiting up on me. She looked worried so I pretended not to be as tired as I felt. I went straight up to my room and got ready for bed.

I could smell the wood smoke in my clothes as I undressed. It was a pleasant reminder of my evening with the guys. I wished I could hang out with them more often, but I didn't like lying to cover up my tracks. I hadn't exactly lied, but I hadn't told the whole truth either. I didn't like telling even a partial lie. It felt like a betrayal of trust.

Even if my parents knew I was gay and were okay with it, I couldn't have spent time with most of those guys because they were college boys. Casper said this was the first time they all came home at the same time. I had witnessed a reunion of the old gang. Still, those who were still at VHS were guys I wished I had a chance to know better. If only I had more time…

As I slid between the sheets, I wondered if I should tell my parents I was gay. I had not wanted to tell them before, but having to lie, even partially, made it seem as if being gay was wrong. I had reached the conclusion that not only was it no sin to be gay, but it was the way God intended me to be. Wasn't it therefore wrong to hide the truth?

I wanted to know if my family would still love and accept me if they knew about me. I didn't think my parents would toss me out, but I wasn't sure how they would react. I had wonderful, loving parents, but I wondered how much their minds had been poisoned by the teachings of our church. Their reaction to Pastor Walker's recent diatribes gave me hope, but could they make the jump from thinking of homosexuality as a sin to embracing it as God's will? I'd made that leap, but it had not been easy. I could feel in my soul that I was exactly as God intended me to be, but it was still hard to undo the damage wrought by my church. How much more difficult would it be for my parents and my brothers?

Maybe I was being selfish with my need to know. My parents already had enough sorrow. They didn't need a moral dilemma dumped on them too. Thomas and Mitch would soon know I was dying. How could I add to the pile of their troubles just to satisfy my need to know?

I was too sleepy to ponder it further. Even staying up for hours wouldn't have helped me make a decision. I let the dilemma flow from my mind. I slowly drifted off with the scent of wood smoke in my nostrils and images of the campfire and my new friends in my mind.

Chapter Twelve

I longingly gazed toward the homo table as I stepped out of the lunch line. Banshee was laughing. Tim had his arm around Dane's shoulder. The rest were talking and smiling. I smiled as I headed for the football table. As much as I wanted to join Banshee and the others, I just couldn't give up what I'd worked so hard to gain. I'd truly miss Lucas, Cody, and the others too. They had become my friends.

"Tough night?" Cody asked as I sat down.

"No, why do you ask?"

Cody looked uncomfortable, but then I remembered the pale face that had looked back at me out of the mirror that morning.

"Oh. I feel better than I look."

Cody still looked uncomfortable.

"Don't worry about it Cody. I never looked that good to begin with." I grinned.

"I wouldn't say that," Lucas said.

"Yeah, you weren't hideously ugly like Lucas," said Cody. "The only way to get girls interested in him is to put a bag over his head."

"Why don't you try putting a bag over your head Cody? Make it a plastic one and seal it up tight," Lucas said.

Cody laughed. Lucas and Cody bickering reminded me of Brandon and Jon going off on each other at the wiener roast.

I wasn't feeling so good. After lunch I took one my aspirin-on-steroids and another capsule my doctor had prescribed for nausea. I felt better, but when P.E rolled around I sat most of it out. We had moved into a unit on soccer. I played for a while but stuck to defense because I was having trouble catching my breath. I had to quit before the end of the period. I walked over to the bleachers fighting back tears. I felt stupid for crying, but I was angry and frustrated. I didn't have much time left and I couldn't even play soccer for more than a few minutes!

I was mad at myself for getting upset. I spent the reminder of P.E. getting my emotions under control so I could pretend nothing was wrong. There was no fooling Banshee. He left the game a little early and came over to sit with me. I noticed Mr. Wells said nothing to Banshee about leaving the field. He knew we were friends.

"I guess you football players don't care much for soccer."

"I like it. I'm just especially tired today."

"Maybe it's all that fresh air from last night."

"Yeah, that stuff will kill you."

I grinned. I knew Banshee was worried, but he didn't mention it. I breathed in deeply.

"It smells like autumn."

"Perhaps because it is?"

"The calendar may say it's fall, but the trees are just beginning to turn. I love this time of year. I love the cool nights and warm days and this scent."

"I love winter with all the snow."

"Sicko," I teased.

"There's also Christmas."

"Good point. I love Christmas! I like Halloween almost as well with the jack-o-lanterns, witches, and ghosts."

"How about the ghost stories?"

"Actually, I like reading ghost stories that are supposed to be real."

"Even after Jon's story last night?"

"Yeah. Jon and Brandon are big jerks, but I like them."

"I don't know if I'm looking forward to autumn this year or not. Last year was just a little too scary."

Banshee was talking about the murders. Three high school boys had been killed, and some sicko dressed up their corpses as scarecrows and hid them in cornfields. A lot of people saw scarecrows walking around too. An explanation had never been found for that.

"Yeah, my parents wouldn't allow me to go anywhere after dark. I couldn't even go out during the day unless Mom, Dad, or Mitch went with me. They never caught the murderer, did they?"

"No, but the cops chased him into the old Graymoor Mansion and he never came out again as far as anyone knows. That place is evil. The murderer was as good as dead himself the moment he went in there. He would've been better off in prison."

"It's creepy that he might still be around. Thanks for ruining autumn for me, Banshee."

"You don't have to worry about him. He's as dead as the boys he killed. Trust me. If a tenth of the stories I've heard about the Graymoor Mansion are true, going inside is suicide."

"Would you spend the night inside for a million bucks?" I asked.

"No way! A million bucks is no good when you've been driven insane or killed by evil spirits."

"I'm beginning to think you believe in ghosts."

"Of course I do! We have one in our house."

Mr. Wells blew his whistle. It was time to go in. Banshee and I got up off the bleachers and followed the others back to the gym.

"Do you really have a ghost in your house, or are you just checking to see how gullible I am?"

"We really do have a ghost. His name is Jared and he's fifteen."

"How do you know that?"

"You can feel it when he's near. It's just there. He also looks fifteen."

"So, you've seen him?"

"Oh yeah, everyone in my family has seen him. Quite a few visitors have spotted him too. He's almost always wearing a Union Civil War uniform."

"That's really cool. You're not making this up?"

"I swear to God I am not making it up. Don't you believe in ghosts?"

"Yeah, I do. I don't think I'm supposed to. According to my church, everyone who has died is lying in their graves waiting for judgment day, but then there's also talk about evil spirits, so the stories don't match. A lot of things don't match."

"That's why I don't go to church."

I was a homo and my best friend wasn't a church-goer. I wondered what my parents would think. That reminded me of my dilemma. Should I tell my family I'm gay or not? I didn't want to think about that now.

"Do you see him often?" I asked to get my mind off my other thoughts.

"Fairly often. Sometimes, I just feel that he's there, but often I can see him. Sometimes, he looks so real and solid you would swear he's alive."

We entered the gym and then the locker room so we stopped talking about ghosts. We undressed and headed for the showers. Banshee looked good naked, but I didn't think about that much. I thought of him as a friend and almost as a brother. Somehow my feelings for him short-circuited the lust I so often felt for attractive boys, especially when they were naked and wet in the shower. Banshee was attractive, but he was much more to me than just a sexy boy.

My afternoon classes passed quickly. Soon, I was back in the locker room dressing out for football. The contrast been the builds of the boys in my P.E. class and those of my teammates was extreme. It was difficult to believe guys could actually have muscles like Lucas and Cody. They even had abs! I felt a little wicked doing so, but I allowed myself to carefully check out my teammates. I stored up mental images for later. I felt a little wicked for that too, but what did admiring God's handiwork hurt?

I didn't run before practice. Today was a weight-room day and I wanted to save my strength for lifting. I knew saving my strength was a waste of time when I began working out. The weight I had to use for bench presses was so pathetic I won't even mention it. Oddly enough, I didn't let it get me down. I just lifted the weight I could handle and went on to the next exercise. That's what I'd done when I'd started lifting with my brother's weight set at the beginning of the summer. The difference was that I slowly got stronger back then and I was slowly getting weaker now. I was determined to hold onto what strength I had for as long as I could. The day would come when I couldn't lift weights anymore and I wanted to enjoy it while I was still able.

None of the guys teased me for the low weight I was using, but they often taunted each other for being weak. I almost laughed when Lucas made fun for Cody for *only* using 220 pounds on the bench press. I bet not one guy in ten could do that.

I wasn't sure how I felt about not being teased. On one hand, it would have hurt my feelings because I really was lifting as much as I could handle. On the other hand, not being teased made me feel less like one of the guys. I knew I shouldn't feel that way, but sometimes emotions are not rational.

I was completely drained by the end of our session. I was almost too tired to walk. I lingered in the weight room for a few moments, waiting for everyone to clear out before I headed downstairs. Kevin stayed behind also, and stepped in beside me as I left the weight-room.

"I really admire you for not quitting. I was watching you in there. I saw how much you were struggling and how it tired you, but you kept right on trying. I don't know if I could do that."

"Thanks," I said.

"Everyone is impressed with you, Elijah. They talk when you're not around. Most of us thought you were way too small to be on the team, but no one thinks that anymore. In a lot of ways, you're bigger than any of us. I thought you should know."

"That means so much to me."

Tears filled my eyes and I had to fight them back. Kevin's words meant more to me than I could put into words. My feelings of not being one of the guys completely disappeared.

I was so tired I had to sit down on the bench in front of my locker and rest after I undressed. To hide my current weakness, I joined in the conversation that was forever going in the locker room. The topic was football of course, and I now knew enough I could talk about it without looking like an idiot.

When I made my way to the showers, most of the guys had already come and gone. Cody was one of the few that were left. There was a time I would've rushed my shower for fear of being in there alone with him, but I no longer had worries about Cody beating me up. Even if we hadn't made peace, my condition made me off-limits. Beating up a boy with terminal cancer would be considered about as low as pushing over a kid in a wheelchair or pummeling a boy with Down's Syndrome. Even the worst bullies weren't that low.

I paused for a moment. I had little bouts of feeling sorry for myself, but thinking of others made me realize I was being a whiner. I was lucky enough to have fifteen good years with nothing really wrong with me. There were boys who had been stuck in a wheel chair their entire life. They'd never had the chance to walk, let alone run or play in a football game. What about all those with Down's Syndrome? I didn't know a lot about the syndrome, but I knew those who had it didn't live as long as others. There were countless other examples, but I didn't want to think about all the suffering in the world. Yeah, my cancer was serious, but at least I'd had my time. There were many who didn't even have that.

I reveled in the hot water coursing down over my body. The soapsuds felt so good, and my peach shampoo really smelled like peaches. My muscles relaxed and I luxuriated in my own little spa there in the shower room.

When I opened my eyes I caught Cody checking me out. He looked away quickly, but I knew what he'd been doing. I was sure of it. He hadn't mentioned the night we'd fooled around since it happened. He hadn't given the least hint he was interested until now. I was surprised to say the least. I'd written off what had happened as a drunken encounter that Cody either didn't remember or didn't want to remember.

I was even more surprised Cody displayed any interest in me. There weren't that many guys in the shower room at the moment, but I was sure I was the least hot among them. My ego got a little boost, but mostly I was confused.

I rinsed off, retrieved a towel, and dried myself on the way to the locker room. I was still just as tired, but I felt better after my shower. My hair even smelled of peaches. I dressed and grabbed my backpack out of my locker.

"Need a lift? Cody asked.

"Yeah, I'm kind of tired."

I didn't mention it, but I'd just been thinking that I was too tired to walk home. If Cody hadn't offered me a ride I would've been searching for places to rest so I could make it all the way there.

I walked with Cody out to his black Trans Am. It was a relief to sink into the seat.

"This is one sweet car. Some guys have it all," I said.

"Yeah, no one deserves stunning good looks, an incredible body, and a killer car, but if anyone is going to have it all, then it might as well be me," Cody said with a grin.

"You forgot to mention your incredible modesty."

"I'm too modest to mention it."

"Of course you are."

"Hey, you wanna get something at Ofarim's? I'm starved. I'll buy," Cody said.

"Sure. Since you're buying I'll have one of everything."

"If you can eat it, you can order it."

"I think your wallet is relatively safe."

The drive to Ofarim's was short. Cody parked his Trans Am out front and we walked inside. We picked out a booth and in a few moments Shawn came over with menus and ice water.

"You got here fast," Cody said.

"The varsity team is so good we don't even need to practice," Shawn said.

"Bullshit."

Shawn laughed.

"You need some time or are you ready to order?"

"I'm ready, how about you?" Cody asked me.

"I will be by the time you're finished ordering."

"Okay, I'll have an Ofarim burger, a large order of fries, a fish sandwich, a large order of onion rings, a chocolate milkshake, and a Coke."

"That's all?" I asked. My mouth was hanging open. Cody was going to eat all that?

"Yeah, I'm on a diet."

I laughed.

"I'll have a cheeseburger, small fries, and a Coke."

"He will also have a milkshake. What flavor do you want?"

"Uh, chocolate, but I don't really need…"

"You're getting one, so shut up."

"Hmm, I've never witnessed belligerent generosity before. He's buying," I explained to Shawn.

"Shut up or you're getting a sundae too," Cody said.

"No please! Anything but that!"

"You guys are just a little odd," Shawn said.

"Your point would be..." I said.

Shawn laughed and went back to the counter.

"You look beat," Cody said.

"I am. Today has been kind of rough."

"I'm sorry."

"Whenever I think about throwing myself a pity party I just think of those who are worse off," I said.

"Yeah, but if you start thinking about all that is wrong with the world it's easy to get depressed. Luckily, I'm blond and built so I'm not required to think."

I laughed.

"You've changed a lot, Cody. When I tried out for the team you didn't like me at all. After I made the team you told me I might as well quit."

"I was being a jerk. I was pissed off at everyone because I got cut from varsity."

"Lucas said not to pay you any mind because you were angry at the world."

"Don't tell him I said so, but he was right. I was pissed off because I had to play on a team where half the guys were new and didn't know what they were doing. It was my own fault for getting kicked off varsity. It's not like I wasn't warned... repeatedly."

"About drinking?"

"Yeah. I thought I was such hot shit the coaches wouldn't dare to cut me, but I was wrong. If I'd been sober I would've realized I was being a stupid fuck. I don't drink as much as I used to. Drinking cost me my spot on the varsity squad. Who knows what else it would've cost me if I'd kept on going? I still drink and sometimes get drunk, but not like I did. I was an idiot. I'm sure I can trust you not to tell anyone what I'm telling you, although I guess it's hardly a secret."

"I won't tell. I'll take the secret to my grave so it won't be long before your words will be buried."

"How can you joke about that?"

"It's better to laugh than to cry."

"I guess, but..."

"I'll admit something too. I cry more than I'd like."

"You've got a right, man. No one will think less of you if you cry. Shit. What you're facing... I don't think I could be as brave. Don't be telling anyone I said that either."

"What's said in Ofarim's, stays in Ofarim's."

I sighed.

"What?" Cody asked.

"I'm not going to get to play again."

"You might."

I shook my head. Tears welled up in my eyes even as I fought them back.

"Don't tell anyone this, but I'm getting *a lot* weaker. I was using low weights today and cutting back on reps and sets, but it left me exhausted. I couldn't have walked all the way home without stopping to rest a few times. I'm not going to get to play again because I just can't do it."

"I'm really sorry, man."

"At least I got to play once, right? I almost scored!"

"That freaking amazed me. I still can't believe you did that."

"Being little is sometimes an advantage."

"Not everything about you is little."

Whoa. There it was again. If Cody meant what I thought he meant...

"I'm not exactly big *anywhere*."

"Big enough."

I didn't know what to say, so I went silent.

"Thanks for not saying anything to anyone about what happened at the party. I was kind of drunk. We both were."

"Yeah. I guess sometimes things just happen."

"Yeah."

Cody sat there and twirled the paper from his straw through his fingers. He looked thoughtful.

"What happened that night... I've been telling myself I was just drunk but... being drunk only gave me the courage to do what I wanted to do."

Cody looked at me fearfully, as if worried he'd said too much.

"It's okay," I said. "I... liked it."

I nervously laughed for a moment.

"Listen, if you'd rather not talk about this, I understand," Cody said.

"No. It's fine. We are friends, right?"

"Yeah," Cody said and grinned.

"We might want to wait until we can talk in private."

"Probably a good idea."

"Yeah, and here comes Shawn with our food. I'm amazed he can carry it all," I said.

"Hey, it's just a snack!"

"For who? The Jolly Green Giant?"

"Here you go guys," Shawn said, unloading a tray onto our table. Cody's plates covered his side of the table and some of mine.

"I'll bring your shakes out next. You'd better finish yours Elijah, or Cody might hurt you."

I laughed.

Cody and I stopped talking so we could eat. I enjoyed just sitting there with him. My mind was spinning with Cody's admission. Not only did he remember what had gone down at the party, it had obviously been much on his mind.

I had no trouble finishing my cheeseburger and fries while Cody worked through his enormous supper. I almost asked if he always ate like that, but then I remembered that not so long ago I was eating unbelievable amounts of food. Football practices burned up lots of calories and so did working out. Lately, I hadn't had as much of an appetite.

I sipped on my chocolate milkshake as Cody talked about his plans for getting back on the varsity team his senior year.

"I think I can do it. Coach Jordan said I almost made quarterback instead of Lucas. He said it was a difficult choice and that he wasn't just telling me that to make me feel good. He also said that if I stay out of trouble and don't drink I have a great chance of making varsity next year."

"You still drink," I said.

"Yeah, but not like I did and I'm cutting back even more. It's taken me a while to admit to myself that getting cut from varsity was my own damn fault. I think getting cut was a good thing. If the coach hadn't cut me I might've been an alcoholic by now. I was actually kind of afraid I was one, but I don't drink alone anymore. When I do drink I stop when I start getting a slight buzz. Sometimes I go to a party and just have one drink. I've even gone to a couple and not drunk at all."

"I think you're making some smart choices."

"I don't want to end up being a loser. My uncle was a big football stud in high school. He looks incredible in his yearbook photos, but now he's grossly fat and spends his spare time lying on the couch drinking beer. I'm not saying he's a loser. He has a good job and he's a likeable guy, but he's totally let himself go physically. That could easily be me, only worse. I could be the fat couch potato only with no job and a drinking problem. I don't want to be that."

"You're ruining the whole dumb blond stereotype."

"I'm not the sharpest tool in the shed when it comes to intellectual stuff, but I manage decent grades. I bet you're a straight-A student, aren't you?"

"Pretty much."

"Jerk."

I laughed.

"I'd trade my brains for your body any day. I wish I would've started working out a lot earlier."

"Ah, you look good, man."

"Not compared to you, but then most guys don't look good compared to you."

"Thanks, but be careful. Most guys think I have excess-ego as it is. You don't want to make me worse."

"Oh, I don't think you can get any worse."

"Hey!"

I laughed again.

"You know it's not smart to make fun of someone who is your ride. You could find yourself walking home."

"I live for danger."

"Yeah. Yeah."

Cody actually finished off everything, down to the last fry and onion ring. He paid the check and we walked back out to his Trans Am.

"You want to go somewhere and talk?" I asked.

"Yeah."

Cody didn't say anything as he pulled onto the street and drove through town and out into the country. He turned into an overgrown lane and then turned again and parked behind a dilapidated brick house. It looked like it was built in the 1800s and it was a wreck. The roof had caved in, the windows were broken, and the only evidence there had been a back porch was the foundation stones. It completely screened us from view. One thing was for sure; no one would overhear us out here!

Cody cut the engine and just sat there for a few moments. The silence grew uncomfortable.

"So... You want to talk about what happened at the party?" I asked.

"Yeah. I need to talk to someone and I sure can't talk to any of the other guys."

"They might surprise you. Everyone seems cool with Shawn and Tim. My brothers really admired Brendan and they're friends with him now. He was almost a god at VHS."

"I'm not gay, okay!"

I flinched at Cody's outburst. It took me by surprise.

"Sorry," I said.

"No. I'm sorry. I shouldn't have yelled at you like that. I'm just... frustrated and confused. I have this image of myself... football player, stud with the girls; someday I want to have a family. What happened that night doesn't fit, but I wanted it to happen."

"Maybe you're bisexual."

"I don't know. I really like girls and I'm not just saying that. When I see a girl like Darcie Swanson I just wanna... well, you know."

"I can guess," I said with a grin.

"Sometimes, I get these feelings when I'm around another guy... I don't understand it. I've had sex with quite a few girls and it's the best, but then I'll look a guy and I just want to do him."

It was dark enough I couldn't see Cody's face clearly, but I was pretty sure he'd just turned red with embarrassment.

"You can't tell anyone about this, okay? I'll kill you if you tell anyone," Cody said.

"You know I won't, but a death threat against someone who only has weeks to live isn't much of a deterrent."

"Shit. I forgot. Hell. I shouldn't be laying my problems on you. I'm sorry, man. Just forget I said anything."

Cody moved his hands to the keys, but I grabbed his wrist.

"No. Let's talk."

"You sure?"

"Yes."

"I'm sorry I came onto you at that party. I shouldn't have done it and I shouldn't have... well, you know. That's one reason I haven't talked about it until now. I didn't want to acknowledge it happened, especially to you. I should not have taken advantage of you when you were drunk like that."

"I wasn't that drunk."

Cody looked at me.

"No?"

"I drank a little and even a little too much, but I was mostly pretending to drink and pretending to be kind of drunk. I wanted to fit in."

"So, you don't hate me for what I did?"

"Do I act like I hate you? Seriously, I didn't even try to stop you that night did I? We've been joking around and talking to each other and hanging out. Why would I do any of that, or accept a ride from you, or go out to eat with you if I hated you? I didn't like it when you were riding me for being friendly with Banshee. I thought you were a jerk for picking on him, but I've never hated you."

"I was an asshole. I guess I was just trying to cover my tracks. I was afraid you might tell someone what I'd done."

"So you decided to act like a homophobe and make Banshee's life hell so you could deny what you did?"

"Yeah, and talking shit like that just comes naturally, you know?"

"Well, it shouldn't. Do you know how much calling people names and humiliating them hurts? Did you ever think about what you were doing to Banshee or to any other kid who might be gay and hear you trash guys just because they're into other guys?"

I realized I was practically yelling.

"Maybe I am just a dumb blond."

"No you're not. I don't like what you did or the way you acted, but I can at least understand it."

"Now I feel worse."

"Remember the feeling. You were a jerk. You're cutting back on your drinking. I bet you can cut back on being a jerk too."

"You're kind of tough, but I guess I should've known that already," said Cody.

"I just don't like to see others in pain, but let's forget about it. I know you're basically a nice guy. Even Lucas said so when you were at your worst. You haven't bothered Banshee in a long time and you've become a good friend to me, so let's leave all that in the past."

"I am sorry."

"Good. Let's talk about what we really came here to talk about."

"You don't mind?"

"I only mind that you keep asking if I mind."

"Okay. Okay. I'm just confused. I'd never done anything with another guy before that party and I haven't since. I guess I've thought about it. Okay, I *have* thought about it. I wanted to what I did, but I don't know why I wanted to do it. I just really wanted to and I couldn't stop myself. Maybe I've been deluding myself. Maybe I'm doing it right now. Why can't I just admit to myself that I'm bi?"

"It sounds to me like you just did."

"I guess. I guess I am bi. Why can't I just say it? I'm bi. There. I said it."

"Feel better?"

"Actually, I do. I feel like... like I don't have to keep thinking about it and trying to explain it away. I don't have to keep wondering. I can just relax and quit worrying about it. I don't know if I'll ever tell anyone else, but it feels good to admit it to myself and to you."

"That took courage," I said.

"More than facing a 225-pound linebacker with an urge to kill?"

I laughed. "I know what that's like."

"Yeah, you're brave as hell, man. I really do like girls," Cody said. "I know that for sure. I'm not trying to cover up being gay. I'm not deluding myself either. I *really* like them. Mmm."

I giggled for a moment.

"I think that much is certain."

Cody looked at me and grew silent. We just sat there for a few moments gazing at each other. Night had come, and the only light was from the stars, the moon, and the fireflies that communicated with each other under the trees. I unfastened my seatbelt and turned toward Cody. He moved in and then he kissed me. He drew back for a moment only, then pressed his soft lips against mine once more. We began to make out. Cody slipped his tongue into my mouth and we kissed more deeply. I grew bold and ran my hands over the muscles of his chest. His pecs felt hard as iron and yet soft under his shirt. Cody kissed me more deeply still as I ran my hands over his torso. We made out for several minutes, then stopped.

"You want to get in the backseat?" Cody asked.

I nodded.

We got out of the car and quickly back in again. It was chilly outside and it was good to get back into the warmth of Cody's Trans Am. Cody drew my face to his and kissed me again, then leaned back and pulled off his shirt. I pulled off mine too. We went right back to kissing.

Now, my hands wandered over Cody's bare skin and I felt his fingers explore my torso. I'd see Cody shirtless plenty of times, but actually getting to touch him was something I never thought would happen, even after that night at the party. His skin was so very soft but the muscles underneath so firm. After a few moments of kissing and caressing I pulled my lips from Cody's and lowered my face to his chest. I licked him and then sucked on his nipples. Cody moaned and I continued even lower, exploring each row of his hard abdomen. Cody unfastened his belt and quickly got out of his jeans and shorts. I reached out and grasped him. He was hard as a rock.

A moment had come that I never thought would come. I leaned down and took Cody's penis in my mouth. Thoughts of what a horrible sin I was committing tried to force their way into my mind, but I wouldn't allow it. I knew this was no sin.

I didn't know what I was doing and yet I seemed to have an instinct for it. Cody's moans and groans made it clear I was doing something right. I couldn't take even half of him in, but I did my best. After only a very few minutes Cody pulled my face up to his and kissed me again. We made out more feverishly and with greater need. The windows steamed up as we explored each other's body.

Cody unfastened my belt and worked his way through my button and zipper. I had never been so aroused in all my life. I quickly shucked my jeans and shorts, and then we made out some more, completely naked.

Our hands roamed everywhere. There was no place Cody would not allow me to touch. I felt privileged and also so very grateful that I had the chance to have such an experience before it was too late. I would have remembered this night forever, even if I had a hundred years yet to live.

Cody licked his way down my body, then drew me into his mouth just as he had on the night of the party. I squirmed with delight. God would not have made such actions feel so good if they were wrong. I'd been lied to about sex my entire life. I'd been taught it was sinful if it wasn't an act of procreation. I wondered how much damage had been done by such false teachings. How many had suffered from guilt for something that was not wrong? I also wondered in what other ways my church had lied to me, but I had no time for such thoughts now. One of the hottest guys at VHS was giving me head!

I fought to maintain control, but it wasn't easy. Just when I thought I'd lose the struggle Cody stopped, kissed me again, and gazed deeply into my eyes.

"Can I fuck you?"

The f-word sounded so harsh. It was a word I did not use. I thought it vulgar. I knew that is not how Cody meant it, and I wanted to experience what Cody offered more than anything.

"Yes."

Cody pulled a condom out of his pocket and unrolled it over his large penis. I watched in fascination. I'd never seen a condom outside of the package before. He also pulled out a very small tube. I didn't know what it was, but then he squirted it into his hand and stroked himself for a moment.

"I've never done this with a guy before, but I'll go slow. Okay?"

I nodded.

I had no idea what I was doing. I only knew I wanted to do it.

Cody was more expert. I guess guys weren't all that different from girls. He pulled my legs up over his shoulders and pressed against me. After several moments of nothing happening, I cried out as blinding pain shot through me.

"I'm sorry," Cody said.

I thought this was supposed to feel good, but so far it just hurt. I thought about telling Cody to stop, but I wanted to experience this. If all there was to it was pain then I just wouldn't do it again. I was unlikely to repeat the experience no matter how it felt. I'd never get another chance.

"Just go slow," I said, trying not to grimace.

Cody pushed in deeper and deeper. I didn't think I could stand it, but suddenly he was all the way in and the pain almost disappeared. It came back when he pulled out and pushed in again, but it wasn't nearly as bad. I concentrated on Cody's incredible body and handsome face. His muscles flexed and the expression on his face was one of ecstasy. I took pleasure in giving him pleasure and soon I experienced it for myself. What Cody was doing began to feel good.

"Faster. Harder," I said.

Cody grinned and did as I asked. The windows of the Trans Am were completely fogged up and the car was filled with moans and groans. Cody pumped into me harder. He kept going and going, filling me with pleasure until a few minutes later he moaned loudly.

I could feel him inside me. I could feel him throbbing. I lost control at that moment and my eyes rolled back into my head in ecstasy. I felt as if I'd seen God.

A few minutes later we were dressed and once again sitting in the front of Cody's car.

"Are you okay with this?" Cody asked.

"Yeah. I would never have been able to experience this without you."

"Glad I could help," Cody said and laughed.

"How do you feel?" I asked.

"Mellow."

"I mean emotionally."

"I feel good about it. I feel like I finally found the courage to admit what I wanted and to go after it."

"I bet I'm going to be walking funny tomorrow," I said.

Cody burst out laughing.

"Sorry I'm so huge."

"Oh please," I said.

"Elijah, can I ask you something personal?"

"After what we just did together I think you can ask me anything."

"Are you gay?"

I gazed into Cody's eyes before answering.

"Yes. I don't imagine many straight guys would let you do to them what you just did with me."

"Good point. Listen, I'm really sorry for all the shit I said and for being a homophobe. I was afraid of what I might be and afraid someone else would realize what was I was, but that's no excuse. I'm so sorry I hurt you and so glad you escaped the day I was going to beat the crap out of you."

"We all have our own devils to fight I guess. I accept your apology."

"When did you know?"

"I'm not sure. The feelings have been there for a long time, but I so camouflaged and denied them that I don't know when they started."

"Do you have any interest in girls?"

"No. I don't. I'm not bi. I'm gay."

"Are you okay with being gay? You seem like you are."

"I am now, but that's a recent development. I wasn't okay with it at all for a long time. According to my church it's a horrible sin, but things have been happening lately to make me reevaluate practically everything. I've come to the conclusion that there is nothing wrong with what I am at all. I am as God meant me to be. The same is true for you."

"Do you mind if we talk sometimes? We don't have to do anything, just talk. I need someone to talk to."

"Of course we can talk. For as long as I'm around we can. After I'm gone, you might think of Banshee. I bet he'll talk to you too."

"I don't see why he would."

"He will forgive you."

"I hope so. I owe him an apology."

"He will. He is wonderful."

"Are you in love with him?" Cody asked.

"No. I love him, but I'm not in love with him. We're friends. Maybe if I had more time we could be boyfriends, but I don't think so even then. I think Banshee and I are best as friends."

"I can understand that. I have a girl who is a friend, but not a girlfriend. We don't have sex. It wouldn't seem right."

"That's the way it is with Banshee and me. We have kissed a couple of times, but I don't think anything more with ever happen. We're best exactly as we are. Remember Banshee when I'm gone. He will be there for you. I'll ask him to do it for me. He won't deny me a dying wish anymore than you did. He would be there for you anyway. I know he would."

"I used to want to kill you. Now I'd do anything to save you," Cody said. "It isn't fair." Cody actually began to cry. He reigned in his emotions after only a few moments, but he'd cried—for me.

"It's okay, Cody. It really is. I don't want to die, but I've been thinking how good my life has been for fifteen years. It hasn't been perfect, but I've been able to do and see so much. My family has always been good to me. I've had it easy. I'd rather live a short and happy life than a long and unpleasant one. I don't believe death is the end either. I don't know what's waiting for me, but I know I will go on."

"Damn, you have balls."

I laughed. It was such a bizarre comment.

"I mean it," Cody said.

"Thank you. When I'm gone, remember that I wasn't scared to die and remember also that I'm happy. Don't mourn for me. Just remember me, okay?"

"How could I forget you?"

"And don't mourn for me before I'm gone either. I'm not dead yet!"

"Stop making me laugh, dude."

"I want you to laugh. I plan to laugh a lot before the end. You can never laugh too much. Now, drive me home. I'm tired."

Cody did something truly sweet then. He leaned over and kissed my cheek.

We didn't say much on the drive back into town. Before long Cody let me out in front of my house. He stayed and watched until I was safely inside. I was exhausted, but it was perhaps the best night of my life.

Chapter Thirteen

The rest of the week didn't go so well. I woke up tired in the mornings, no matter how early I got to bed. Halfway through the mornings I was exhausted. I didn't eat much. Food didn't taste good to me anymore. Maybe it was because of the drugs. I was hitting the hydrocodone pretty hard. I was popping one every four hours. I knew I was going to have to ask Dr. Peters for something stronger soon, but I put it off. I didn't want my parents to know the pain was increasing. I knew it would scare them. It was scaring me. The very thought of food made me nauseous. I was taking a lot of my anti-nausea medication. It helped, but not enough. The headaches were my real problem. It was hard to concentrate in class when my head was pounding. It was also hard to enjoy lunch with the guys. Cody and Lucas didn't say anything, but they could tell I wasn't feeling well. They also noticed that my tray was barely touched when I dumped it.

On Wednesday, Mr. Wells let Banshee sit with me during P.E. That's all I did in P.E. now—sit. I wasn't being a slacker or taking advantage of my condition. I really was too tired to do even a single jumping jack. The very thought of jumping up and down made my head hurt.

Banshee and I talked quietly during class. He told me stories about the homo table. Some of them made me laugh. That made my head hurt too, but laughing made me feel better. I think Banshee knew it. He tried to make me laugh a lot.

My mind wandered while Banshee talked to me, but not as much as during classes. I got up at the end of some of my classes with only the vaguest idea of what we'd been discussing. Sometimes, I forgot what period it was and had to ask. That was kind of scary and made me feel foolish. It was easier to concentrate while Banshee was telling me stories, but I know I missed out on a good deal.

I lay down on the bleachers and gazed up at the ceiling far, far above as I listened to Banshee talk about Tim and Dane making out every time the lunch monitor wasn't looking. I was so tired I closed my eyes and felt myself drifting off. Falling asleep felt different this time. I felt as if I was floating out of my body. I wondered briefly if I was dying. If this was dying it wasn't so bad.

"Elijah. Elijah!"

"Huh? What?" I said waking.

Banshee was leaning over me. His eyes were wild with fear. Tears ran down his cheeks.

"What? What's wrong?" I asked, sitting up too quickly. "Oww." I grabbed my head. It throbbed.

"I couldn't wake you up. I thought..."

"You thought I was dead?"

"Yeah."

Banshee was upset, but I wasn't sure what to say to him to comfort him. My head hurt so much just then that death would've been a relief, but I knew I couldn't tell him *that*.

I started to get up, but I was dizzy.

"Could you help me over to the water fountain?" I asked.

"Of course."

Banshee studied me as I walked across the gym floor. I stared straight ahead in an effort to keep my balance. When we reached the water fountain I took out a hydrocodone and swallowed. I'd taken one only a couple of hours before. I was going to have to see Dr. Peters very soon.

"You aren't feeling very good, are you?"

I shook my head.

"Maybe I'm coming down with something," I lied.

"You should probably see your doctor soon."

"Yeah, I think I'm going to have Mom schedule an appointment. In fact, um..." I closed my eyes as a flash of pain assaulted my brain, then reopened them. "Could you ask Mr. Wells if you can take me to the office. I think I need to call home."

I felt guilty. Banshee looked so worried. He hurried away and was back with Mr. Wells in seconds.

"Would you like someone else to help you as well?" Mr. Wells asked as he approached.

I shook my head.

"Banshee will be enough. I'm just a little dizzy and my head hurts. I'm going to call home and have Mom see if she can get me an appointment today."

"I hope you feel better," Mr. Wells said, gripping my shoulder.

"Thanks."

Banshee led me across the gym floor toward the exit doors. I grimaced now and then when a flash of pain ripped through my skull. The pain hadn't been this bad before. I felt the eyes of my classmates on me. They were stealing glances as Banshee led me out of the gym. I didn't care. I just wanted my head to stop hurting.

The journey to the office wasn't all that long, but it sure felt like it. I was getting really dizzy and my headache increased in intensity. I had to fight back the tears. I leaned on Banshee so heavily he stumbled.

"Sorry," I said.

"It's okay."

A sob escaped my lips and tears welled up in my eyes as we struggled along.

"I don't feel very good. Take me to the nurse instead," I said.

Banshee looked really worried. I was getting pretty worried myself. I wondered if this was end. I was having a lot of trouble walking. The pain in my skull was so bad I couldn't concentrate on putting one foot in front of the other. I would've gone down if Banshee hadn't held onto me.

"Cody, help!" cried out Banshee as I almost slipped from his grasp.

I saw Cody run towards us. He scooped me up in his strong arms and carried me down the hallway as Banshee rushed to keep up. He carried me all the way to the nurse's office and laid me down on the examination table. I lost sight of Banshee and Cody as the nurse took out her stethoscope and listened to my heart.

"Tell me what's wrong," she said.

"My head really hurts and I'm very dizzy. Can you call my mom and see if she can get me a doctor's appointment—soon."

The nurse checked my pulse.

"Have you taken your hydrocodone recently?" she asked. She knew all about my condition and the medications I was allowed to carry with me.

"Yes, five minutes ago. It's not helping." I fought back another sob. I was tired of crying.

"Just lie still. I'll call your mom."

I could hear the nurse on the phone in the other room, but I couldn't tell what she said. She was back in minutes.

"Your mom is on her way. I called your doctor and let him know you're coming in."

"Thanks. Are Banshee and Cody still here?"

"Yes, they're in the waiting room. They'll help your mom take you out to her car, unless you think you need an ambulance?"

"No. Can I talk to Banshee for a moment?"

"I'll send him in, but just for moment."

I waited and soon Banshee was looking down at me, his eyes filled with worry. He took my hand.

"I will be okay," I said. I didn't know if I believed that myself, but I sounded convincing. The effect was somewhat ruined when I grimaced in pain. "Listen, I don't want Cody to carry me to the car. If you both help me I can walk, okay? My legs work fine. I just got really dizzy before and my head hurt. Mom will get scared if he carries me."

"We'll get you there," Banshee said, trying to smile.

"Thanks and tell Cody thanks for carrying me here."

"I guess all those muscles of his do serve a purpose beyond looks," Banshee said, trying to lighten the mood.

I smiled.

"The nurse said I could only stay a minute. Anything else?"

"No. That's it, but don't worry. I'll be fine."

Banshee squeezed my hand, then leaned over and kissed my cheek. He left me alone in the room. I closed my eyes. I could hear the nurse moving about. I felt better now that I was lying still. I hoped my medication would take effect before Mom arrived. If I was lucky I wouldn't need any help to the car.

I gave Mom a smile when she came in. It was my attempt to put her at ease. I downplayed the pain I was experiencing and only told her I'd been a little dizzy. She didn't look convinced.

I sat up slowly just in case the dizziness returned. It did, but not nearly as severely as before. Banshee and Cody came in.

"We'll just steady you," Cody said. I smiled my thanks. He was also downplaying the situation. I appreciated it.

Banshee and Cody steadied me as we walked to the car. My dizziness got worse, but the pair did a good job of hiding it from my mom. A couple of times, Cody was supporting most of my weight, but you'd never have known it.

"Thank you boys so much," Mom said when we reached the car.

"You're welcome."

"See you later," Banshee said, trying to sound upbeat.

"I'll tell Coach you're being a slacker today," Cody teased. I grinned.

Mom looked too worried on the trip to the doctor's office. I wanted to close my eyes and rest, but I kept them open and smiled as much as I could.

"Have the headaches been really bad?" Mom asked.

"They're just... a little worse. The hydrocodone isn't doing quite enough. I just need something a little stronger," I lied. I figured God would forgive me for lying since it was to make my Mom feel better.

Mom helped me into the doctor's office. I used all my strength and the railing to hide my difficulties as much as possible. We didn't have to wait when we walked in. A nurse ushered us straight into an examining room. Doctor Peters came in almost immediately.

"Can you wait outside?" I asked Mom. "I have something kind of... personal I want to ask about. It's nothing serious. I promise."

I could tell Mom was reluctant, but she agreed.

"I didn't want her to hear how bad it is," I told Dr. Peters as soon as she left.

"Tell me the problem."

I told Dr. Peters how I'd been feeling and how Cody had to carry me to the nurse's office. I also told him how Mom didn't know that part and how I was downplaying the pain for her benefit.

"You're very thoughtful to want to spare your parents worry, but you can only hide your symptoms from them for so long."

"I know. Am I... am I getting close to the end?" I asked.

"I can't say for sure without another CT scan, but with every day that passes you are getting closer."

I figured that translated to, "Yes, you're going to die soon."

We talked for a while. Dr. Peters prescribed stronger pain medication and a stronger medication for both dizziness and nausea.

"If this doesn't take care of the headaches, let me know immediately. The next step will be morphine. We want to delay that as long as possible. Once on it you'll be only semi-coherent."

I figured that meant I'd be a serious space cadet and probably wouldn't be able to go to school. I wanted to put that off as long as possible. Once I was serious enough I couldn't go to school or football practices my life would hardly be worth living.

"We should probably bring your mother back in. I need to inform her about the medication changes."

"Make it sound as good as you can," I said.

Mom came back in and Dr. Peters told her about the stronger medications but emphasized there was no need for heavy medication yet. There was no way he could make the situation sound good, but Mom didn't look overly worried. I wanted the time we had left together to be as pleasant for her as possible and I wanted to enjoy it too.

We went to the drug store next, but I waited in the car. I wasn't feeling at all well and wasn't sure I could walk that far. That's not what I told Mom, of course. I told her I'd rather sit and watch people walk by than stand in a drug store that smelled of vitamins. I also asked for a Hershey bar hoping to fool her into believing I felt good enough to be excited about chocolate. Cancer had made me a devious boy, but it was for a good cause.

When we returned home, I made it inside through sheer force of will. I asked Mom to make me some hot tea. I thought it might make me feel better, but mostly I wanted her out of the room while I tried to make it up the stairs.

The stairway was an ordeal. Each step made my head hurt. Worse, I was getting really dizzy. To keep from falling I leaned way forward while I gripped the handrail. I made it up to my room and immediately took my new medications into the bathroom. I took one of each and sat down on the edge of my bed. Mom brought in my tea and asked if I wanted anything else. I told her I thought I'd take a little nap.

As soon as Mom left the room I drank my tea, then lay back on the bed and tried to hold perfectly still. My head pounded, but not as bad when I was moving about. I feel asleep and didn't awaken until about 7 p.m. I felt better. My headache, dizziness, and nausea were gone. I was very tired, but I felt so much better I didn't have to pretend to be feeling good when I went downstairs.

Mom had made pizza and I actually felt like eating for once. I only had one slice, but I told Mom I'd pigged out at lunch. The truth would not do. When I finished, I told my parents I was heading back upstairs to do my homework. That was more or less true. Most of my books were at school, but I did some reading for English. By 9 p.m. I was back in bed. I slept the entire night. I felt pretty good when my alarm woke me up.

***

"Elijah!" said Banshee the moment he saw me in the hallway the next morning. He grabbed me and hugged me. "I didn't think you'd be in school today!"

"I'm feeling better. The doctor gave me some serious drugs. If I laugh for no reason don't worry. The painkiller I'm on now makes me a little giddy. This one makes hydrocodone look like children's aspirin."

"Are you okay?"

"Eh. I feel okay, other than being really tired."

That was the best answer I could give. It was mostly true. Compared to the day before I felt great!

Cody was just as surprised to see me in school as Banshee. He grinned when he spotted me later in the day.

"Yeah, I knew you were faking to get out of football practice," he said, but I could tell from his expression he was still concerned.

"Shhh," I said. "Don't tell anyone. Thanks for giving me a lift to the nurse's office yesterday."

"You scared the shit out of me. When I heard Banshee cry for help and then got a look at you I almost panicked."

"I guess I wasn't looking pretty, huh?"

"I was worried you were... that you were in a lot of pain."

"My head felt like someone shoved it in the weight stack and then did bench presses," I said.

"But you're better now?"

"Well, I'm the same, but I'm on some serious pain killers. Right now you could hit me in the face as hard as you wanted and I probably wouldn't feel it!" I giggled, then looked around. "Sorry, being silly is a side effect."

"I'll walk you to class."

"Sure you don't want to carry me?"

"Only if you really want me to."

"I'll walk this time."

Cody kept an eye on me, but I wasn't dizzy so I didn't sway or stumble. He looked relieved, but he knew there was no real getting better for me. I was just thankful not to be in pain. I don't like pain. It hurts me.

I was a little loopy during lunch, which helped the guys forget I was terminal. I didn't have much of an appetite, but I did eat some of my chili and half of a peanut butter sandwich. It was more than I wanted, but the doctor said not eating would only hasten my demise. Okay, he didn't say it quite like that, but that's what he meant.

I sat out during P.E. again. My head wasn't hurting, but I had no energy. If I tried to run they'd be calling me snail boy. Okay, my classmates probably wouldn't have been that cruel, but I wouldn't have been moving fast or far.

I was pleased to be back in the locker room for football practice after school. They guys welcomed me back like I'd been gone for weeks. Lucas hung back and walked with me out to the field while the others ran on ahead.

"Cody called me last night. He was really worried about you. He said you collapsed and he had to carry you to the nurse's office."

"I was still conscious, but yeah, he had to carry me. Banshee was helping me there, but my headache got so bad I couldn't stand it and I was so dizzy I couldn't walk."

"I think Cody likes you."

I looked quickly at Lucas.

"What do you mean?"

"Remember how he hated you at the beginning of the year? I swear he'd been crying last night when he called. I'm glad you two have become friends."

"Oh!" I said relieved. I feared for a moment Lucas had figured out that there was something between Cody and me. "Yeah, he's been really cool here lately. You've been cool all along. I haven't forgotten that."

"Hey, I'm always cool."

"Yeah, and about as modest as Cody."

"Ouch!"

I giggled, then put my hand over my mouth.

"What was that?"

"It's the pain killers. They make me a little silly. Right now I've got a little bit of a headache, but I don't care!" I laughed.

"Yeah, right. I think you've got some vodka hidden in your locker."

"You wish."

"I better catch up. Some of us are required to run."

I grinned. Lucas ran ahead. I kept walking. I thought about walking around the track while the guys ran, but by the time I reached the field I was too tired.

I watched my teammates practice as I sat on the bench. I was so thankful I'd been allowed to play in the first game. I didn't know it at the time, but that was my only chance to play football in a real game. There was no way I could do it now. I don't think I could've made a touchdown if the other team stood to the side and let me pass.

Sadness touched my heart knowing that I'd never again experience the thrill of having fans cheer for me. I was itching to get out on the field and run. I wanted to race down the field and catch a pass, just as I'd done on that night that now seemed so long ago. I would've been happy just to practice with my teammates, but now I had to be content just to sit on the sidelines. I wasn't going to let sadness overwhelm me. Instead, I was thankful that I'd run and worked out all summer. I was thankful I'd given my best during tryouts. I was thankful I'd made the team and played in a real game. I would always have that.

I didn't bother to shower after practice. As much as I wanted to see the sights in the shower room I was too tired to make the effort. I wondered how long it would be before I was too tired to walk and ultimately too tired to get out of bed. I began to feel sorry for myself, but then I sucked it up and was thankful that I could still walk.

Cody offered me a ride home and I accepted. If no one had offered me a ride I would've called Mom. The house was too far away from school for me now. Making it that far required too much effort.

"How did today go?" asked Cody as we sat in his car.

"Good, mostly. "My head hurt a little now and then, but not like it did yesterday. Mostly, I'm just tired all the time. I constantly feel like I just want to lie down and take a nap."

"I guess fighting off the cancer is hard on your body."

"Yeah and I don't eat much."

"You should eat more."

"I know, but the thought of food is just... eh."

"You aren't giving up on me, are you?"

"No, but I know I don't have much time left. I can feel it."

"Don't say that."

"It's true. The new meds are working well against the headaches, but my head still hurts sometimes. The next step is morphine. Once I get to that point it's all over."

"Damn."

"Sorry to be depressing."

"No. We can talk to each other about everything, right?"

"Yeah. I have some juicy secrets to take to my grave."

"Just don't be taking them too soon. I'm gonna miss you."

"It's hard to imagine that I used to think of you as a complete jerk."

"About as hard as it is to imagine that I used to think of you as a useless little wannabe."

Cody and I both laughed. Cody stopped the car in front of my house. He looked around for a moment, then leaned over and gave me a kiss on the lips. The kiss was more caring and loving than sexual.

"Thanks, Cody, and thanks for the ride."

Once again, Cody watched until I went inside before he drove away. Mom heard me come in and called me into the kitchen. She had fried chicken, green beans, and cream gravy ready. I was hungry, but the thought of food wasn't all that appealing. Still, it was fried chicken, and I'd always liked Mom's cream gravy spread over pieces of bread. Cody was right. I did need to eat. I was sure the gravy was packed with fat and calories. I sat down and ate while I talked to Mom. Dad came into the kitchen and had a cup of coffee and some apple pie. It was nice sitting there with my parents, but they looked sad. I felt so sorry for them. I felt guilty for leaving them, but there wasn't much I could do about that.

After supper, I headed for my room, but stopped before I reached the stairs. Dad had just turned on a news program and my ears pricked up when Chicken Fillets was mentioned. Mick Huckster, a well-named windbag politician from the south, was speaking.

"I ask you to join me in speaking out this Saturday on "Chicken Fillets Appreciation Day." The goal is to support a business that has the courage to operate on Christian principles and whose C.E.O. has taken a stand for Godly, moral values. Too often, the left makes corporate statements to show support for gays, abortion, profanity, or other immoral acts, but if Christians affirm traditional values, we're considered homophobic, fundamentalists, hate-mongers, and intolerant. It is time that we, who occupy the moral high ground, fight back."

I had never liked Huckster. He tried blaming natural catastrophes on groups he didn't like—gays, blacks, women, whoever he was currently spouting off against. This time, his attack struck too close to home. Many groups who were against prejudice and hatred no longer ate at Chicken Fillets to protest the enormous donations made by Cathy Daniels, President and C.E.O. of Chicken Fillets, to anti-gay and other hate groups.

"Moral high ground my butt," I thought as I continued on up the stairs.

Huckster was a hate-monger who carefully worded his attacks. I noted he inserted "profanity" and "immoral acts" into the same list as gays. I knew what he was up to. Huckster and those like him worked very hard to demonize gays. I felt like a fool, but I'd fallen for such tricks before my eyes were opened. I'd never fallen for Huckster's slimy tactics. I wasn't that big of a fool, but I had been a fool back when I wasn't thinking for myself. Like many, I was too lazy to uncover the truth.

I felt more anger for Huckster and those like him than I should, but how much damage had he and his kind done to me, and to those like me? How long had I denied my true nature because of such people? How much had I hated myself because of them? What made me truly angry is that such hate mongers misrepresented themselves as Christians. They weren't Christians at all. They were Anti-Christians. I wondered if Huckster and those like him were the Anti-Christ that the Bible warned about.

Cathy Daniels had donated money to my church. I wasn't surprised, especially with the hatred Pastor Walker had recently been spewing. Daniels, Walker, and Huckster—they all disgusted me.

I put them out of my mind and turned to my homework. They couldn't hurt me anymore. Jesus had led me to the truth. I paused for a moment and thought of Jesus. Would he return to our church on Sunday? I certainly hoped so.

***

The big news hit the next day. Mick Huckster and Cathy Daniels were coming to Verona on Saturday! The gay boys of Verona had staged a protest against Chicken Fillets shortly after the wiener-roast. It was the day I'd marched in and quit my job. I arrived to see Shawn, Tim, Casper, Nathan and many others holding up signs to protest the donations Chicken Fillets made to anti-gay groups. Later, Skip told me business was down by 80% and it was staying down. The gay boys had told their friends and family about Cathy Daniel's anti-gay donations. Those friends had told their friends, and so on. I guess Huckster and Daniels didn't like that and had decided to target Verona. Rumor was there was to be national news coverage, but I guess I'd just have to wait and see.

I found out later in the day that Huckster and Daniels would be attending services in my church on Sunday. I hoped more than ever that Jesus would show up. Walker, Huckster, and Daniels would all be there. We needed Jesus to combat the antichrists.

My headaches came and went. They weren't nearly as severe as they had been before Dr. Peters had prescribed my new meds, but when I had one it made my life unpleasant. Luckily, I was headache free more often than not and the absence of that pain was pure pleasure. I was always tired, but I napped some, even in classes, and that helped. My teachers normally would not have allowed napping, but they knew what was wrong with me. Everyone around me was very kind and considerate. I was glad I had such examples in my life. Most of my teachers and classmates didn't go to church, but they were far more Christian in their actions and attitudes than many who did attend services. There were too many like Huckster, Daniels, and Walker out there. It was good to know that most people were not like them.

Something incredible happened at lunch on Thursday. I was sitting with the other football players when Banshee walked up with his tray.

"Mind if I sit with Elijah?" he asked.

Some of my teammates looked at him like they couldn't believe he had the gall to ask to sit at the football table. I feared one or more of them would tell him off.

"You can sit by me," Cody said. "Move your big ass, Beck. We need some room for Elijah's friend."

"You mean move my hot ass," Beck said and scooted down.

I just about cried. The guys were doing this for *me*. I was so touched I almost lost it.

"Guys," I said. "This is Banshee. As Cody said, he's my friend. Banshee, these are the guys."

"Wow. I can't believe you guys let me sit here. Thank you so much!"

"No one else has ever had the balls to ask to sit with us," Lucas said. "Of course, we would've told anyone else to take a hike."

"Or, we would've grabbed him by the seat of the pants and tossed him across the cafeteria," Cody said. "But, any friend of Elijah's is a friend of ours, or at friend of mine at least."

"So, you're really a queer?" Kevin asked Banshee.

"Kevin!" Cody warned.

"I'm just asking. He sits at the homo table."

"Yeah, I'm gay." Banshee looked around nervously. "Are you guys gonna kill me now?"

"Nah, we all know some queers, such as the quarterback of the varsity team, and the former quarterback of the varsity team. Hmm, it's almost as if one can't be the quarterback without being a homo. You have anything you wanna share with your buddies, Lucas?" Beck asked.

"You wish! Sorry to disappoint you, Beck, but you're not my type."

Beck laughed. I released a sigh of relief. I never dreamed Banshee would dare to sit at the football table or that it would be such a non-issue.

"What's it like taking it up the butt?" Kevin asked. "That's got to hurt."

"Dude!" Beck said.

"Hey, I'm curious okay?"

"Closet homo," Lucas coughed into his fist.

"I don't want to try it. I'm just curious!"

"Bi curious?" Beck asked and laughed.

"No!"

"I can't answer your question. I don't know. I've never uh…"

"Taken the sausage?" Cody asked, and then laughed.

"Yeah."

"Can we talk about something else now? I'm eating. No offense, but I just don't get the homo stuff," Beck said.

"Okay. I'll change the subject. It's too bad Elijah hasn't been able to play again. You guys might have won a game if he was on the field," Banshee said.

"Now we're going to kill you," Kevin said.

"Maybe we'll just give him a swirlee," Lucas suggested.

"I say we run his underwear up the flagpole... while he's wearing them," Cody said.

"Should I run for it?" Banshee asked me with a grin.

"It wouldn't do any good. They're too fast. They would catch you," I said.

My teammates actually seemed to like Banshee. I would never have believed it if I hadn't seen it. I have no doubt he would never have been allowed to sit there if he wasn't my friend and if I wasn't terminal, but Banshee impressed the guys with his smart mouth. Thankfully, it kept them from talking about girls.

I enjoyed the rest of the day. I was headache free. I was tired, but not so tired that it was a mammoth effort just to walk from one class to the next. I sat out of P.E. and Banshee kept me company. We spent the period talking about Banshee joining the football table. I was very pleased he had done so. It allowed me more time to spend with him. I knew what he was giving up to be with me.

I walked into the locker room before practice and sat down on the bench. My teammates were stripping off their clothes and changing into their uniforms.

"Aren't you going to dress out?" Lucas asked.

"There's no real need. It's not like I'm going to do anything."

I must admit I was having a little pity party for myself just then, but Lucas wouldn't allow it.

"Bull shit. Get in a uniform. You're a member of the team. Do it! Now!"

I didn't have to be told twice. I smiled. Lucas snapped me out of my funk. I was a member of the team. I couldn't play anymore or even practice, but I'd earned my spot. I'd die a football player.

A wonderful surprise was waiting for me Friday when I got home from school. There was no practice, but Cody drove me home anyway. He kissed me again just before I got out of the car. I walked up the sidewalk smiling.

Mom called me into the kitchen as soon as I came in the front door. When I entered everyone yelled "Surprise!" There was a large birthday cake on the table, which was a big surprise since it wasn't my birthday. The biggest surprise was that my Mom and Dad weren't alone. Mitch and Thomas were there too! They had come home from IU for a visit.

"Why didn't anyone tell me you guys were coming?" I asked.

"That would have ruined the surprise," Thomas said.

"Why is there a birthday cake?"

Mitch rolled his eyes.

"It's not a birthday cake. Look," Mitch said.

I drew closer. The cake was in the VHS school colors of blue and white. Written on the white frosting in blue was "Elijah. Congratulations on Your Football Success." There were football goals at both ends and a player that I supposed was me running down the field with the ball.

I looked up and smiled. I noticed then that both of my brothers had tears in their eyes.

"You know don't you?" I asked.

Mitch just about lost it, but hugged me instead. Thomas joined the hug, then Mom and Dad.

A Parrot Pizza box sat on the counter. Dad sat me in my usual place while my brothers got out plates, forks, and napkins. Mom poured glasses of Coke and then served up the pepperoni with extra cheese pizza. It was just like old times. Mom, Dad, Thomas, Mitch, and I all sat around the kitchen table eating together.

I only had one piece of pizza. I wanted some cake and I knew I wouldn't be able to eat much. Mom and Dad each also only ate one piece. Thomas and Mitch finished off the rest between them. I looked at my brothers while we ate. I'd almost forgotten how big they were. Both of my brothers were as big and built as Lucas or Cody, even more so. I was tiny compared to them.

Once the pizza was demolished, we hit the cake. Mom had bought vanilla ice cream to go with it. I had a big slice. My taste had been off for some time, but the cake nearly tasted normal. It was close enough that I thoroughly enjoyed it.

My brothers had to hear me tell all about my almost-touchdown. Each of them had accomplished much greater things, but I could tell they were both proud of me.

I was glad Mom and Dad had already told my brothers that I was dying. I didn't want to be around for that. I wouldn't have wanted to find out Thomas or Mitch had cancer, so I knew it would be rough for them to find out about me. Throughout supper both of my brothers acted upbeat, but neither could quite hide the stunned look on their face. I don't know when my parents had told them I was dying, but my brothers looked like they couldn't quite believe the truth. I felt sorry for them.

I was tired out by the time I finished my cake so I went to my room—our room that is. I smiled as I walked up the stairs. Thomas and Mitch were back, for a night at least. I knew I'd sleep better with them in the room. I always felt safe when my brothers were around.

I took a nap. I woke up only when Thomas and Mitch came up. I propped myself up with my pillow. My brothers sat on the edge of my bed.

"How are you feeling?" Thomas asked.

"I get headaches and I tire easily. Sometimes, I get nauseous. The drugs help."

"I'm so sorry, Elijah," Mitch said.

"Are you guys mad because we didn't tell you sooner? Mom, Dad, and I thought it would be best if we didn't tell you until we had to."

"We would have come home sooner," Thomas said.

"Maybe it was the best thing. Part of me would rather not know," Mitch said.

"That's what I thought."

I looked at both of my brothers. I hadn't planned to do it, but I made a decision right then as they both sat on my bed.

"I've uh... got something to tell you," I said. "You may not like it, but... I just..."

My lower lip began quivering and my eyes filled with tears.

"Hey. Hey. It's okay," Mitch said. "You know you can tell us anything. We're brothers. We're the Three Musketeers."

Wow. I'd forgotten about that. When I was little and feeling left out because I couldn't do what my big brothers did, Thomas and Mitch would tell me we were the Three Musketeers. Sometimes, we'd even played at it using sticks for swords.

"I'm gay," I said.

It was the hardest thing I'd ever had to say to my brothers. The fear that they'd reject me or hate me was enormous.

"It's okay," Thomas said.

Thomas hugged me. I hugged him back and held him. Tears flowed from my eyes. I couldn't help it. After a bit I stopped crying and Thomas released me.

"We... kind of already knew," Mitch said.

"How? I didn't even know it!"

"He never was too bright, was he?" Mitch said to Thomas.

"Hey!"

Mitch laughed.

"I'm kidding. It was just little things."

"Remember that time we took him in the locker room?" Thomas asked Mitch, and then turned to me. "I think you were in the sixth grade. We took you in the locker room with us because Dad had to leave the game early and wanted us to take you home because it was late. Eric Pemberton was the quarterback and you stared when he took off his shirt."

"I did?"

"You were practically drooling. I had to shove you to get your eyes off him," Thomas said.

"I don't really remember that."

"It happened. I was pretty sure you were gay then."

"You also never sneaked looks at our Playboy stash when we were gone," Mitch said.

I knew about that stash. I remember thinking that if Mom found out there would be hell to pay.

"How could you tell I never looked at them?" I asked.

"We always left a tiny strip of paper in the crack of the paneling. That way we could tell if Mom or Dad were nosing around and move our stash to a safer location. The paneling was never disturbed and we knew you knew what was in there."

"Are you guys okay with it? At church..."

"Forget church. Half of what is said there are lies. I figured that out when I was much younger than you. You are our brother, of course we're okay with it," Mitch said.

"You've really known all these years?" I asked.

"We highly suspected. We were almost sure," Thomas said. "We didn't think about it much and I think discussed it only once. It doesn't really matter to us."

"Well, I wish you would have told me I was gay. It would've saved me a lot of denial."

My brothers laughed. I wasn't amused. I was, in fact, angry.

"Come on. Think about it," Mitch said. "What would you have done if we'd told you that you were gay?"

"I guess I'd have been upset and hurt and angry. I wouldn't have believed you."

"See?"

"It's the kind of thing you have to figure out for yourself," Thomas said.

"Do Mom and Dad know?" Mitch asked.

"I'm afraid to tell them and I feel telling them would be selfish."

"Why?"

"They've got plenty to worry about now. I kind of want to tell them just to make sure they'll still love me if they know, but that seems selfish. They won't like it and it will cause them pain. It's selfish of me to hurt them just to know for sure they'll still love me."

"You should already know they will," Mitch said.

"Yeah, but... in church..."

"Would you forget that? Mom and Dad are devout but not stupid. They may be upset and they'll be worried, but then they'll think about it and be fine with it. It's up to you whether you tell them or not, but they won't stop loving you for it."

"I might tell them. I don't know. There is so much going on now."

I told my brothers about Pastor Walker, Jesus, Cathy Daniels, and Mick Huckster. They already knew about Daniels and Huckster coming to town. It was big news. They didn't know anything about Pastor Walker's rants or Jesus.

"It doesn't surprise me. Walker is a nut case," Thomas said.

I was surprised to hear Thomas talk about a pastor like that.

"I think he may be a child molester. He's just got that look to him," Mitch said.

I didn't know what that look could be, but I was glad both my brothers thought there was something wrong with him. It made me more certain about my own thoughts and feelings about him. The Three Musketeers were back.

Chapter Fourteen

Saturday was Huckster's Chicken Fillets Appreciation Day. Mitch drove me downtown to see all the excitement, but first we stopped and picked up Banshee. Mitch gave Banshee a significant glance and I knew he wondered if we were a couple.

Mitch had some difficulty finding a place to park because the area near Chicken Fillets was crowded. My heart sank when I saw the size of the crowd. I'd hoped people in Verona would be smarter than to fall for the manipulation of a political charlatan. When I drew closer my heart rose. There were TV cameras from NBC, ABC, and CBS and there was a big crowd, but no one was going inside.

I spotted Mick Huckster and Cathy Daniels near a small stage that had been built for the event. It was festooned with red, white, and blue bunting. The cameras panned the audience and then settled on the stage where Huckster and Daniels were soon scheduled to speak. Mitch helped me up onto a mailbox so I could sit and watch. Both he and Banshee were tall enough to see without a problem. Huckster took the stage.

"Freedom of speech is the American way. There has been a concerted effort by certain groups to suppress the basic American rights of the good, wholesome, Christian business located behind us. I'm pleased so many have shown up today to show their support for..."

"Donating to groups that spread messages of hate isn't a right! It's a disgrace!" someone shouted.

"It seems we have a member of one of those groups right here," Huckster said, then laughed.

No one laughed with him. The crowd was completely silent. Huckster looked uncomfortable and cleared his throat.

"Chicken Fillets has shown great courage in standing up for Freedom."

"By selling chicken, paying its workers minimum wage, and donating to groups that discriminate?" the same voice called out.

The audience laughed. Cathy Daniels sneered. Huckster's face darkened with anger.

"What would you know about standing up for freedom? Chicken Fillets..."

"I'll tell you what I know."

The speaker finally stepped out and I recognized him. I was expecting one of the gay boys of Verona perhaps, but the man who'd spoken was much older. He was in his late-50s or early 60s. It was Mr. Van-Patterson-Patton. His last name was so long it had always stuck in my memory.

"Excuse me, but this is a press conference," Huckster said, trying to dismiss Mr. Van-Patterson-Patton.

The press had other ideas. From my vantage point I saw Shawn talking quietly to one of the reporters. The reporter quickly walked toward Mr. Van-Patterson-Patton with a microphone and the NBC camera was soon focused on him. The reporter began speaking. I couldn't hear what he was saying, but it looked as if he was interviewing Mr. Van-Patterson-Patton.

Mick Huckster trembled with rage and Cathy Daniels looked indignant.

"This is a press conference. We are here to..." Huckster began.

No one was paying attention. All the cameras were now turned on Mr. Van-Patterson-Patton. I wished I could hear what he was saying for every once in a while the crowd cheered.

Huckster stomped off the stage in a huff and disappeared with Cathy Daniels into Chicken Fillets. I noted they were the only ones going inside.

"Come on. We'll have to watch the news to see what happened," Mitch said.

Mitch helped me down off the mailbox. I was feeling especially tired. Banshee stepped in beside me and put his arm around my waist. I leaned into him. Mitch looked worried. The car wasn't far away, but I was exhausted by the time we got there.

"Can you just take me home?" I asked Mitch. "I'm not feeling so well."

The truth was I felt awful. I wasn't nauseous and had only a slight headache, but I felt like I could pass out at any moment. I also felt bad because the three of us had planned to go to Ofarim's after checking out the action at Chicken Fillets. When we drove past it looked like that was not a good idea anyway. The place was packed and there was even a line outside. I wondered what as up with that.

I caused a scene when I got back home. Mitch and Banshee practically had to carry me. When Mom saw them bring me in she freaked out. I told her I was just really tired, but I think she thought I was dying. I wasn't entirely sure I wasn't but I assured her that I just needed to sleep.

Everything was a bit foggy. I could feel myself being lowered into my bed. I feel asleep and didn't awaken until hours later. I don't know when Banshee left, but he was gone when I woke up. When I opened my eyes I turned and there was Thomas, sitting in a chair, watching me.

"Hey," I said.

"Hey."

"What time it is?"

"Almost 5 p.m."

I felt disorientated, but then the memories came flooding back.

"I want to watch the news!" I said.

I sat up too fast and got dizzy. Thomas looked worried.

"I just sat up too fast. Let's go downstairs."

"Are you sure?"

"We're just going downstairs, not trekking through the Amazon."

I was trying to sound brave, but I wasn't sure I could make it downstairs. The truth would not do because then I probably wouldn't get to see the news and I wanted to see what had happened downtown.

Thomas walked beside me as I made my way downstairs. I moved slowly, but I made it. I sat on the couch and Mitch and Thomas sat on either side of me. Mom and Dad joined us. Mom fussed over me until it was time for the news to start.

"I told you I was just tired. I'm okay," I lied.

I knew I wasn't okay. I didn't have much time left. I was down to days, perhaps hours. I could feel it in my heart.

Mitch had the NBC station on. I didn't usually watch the news, but I wanted to see this. There was some stuff I didn't care about first and then Tom Brokaw began to speak about Huckster.

"Across the country today, customers lined up support the Chicken Fillet restaurant chain during "Chicken Fillets Appreciation Day" created by Mick Huckster, Senator from Tennessee. Chicken Fillets across the country reported record business except in one small Indiana town.

"It was supposed to be the focal point of Huckster's counterstrike against those who have criticized C.E.O. Cathy Daniel's donations to groups who many call discriminatory, but in Verona, Indiana, Huckster met with unexpected opposition."

The scene switched to the Chicken Fillets in Verona. It was weird watching on TV what I'd seen in person only a few hours before. There was Huckster, beaming at the crowd and spouting his crap. There was Cathy Daniels smiling at the cameras. Then, the good part came. The camera left Huckster right after he said, "What would you know about standing up for freedom?" and turned to Mr. Van-Patterson-Patton.

"I stood up for freedom in 1944 when I set out to flank machine gun positions that were firing on my fellow soldiers near Carano, Italy. I went through a minefield, took out three enemy machine gun positions, and returned to my comrades.

"How dare you stand there and defile the term "freedom" by applying it to a greedy corporation that takes advantage of its workers and donates to hate groups! You, Mr. Huckster, and all those like you who twist patriotism to advance your agenda of hate, dishonor all those who are true patriots. You disgust me."

The crowd cheered and then the tape went back to Tom Brokaw.

"What Mr. Van Van-Patterson-Patton did not say is that on the same day he destroyed three enemy machine gun positions, he also destroyed three tanks that were sent to retake those key positions. Van-Patterson-Patton also saw action in Korea and Vietnam, and received the Congressional Medal of Honor.

"While Senator Huckster is proclaiming his "Chicken Fillets Appreciation Day" a success, it was certainly not so in one small Indiana town where an angry Congressional Medal of Honor winner gave Senator Huckster what Van-Patterson-Patton called "a good old-fashioned dressing down." I'm Tom Brokaw for NBC News."

I laughed out loud and so did my brothers. Mom and Dad seemed pleased too.

"They shouldn't have riled up old Van," Dad said.

"I didn't know he was a Congressional Medal of Honor winner," Thomas said.

"He doesn't talk about any of that much," Dad said. "I only knew because my father told me. It was big news when it was awarded."

"I wonder if he'd let us see it," Mitch said.

"You can ask, but don't go bothering him right away. There will probably be a flood of reporters and well-wishers at his door. Ask him on your next trip home."

"Who is up for hamburgers?" Mom asked.

"No Chicken Fillets takeout?" Mitch asked mischievously. I hit him in the arm, but I doubt he felt it. "Just kidding! I'll take two!"

"Me too!" Thomas said.

"I'll stick with one," Dad said.

"Me too," I said.

"Fire up the gas grill," Mom said.

"Oh, I see. It was a trick. It's my night to cook," Dad said.

"I'm making French fries and there is blackberry cobbler cooling on the counter."

I loved blackberry cobbler!

We turned off the TV. Mom headed for the kitchen and Dad went outside. Thomas and Mitch stayed on the couch with me. I tried to act like I felt better than I did, but they weren't buying it.

"Mom and Dad are gone. You don't have to pretend with us," Thomas said.

I lay my head back and closed my eyes.

"I feel really, really bad," I said.

"Maybe you should see Dr. Peters again?" Mitch asked.

"He can't do anything. I've already got my meds. The pain isn't too strong right now. I just feel really, really weak."

I didn't add that I felt like I was slipping away. I knew that would scare them.

"I think we should stay home from school for a while. I'd rather spend time with you," Mitch said.

"Yeah, IU won't miss us," Thomas said.

"You guys can't put your lives on hold just to spend time with me. You have school and what about football?"

"Screw football," Thomas said. "You're more important."

"I can't let you do that."

"What makes you think you have a say in the matter?" Mitch said. "We explained this to you years ago. We're bigger than you so that makes us right."

"Being bigger does not make you right."

"Oh, but it does," Thomas said. "Since you're ill we won't prove it with the usual tickling."

"I'm gonna miss you guys," I said. "Well, I guess I am. Hey..." I grinned.

"I don't like the look of that grin," Mitch said.

"Me either. He's thought of something nasty."

I smiled at my big brothers.

"I'm going to come back as a ghost and haunt you. I will pay you back for every time you tickled me."

My brothers laughed for a few moments, but then Mitch began crying. I put my hand on his leg and Thomas hugged him with one arm. Mitch wiped his tears away.

"I'm sorry. I just..." He lost it. Pretty soon we were all crying. There we were, three football studs, crying like babies. My brothers were crying because I was dying and I was crying because they were crying. Thankfully, Mom didn't hear us. We settled down soon enough, but I don't know what Mom would have done if she'd walked in and seen us.

"Listen. I'll tell you what I told a couple of my friends. I'm not afraid to die. I don't want to die, but I'm not afraid. I think I'll go on somehow. Maybe there is a Heaven or maybe there's not, but there's go to be something and I get to find out soon. What upsets me is the pain my death will cause you, Mom and Dad, and my friends. I guess I can't ask you not to be sad when I'm gone, but don't worry about me okay? I'll be fine. I want you guys to go on with your lives. Have fun. Score some touchdowns for me. Take care of Mom and Dad. You know how hard this will be for them."

"You're making us look bad," Thomas said. "You're the one with cancer, but you're the one being brave while we cry like babies."

"I won't tell... probably."

"I love you little brother," Thomas said and hugged me.

"Me too," Mitch said.

We all hugged.

"I love you guys, too."

The emotional scene with my brothers wore me out. I could not keep my eyes open.

"Can you guys help me upstairs? I need to sleep for a while."

My brothers did more than help. They carried me and put me in bed.

"I'm going to go to sleep now. It's okay. I'll just be sleeping," I said.

I closed my eyes. I felt Thomas kiss my forehead and then Mitch. I nodded off in moments, hoping that I was just going to sleep. I didn't want to die, not yet.

***

I woke up the next morning. That made me happy. I wasn't sure I'd wake up, despite what I told my brothers. When I opened my eyes I saw Thomas getting dressed. His torso was lean and muscular. Mitch came back from his turn in the shower wearing only a towel around his waist. He was a year younger than Thomas, but just as built. My goal had been to someday be as studly as my brothers. It was a goal I'd never reach, but I guess that didn't matter now.

"It's about time you woke up, lazy," Mitch said. "We were going to wake you soon. It's time to get ready for church."

"You're going?" I asked.

"Yeah, it makes Mom happy."

I smiled, got out of bed, and stumbled off to the bathroom. I wondered what my brothers would make of Pastor Walker's rants. I sure hoped Jesus would show up. I didn't want them to miss him either. Senator Huckster was going to be there as was Cathy Daniels. It was going to be an interesting service.

I had to rest on the toilet after my shower. I'd been up for ten minutes and already I was too tired to walk back to my room without a rest. To make matters worse I was dizzy and my head pounded. I popped my pills and hoped they'd get me through the church service.

Once rested, I headed back. Thomas and Mitch had finished dressing. They looked really sharp in their long-sleeve shirts and ties.

"I need you guys to do me a favor," I said, as I slowly dressed.

"Anything," Thomas said.

"First, I need you to help me downstairs, but mostly I need you to get me out to the car while Mom and Dad aren't watching."

My brothers looked concerned.

"Maybe you shouldn't go," Thomas said.

"No. I want to go. I have to go."

I briefly filled my brothers in on what had been going down at church. I said nothing about my suspicious that Jesus was THE Jesus; I only said he was a boy from school named Jesus.

"If Mom and Dad see how weak I am, they won't let me go," I said.

"I think maybe you shouldn't," Mitch said. "It won't be good for you."

"Mitch, please. Nothing can save me. I want to do this. Besides, I'm talking about sitting in church, not climbing Everest."

That made Thomas and Mitch laugh.

"Please." I used my best puppy-dog eyes.

"Stop. Just stop. Okay. We'll do it!" Thomas said.

"Thanks!"

"Using that pathetic expression is so unfair," Mitch said.

"Like using that you're bigger is?"

I thought my brothers were going to change their mind when they noticed I had to rest in between pulling on my pants and putting on my shirt. I had no energy and little strength anymore. They both looked extremely worried. I didn't tell them I sensed the end was near. Oddly, it was a relief that it would all soon be over. I just hoped I had a chance to say goodbye to Banshee, Cody, Lucas, and the guys before I died.

After Mitch made sure the coast was clear, Thomas scooped me up in his arms and carried me down the stairs. He sat me down at the kitchen door and then the three of us entered together. My brothers stuck close until I was seated. I was glad. I wasn't steady on my feet.

Mom had made pancakes, scrambled eggs, and bacon. I knew none of it would taste right, but I was determined to force myself to eat. My brothers pigged out, but then that was nothing new. The eggs tasted really strange to me... not bad, just odd. The bacon had no taste at all and the pancakes were bland. The syrup tasted mostly normal, so I focused on it as I ate. I put it on everything.

There wasn't a whole lot of talk at breakfast. Mom asked how I was doing, of course. I lied and said I was okay. Cancer had turned me into a big liar, but at least it wasn't a bad kind of lying.

After we finished eating, Dad went into the living room but Mom lingered in the kitchen. Thomas and Mitch lingered too, nibbling so it didn't look like they were just hanging around.

"You two hurry up. I have to finish getting ready. I'll be back downstairs in five minutes," Mom said.

The moment Mom left the room my brothers lifted me in their arms, carried me out the back door, and to the car. I was in the middle of the backseat before either Mom or Dad came out. *So far, so good*, I thought. *Now, if I can just make it inside the church.*

There weren't any parking spots near the church, but Dad let us off right in front and went in search of a space. There were a lot more people going into the church than usual. It was the size of crowd one could expect at Easter or Christmas, rather than a

Sunday in October. Thomas and Mitch walked close on either side of me and took my hands. I was dizzy, but with my brothers beside me, I didn't have to worry about falling. I pressed down hard on their hands, letting them support most of my weight. Still, it was a tremendous relief when we made it to the pew and sat down. I couldn't have done it without Thomas and Mitch.

I could tell my brothers were upset. They knew I wasn't doing at all well. I didn't tell them, but I was taking all my meds far more often than I was supposed to. I didn't think there was much danger. What was the worst that could happen? I'd accidentally kill myself? Big deal!

I knew that very soon I'd have to ask my parents to take me to see Dr. Peters again. I couldn't make it much longer without going on morphine. Even as I sat in the pew I was assaulted by blinding flashes of pain in my head. It wasn't constant, but ever so often it hit and I struggled to keep the pain from showing on my face.

The church was packed. Mick Huckster came in accompanied by Cathy Daniels. Maybe it was because I knew what they stood for, but I didn't like the look of either of them. They appeared arrogant and smug. I'd never cared for either of those characteristics. I knew I was supposed to love everyone, but I couldn't manage it with those two. I couldn't even get myself to like them.

We sang a hymn and then Pastor Walker took the pulpit and gazed out at the audience.

"Today, we have two extra special guests; Cathy Daniels, who has donated so generously to our efforts to battle against those demanding "gay rights", and Senator Huckster, who is known for standing up for good, old-fashioned, family values. I feel a special connection to our honored guests, for they have recently come under fire for their efforts to fight against the rising tide of perversion and indecency in America. As those of you sitting here know, I too have come under fire for my sermons on the evils of homosexuality. It has forever been so. Those who stand up to fight the good fight are always the targets of the immoral and the depraved.

"I am here to assure all of you that I will never back down. I will never give up the fight, no matter the opposition. That is why I am doubly glad to have two such esteemed guests. Neither of them will back down in the face of opposition either. We must all support them in any and every way we can. The good, upright, moral people of this country must stand together, or our immoral foes will overwhelm us."

I almost laughed out loud when I saw Mitch roll his eyes, but a blinding flash of pain in my mind prevented it. It was the only time I was ever thankful for pain.

"In my latest sermons I have stressed the big picture. I have talked about what needs to be done on a national level to combat the spreading disease of homosexuality. These big battles are important and we must be ready to fight, year after year, until we wear down and ultimately destroy our opponents. Today, I wish to talk to about something far more important than the big battles, and that is the action of individuals. Each of us must do our own part to fight the good fight in our schools, the businesses of our town, and even in our own homes.

"The homosexuals have infiltrated our schools. Openly homosexual athletes parade upon the playing fields and are even showcased in our local paper! This glorification of evil must stop and it must stop now! We must demand that homosexuals be banned from sports teams. Do we wish our community to be represented by these disgusting perverts? Do we want them in the locker room and the showers with our boys who are every day in danger of being molested? No! It is up to us to demand change. It is up to us to assail the school board until these perverts are put back in their place. Many of you here own businesses. Do you want to advertise in a newspaper that glorifies perversion? Tell the editor of *the Citizen* that you will no longer support him with your ad dollars if he continues to support the immoral."

I grew angrier and angrier as I sat there. I thought of Shawn, Tim, Brendon, and Ethan. I thought about the kind of guys they were and all they'd done to help others. Not so long ago I'd thought to myself that their actions were far more Christian than the actions of those who called themselves by that name. To have Pastor Walker stand in front of the congregation and not only demonize them, but try to incite the congregation against them infuriated me.

Pastor Walker's words were making me sick. My head pounded, I felt nauseous, and dizzy. I kept looking toward the back of the church, waiting for Jesus to come. He needed to be here. He needed to show these people what a truly hateful man Pastor Walker had become.

"Businesses that support homosexuals in any way must be made to pay! We must make it known that we will not patronize any business that supports the immoral and the unholy! Would you patronize a business that donates money to a satanic "church"? Of course not! So why would you patronize any business that supports perverts who perform immoral acts on a daily basis?"

"I am very disappointed by the lack of support Chicken Fillets received in this town yesterday. Across the nation moral individuals stood up for freedom of speech, but here not one person stood up for what is right. I am ashamed that our town was not there when Chicken Fillets needed us, but Christianity is about forgiveness. I expect all of you to patronize Chicken Fillets at the first opportunity and as often as possible afterwards. Do not take your business to Ofarim's. A lesbian owns it and at least one known homosexual is employed there! Café Moffatt also is known to employ a homosexual as a waiter! Will you support these immoral establishments while you will not support the restaurant that is an openly Christian business?

"Enough said about that. I know you will all do what is right. The most important battles are those fought in the home. If each of us looked to the spiritual welfare of our own home the battle against depravity and immorality would be won. You know of what I'm speaking. I know it is painful to contemplate for it is the most difficult battle of all. We all love our children, but I must remind you of the old rule, "Spare the rod and spoil the child." The rule is true and is too often ignored. Where homosexuality is concerned the stakes are much greater. Spare the rod and damn the child's soul.

"I sure there are many here who have suspicions about their sons; Boys who do not play sports; Boys who are quiet; Boys who seem feminine; and Boys who show no interest in girls when puberty begins. Action, harsh action, must be taken when even the least sign of possible homosexuality presents itself. Boys who do not volunteer to participate in sports must be encouraged and, if need be, forced to participate. Boys who are quiet must be taught to be outgoing. Boys who are feminine must be punished."

I looked to the back of the church again. Where was Jesus? How could he allow such statements to go unchallenged? How could he let this despicable man lead an entire congregation astray? Pastor Walker was sowing the seeds of suspicion. He was attacking the freedom to choose. Forcing boys to play sports? Punishing boys who didn't measure up to his standard of masculinity? I could not believe what I was hearing.

"When any sign of femininity is observed in boys it must be quickly corrected and punished. It is better to slap a boy than to allow him to speak in feminine tone. It is better to break his arm, than allow him to play with dolls. If any boy is caught with another boy, he should be severely beaten."

My head was splitting with pain. I trembled with rage. Pastor Walker was an evil, evil main. I looked to the back of the church. Why did not Jesus come?

"Much has been said against bullying in the schools, but that bullying makes boys tougher. It should not only be tolerated, it should be encouraged. There is no evil greater than homosexuality. We must all take action against homosexuals. They must be hunted down, beaten, and killed if they will not repent. If one of them was in this congregation, I would beat him and toss him out the doors myself."

I looked back to the entrance again, but Jesus did not come. Pastor Walker opened his mouth again to spread more of his spiteful hate.

"Try it then!" I called out.

I struggled to stand. My legs trembled with the effort. I had to steady myself on my brother's shoulders as I arose unsteadily.

"Try it because I'm gay and I am sick of your hateful lies! You are nothing but a bigot. Every word that slips from your tongue is a message of hate! Every human being is created in the image of GOD. There are no exceptions! Jesus commanded us to love all others, not all others except the blacks or the Jews or the gays—ALL OTHERS and yet you stand there and preach hatred and abuse. You are despicable!"

Pastor Walker smiled almost evilly.

"I see now why God struck you with cancer. Here is an example of God's wrath!" the pastor said, pointing at me. "God has recognized the perverted and impure in our midst and has protected us by striking him down."

My father jumped to his feet, as did my brothers. Thomas and Mitch looked ready to tear the pastor apart. Mom was crying. She looked upon Pastor Walker with revulsion.

My head hurt so bad it was all I could do not to scream. I knew I had only minutes left.

"Why are you so upset?" I asked. "Why do gays bother you so? Why are you so emotional you clothe your anger with the Bible and justify your bigotry with scripture? Why do you have to do it? I've met several boys like me in the last few weeks and every single one of them is more Christian than you! They don't go to church, but they're good and kind. They help those who are in need. There was a boy who sat all alone at lunch, every day he sat there, and it was a gay boy who came to him and befriended him and made him feel good about himself. You speak in ignorance and hatred. You are not fit to stand behind that pulpit. Your hatred and your lies have no place in a church!"

"Remove him!" ordered Pastor Walker.

"Try it," Thomas said. My brothers were tensed and ready to take on anyone and everyone who dared try to touch me, but no one stepped forward.

Blinding pain flashed in my mind and I screamed. I toppled forward and would have fallen, but my brothers caught me. I was in such pain I cried. I couldn't stand anymore. I slumped down. Thomas and Mitch carried me into the aisle and laid me down. Mom and Dad rushed to my side. I looked up at them and tried to smile, but I felt like my head was splitting open.

"I love you all," I said between my sobs.

I thought those were going to be my last words.

"God's vengeance is swift," announced Pastor Walker.

"Amen," said both Huckster and Daniels.

"You will be silent."

I recognized the voice. The crowd who had gathered around me parted and Jesus came and knelt by my side. I looked up at him and smiled. He'd come to take me away. I knew it was him. I knew he was THE Jesus.

"I order you to leave..." Pastor Walker began.

Jesus, his visage stern, gazed at the pastor. The sky darkened outside and thunder rumbled and shook the panes of the stained-glass windows. The whole church seemed to tremble, but I was in such pain I could no longer trust my senses. I tried to raise my head, but I couldn't get my muscles to work. I was losing control over my own body, but it was okay. I was at the end. I wouldn't have to suffer much longer. My family surrounded me and Jesus himself had come to take me now to whatever awaited. I knew that everything was going to be okay. In my heart I always knew it would be so.

Jesus turned his gaze on me and smiled.

"You've been so brave and have done so well. I'm very proud of you."

I could die happy. One thing only troubled me.

"Please take care of my parents, my brothers, and Banshee and Cody and the others..."

"Shhh. It is not time for you to go. You can take care of them yourself."

Jesus touched my brow and all the pain instantly disappeared, as did my grief, and sadness. As I lay there I felt... fine. I sat up, and then stood up. The entire congregation gasped. My Mom cried hysterically for a moment, but then grabbed me and hugged me. She covered my face with kisses. Dad, Thomas, and Mitch hugged me too.

"An act!" Pastor Walker said. "He is a charlatan and this boy is in league with him!"

Mick Huckster and Cathy Daniels nodded their agreement.

"Silence," Jesus said, walking toward the pastor.

Pastor Walker's eyes grew wide with fear. He opened his mouth as if to speak, but no sound issued forth.

"You have abused your position. You have misled your flock. You have lied and you have twisted the truth for your own foul purposes."

"How dare you..." began Cathy Daniels.

"Why do you use your wealth to harm others?" Jesus asked, turning toward her. "When did you lose your way? You were not always so. You have used your wealth to harm a group who has done no harm to you, no harm to anyone. There are so many that desperately need your help. There are those without food, those without homes, and those who are dying because they cannot afford care. Here you stand in arrogance, pronouncing judgment on others. You claim to be a Christian and yet your ways are evil. You *are* the Antichrist the Bible mentions, you and all those like you."

Cathy Daniels shut her mouth and actually looked ashamed. Mick Huckster said not a word, but instead stared at the floor. Jesus turned back to Pastor Walker.

"Minorities were put upon the Earth for many reasons. One of those reasons is to test those who call themselves Christians. You were commanded to love all and reach out your hand to those in need, but instead you have spread hatred and raised your hand in violence. You have failed the test. You are not a Christian. You are an Antichrist. I warn you now; change your ways before it is too late."

Jesus turned back to me and smiled.

"Always follow your heart, Elijah. It will not lead you wrong. When others try to lead you astray your heart will show the way."

Jesus turned and walked from the church. The crowd parted for him and watched him in silence. He disappeared through the doors and then the entire congregation began talking at once.

I was the center of attention. Everyone wanted to see me and many wanted to touch me. I was not afraid. My parents hovered over me, gazing at me in wonder. If I looked as good as I felt I knew my appearance must be drastically changed. Mom couldn't stop crying. Thomas and Mitch didn't quite know what to do, but they were smiling.

As soon as we could, the five of us made our way to the exit. The crowd let us through, but many reached out to touch me as if I would bring them good luck.

I breathed in deeply as we stepped outside. The autumn air smelled wonderful. Being able to walk unaided was delightful. Being free of the pain, dizziness, and nausea was magnificent. It had been so long since I'd felt good that I felt as if I had gone to Heaven.

Later, I called Banshee and asked him to meet me at the football field. I made sure to arrive before him so that I was sitting on the bleachers waiting when he arrived. As he neared I stood up and grinned at him. His steps faltered and then he stopped.

"You... you look incredible!" Banshee said. He ran to me, hugged me, and cried. "What has happened?" he asked when once more he was able.

"Let's take a walk and I'll tell you," I said.

We headed across the football field, onto the soccer fields, and beyond onto the paths that ran through the woods. I told Banshee everything that happened earlier that day at church.

"I... I... that's completely unbelievable, or it would be if you weren't walking by my side right now. I was so worried about you. The last time I saw you... you looked so terrible. I was afraid that it really was going to be the last time I'd ever see you."

Banshee's eyes filled with tears and he began to cry.

"It's okay, Banshee. I'm here and I don't think I'll be dying any time soon. Mom called Dr. Peters and scheduled another CT Scan, but I already know the cancer is gone. I feel wonderful!"

I twirled around, looking at the golden autumn leaves overhead, then looked back at Banshee. I took his hand and we continued walking along the forest path. His tears were gone and he was smiling.

"You really think that was Jesus then? I mean THE Jesus from the Bible? That's just... Stuff like that doesn't happen, not really. No one will ever believe it. It's crazy!"

"Crazy, but true. I knew who he was before he touched me and took away my cancer. I knew it was him. I could just feel it. I had a hard time accepting it, but in my heart I knew it. That's what he told me, to always trust my heart, and I always will."

"No one else will ever believe it."

"That doesn't matter. I'm going to tell the truth. People can believe me or not. They can think I'm crazy if they want. They can think I faked my cancer, although I have the CT scans to prove it was there. I know what really happened. The congregation of my church knows too. They were there. They *saw*. They all wanted to touch me after I'd been healed because I had been touched by Jesus."

"You're a holy relic now," Banshee laughed.

"You can laugh. It could become a problem. I don't mind. I'm just glad to be alive. I wasn't afraid to die. I was ready, but I'm so glad I have the chance to go on living. There's so much I haven't done yet, so much I haven't seen, and then there's just living, getting up in the morning and going to school, spending time with you, going to football practices, and maybe even getting to play again."

"Well, you've blown your excuse for getting out of P.E. I hope you realize that."

"I can't wait to do jumping jacks and to run! I can't wait to do pushups and sit-ups."

"You really are glad to be alive, aren't you?"

"Yes!" I said and giggled.

We walked along, breathing in the scent of autumn, chatting and laughing. I couldn't remember when I'd enjoyed a day so much.

We spent a long time walking in the woods. As evening came on Banshee walked me home. My family was waiting on me. I was utterly and completely happy.

***

The next day my parents drove me down to Indy for another CT Scan. The doctors there simply could not believe it. They ran a diagnostic on the machine, checked the machine by scanning another patient, and then ran the scan on me again. The doctors could not explain it, but the tumor in my brain was gone.

Mom took me to see Dr. Peters when we arrived back in Verona. He too was amazed. Of course he had already heard the rumors, and I confirmed them. I told him that Jesus touched my brow and took my cancer away. He looked at both CT Scans and he examined me. I expected him to be skeptical and offer some scientific reason my cancer was gone, but he took me at my word.

My first day back at school was bizarre, to say the least. I was the center of attention, as you might imagine. I don't think most of my classmates or even teachers knew what to make of me. Some kids reached out and touched me as they passed. Some stared at me in awe, but most just plain stared. I knew they'd all heard about what had happened on Sunday morning in my church. Whenever anyone asked what happened I told the truth. Some looked at me like I was putting them on, but others believed.

Everyone had known about my cancer. Everyone had seen me slowly, and then not so slowly, growing weaker and sicker. Perhaps some thought I'd put on an act, but I doubted anyone was that good an actor.

Banshee met me at my locker before lunch and we walked down to the cafeteria together. We went through the line and came out with hot chili soup, peanut butter & jelly sandwiches, apple crisp, and orange Jell-O. It all smelled so good I couldn't wait to eat it. We walked over to the football table and joined the guys.

I'd passed some of them in the hallways, but this was the first time they'd gotten a good look at me. I grinned as I sat down.

"Is it true?" Cody asked. "I heard your cancer is gone. I thought it was a crazy rumor, but you look incredible. The last time I saw you, you looked like death warmed over."

"It's true. My parents took me to Indy for another CT scan. The tumor is completely gone."

"How is that possible?" Lucas asked. "I would suspect there was some kind of mistake and that you'd never had cancer at all, but I know that's not true. I saw what it did to you. I wasn't looking forward to your funeral and I expected it to be very, very soon. To be honest, I thought the last time I saw you would be the last time I saw you alive."

It was just what Banshee had said.

"You might have heard the rumor about what happened at my church on Sunday morning," I said. "That rumor is true. Jesus was there. He touched me and took my cancer away."

The table was silent, which was quite unusual for the football table. I think most of them didn't know what to say. They could tell I was completely serious.

"I know some of you, or perhaps all of you, will have trouble believing that, but that's exactly what happened. Some of you may even have had a class with him. He goes to school here."

"Jesus, THE Jesus, goes to VHS?" Cody said.

"Yeah, I know it sounds crazy, but it's true."

"You mean that kid with the curly black hair and the dark complexion?" Kevin asked.

"Yeah. That's him. You have classes with him?"

"No, but I've seen him. There *is* something about him. He spoke to me once. I was... well, it was last week and I was getting really upset because you were dying. Mostly, I was angry with God. Jesus walked up to me in the hallway. I didn't know that was his name, but he just came up to me and said, "Everything happens for a reason. Be patient. All will be well." I felt... at peace when he left. I turned to ask him his name, but he was gone. There was no way he could have slipped out of sight so fast, even if he sprinted, but *he was gone*. It was kind of spooky, like he was a ghost, but yet not. I felt... better."

"So you actually believe Jesus, the dude who walked on water and all that, is a kid at our school?" Beck asked. Kevin looked him in the eyes.

"Yeah, I do. There was my encounter with him and Elijah's cancer is gone. Cancer doesn't just disappear and we all know how sick Elijah was. We were all worried about him. We all knew he was going to die soon. Now look at him. He looks perfectly well. I'd even say he's glowing. It's as if he's been touched by the hand of God."

The table grew silent. I figured enough had been said about my miraculous recovery for the moment. I looked around at the guys.

"I have something to tell all of you. Since I'm going to be sticking around there's something I want you to know about me. I'm gay."

I felt no fear. I didn't know how my teammates would react, but I was not afraid. After staring death in the face for so long something like telling my buddies I was gay held no terror for me.

"So, are you two..." Lucas said, indicating Banshee and me.

"We're just really good friends," I said.

"But I am gay too. You might have noticed that I came from the homo table. I am a member."

"Well, not everyone at the homo table is necessarily a homo," Kevin said.

"And not all homos sit at the homo table," Beck said, shooting Cody a significant look. I wondered what he knew.

Cody looked around fearfully at his teammates. His face reddened slightly. His eyes met mine and he smiled.

"I'm bisexual, okay? I like girls, but... some guys are kind of hot."

"Whoa! I never saw this coming," Kevin said. "You're bi? Really? No way!"

"You want me, don't you, Cody?" Lucas said with an evil grin crossing his face.

"You wish! I think *you* want *me*, or maybe you're just insanely jealous of my incredible body and big dick."

"That's a laugh!" Lucas said.

"Okay, who else is a homo? Let's just get it out in the open. The quarterback of the varsity squad is a homo and so is his brother. The previous varsity quarterback was a homo too. It's not a big deal," Beck said.

"Hey, let's not ruin my moment of courage," Cody said.

"Courage my ass. You only came out as bi *after* Elijah told us he was gay. He took a big risk. Any of us can beat him up with ease."

"Hey!" I said.

"We still like you," Beck said with a grin.

No one else spoke up so it looked like I was the only full-fledged homo on the team. I really think anyone who was gay would have spoken up at that moment.

"So I guess we only have to be careful about dropping the soap in the showers around Elijah and Cody," Lucas said.

"Ha! I bet you'll be dropping the soap all the time, just hoping!" Cody said. "I hate to bust your bubble, but I am mostly interested in girls."

"There's still Elijah," Kevin said.

I turned red.

"Let's not pick on Elijah. He's my bud and he is a personal friend of Jesus. Mess with this dude and you might get struck by lightning," Lucas said.

The rest of lunch passed pleasantly. The food was delicious. It actually tasted like it was supposed to taste. I ate everything on my tray. I talked and laughed with the guys and just enjoyed being alive.

During P.E., I ran with the rest of the class and then did calisthenics. I laughed as I did jumping-jacks. I played four games of ping pong and lost every single one. I'd never had such fun in P.E. before.

For the first time in a long time, I ran out to the track with my teammates for football practice. I was right back where I had been before I knew I was sick. In fact, I felt as if I ran faster and with greater ease than I ever had in my life. Maybe it was just my imagination, but I didn't care. I could run again!

Practice was brutal, but I didn't back off. I bounced off the tackling dummies, but that only made me laugh. I didn't take it easy for a moment. I put everything I had into practice as if I'd never been sick at all. When practice ended I returned to the locker room tired, but practice was nothing compared to just walking from the bed to the bathroom in the last days of my illness.

If any of the guys were uncomfortable about a homo and a half-homo being in the showers with them they didn't show it. Cody didn't say anything about what we'd done together and neither did I. That was our business and no one else needed to know. I doubt they even guessed and I didn't think they'd really care.

Cody drove me home. I kind of wanted to walk, but I figured I could go for a walk later. I had plenty of time for walking now!

"I was surprised you told the guys you're bi," I said.

"It was time. I've been thinking about telling them for a while now, but it's not easy to admit. If I went to school somewhere else, I would probably never have told anyone, but it's different in Verona you know? There are jerks who make trouble, but you saw how the guys handled it. Besides, after your announcement and miraculous recovery admitting I'm bi was anti-climatic."

"Yeah, it's not every day one announces he's been healed by Jesus and can prove it."

"I can't argue with that. I can't tell how glad I am you're okay. I'll be honest, I cried sometimes because I didn't want you to die."

"I'm glad you like me so much."

"Eh, I just enjoy picking on you."

I gave Cody the evil eye. He laughed.

"Okay, I'll tell the truth. You're an incredible guy, Elijah. I don't think you realize just how much you have going for you. Yeah, you're small for a football player, but that's your secret weapon. Guys don't expect you to be tough, and they sure don't expect you to get past them. You have more courage than any other guy on team. I can't believe how long you kept going. You kept getting sicker and sicker, but you kept going. You kept doing what you could do, even though you expected to die. I didn't know how I was going to handle losing you. Now, I can look forward to being your friend for a long, long time."

"Thanks, Cody."

"You don't happen to have a sister, do you?"

"Nope, only brothers."

"Damn."

"Why?"

"Well, if you had a sister and she was anything like you I'd be interested. Of course, your brothers are downright hot. Are either of them..."

"I really don't think so," I said.

"Shame."

"Hey! Those are my brothers you're talking about."

"Your brothers are hot, man."

"Let's talk about something else."

Cody laughed, then looked at me and grew serious.

"I'm glad you're okay and that you'll be sticking around. I would have missed you and it would've had nothing to do with what's happened in this car."

"Thanks, Cody. I'm glad I'm sticking around to be your friend too."

We were at my house by then. Cody let me out. I walked inside. I had homework to do. I couldn't wait!

***

My life kept getting better after that. I'm not saying everything was perfect. Nothing is ever perfect. I didn't get to play during our next few games, but considering I didn't think I'd be alive to even see the next game I didn't mind. I knew it might be a long time before I got to play again, but I was going to keep practicing and keep working. I'd made it this far and I was determined to go on.

Jesus disappeared. He simply vanished. I didn't see him at school again. I asked around, but no one else had seen him either. I wanted to talk to him. I had a lot of questions, but he was gone. I wasn't surprised, but I was disappointed. After all, it's not every day one gets the chance to talk to Jesus.

Pastor Walker disappeared too. He vanished without a trace. We had a substitute pastor for a couple of Sundays and then the new one arrived. I liked him a whole lot better. His first sermon was on the duty of Christians to love all others. I knew we were going to get along fine.

My church was a better place. The atmosphere was more accepting. Some parishioners never returned, but most did and they seemed, well... more Christian. There was no more talk of concentration camps or battling homosexuals. There were no more hateful songs sung by children. Instead, plans were made to open the church to the homeless during cold winter nights and there was talk of providing Thanksgiving Dinner for all those who couldn't afford one. I was once again glad to attend church. After services I felt like I'd touched base with God. Our church had finally returned to what churches were all about—helping others.

My life returned to normal, or at least as normal as it can be when everyone knows Jesus himself healed you. There were plenty of unbelievers, but that didn't matter. In Verona, a lot more people believed in Jesus than had ever believed before. We even had a lot of new people showing up at church. Oh, and Chicken Fillets closed down in Verona. No one would go there anymore. As for Cathy Daniels and Mick Huckster, I don't know if they have changed their evil ways or not. I'll just have to wait and see.

I can't tell you I lived happily ever after. I'm not an old man near the end of his life who is looking back on his youth. I'm fifteen-years-old, so hopefully I have a lot of living still ahead. No matter how much time I have, I'm determined to appreciate every moment of my life. When my time does come I won't be afraid because I know my friend Jesus will be waiting on me.

The End

The Gay Youth Chronicles

Listed in suggested reading order

Also look for audiobook versions on Amazon.com and Audible.com

Outfield Menace

Snow Angel

The Nudo Twins

The Soccer Field Is Empty

Someone Is Watching

A Better Place

The Summer of My Discontent

Disastrous Dates & Dream Boys

Just Making Out

Temptation University

Fierce Competition

Scarecrows

Scotty Jackson Died... But Then He Got Better

The Antichrists

The Picture of Dorian Gay

Someone Is Killing the Gay Boys of Verona

Keeper of Secrets

Masked Destiny

Do You Know That I Love You

Altered Realities

Dead Het Boys

This Time Around

Phantom World

The Vampire's Heart

Second Star to the Right

The Perfect Boy

The Graymoor Mansion Bed and Breakfast

Shadows of Darkness

Heart of Graymoor

Yesterday's Tomorrow

Boy Trouble

The New Bad Ass in Town

Christmas in Graymoor Mansion

A Boy Toy for Christmas

Also by Mark A. Roeder

Homo for the Holidays

Ancient Prejudice*

*Ancient Prejudice is an early version of *The Soccer Field Is Empty*, which is recommended by the author instead of *Ancient Prejudice*.

Information on Mark's upcoming books can be found at markroeder.com. Those wishing to keep in touch with others who enjoy Mark's novels can join his fan club at http://groups.yahoo.com/group/markaroederfans.